THE SWEET FORBIDDEN

Chase knew it was time to leave, but he really didn't want to go. He looked at Rebecca's hair, shining with red and gold highlights in the lamplight. As if it had a will of its own, his hand rose, touched a soft wave at Rebecca's temple, then dropped to a curl lying on her shoulder, fingering it.

Rebecca's heart beat crazily in her chest. She desperately wanted him to kiss her. Unconsciously, she raised her head, her lips parting in silent invitation.

Chase gazed down at her face, his eyes locked on her soft, full mouth. He'd promised himself he wouldn't touch her. He'd stayed away from the wagon, trying to put distance between him and temptation. But now he could feel her heat, her sweet scent filling his senses, her mouth looking so inviting. He framed her face in both his hands, lifted it, and Rebecca stood on tiptoe, meeting him halfway. . . .

TO
LOVE
AN
EAGLE

Joanne
Redd

A DELL BOOK

Published by
Dell Publishing Co., Inc.
1 Dag Hammarskjold Plaza
New York, New York 10017

Dell ® TM 681510, Dell Publishing Co., Inc.

ISBN: 0-440-18982-9

Printed in the United States of America

August 1987

10 9 8 7 6 5 4 3 2 1

WFH

For Gwen. This one is for you. You earned it.

Special thanks goes to my daughter, Denise, for giving me the title of this book and to Pat, my agent, whose belief in this book never faltered.

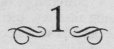

Natchez, Mississippi—December 1835

"THAT IS THE MOST ASININE SCHEME I'VE EVER heard."

The words were said in a calm, cool tone of voice, with just a hint of mockery, and for that reason had more bite to them than if they'd been said in heat.

Paul Blake gazed across his comfortable, well-furnished drawing room at the man who had made the soft-spoken yet stinging comment. Chase Winters stood beside the fireplace, one elbow casually propped on the mantelpiece, a glass of bourbon in his slender hand, his finely tailored suit straining across his broad shoulders and fitting his tall, lithe body like a second skin. The firelight played over the bold adventurer's dark hair and bronze skin, casting half of his rugged features in shadow and giving him a dangerous, almost diabolical appearance.

A shiver of fear ran up Paul's spine as he felt the barely suppressed savagery that rippled just below

7

the surface of this man. And Chase Winters was a savage, at least in part. He was the son of an Anglo adventurer and a powerful Comanche chief's daughter, something that few men knew, for the twenty-seven-year-old Chase was closed-mouthed, a man clothed in mystery.

Paul was aware of those black, penetrating eyes on him and knew that Winters was awaiting a response. "Why do you think the plan is stupid, Chase?"

"Because taking cannons to the Alamo would be a waste of my time and your money, Paul," Chase answered. "Just because a group of hot-headed Texians captured the Alamo doesn't mean that they can hold it. Whether they like it or not, they're citizens of the Mexican state of Texas-Coahuila, and Santa Anna will do everything in his power to see that they remain Texians. They're fools if they think they can fight against him."

"But the Alamo is a fortress," Paul objected, "and Santa Anna can't take East Texas until he's captured it back. He'll need it as a base. If the Mexicans can be held back at Bexar, Texas can raise an army."

"From what?" Chase spat. "That bunch of rabble-rousers who are gathering on the Texas border? Hell, when those glory-seekers get a glimpse of Santa Anna's army, they'll turn tail and run. Christ! Do you have any idea how big the Mexican army is? And its troops are battle seasoned, the officers some of the best in the world, men who were trained by Napoleon himself. By capturing the Alamo, all those hotheads have accomplished is to make Santa Anna even angrier. He'll never forgive the Texians for taking it and sending General Cos—his own brother-in-law—back to the Rio Grande. Those fool Texians have added personal insult to rebellion."

"And that's precisely why we've got to fortify the Alamo," Paul countered. "The Texians aren't fighting Mexico for separate statehood anymore. It's gone beyond that. They're fighting for independence! And the American settlers in Texas won't give up their land, Chase. They'll fight to the death, if necessary."

"All right," Chase conceded, "so the American settlers in Texas will fight. What's that got to do with you?"

Paul stiffened. His voice was thick with indignation as he said, "Those are fellow Americans. I and the men that I represent feel it our duty to support them in any and every way that we can. We want to see Texas as part of the Union. And so does President Jackson. We're hoping he'll back the Texians' rebellion."

Chase knew that Paul spoke the truth. Andrew Jackson was an expansionist who envisioned the United States stretching across the entire continent, from the Atlantic to the Pacific oceans, and had had his eye on Texas for some time. But, while Jackson wanted to see Texas become a part of the United States, there were others who didn't—specifically those northern states that wanted no more slave states brought into the Union. Yes, Jackson would meet with fierce opposition from within if he tried to invade Texas and challenge Mexico for

9

it, and the President needed the consent of Congress to do that.

Chase sat in the chair opposite Paul's and asked, "And what if Jackson won't, or can't, back the Texians?"

"Then they'll fight alone!" Paul answered passionately. He leaned forward, saying emphatically "That's why it's of the utmost importance to get those cannons to the Alamo. The Texas army will need artillery."

"The Alamo was a *presidio*, a Mexican fortress," Chase pointed out. "What about the cannons that were already there? Didn't the Texians capture them too?"

"To be perfectly honest, Chase, we really don't know. It's possible. Or General Cos might have destroyed the artillery there before he surrendered. But even if there are a few cannons at the Alamo, Texas is going to need more. For that reason we have set up a second, alternative destination for our cannons. If they are not needed at Bexar, then deliver them to the nearest Texas army post."

Chase let out a long, disgusted sigh and said, "All right. It seems that you're determined to get those cannons into Texas, and if you want to waste your money by hiring me to get them through, then it's no skin off my back. But what's all this hogwash about taking them, dismantled and hidden in a false wagon bottom—on a wagon train, no less! Christ! Do you realize how slow those trains move? Why don't you just let me drag them to the Alamo behind a team of fast horses?"

"That's been tried before. You see, we've attempted to slip cannons into Texas twice already. The first time we didn't send them on carriages. The rough Texas roads broke off the wheels before they had even gotten twenty miles from the Sabine, and the guns had to be abandoned. The second time we sent the cannons on carriages, but they never arrived. We assume that the men we hired to deliver them were attacked by Indians and wiped out, as there are no Mexican soldiers in East Texas since they were pulled out back in '32. That's why the men who I'm representing *insist* that it's got to be done by wagon train this time. There's safety in numbers. Indians aren't as likely to attack a large wagon train. And speed is of no importance. Everyone knows that Santa Anna won't make his drive across Texas until the spring."

"Oh? And why not?" Chase asked in a voice dripping with sarcasm.

"Hell, man!" Paul spat in exasperation. "Santa Anna would be a fool to march his army across that desolate stretch of land between the Rio Grande and Bexar in the winter, with no forage for his animals."

Chase leaned forward in his chair, saying in a hard voice "Don't make the mistake of underestimating López de Santa Anna, Paul. He didn't become the greatest general Mexico has ever had by doing the expected. Like Napoleon, he's a brilliant tactician and a charismatic leader. If he decides to march in the winter, he'll get his army to Bexar, even if he has to kill half of his men in the process. Your hotheads at the Alamo just might be surprised to find Santa Anna standing on their doorstep sooner than they think." Seeing Paul's face drain of all color at his dire prediction, Chase pressed his advantage. "Now, I can set up a relay of fast horses and armed guards along *El Camino Real* and have those cannons in Bexar within two weeks."

Paul rose from his chair, walked to the window, and stared out at the bare fields of his cotton plantation. He was very tempted to agree with Chase's proposition. Having been born in Texas, Chase knew both the land and its people, and he certainly knew the Mexicans better than Paul or his associates. But Paul wasn't in the position to change the plans that were already set in motion.

He turned, saying "If this were just between you and me, I'd say go ahead, Chase. But it isn't. My associates don't want to take any risks this time. And after two failures, you can hardly blame them. After all, cannons are expensive pieces of equipment. No, they want their investment protected. That's why they're determined to send them by wagon train. Besides, it's too late to change our plans. The wagon and cannons are already in Natchitoches—as is the woman we've selected to accompany you."

Chase's dark head snapped up at Paul's last words. "Woman? What woman? What in the hell are you talking about?"

"Calm down, Chase. I would have told you earlier, but you interrupted me. We've carefully screened all of the wagon trains being assembled in Natchitoches right now. The one that we've chosen for you to travel on is the only well-organized train in the entire lot. Its wagon master is a man who won't take any foolishness from anyone, and every man on that train is a sharpshooter. If the Indians attack it, they'll regret it. Besides that, this train has already decided where they're going to settle in Texas—on the upper Guadalupe River, which would place you close to Bexar when you have to leave them."

Chase slammed to his feet. "Damn it, Paul! Stop hedging! What's this business about taking a woman along?"

"I'm getting to that!" Paul snapped back. "If you'd stop interrupting, I'll tell you."

Chase sat back down, glaring at Paul with a look that made the Natchez planter's nerves crawl. He cleared his throat nervously before saying "As I said, the wagon master on that train is very strict. He insists that he'll only take families. No single men. He feels, and justifiably so, that married men are more stable and reliable, less likely to take off on their own. He doesn't want to find himself in the middle of Texas, surrounded by hostile Indians, with only a few wagons left. That's the reason for the woman. She'll pose as your wife."

"You're crazy if you think I'd take a woman along with me!"

"Why not?"

"Why not?" Chase asked in an incredulous voice. "I'll tell you why. Because if we run into Santa Anna's army, I'm leaving that god-damned wagon and those cannons right there and running like hell. And I'm not going to drag some female with me when I do!"

Chase rose and headed for the door, saying over his shoulder "Find yourself another man, Paul. I'm not interested."

"I wouldn't be so fast to turn the job down, Chase," Paul said in an ominous voice. "Not if you care about what happens to your brother."

Chase stopped in midstride, then turned, a scowl on his face. "What's Jim got to do with this?"

"Your brother got himself into another scrape, Chase. A real mess this time. He stole a valuable Thoroughbred from a wealthy, influential man in Kentucky and rode the animal down while trying to escape. He's been sentenced to hang." Paul hesitated. He had hoped that he wouldn't have to use this weapon on Chase. Then he took a deep breath to fortify himself and said, "My associates in this venture are influential men. If you'll do this job for us, they'll see that Jim's sentence is commuted to a brief prison term."

Chase didn't like being cornered, and he certainly didn't like being forced into something by a bunch of armchair generals. His dark eyes narrowed menacingly. "You'd hold my brother's life over my head?"

Paul shivered at the murderous look in Winters's black eyes. He had seen the adventurer angry before, but what the planter now saw was Chase's savage side. It was a terrifying sight that made Paul's blood run cold. He'd been a fool to threaten this half-breed.

When Chase walked across the room, Paul stepped back in fear, then almost collapsed with relief when the tall Texian slumped back down in the overstuffed chair. Paul watched warily while Chase sat staring out into space, a deep scowl on his face.

So, Chase thought, Jim has gotten into another jam, and as usual, he was expected to pull his brother out. The pattern had been set when they were boys and had continued into their adult lives. Chase fervently wished that he had never laid eyes on his half brother; if it hadn't been for fate, he probably would never have known about Jim.

When he was eight years old, his Indian mother died. His Anglo father had taken Chase back to Missouri. That was when Chase had learned of his father's "white" family and of the existence of his younger half brother.

His stepmother had taken Chase into her home, raising him like her own son, a remarkable feat for she must have been shocked to learn that her husband had an illegitimate child—a half-breed, no less. It was Blanche, and not his wandering father, who taught Chase English and the ways of the white man, who educated him, who tried to protect him from the hatred of their neighbors who thought that the only good Indian was a dead one. Her death, when he was thirteen years old, had been a crushing blow to Chase.

It was because of his gratitude to this kindly woman that Chase repeatedly pulled his half-brother out of trouble, not because he had any great love for Jim. Like Chase and their father, Jim was a mustanger and an adventurer, a bold, daring breed of men who laughed at danger. But Jim was too reckless, going from one madcap scheme to another, flirting with the law and death. And this time Jim had gone too far. Chase was tempted to let them hang his half-brother, but he couldn't. He owed that much to Blanche.

Chase looked up. "Why me, Paul? You can get any number of men to take those cannons to Bexar for you. With the price you're offering, you're bound to find some fool who'd be more than willing. Why are you going to such extremes to force me into it?"

"Because taking those cannons to the Texas army is only half the job, Chase, and only you can do the other half. We want you to talk to the Comanches for us."

"The Comanches?" Chase asked in surprise. "What have they got to do with all this?"

"The provisional government in Texas is worried about how the Indians are going to react to this rebellion. They're afraid some of the tribes in Texas will side with the Mexicans. There have been rumors of Santa Anna signing an alliance with the Comanches, and the Texas army can't fight two enemies at once."

"That's ridiculous! The Comanches would never sign an alliance with the Mexicans. They hate them with a passion. And the Comanches don't consider the Anglos their enemy. The American settlers are too far east for them to concern themselves with. If anything, the Comanches are indifferent to them."

"I sincerely hope that you're right. And if anyone should know, it's you. Which is precisely why we need your help. The Texas government is sending emissaries to all of the tribes in Texas to solicit peace treaties, men like Sam Houston who have friends among the various tribes. But they didn't have anyone to send to the Comanches. I suggested you, since you're half Comanche yourself and your grandfather is a powerful Comanche chief. Surely he has influence with the others."

Chase frowned. "I'm not so sure that even my grandfather would agree to a peace treaty with a people he knows nothing of."

"We're not demanding results, Chase. All we're asking you to do is talk with them, present our proposal." Paul paused, then asked in a hesitant voice, "Will you do the job for us, Chase?"

Chase scoffed, saying bitterly "It doesn't look like I have any choice."

Paul sincerely regretted having to force Chase into this position. "Try to understand our viewpoint, Chase. Texas must be freed from the Mexican yoke. We're fighting for important things here: Liberty. Justice. Freedom. The same things our forefathers fought for."

"And you won't let anything or anyone get in your way, will you?" Chase rejoined. He laughed harshly. Then, his voice heavy with contempt, he said, "That's what I've always liked about you patriots, Paul. To you, the end always justifies the means, even if those means are less than honorable. You don't care how dirty your tactics are, or who gets hurt in the process. Tell me, are you holding something over her head too? The woman who's going along with me?"

"Of course not!" Paul answered indignantly.

"Rebecca Dryer was more than happy to help our cause. She's just as anxious as we are to see Texas freed from Mexico. She hates the Mexicans with a passion. They deported her from Texas five years ago—after they had confiscated her family's land and killed Mr. Dryer and her brother. The Mexicans claimed they had no right to be there," Paul ended bitterly.

So, Rebecca Dryer's family had been squatters, Chase thought, dirt-poor farmers who had sneaked illegally across the border and claimed a piece of Texas land for their own. No wonder she had been kicked out of Texas!

"And just what am I supposed to do with her after I deliver the cannons to the Alamo?" Chase asked. "Drag her into Comanche territory with me and then back across the Sabine?"

"Into Indian territory?" Paul asked in a shocked voice. "My God, no! Rebecca will stay with a friend of mine and his family in Bexar until the war has ended."

Chase nodded. "When does the wagon train leave?"

"In two days."

"Two days?" Chase repeated in disbelief.

"I would have given you more time, but we had a little difficulty in making the arrangements for Jim. Besides, the way you ride you can make it in that time, and Rebecca has already taken care of buying the provisions and the stock for the trip."

"You let a *woman* buy stock and provisions for a trip like that?"

"I certainly did. I told you that she's traveled to

Texas before. She knew what was needed, probably better than I."

"But the merchants might have cheated her. Sold her bad goods."

"Not Rebecca," Paul answered in a confident voice.

Chase looked thoughtful for a minute. "Well, I guess if she's a widow woman, on her own now for five years, she's learned how to deal with sneaky merchants."

Paul's head snapped up at Chase's words. Where in the hell did Chase get the idea that Rebecca was a widow? he wondered. Then he remembered that he had called Rebecca's father Mr. Dryer. Chase must have assumed that Mr. Dryer was her husband.

Chase didn't notice Paul's reaction to his words and continued. "And I'll have to say one thing for those squatters' women. They may not be much to look at, old before their time, scrawny and hatchet-faced, but they are hard workers and good managers. And they know their place too. You won't see any of them sticking their noses into men's business."

Paul's eyebrows rose. Chase's description of Rebecca was no more accurate than his assuming her a widow. Rebecca was a hard worker and a good manager, but she was certainly none of those other things. Paul wondered if he should tell Chase that Rebecca was a beautiful, well-bred young woman, that her father hadn't been a squatter but a planter who the Mexicans had wrongly accused of being in Texas illegally. And if Chase thought Rebecca was going to be one of those meek, docile women, always subservient to the male, he was going to be in for a big shock. Even though she was only nineteen, Rebecca was the most fiercely independent and outspoken woman he had ever known.

For a brief moment Paul considered correcting Chase's misconceptions, then decided against it, for fear Chase would back out. No, he'd leave Chase to Rebecca. As determined as she was to complete this mission, she'd see that Chase followed through with the delivery of the cannons. Of that much he was positive.

Paul walked to his desk and opened a drawer, pulling out an oilskin packet. Handing it to Chase, he said, "This is the peace treaty. It's already signed by Governor Smith. If the Comanches agree, all they have to do is make their mark."

Even though he seriously doubted that the Comanches would sign, Chase accepted the packet and slipped it inside his frock coat. "What does this Rebecca Dryer look like? I'd hate to make an ass of myself going around and asking every woman on that train if she's supposed to be my wife."

"You can't miss her. She's a redhead."

One of those carrot tops? Chase thought in disgust. Christ, it was bad enough that he was going to be saddled with a woman for the next six to eight weeks, but the thought of having to live with this Rebecca Dryer day after day was downright depressing. The least Paul could have done was pick a woman who was easy on the eyes.

"And the name of the wagon train?" Chase asked.

"It's the McPherson train. Jamie McPherson is the wagon master."

Chase turned and started for the door.

"Chase?"

He whirled around, his dark eyebrows rising in a silent question.

"I know that you don't have any interest in this revolution, that you think the Texians are just a bunch of hotheads playing a fool's game . . . but don't you think Texas has at least a chance at winning their independence from Mexico?"

"Sure they've got a chance," Chase replied. He watched as a broad smile spread across Paul's face, then added grimly, "About the same chance as a snowball in hell."

With that, Chase walked from the drawing room, leaving Paul staring in dismay at his broad back.

REBECCA DRYER SHOVED THE HEAVY BAG OF flour into its place on the wagon and then stood, rubbing her aching back wearily. Thank God, that was the last of the supplies to be loaded, and not a minute too soon, she thought. Tomorrow the wagon train would leave for Texas.

Where the devil was he? Rebecca thought angrily, pushing her way through the crowded maze of crates and barrels to the front of the wagon. Paul had promised her Chase Winters would be there in plenty of time, and she had seen absolutely nothing of her mysterious traveling companion. It was bad enough that she had had to purchase all of the supplies and load the wagon herself—a backbreaking chore—but now Mr. McPherson was threatening to take their place on the train away from them if her "husband" didn't show up soon.

Rebecca sat down on the wagon seat and scanned the area. Then she shook her head in disgust. It wouldn't do her any good to look for him because she hadn't the slightest idea of what he looked like. In fact, she knew very little about the man she would spend the next weeks with. Paul had told her Winters was an adventurer and assured her that he was capable and the perfect man for the job since he knew Texas so well from his travels. But now Rebecca was beginning to wonder about hiring such a man for an important mission. From what she had seen, those adventurers were an irresponsible, shiftless, lazy lot, more interested in chasing some get-rich-quick scheme than putting in an honest day's labor. Undoubtedly, Winters was dallying someplace, probably a tavern, getting stinking drunk. Damn it, if he missed this wagon train and ruined the mission, she'd take a bullwhip to him—if the bastard *ever* showed up!

Rebecca had been elated when Paul had approached her about posing as Winters's wife. She had known of Paul's and his friends' disastrous failures to deliver cannons to the Texians and that they were planning to try again, but she had never dreamed that she—a woman—might be able to participate in their venture. It had seemed the answer to her prayers. Ever since her father and brother had been killed by the Mexicans and she had been brusquely deported from Texas, she had burned for revenge. That, and her determination to get back her father's land in Texas, rather than any feelings of patriotism, had driven her to join the firebrands who were encouraging rebellion in Texas. Her maiden aunt, whom she had been forced to live with in Natchez after her mother's death, had been shocked by Rebecca's behavior, saying it was outrageous for a woman to involve herself in men's business. Even some of the men in the group had been disapproving, feeling her interest in war and revolution not at all appropriate for a well-bred young lady. But Rebecca hadn't given a tinker's damn what any of them thought. Independence for Texas and her revenge were the only things that mattered to her. She wouldn't rest until she saw every Mexican in Texas pushed back across the Rio Grande.

So, when Paul had tentatively approached her about the mission, Rebecca had jumped at the opportunity. She pushed aside his concern for her safety and reputation, ignored his warning that it might be dangerous. Then, when Paul had been plagued by doubts, Rebecca had been terrified that he would change his mind and send an older, more mature woman instead. But she had insisted that she be given the mission and Paul, worn down by her determination, had agreed. Rebecca had announced to her aunt that she was going for a prolonged visit to her father's relatives in Montgomery and departed for Natchitoches instead. She had arrived in the western Louisiana town a week ago. The wagon, with its dismantled and concealed cannons, had been delivered two days later. Since then she had made a reservation on the McPherson train and bought all of the supplies and provisions they would need, including the six oxen needed to pull the heavy wagon. Now all she was waiting for was Chase Winters's appearance.

"Miz Winters?"

Lost in her thoughts, Rebecca totally ignored the bearded, rangy man calling up to her.

"Miz Winters!"

Startled, Rebecca jumped. She glanced down and saw the man standing beside her wagon, an irritated look on his craggy face. "Oh, I'm sorry, Mr. McPherson. I was preoccupied."

"I dropped by to see if your husband has arrived yet."

"No . . . no, he hasn't," Rebecca replied nervously. "But I'm sure he will be here any minute now."

"We're pulling out tomorrow, you know, and your husband hasn't even signed on yet."

"I know," Rebecca replied, and then, as a sudden inspiration hit her, said, "But if signing on is what is worrying you, I can sign in my husband's place. And then, if he isn't here in the morning, I can drive the wagon until he catches up with us."

Jamie McPherson's mouth gaped open at Rebecca's suggestion. Why, a little woman like her couldn't possibly drive a wagon the size of hers or handle a triple yoke of oxen. One of their Kantuck women might be able to, but they were used to hard work, helping their husbands fell trees and lift heavy rocks out of their fields. This young woman was much too delicate, even if she did have more flesh on her than their women. He'd made a mistake when he'd promised her a place on the train. She wasn't their kind of folks. Obviously she came from wealth. Just look at that wagon she had, twice as big as any of theirs. He'd heard it was crammed full of crates of furniture for her new home; that's what she'd told some of the members of the wagon train. Why, even her calico dresses were brand new, not worn and faded like the other women's. Besides, you could tell she was a high-classed lady by the way she talked. Why, she'd probably fall to pieces a week out on the trail and be begging her husband to turn back. *If* she had a husband, Jamie thought to himself.

"No, ma'am, I ain't takin' no lone woman along on my train," he said in a firm, determined voice. "Either your husband shows up—or you're off my train! And he's got till sundown to sign on."

"Until sundown?" Rebecca asked in dismay. "But that's just two hours away! Can't you at least give him till morning? The train doesn't leave until then."

"Nope. If you ain't goin', I've got three other families clamorin' to get on my train. Whoever I pick will have to know by sundown if they're going or not."

Jamie McPherson turned and walked away, calling over his shoulder "Till sundown, Miz Winters!"

Rebecca bit her bottom lip. Tears of frustration and anger burned her eyes. "Damn you, Chase Winters!" she muttered. "Where in the hell are you?"

Chase was at that very minute riding into the clearing where the McPherson train was camped. He had been in the saddle for almost forty-eight hours, stopping in Natchez only long enough to pick up his belongings. Since then he had ridden straight through, except for taking care of those three cutthroats who had tried to ambush him on a lonely, deserted stretch on the trail. Now he was hungry and bone-tired.

After he had reached Natchitoches, he had spent another two hours looking for the McPherson train among all the trains assembling on the outskirts of town. He had never seen so many wagons in his entire life. To him, it looked as if every farmer in the South were moving to Texas.

As a whole, they were a motley crowd. Like him, they had seen the handbills posted in all the cities and towns, soliciting volunteers for the Texas army and promising eight hundred acres of free land to every man who would join up. But all they had seen—or chosen to see—was the promise of free land. Most had no intention of signing up with the army, and those who did plan on it didn't expect to fight. They all thought the war had ended when the Alamo had been captured by Ben Milam and his Texians. Milam had snatched the command of the militia away from Steven F. Austin, when Austin couldn't make up his mind on whether to attack the fortress or not. All through his long ride through Louisiana, Chase had seen the scraps of paper tacked on cabin doors with GTT—Gone to Texas—scribbled in big letters.

That the settlers were moving into Texas under the misconception that the war was over was bad enough, but what was worse was that they had no better understanding of the preparations necessary for such an arduous, dangerous trip than they had of the true political situation. Most wagons were in a sad state of disrepair, many not even covered to offer protection from the elements. The majority of the livestock were half-starved creatures that would die long before the destination was reached, leaving the settlers stranded. All too often the precious space on the wagon beds, needed for the bare essentials necessary for survival, was crammed with household furnishings instead. Chase had been shocked to learn that some of the settlers didn't even carry arms.

The trains were poorly organized. No one seemed to know which train was assembling where, much less what their destinations were or when they would be leaving. To add to this muddle and confusion, some of the trains had no single official leader, while in others the members argued over who would be wagon master, sometimes settling their disagreements with their fists. Wagons were parked at random and children ran wild through them while untethered animals roamed in search of grass. Chase had been stopped more than once during his ride by a farmer wondering if he had seen his cow or horse, or a frantic mother looking for a lost child. After almost two hours of inquiries, Chase had learned that the McPherson train was assembling north of the town, away from the others.

When Chase rode into the clearing where the train was camped, he could understand why Paul had insisted that he travel with this train. It was a stark contrast to the others. The wagons, all covered and all in good shape, were lined up in a neat row along a wooded creek. All of the animals were in a roped-off corral to the back of the camp, and, while everyone was busy making last-minute preparations, there was none of the chaos he had seen earlier.

Chase reined in his horse and scanned the area. To his dismay, in this assembly of predominately Scots-Irish, there were redheads everywhere, and a good third of them were women. Chase cursed himself for not having asked for a more detailed description of Rebecca Dryer. His dark eyes locked on one redheaded woman. Tall and reed-thin, her frizzled, carrot-color hair was streaked with premature gray, her skin brown and leathery from years of exposure to the sun. When she glanced up and gave Chase a sour look, his spirits sank even lower. And then, when a small child toddled up to her and yanked on her faded, crumpled calico skirt, Chase felt a wave of relief wash over him. He pivoted his horse and rode away.

As he approached a young boy leading a cow to the corral, Chase asked, "Do you know where I could find the Winters's wagon?"

The boy looked up, his entire face covered with freckles, and grinned. "Sure do, mister. Ain't no one on this train don't know that wagon. It's that big 'un down there."

Chase looked in the direction the boy was pointing and saw the wagon. As the boy had said, it was big, almost twice as long as the others. "Thanks," Chase said, kneeing his horse into a trot.

When Chase reached the big wagon, he dismounted and looked around him, seeing no sign of a woman. He tied his stallion's reins to one of the wagon wheels and then examined the wagon.

The wooden wheels were seven feet across; the rims, guarded round with iron hoops, were ten inches wide and four inches thick, the spokes the size of a man's forearm. The wagon was made of cypress—a strong yet lightweight wood, valued for its resistance to water—and not of the cheap pine, which warped badly. It was put together with wooden pins instead of iron nails that would pull loose and drop out over rough roads. He bent and looked under the wagon at the sturdy axles, nodding his head in approval. Rising, he looked up at the canvas covering, then fingered it. It was heavy grade, not the thin canvas that would tear easily or rot after a few weeks of being exposed to the sun and rain. Then he stood back and scrutinized the base of the wagon. From the outside he couldn't see any hint of a false bottom, and certainly not one in which the parts of three eight-pounders could be hidden. Yes, he had to hand it to Paul and his associates. They certainly hadn't scrimped on the wagon. It was the best constructed he'd ever seen, obviously custom made by a master craftsman.

Chase walked to the back of the wagon, intent on looking inside, but when he rounded the corner, he came to a dead halt, surprised to see the wagon tailgate was already down, as were the fold-down wooden steps. He peered into the dim interior and was just able to see the outline of a woman inside.

"Rebecca?" he asked.

Rebecca whirled around at her name. Then, when she saw Chase, her eyes widened. Who was *he?* she thought. Why, she hadn't noticed him around camp, and he was a man who would stand out in any crowd, with his dark, rugged good looks and tall, commanding physique. Her eyes quickly swept over him, across the broad shoulders, the wide chest and slim hips, the long, muscular legs. Dressed in buckskins, a powder horn and two leather pouches hung from his neck and rested on his chest, just below the V of bronzed skin where his tunic was open. At his right side, attached to a wide belt and sheathed in a leather scabbard, hung a long knife. Despite herself, Rebecca stared at the stranger. He oozed masculinity and power.

"Are you Rebecca Dryer?" Chase asked.

Dryer? Rebecca thought. Why, no one in Natchitoches knew her real last name. Then this must be Chase Winters! But she had expected someone older, someone ordinary, someone not so—so overpowering!

Still a little shaken at finding Chase Winters not at all what she had expected, Rebecca walked to the end of the wagon and stepped out onto the tailgate, wondering why her legs felt so weak.

Then it was the Texian's turn to be shocked. Rebecca's hair was red, but not the bright brassy color he had expected. Waving softly around her face and pulled back and tied at the back of her neck with a ribbon, the color was breathtaking, remarkably changing from gold to red, then back again as the light played over it, as elusive as the flames of a fire. Chase had never seen such beautiful hair.

His eyes dropped to Rebecca's face. Her complexion was soft and creamy, a smattering of faint freckles across the bridge of her saucy, upturned nose. Her eyes were a vivid dark blue, startling in their clarity and fringed with long, dark lashes, the eyebrows above them delicately arched. He glanced quickly over the rest of her, the pretty mouth, the graceful neck, the high, shapely breasts, tiny waist, and softly curved hips. Chase couldn't believe his eyes.

Rebecca was very much aware of Chase's dark eyes sweeping over her. She had never been scrutinized so boldly, and it left her feeling stripped to the bone. A flush rose on her face and, with it, her ire.

"Are you Chase Winters?" she snapped.

Chase nodded mutely, still engrossed with the unexpected vision of loveliness before him.

"Well, it's about time you got here! Where in the blazes have you been, anyway?"

Rebecca's sharp rebuke snapped Chase from his state of shock. If there was one thing he couldn't stand, it was a waspish woman. His own anger rose. "In the saddle for the past two days!"

"Well, you certainly took your time getting here. You were supposed to be here days ago. Do you realize we've almost lost our place on this train because of your dallying?"

"Back off, lady!" Chase yelled. "I haven't been dallying. When I said I'd been in the saddle for the past two days, I meant it! If you can find anyone who can ride from Natchez to Natchitoches in less than forty-eight hours, then you're welcome to them."

"Two days?" Rebecca asked in disbelief. "You rode from Natchez in that time?"

"Two days—and two nights!"

"Well, then, why did you wait till the last minute to get started?"

"I didn't wait till the last minute!" Chase snapped. "I didn't know a damned thing about this crazy scheme until then."

"Crazy scheme?" Rebecca gasped indignantly.

"Yes, crazy scheme," Chase ground out. "Dragging a bunch of cannons halfway across Texas, in the middle of the winter, to a bunch of hotheads who fancy themselves as soldiers—on a wagon train, no less. Lady, that's the most stupid thing I've ever heard!"

"Well, if you think it's so stupid, then why did you take the job?" Rebecca asked hotly.

"Because if I didn't, they were going to hang my brother!"

No sooner had the words crossed his lips than Chase wondered what in the world had possessed him. He was a man who fiercely guarded his privacy, accounting to no one for his actions. So why had he offered an explanation to this little chit? Chase knew the answer. Rebecca infuriated him so that he had let his guard down and blurted out the information before he had even stopped to think.

Rebecca had recovered from Chase's shocking revelation. "Hang your brother? Who's going to hang your brother?"

"Oh, so you didn't know about that little bit of extortion? Well, I'm glad to know Paul doesn't single me out as the only recipient of his surprises."

"Paul? Paul was going to hang your brother if you didn't agree to take this job?"

"Paul and his friends."

"They'd murder him?" Rebecca barely whispered.

"No, they'd allow him to be hanged."

Rebecca could only stare at him, confusion added to her shock.

"He's been sentenced to hang for stealing a horse. If I agreed to take this job, they'll arrange to have the sentence changed to a brief prison term."

His brother was a common horse thief? Rebecca thought. My God, what kind of a man had Paul sent? Why, he was nothing but—but trash!

Chase saw the look of disgust on Rebecca's face and knew what she was thinking. He had been stunned to find that his traveling companion was young and beautiful. And obviously she was well bred, for there was a certain haughtiness to her carriage, and her voice was cultured, despite its sharpness. As much as he had dreaded spending his time with the skinny hag he had imagined Rebecca to be, that woman would have been tough and used to hardships. Christ! Paul must be out of his head to send a woman as delicate as this one on such an arduous, dangerous trip. Didn't he give a damn what happened to her? Besides that, this woman had been pampered and spoiled all her life. She'd be a liability to him, whining constantly, expecting him to wait on her hand and foot, while all the time looking down on him as if he were the scum of the earth just because his damn brother was a horse thief. What would she think if she knew *he* was a half-breed!

A sudden glimmer came into Chase's eyes. That was it! He'd tell her. No high-class woman would be caught dead in the company of a half-breed, particularly one as snobbish as Rebecca. And she'd probably be terrified too. He'd seen the fear in people's eyes when they discovered he was half Indian, as if they expected him to pounce on them and scalp them any minute. Yes, when she knew the truth about him, she'd back out quick enough, and the mission would have to be cancelled for the time being. By the time Paul and his friends had made other arrangements, he'd have found that stupid brother of his and broken him out of jail. Then Paul and his friends could go to hell!

Chase smiled smugly and said, "I don't know why they're making such a fuss about Jim stealing one horse, anyway. Hell, I've stolen thousands of them."

"You've what?" Rebecca asked in a shocked voice.

"Oh? Didn't Paul tell you how I made my living? I'm a mustanger. I steal whole herds of horses and drive them across the Texas border."

"But—but mustangs are wild horses. That's not stealing."

Chase grinned, saying "Well, to be honest with you, they're not all wild horses. Sometimes my Indian relatives and I help ourselves to a few of the settlers' horses too."

"Indian relatives?" Rebecca choked out.

"Sure. Didn't Paul tell you I was a half-breed?"

Chase couldn't have shocked Rebecca more if he had told her he was the devil himself. Her knees buckled, and she weakly caught the edge of the crate beside her. Her heart raced in a mixture of horror and fear. My God, Paul must be insane, she thought wildly. Why, she could be murdered in her sleep!

"Look, if you're afraid to travel with me because I'm a half-breed, maybe we'd better call the whole thing off," Chase said, struggling to hide his smile and trying to look offended.

But we can't do that, Rebecca realized. It would take weeks for Paul to make other arrangements, and time was critical. The Texians needed the cannons as soon as possible. Suddenly she felt disgusted with herself. Paul had warned her the mission might be dangerous, and now, here she was being frightened off at the first sign of danger. And this man was dangerous. She had sensed that before he had even told her he was half Indian. But she couldn't let her fear override her purpose. With this mission she was being given the chance to have revenge on the Mexicans.

"Look, if you're one of those Indian haters . . ." Chase began.

"Oh, no, it's not that," Rebecca interrupted quickly. "It's just that you surprised me."

"Then you're not afraid of me?"

"No, of course not," Rebecca lied bravely.

Chase frowned. He had seen the look of fear in her eyes. What had happened?

"Mr. Winters, I really don't care who you are, or what methods Paul used to get you to agree to accept this job. All that's important to me is getting these cannons to the Alamo. Now," Rebecca said, quickly descending the steps, "the first thing

36

you have to do is get over to Mr. McPherson's wagon and sign on."

Chase was a little stunned by Rebecca's sudden recovery from the startling things he had just told her. He stood staring at her in disbelief as she walked away.

Realizing that he wasn't with her, Rebecca turned and snapped, "Well? What are you waiting for?"

Once again Rebecca's sharp words irritated Chase. If she thought she was going to lead him around like a stupid cow with a ring in its nose, she was dead wrong. No one bossed Chase Winters!

"I'll sign on later," Chase announced. "After I've rubbed down my horse and watered him."

"But you don't understand! Mr. McPherson said if you didn't sign on by sundown, he'd give our place on the train to someone else."

"It's still another hour until sundown."

"But—"

"I said later!"

The words were soft spoken, but there was steel beneath that velvet. Rebecca glanced up into Chase's eyes. Before they had been coal black, but now, unbelievably, they were even darker. And they were glittering dangerously. A shiver of fear ran through her.

Without another word Chase turned and walked to his horse. Rebecca was forced to wait while he dried the sweat from the animal, then walked him to cool him down, then watered him. The sun sank lower and lower and Rebecca pulled her shawl closer and shivered in the cool air. As Chase drew the procedure out, Rebecca knew that he was doing it deliberately to irritate her. By the time he had finally finished, Rebecca could have scratched his eyes out—half-breed or not!

Chase gave a curt nod to signal he was ready to go, and Rebecca flipped her head angrily and whirled away. As she walked, Chase was momentarily occupied, engrossed with watching the provocative sway of her hips. Then, realizing that she was leaving him behind, he caught up with her in a few quick, long strides.

As they walked to the McPherson wagon at the head of the train, Rebecca fumed silently. Why, he's no different than other men. Stubborn, arrogant, determined to lord it over a woman. Well, he wasn't going to dominate her. And she'd be damned if she'd let him frighten her any more!

Jamie was sitting beside his wagon, behind a makeshift table of several rough pine planks and two barrels. Standing before him, Rebecca said, "Mr. McPherson, my husband is here to sign on."

McPherson looked up at Chase and then scowled. Chase knew what he was thinking. He had seen that look too many times. McPherson thought he was Mexican because of his dark coloring and European features. On the west side of the Sabine, Chase was often mistaken for a Mexican, on the east side of the river, for Creole. Chase never bothered to correct them. It wasn't that he was trying to hide his Indian blood. He was proud of it. If anything, it was his Anglo blood that sometimes made him ashamed. It was the white men, not the Indian, who were deceitful, greedy, hypocritical, and bigoted.

"What did you say your first name was, Mr. Winters?" Jamie asked in a suspicious voice.

Chase was tempted to answer Juan, just to see how the rangy wagon master would react. Then he wondered ruefully if he should give McPherson all of the first names he had been given. His mother, in typical Comanche fashion, had given him his pet Indian name, Chasing Wolf, after the first thing she had seen following his birth, a wolf chasing a rabbit. Later in his life, at the naming ceremony, his grandfather had named him Soaring Eagle, because eagles had more powerful medicine than wolves. His Anglo father had simply shortened his mother's pet name to Chase.

"Chase."

"Where you from?" Jamie asked, still suspicious.

Chase didn't consider himself from anywhere in particular. He roamed all over Mexico and the country west of the Mississippi. He had never put down any roots. Nor had he any desire to do so. He liked his life the way it was—with no ties. Realizing that McPherson was waiting for an answer, he said, "Louisiana."

Maybe he was Cajun, McPherson thought. They were dark-skinned, although Winters didn't talk like any Cajun he'd ever heard. But the Cajuns were tough, hard-working people, good fighters and excellent woodsmen, and that's what he was interested in. McPherson eyed the callouses on Chase's hands and his muscular arms, then looked at his buckskins. The skins were a dark brown, showing that they'd been well worn.

The wagon master gave a curt nod of his head. "All right, Winters, let's get somethin' straight right off. I'm the boss on this train. I'm the one that says when we leave in the mornin's and when and where we camp at night. And I choose the route. If there's rivers to be forded, I'm the one that decides where and when. Now, if you've got suggestions, I'll listen to 'em, but I'm the one that makes the decisions. Any objections so far?"

Chase shook his head.

"We've got rules on this train, and I expect everyone to obey 'em," McPherson said in a firm voice. "First one's no fightin' or squabblin'. You got a disagreement with someone, you come to me. Second, everyone pulls his own weight. You're responsible for your own wagon and animals. At night all of the animals will be corraled with a watch set over 'em, and you'll be expected to take your turn standin' watch.

"Bring provisions for at least a month. We'll stop only once, at Nacogdoches. And I want every family to have at least two rifles and plenty of powder. If Injuns attack us, every grownup is gonna fight. That means you'll have to teach your wife how to shoot."

"That won't be necessary," Rebecca said. "I already know how to shoot, and I have my own rifle."

Both Chase and McPherson looked at Rebecca in surprise. Then, remembering that he was supposed to be her husband and should already know that, Chase quickly hid his expression.

"That's fine, Miz Winters," the wagon master said, then returned his attention to Chase. "We've got twenty wagons in this train, and we're lined up in the order that we're gonna leave here tomorrow mornin'. But that don't mean that will be your position in the train the entire trip. Every day when we stop for the night, the lead wagon will go to the end of the line. That way everyone gets his turn at eatin' dust. And somethin' else. We'll take days off to rest the animals and make repairs, but it ain't necessarily gonna be on Sunday, and it may not be as often as once a week. It'll depend on when we hit the rivers. So if you've got objections 'bout travelin' on the Lord's day, you find yourselves another train."

McPherson took a deep breath and stuck out his chin, giving Chase a challenging look. "Now, if you're wonderin' why I've set myself up as wagon master of this here train, I'll tell you. I fought with old Andy himself in the Creek Wars, and I know Injuns. Hell, I can smell one of those stinkin' bastards a mile away. And Injuns are gonna be the biggest danger we're gonna face. I've heard those Texas savages are jest 'bout the meanest red devils in this country." He glanced briefly at Rebecca, saying "Now, if my language offends your little wife here, I apologize. But I don't believe in mincin' words."

Rebecca wasn't in the least bothered by a few curse words, but she was terrified that Chase might take offense at the wagon master's insults. She glanced at Chase, expecting to see that hot, fierce look in his eyes again, but his expression was totally inscrutable.

Chase wasn't angered by McPherson's derogatory remarks. All men, including the Indians, called their enemies ugly names. If anything, Chase was amused by the old Indian fighter's claim that he could smell an Indian a mile off. If that was true, why couldn't he smell the Indian blood in him? But McPherson did have a point. There were a lot of Wichitas, Wacos, and Tawakonis between here and Bexar. But Chase didn't agree that Indians were the biggest danger they might face. He was a lot more worried about Santa Anna and his army. A well-formed wagon train could fight off a band of raiding Indians, but the only thing they could do if they ran into the Mexican army was turn tail and run like hell.

"You got any questions, Mr. Winters?" McPherson asked.

"No," Chase answered.

"Any objections about me being boss?"

"No."

McPherson was a little surprised at Chase's answer. Winters didn't strike him as a follower. He'd figured the man for one of those fiercely independent men who lived by his own code of rules. The wagon master gazed at Chase thoughtfully, still puzzled by this enigmatic man standing before him, then reached for a paper sitting on the table before him. "Okay, Winters, make your mark here."

McPherson shoved the contract across the table,

and Chase picked up the quill pen and signed it, surprising both McPherson and Rebecca when he wrote his name in excellent penmanship instead of the childish scrawl or simple mark that most frontiersmen used.

As they walked away from McPherson's wagon, Rebecca felt immensely relieved. Their place on the wagon train was finally secured.

"What do you think of Mr. McPherson?" Rebecca asked Chase. "Do you think he'll make a good wagon master?"

Chase was surprised that Rebecca would even ask his opinion—and pleased. He puzzled briefly over the latter. He wasn't a man who worried about pleasing others. Then, brushing his puzzlement aside, he answered, "Yes, I do. He's a strong leader. He'll be tough but fair. And after seeing those other wagon trains being assembled today, I'm relieved Paul chose this one. Half of them probably won't even make it to the Sabine."

Chase veered sharply from the path they were following. "Where are you going?" Rebecca asked. "Our wagon isn't in that direction."

"I want to see the draft horses you bought while it's still light."

Rebecca came to a stop, saying "I didn't buy horses. I bought oxen."

Chase was a strong horse man. Being half Comanche, to him the only animal of any value at all, for riding or pulling, was a horse. "Oxen? Why in the hell did you buy them?"

"Because oxen can pull heavier loads than horses," Rebecca answered, irritated by his criticism. "My God, do you realize how heavy those cannons are? Besides, oxen have more endurance. They can go from dawn to dusk without a drink of water if necessary."

"Yeah, and they're also stupid, stubborn, and hard to handle. Besides that, they're the slowest creatures on earth. Even a turtle can move faster than them, if it's in a hurry." Chase turned and walked away.

Rebecca ran to catch up with him. "Don't you want to see them?"

"Hell, no! There's no need for me to look at them. I wouldn't know a good one from a bad one."

When they reached the wagon—Rebecca had to practically run to keep up with Chase's long strides—Chase said, "I guess I'd better check our supplies over. If you didn't show any better sense buying them than you did those oxen, we're going to be in a hell of a mess."

Rebecca's eyes flashed dangerously. "Mr. Winters," she said in an icy voice, "I did *not* make a mistake when I bought those oxen. And I can assure you, you won't find anything wrong with the supplies I brought either."

"That remains to be seen!" Chase vaulted to the top of the tailgate and walked into the wagon. Then, realizing that it was too dark to see anything, he asked, "Where's the lamp?"

Rebecca walked up the wooden steps. "Right over you."

"Where?" Chase asked irritably, then turned, bumping his head on the lamp hanging from a cross rib. "God damn it," he muttered, rubbing his forehead.

Rebecca smiled smugly. "I believe you found it."

Chase shot her a hard look, took the lamp down, and lit it. Hanging it back up, he looked at the heavy packing crates in disbelief. "What in the hell is in those crates?"

"Sssh, lower your voice! Someone might hear you."

Chase glared at her.

"They're empty," Rebecca informed him. "As I told you, those cannons are heavy. This wagon is going to make deep ruts. How could we explain that and those six oxen needed to pull it if we just carried ordinary supplies? So Paul had those crates built and put into the wagon. I've been telling everyone they contain heavy furniture I'm taking for my new home."

"So the wagon master doesn't know we're carrying concealed cannons?"

"Of course not! He thinks we're planning on settling on the upper Guadalupe with everyone else on the train. If you had read that contract you just signed, you would have known that was part of the agreement. He doesn't know our plans, and if he did, I don't think he'd like the idea of us using his train simply as protection for those cannons."

Chase didn't think McPherson would be too happy about it either, and the wagon master was one man Chase didn't want to rile.

He turned his attention to the barrels and sacks crowded in among the crates. To his surprise, Rebecca seemed to have thought of everything. At least, as far as food supplies went. But then, a woman would remember those things.

"Where's the gunpowder?" he asked.

"In that barrel over there," Rebecca answered, pointing.

"Axle grease?"

"In that corner," Rebecca replied, pointing in the opposite direction.

"Axes and tools?"

"In the tool box next to it."

"Did you buy grain? At this time of the year, grass will be scarce in some places."

"Yes, those big sacks over there have grain in them." Rebecca was tired of Chase's questions. "I also bought a spare yolk, extra harnesses, ropes, and canvas for patching. The bandages and medicines are in that box over there, the lamp oil in that barrel, the—"

"All right!" Chase interjected. "So you bought everything!" He was surprised and strangely irritated at Rebecca's efficiency.

For a moment they stood in strained silence. Then Rebecca said, "Well, I guess I'd better get a fire started for supper."

"I'll start it."

"No, thank you," Rebecca replied coldly. "I'm perfectly capable of starting a fire." She shot him an angry look, still smarting from his criticism of the oxen and his cross-examination. What did he think she was? she thought as she climbed down the stairs on the tailgate. A child?

Chase frowned as he watched Rebecca leaving

the wagon, thinking what an independent cuss she was.

When they were outside, Rebecca carried the wood to the circle of ashes where she had built her other fires. Chase stood by, feeling unneeded and ridiculous.

Rebecca glanced to the front of the wagon and, seeing Chase's horse still tied there, said, "You'd better take your horse to the corral."

Chase always kept his horse close by, particularly when he was in the wilderness. Again, it was his Comanche blood coming out in him. The warriors always tethered their favorite warhorse just outside their tepee, or nearby if they were on the trail, just in case an enemy should suddenly attack.

"No. My horse stays with me."

"But you heard what Mr. McPherson said. All of the animals were to be corraled at night."

"That's because he's afraid of thieves. No one will steal Lightning. I've trained him so he can't be stampeded, and he won't let anyone mount him or touch his reins."

"But it's a rule. You don't want to provoke Mr. McPherson by breaking the rules."

"My horse stays with me," Chase repeated stubbornly.

Once again Rebecca's anger rose. He was the most critical, mule-headed, stubborn man she'd ever had the misfortune to meet. "Supper will be ready in fifteen minutes," she said, turning to the fire.

"Don't bother cooking for me. All I want is a cup of coffee. Then I'm going to bed."

Rebecca turned, a frying pan in her hand. "You're not going to eat anything?"

"No, I'm too tired to eat."

"But you shouldn't skip meals," Rebecca said in a disapproving voice. "It's bad for your health."

"All I want is a cup of coffee to relax me," Chase insisted, wishing he could have a stiff drink instead.

Suddenly it dawned on Rebecca. "I didn't buy coffee," she blurted.

"How could you forget to buy coffee?" Chase asked in disbelief. "You bought every other possible thing."

"I don't drink it. It's not good for you. I could make you a cup of hot tea, if you like."

"Hot tea?" Chase asked as if she had suggested poison. "No, thanks, I'll just skip the whole thing."

Chase turned and walked back to the wagon. Wearily he sank down to the ground and leaned against the wagon wheel, wondering where he was supposed to sleep. Well, he'd be damned if he'd ask her, like some little kid. God, she was a bossy one. Telling him what to do with his horse, lecturing him about rules and his health.

He leaned back and closed his eyes, aware of Rebecca's rustling skirts as she moved about the campfire. The tantalizing smell of bacon frying wafted through the air, and Chase's stomach grumbled. Now he wished that he hadn't said he didn't want anything to eat, but he'd be damned if he'd tell Rebecca differently. God, he was tired, too tired. He needed to unwind.

He sat up and pulled his last cheroot out of his tunic pocket. He'd saved it for a special occasion, but he needed it now. Maybe a good smoke would relax him. He looked up to see Rebecca watching him, a frown on her face.

"What's the matter?" Chase said angrily. "You going to tell me smoking is bad for my health too?"

"Well, it is, you know! But that's not what I was going to say. I was going to ask you not to smoke in the wagon. It leaves a bad smell."

"I'm not even in the wagon!"

"I know. But I was just warning you."

It was the crowning blow. Chase slammed to his feet, threw the cheroot to the ground, walked to his horse, and tossed his saddle blanket across the animal.

"What are you doing?" Rebecca asked in surprise.

"I'm going into Natchitoches," Chase ground out, throwing the saddle on the animal's back.

"What for?"

Chase turned and shot her a hot look. "For a smoke, a drink—and some peace and quiet!"

"A drink?" Rebecca asked in a shocked voice. Then she glared at him and placed her hands on her hips. "You're going into Natchitoches to get drunk, aren't you?"

"I hadn't planned on that—but I just might!" Chase replied angrily.

Rebecca watched in dismay as Chase turned his back on her and finished saddling his horse. "When will you be back?" she demanded.

"I don't know," Chase ground out between clenched teeth.

"But you *will* come back by morning?"

"I may—or I may not."

"But you've got to be back by then!" Rebecca cried. "That's when the wagon train leaves."

Chase made no comment. He tossed his saddle-bags over Lightning and reached for the reins.

My God, Rebecca thought. Was he going to walk out on her? Were all of Paul's plans and all of her hard work for nothing? In desperation she said, "You've got to come back. Remember your brother."

Slowly Chase turned, and when Rebecca saw the expression on his face, she stepped back in fear. His black eyes had that strange, frightening gleam in them again. His lips were compressed tightly with barely suppressed rage, a slash across his dark face.

"Don't ever threaten me," Chase said in a tight, warning voice.

"I—I wasn't threatening," Rebecca answered in a trembling voice, swallowing nervously. "I—I just wanted to remind you that you have a job to do. You agreed. You gave your word."

"And I'll do it," Chase muttered.

Rebecca let out a long sigh of relief, and then she almost jumped out of her skin as Chase stepped forward, towering over her, then leaned into her face, saying in a carefully measured voice as hard as steel "Let's get something straight right now. No one leads me around by the nose, no one nags me, and no one questions me. Particularly not some little snip of a girl."

Rebecca felt Chase's words like a slap on the face. Forgetting her fear, she drew herself up to her full five feet two inches. "I am *not* a little girl," she said indignantly. "I'm a woman."

Chase's dark eyes slowly raked Rebecca's body, and suddenly her knees felt weak and a peculiar warm curl formed deep in her belly.

"Yes, I guess you are a woman at that," Chase said in a strangely husky voice. Then he looked her straight in the eye. "But that doesn't change anything. I still won't have you sticking your nose into my business. The only reason you're coming along on this trip is because I need a 'wife.' Getting those cannons to Bexar is my job—not yours! You're just coming along for the ride."

With that Chase turned, walked to his horse, and mounted. Rebecca watched dumbly as he rode away into the darkness. Then she turned and rushed to the frying pan she had left on the fire. Using her skirt to protect her hand from being burned, she yanked the pan off the fire and stared down at the blackened strips of bacon. "Damn it," she muttered, blinking back tears of rage and frustration. "Now look what that bastard has done. He made me burn my supper!"

3

WHEN CHASE RODE BACK INTO CAMP EARLY the next morning, the place was bustling with activity. Women stood at a score or more of fires, hastily preparing breakfast, while the men packed the wagons and harnessed the teams of horses and mules or yokes of oxen, then hitched them to the wagons.

When Chase reached their wagon, Rebecca was nowhere in sight. Seeing the fire blazing beside it, he knew she was up and about, but where? He stood in his stirrups and scanned the area, looking for her distinctive color of hair among the people rushing about. Then he saw her coming from the corral and trying, without any success, to drive a triple yoke of oxen to the wagon. Chase dismounted, tied Lightning to the tail of the wagon, and wove his way through the crowd toward her, a smile of smug satisfaction on his face.

As Rebecca caught sight of Chase striding toward her, a wave of relief washed over her. When she had awakened that morning and discovered that he hadn't returned, she had feared that he wouldn't be back, despite his assurances that he intended to do the job.

She had spent a long night, twisting and turning, and had finally admitted that she *had* been waspish with Chase. Her mother had always warned her about her sharp tongue, but Rebecca always said what she thought. She realized that she was going to have to watch her words with Chase. He was a hard man—and a dangerous one, as she had found out last night. A tingle of fear ran through her as she remembered the look on his face. But trying to be agreeable with him was not going to be easy. The dark Texian had a way of irritating her as no one ever had.

After a good night's sleep, Chase was feeling a little mellower himself. Besides, he was confident that he had firmly put Rebecca in her place and that she wouldn't give him any more trouble. He took the harness reins from her hands. "I'll take care of the oxen. Why don't you go ahead and fix breakfast?"

Rebecca was more than happy to turn the intractable animals over to Chase. He was right, she had discovered. The beasts *were* stubborn and hard to handle. She nodded in silent agreement and hurried back to the wagon.

As she passed Chase's white stallion, she noticed the coffeepot tied to the back of the saddle and the sack of coffee hanging beside it. She stopped, staring at them, thinking that she ought to let him make his own damned coffee, if he was so determined to have it. Then, realizing that she was being childish, she untied the pot and sack. Besides, she wanted him to need her, even if it was for something as simple as cooking for him. If she wasn't needed for this mission, if she didn't feel she was contributing some small part to it, then how could she satisfy her need for revenge?

By the time Chase had finished harnessing the oxen to the wagon, breakfast was ready. Rebecca handed him his plate of food and then poured him a cup of coffee. The Texian's only reaction was a slight quirking of his dark eyebrows as he accepted the cup.

They had hardly finished breakfast when a man rode down the line of wagons, yelling "Load up! We're pulling out in ten minutes!"

Rebecca hurried to wash the dishes and load the cooking utensils into the wagon, while Chase put out the fire and unsaddled Lightning, tossing his saddlebags, saddle, and saddle blanket into the rear of the wagon.

They had hardly settled down in the wagon seat when they heard the cry, "Wagons ho!"

Rebecca felt a thrill of excitement running through her. Her big adventure was beginning, and at the end, she would have her revenge. Texas would be freed of the hated Mexicans forever.

Chase, however, was far from excited. The thought of riding on a hard wagon seat and staring at the broad rumps of six oxen trudging along at a snail's pace, day after day, was depressing. He was used to being in the saddle, directing his own course and rate of speed. He didn't like being tied down to a wagon—or anything, for that matter. Besides, it was going to be boring as hell.

But Chase was kept busy for the first hour. The oxen, having been out of the yoke for several weeks, kept trying to stray from the path, enticed by the sight of the grass growing beside the road, and it took a strong hand on the reins to keep them in line.

Sitting beside Rebecca on the wagon seat, Chase was very much aware of her. He hadn't realized the day before how small she was. Probably because he had been too irritated at her to notice, he admitted ruefully. Yesterday she certainly hadn't given him the impression of being little and defenseless, as she did now. Her sweet, womanly scent drifted toward him, and at every breath she took, Chase was acutely conscious of her breasts rising and falling.

He recalled what Paul had told him about Rebecca. At the time, he had not been particularly interested in her, but now he found he wanted to know more about her.

"Paul said that you have lived in Texas before, that you were . . ." Chase hesitated, searching for the right words. He didn't want to say kicked out. ". . . asked to leave."

"We *weren't* asked to leave," Rebecca said in a tight voice. "We were *told* to leave." Her eyes glittered angrily. "In fact, we were physically expelled."

"What happened?"

"We weren't squatters, if that's what you're thinking. My father had every right to be there."

"Then you were settled on one of the land

grants by a legitimate *empresario?*" Chase asked in surprise.

"Yes, we were. We settled in the Robertson Colony, just north of Steven Austin's little colony. My father picked out a large tract of land on the Brazos River and paid Sterling Robertson a good sum for it. He was going to raise cotton, just like he had back in Mississippi."

"Then what went wrong?"

"There was some kind of a mix-up. When the grant was approved by the Mexican government, the agent for the land company at that time put the title in his name and then sold it back to the company, which was perfectly legal. After we had been in Texas for several months, the Mexicans told us we had to leave. They claimed that they had no record of the title being changed. Robertson was the new agent for the company and had no idea there was a problem when he brought us to Texas. He and his family, along with the other settlers, fled to Austin's colony. Robertson planned to ask Austin to intercede with the Mexicans and get the misunderstanding straightened out. But my father refused to leave with the others. He wanted to finish building our home and the slaves' quarters before winter set in, and get the fields cleared for spring planting. He thought Robertson and Austin would get things cleared up in a few weeks."

Rebecca swallowed hard, fighting back tears, before she continued. "For several weeks nothing happened. Then, one day, a patrol of Mexican dragoons came to our plantation and demanded to see the title for the land. My father tried to explain why he didn't have it, what the mix-up was, but the officer in charge wouldn't listen to him. He claimed we were squatters and said he was going to deport us. Then he ordered his men to burn the buildings. When my father saw what they were going to do, he and my brother ran for their rifles, but before they could even prime them, the soldiers shot them. Even after they were dead, the soldiers kept shooting them."

Rebecca choked back a sob and turned her back to Chase. While she struggled to compose herself, Chase sat silent, staring straight ahead, wishing he could do something to comfort her yet sensing that she'd resent any sign of compassion.

After a few moments Rebecca brushed back her tears and straightened in the seat. She sat, staring ahead of her for a long while, and Chase thought that was all she was going to tell him. Then she resumed her tale. "The Mexicans set fire to all of the buildings, even the corral. Then they put me and my mother and our slaves in wagons and took us to Nacogdoches. They wouldn't even let us bury my father and brother. We stayed in a prison there for a few days before we were joined by some squatters the Mexicans had arrested. Then they took us all back to the Sabine, warning us never to come back to Texas again. They kept our slaves and all of our animals, except for the one horse pulling our wagon," she ended bitterly.

Chase had heard stories of isolated incidents much like Rebecca's. He'd never known if they were true or just rumors spread by the war party in Texas to fire the Anglos' hatred against the Mexicans. He did know of legitimate settlers having difficulty getting the titles to their land. Many colonists in Nacogdoches had yet to see them. With the Mexican government constantly changing hands as the country was torn by one revolution after another, officials in Mexico City had repeatedly set aside the legal paperwork for the colonists in Texas. It seemed the Mexican government had more important things to do than worry about the settlers in far-off Texas, which was one of the Texians' grievances against Mexico. They had wanted their own state government, one that would handle such problems and would protect their interests. In short, like the English colonists of almost a century before them, the Texians wanted a government closer to home, a government that they would have a voice in.

"When did all this happen?" Chase asked.

"Five years ago this past fall."

"But that was after Mexico suspended all land grants and prohibited any more Americans from entering Texas. Didn't Sterling Robertson explain that to your father?"

"Robertson didn't know about the decree when he brought us to Texas. The law was passed in April. We crossed the Sabine in May, before the news of it even arrived in Texas. And when we did learn of it, Mr. Robertson said the decree didn't apply to us, that it only applied to those land grants of the *empresarios* that hadn't already settled at least one hundred families in Texas—which he had! No, we *weren't* squatters. We were in Texas legally. The Mexicans had no right to do what they did."

Chase frowned, recalling past events. When the Mexicans realized how many Americans were entering Texas, they had become alarmed, fearing that the Anglos would try to take the land away from them. They had passed a law suspending all land grants and prohibiting the settlement of colonists from the United States. A large group of late immigrants had been caught by the sudden decree. Many were legitimate but had failed to get their titles, like Rebecca's family, but the Mexican government considered them all illegal immigrants, along with the squatters. Then the Mexicans had sent troops to East Texas, claiming it was to protect the settlers from Indians, but the Anglos knew better and resented the military occupation, particularly since the soldiers were common criminals, taken from Mexican jails. The law was later rescinded, and the *empresurios* were allowed to bring families into Texas again, providing they had not already met their quota. But, under the new ruling, the colonists were not allowed to bring their slaves with them, and many of the older settlers feared Mexico was going to abolish slavery, which only added fuel to the fire that was already smoldering.

Chase brought his mind back to the present, saying "So there was only you and your mother left. What did you do? Go back to your old plantation in Mississippi?"

"No. There was nothing to go back to. My father had invested everything he had into the Texas plantation. So we moved in with my mother's sister in Natchez. My mother died six months later. My aunt said she grieved herself to death, which wasn't far from the truth. My mother never recovered from the shock of seeing my father and brother murdered before her very eyes. From that day on, she never spoke another word. She didn't seem to know where she was, or who I was. She just existed, going steadily downhill, until she died. The Mexicans killed her too. Just as sure as they'd put a gun to her head and shot her."

"And what about your aunt? Does she approve of your going on this trip to deliver cannons to the Texians?"

"She doesn't know. She thinks I'm visiting my father's relatives in Montgomery." A fiercely determined gleam came into Rebecca's eyes. "But even if she had known and objected, she couldn't have stopped me. No one could. The day I saw my father and brother murdered, I vowed that I'd do everything in my power to see Texas freed from Mexico, that someday I'd go to Texas and get my father's land back."

Chase could understand Rebecca's motives for getting involved in the Texas revolution much better than Paul's. His reasons were based on patriotism—or so he claimed—a love of country that Chase, with his Indian blood, had difficulty comprehending. The Comanches gave their allegiance to no one except the immediate tribe to which they belonged. They were bonded to people, not the land. But Chase understood Rebecca's reasons only too well. She wanted revenge. It was a powerful emotion, one that had driven men—and women—since the beginning of time.

Rebecca was very quiet for the rest of the day, and Chase knew that she was brooding over the traumatic events of the past. He wished that he hadn't said anything.

When they finally camped that evening, the wagons pulling into a tight circle for protection, Rebecca was exhausted, both from the unaccustomed bouncing on the wagon and her emotional upheaval. She hurriedly prepared the evening meal while Chase unhitched the oxen and led them to the corral for the night.

They had hardly finished eating when Jamie McPherson walked up to Chase. "Winters, I'm assignin' you to first watch tonight. I know that you've been separated from your wife for a while and that you're newlyweds and all, but the other men have been watchin' over your oxen all this time and feel that it is only fair that you take the first watch out. So I'm afraid that you'll have to put your pleasurin' off for a while."

Chase glanced back over his shoulder at Rebecca and saw her blushing furiously. Well, McPherson had warned them that he didn't believe in mincing words.

Chase grinned and replied, "No problem, McPherson. There's always tomorrow night."

Chase heard Rebecca's gasp behind him and grinned wider. Then he picked up his rifle and strolled off with McPherson.

Rebecca watched the two men as they walked away into the darkness, wondering whether Chase had only been playing along with the wagon master or if the Texian had been serious. Did he think that because she had agreed to travel with him, posing as his wife, she was some loose woman and wouldn't object to sharing intimacies—whatever that meant—with him? Well, he was going to be in for a big surprise!

After Rebecca had washed the dishes and banked the fire, she wearily climbed into the wagon, not even noticing the flashes of lightning in the distance. She unrolled the small feather mattress at one end of the wagon. It was the only luxury she had allowed herself on this trip, remembering only too well how hard the wagon floor had been on her first journey to Texas. Quickly she undressed, slipped on her flannel gown, and lay down, pulling the blanket over her. She was asleep almost as soon as her head hit the pillow.

She was awakened by a noise and opened her eyes to see the shadow of a man standing over her. She gasped, sat up, and opened her mouth to scream, but it died in her throat as a strong hand closed over her mouth.

"Don't scream. It's only me," Chase said in a low voice, squatting beside her.

He removed his hand and Rebecca asked irritably, "What are you doing here? I thought you were on watch."

"First watch. I've been relieved," Chase answered, standing up.

Rebecca could vaguely see he was pulling off his tunic. "What are you doing?" she snapped.

"I'm fixing to go to bed," Chase answered calmly.

"In here? No! You sleep outside!"

Chase tossed the tunic aside. "Are you crazy? It's raining outside!"

For the first time Rebecca heard the steady patter of raindrops on the canvas above them. "Then sleep under the wagon."

"It's muddy under the wagon. Besides, it's cold out there. Why should I sleep outside when I've got a perfectly good wagon to sleep in?"

"Then sleep at the other end!"

"Where? Christ, there's not even room to breathe back there, with all those damned crates sitting around. I have to turn sideways even to get through. Where in the hell would I lay down? Or even sit, for that matter?"

Rebecca could see by his shadowy movements that he was fiddling with his pants. "What are you doing?" she asked in alarm.

"I'm taking off my pants," Chase replied in exasperation.

"You're going to strip stark naked?" Rebecca asked in a shocked voice.

"My buckskins are soaked. Have you ever slept in soggy buckskins? It's miserable," Chase replied tightly, yanking the pants off and tossing them on top of the tunic.

"But you can't take off your clothes!" Rebecca objected, feeling panic stricken. "Expose yourself to me like that!"

"Hell, it's dark in here! You can't see anything."

At that minute a flash of lightning briefly illuminated the interior of the wagon, and Rebecca did get a fleeting glimpse of Chase. What she saw didn't repulse her in the least, although she had always imagined the sight of a naked man would. There was a primitive beauty about him as he towered over her, tall and superbly muscled, his wet bronze skin glistening, his black eyes blazing. The sight was strangely exciting.

"If it will make you feel any better, I'll wrap up in this," Chase said, snatching a blanket off the mattress.

"I told you, I don't want you in here. You sleep outside!"

"Damn it, no!"

"If you don't get out of here, I'll—I'll scream!"

"Scream?" Chase asked in disbelief. "And have half the wagon train running over here to see what's going on? And then what will you tell them? That your *husband* tried to crawl in bed with you?"

Rebecca realized that she couldn't ask for protection from the settlers. If she told them the truth, then they'd both be kicked off the train. No, she'd have to defend herself. She pulled her blanket around her and glared up at Chase. "If you touch me, I'll scratch your eyes out!"

"Is that what you're afraid of? That I'll try something? Hell, I didn't come in here to make love to you. I came in here to sleep."

"But you said this evening—"

"I was only teasing!" Chase interjected in an exasperated voice. "For Christ's sake! Can't you take a joke? Now move over."

Rebecca moved to the side. It was either that or be sat on by Chase. She sat, holding the blanket around her tightly, protectively, hovering as close to the side of the wagon as she could possibly get. Chase lay down and rolled over with his back to her.

The minutes passed. The only sounds were the pattering of the rain and an occasional crash of lightning. Finally Chase rolled over and said, "For God's sake, Rebecca, will you stop boring holes in my back and lie down? I told you I'm not going to try anything. Despite what you've heard about Indians, I don't force my attentions on women. I like them warm and willing—and experienced!"

Chase turned his back to her again, and Rebecca stared at his shadowy form for a long time. His assurance that he didn't want her hadn't comforted her in the least; in fact, he had stung her pride and left her feeling inadequate.

When Chase heard Rebecca finally lie back down, he shook his head in frustration. He'd underestimated her when he thought that he had firmly put her in her place the night before, that she wouldn't dare question his actions again or try to tell him what to do. All he was winning in this running battle with Rebecca were skirmishes, and he feared it was going to be a long war.

When Chase heard Rebecca's steady breathing and knew that she was asleep, he closed his eyes. But as tired as he was, sleep wouldn't come. He was too aware of Rebecca's nearness. He could feel her warmth and smell her sweet scent, both tantalizing his senses. Eventually he dozed off, only to become suddenly wide awake when Rebecca, drawn by his body heat, snuggled against him in her sleep.

Chase tensed, lying perfectly still, acutely conscious of Rebecca's soft breasts rising and falling against his bare back and her legs pressed against the back of his, her touch scorching him and leaving him aroused and aching for release. Tormented by mental visions of her soft, kissable lips, he struggled to fight back the urge to turn and take her in his arms, to taste those lips and feel that silky skin that was driving him wild. Finally realizing that he was losing the battle against his rising passion, Chase muttered a curse, rose, dressed in his damp buckskins, and left the wagon, refusing even to look back for fear that he would give in to his raging desire.

4

THE NEXT MORNING CHASE SAT ON THE WAGON seat—alone. He had been stirring around their camp long before Rebecca had awakened. When she had gotten up to prepare breakfast and they ate, she had ignored him, shooting him icy looks when he got too close. As soon as the train had pulled out, she had climbed into the back of the wagon where she was now.

Chase didn't have to turn around and look to know what she was doing. He could hear her shoving the crates around and rearranging the sacks and barrels, clearing an area in the back of the wagon for him to sleep in. God, she was the feistiest woman he'd ever met in his life.

But, he admitted to himself, it was probably a good thing that Rebecca was. After last night he seriously doubted that he could lie beside her and keep his hands off her. Just thinking about it made his heat rise, his throat dry. And he'd be damned if he'd back down and sleep under the wagon, as Rebecca had ordered him to do.

Chase frowned, puzzled by his strong attraction

to her. Sure she was beautiful, with all the curves in the right places, but she was also sharp-tongued, bossy, and obstinate. She wasn't at all what he considered the ideal woman to be—sweet, soft-spoken, even-tempered, serene. Blanche had been that kind of woman—and so had Shining Water. Chase frowned at the thought of the Indian maiden, a fresh pang of regret washing over him as the memories came rushing back.

When Blanche had died, his father had taken his two sons on his mustang raids into Texas. For two years Chase had followed the herds, captured them, and driven them across the Sabine. Then his father had been killed in a stampede. Jim had decided to stay with the mustangers, but Chase had never felt that he really belonged in the white man's world so he had returned to the Comanches.

A month after his arrival he had gone into the wilderness on his visionary quest. For four days and four nights, he fasted and prayed and waited for the sign that would tell him what his guardian spirit would be. He had finally spied an eagle circling high in the sky, and that had become his medicine.

In the three years that followed, he had gone on buffalo hunts and horse raids—and fallen in love. Shining Water had been only fourteen at the time —by Comanche standards, a marriageable age for a woman. She was doe-eyed, with hair as black as a raven's wing, shy, soft-spoken, sweet-tempered. And she had idolized Chase. He would have taken her as his wife had not fate intervened.

A raid into Mexico had been planned for that

September, and Chase had been chosen as one of the warriors to go on it, a great honor for one so young. The war party had swept south, crossed the Nueces River, then the Rio Grande, and ridden deep into Mexico. Their first attack was on a small village, the homes no more than mud hovels. Because of his youth, Chase was assigned a sentry post instead of taking part in the actual fighting.

That night Chase discovered that the raid on the Mexicans was nothing like the earlier raids he had made on the Wichitas and Cherokees, where he had earned his coup marks by touching his living enemy, which the Indians considered much more courageous than killing. No, on those raids the objective had been to steal horses, not to kill. He had been shocked by what he witnessed in Mexico, the rampant murder, rape, and plunder. Chase knew that the Mexicans were the Comanches' old enemies, but what he had seen had not been fighting. It was a massacre of unarmed men, the killing of innocents guilty of no crime against his people— men, women, and children murdered only because they had the hated Mexican blood in their veins. And he had been shocked. To him it was no different from a white man hating and killing an Indian simply because he was an Indian.

There had been other raids, some repetitions of the first and others against large, well-fortified *haciendas*. In most of the later cases, the homes were left burning but still intact, and the Comanches had to content themselves with stealing the horses and cattle instead.

On the long ride back north, Chase had brooded

over what he had seen. By the time the victorious war party had ridden back into their camp, waving fresh scalps over their heads, Chase had known that he didn't belong to the Indians' world either. On the next raid he knew that he would be expected to kill too, and Chase couldn't stomach it. To him, it was senseless. Nothing would be proved or resolved. Deciding to go back East, he had asked Shining Water to accompany him, but she had refused, afraid to leave her people and the only life she had ever known. Chase had left, knowing that she was the only woman he would ever love. He had never returned to his tribe but he carried her memory in his heart.

Since then Chase had moved in a shadowy, in-between world, dealing with both the Indians and the white man and yet never feeling that he belonged with either. He wished that he could totally accept the culture of one, without any doubts or reservations, and firmly reject the other, but he found that he could no more do that than separate the two bloods that flowed in his veins.

The feel of Rebecca jabbing his shoulder with her elbow as she climbed back on the wagon seat brought Chase back to the present. He watched from the corner of his eye as she sat down and folded her hands primly in her lap, staring straight ahead, her small chin stuck out, her back as rigid as a ramrod.

"I've cleared a space in the back of the wagon for you to spread your bedroll," she said in a haughty voice.

"Thank you," Chase replied.

Rebecca shot Chase an oblique, icy look. "You're quite welcome," she said stiffly.

He watched as she inched away from him toward the edge of the wagon seat, as if he were something dirty and she couldn't get far enough away. The act infuriated Chase. She hadn't been so anxious to keep away from him last night, he thought angrily. If she had stayed where she belonged, he wouldn't have had to leave the wagon and might have gotten some much-needed sleep.

Without even looking at her Chase said, "It really wasn't necessary for you to clear me a space though. I didn't mind you putting your cold feet on my bare legs."

Rebecca turned to face Chase so rapidly that he was amazed that she hadn't snapped her head off at her shoulders. "What are you talking about?" she demanded.

"Oh? Don't you remember snuggling up to me last night? Curling your body around me, like a kitten to a warm, toasty fire?"

Rebecca's eyes widened in horror. Had she done that in her sleep? Snuggled up to him? And my God, he had been naked!

Chase slowly turned his head, looking Rebecca directly in the eye. He smiled. "If you get cold at your end of the wagon, you can always join me at mine. But let me warn you, Rebecca. The next time you press that soft, delightful body of yours up against me so intimately, I intend to accept the invitation. Then I'll really warm you up."

Rebecca gasped, her face turning beet red at his implication. She jerked her head away to stare at the six oxen. She desperately wished she could think of some cutting rebuke, but no words came to mind. It seemed that he took pleasure in humiliating her, and she hated him for it.

For the rest of the day Rebecca sat mute beside Chase, not even giving him a sideways look. Chase was so bored he almost wished she was railing at him again. Anything would be better than sitting there, staring at the wagon ahead of them, the dust raised from the animals' hooves choking him and making his eyes water, the only sound the creaking of the wagon and the steady monotonous *clip-clop* of the oxens' hooves on the ground. When Rebecca climbed from the wagon to walk beside it later that afternoon, Chase glared at her, resenting the fact that she could get down and stretch her legs, while he was forced to sit there and drive. He longed to saddle Lightning and take a long, hard ride through the countryside. If he had to go through one more day of this, he'd go crazy!

That night, as soon as her evening chores were finished, Rebecca lay on her feather mattress, her ears straining for the sound of Chase's approaching steps. She halfway expected him to crawl into her end of the wagon, just to spite her. For some reason she couldn't understand, he seemed determined to bend her to his will, and Rebecca was equally determined not to bend.

When she heard him at the back of the wagon, Rebecca felt a strange twinge of disappointment. She briefly puzzled over it, then decided it was only because she wanted the opportunity to put him in his place. Imagine! Suggesting that she had snuggled close to him for something more than warmth. And him, of all men—a half-breed!

Rebecca listened closely, hearing a faint rustling sound. She knew Chase was stripping off his buckskins. My God, did he always sleep in the nude? Of course. He was a heathen, wasn't he? Why, they even run around half naked in the daylight!

Then the memory of Chase standing over her the night before, magnificent and utterly male in his nakedness, came flooding back. Rebecca tried to force the image from her mind, but it seemed to be etched there, as if the lightning itself had burned the vision into her brain for all time. That strange, warm curl formed deep in her belly again and her mouth turned dry. She shivered, a shiver that had nothing to do with fear.

The next morning Rebecca looked around the clearing irritably. Chase was nowhere in sight. His breakfast had been ready for over fifteen minutes, and she'd seen nothing of the Texian. She knew he had to be somewhere close by. The oxen were already hitched to the wagon. If he didn't hurry back, he'd have to skip his breakfast. Everyone had already loaded up, including her.

Then she saw him, riding his stunning white horse and threading his way through the crowded camp. Despite her anger, her breath caught at the sight of him. On foot, Chase was a striking man, with his dark, rugged good looks and his exceptional breadth of shoulders, but mounted, he was magnificent. Chase rode his stallion with an ease and skill that made man and animal seem to blend into one graceful, powerful unit. Rebecca was aware that she wasn't the only one who had noticed. Everyone in the camp had turned and stared in awe.

Rebecca watched while he dismounted, still stunned, and then, remembering her anger at him, demanded, "Where have you been?"

Chase winced at her sharp tone of voice and fought back the urge to yell back, None of your damned business! But he was determined not to start this day off on a bad footing, no matter how much Rebecca irritated him. "Out for a ride," he answered calmly.

A ride? Rebecca thought. He's out for a leisurely ride, while I'm slaving away packing our wagon? She glared at him.

Chase ignored her hot look and picked up his plate. Between bites he said, "I stopped by McPherson's wagon and told him that I've done some traveling in Texas. He asked me if I'd mind doing some scouting for him." Handing her his empty plate, he asked, "Do you think you could drive the wagon?"

Remembering the morning she had tried to drive the oxen from the corral to the wagon, Rebecca seriously doubted that she could handle the big beasts, but she hated to admit that to Chase. Then he might accuse her of being nothing but excess baggage again. "I'm sure I can," she answered with a confidence she really didn't feel. "After all, some of the other women drive."

Chase wondered. True, some of the other women in the train did drive, many with a skill that equaled their husbands'. A few even drove oxen, but none drove *six* of the huge, stubborn animals.

Seeing the look of doubt in Chase's eyes, Rebecca was determined she do it, just to prove him wrong. "I said I could drive!"

Chase longed to do the scouting, to get away from that damned wagon, to be in the saddle again. "All right," he agreed. "We'll see if you can."

Rebecca placed Chase's plate and eating utensils in the back of the wagon. Then Chase slammed the tailgate shut and together they walked to the front of the wagon. When Rebecca was seated, Chase showed her how to hold the reins, wrapping them around her wrists, then her hands, to give her a firmer grip on them. Then he stepped back down and mounted. "I'll just ride beside you, until you get the hang of it."

When the wagon before them pulled away, Rebecca jiggled the reins and called, "Giddy up." The oxen, sensing someone new at the reins, stood, stubbornly refusing to move. Aware of Chase's dark eyes on her and fearing that he would say I told you so, Rebecca stood and shook the reins harder, calling even louder "I said move, you blasted beasts!"

Rebecca never knew if it was her violent jiggling of the reins or her tone of voice that finally made the oxen step forward, but when they did, she turned and grinned with self-satisfaction at Chase.

Rebecca found out that while getting the animals to move was one thing, getting them to move in the direction she wanted was quite another.

"They're straying off the road!" Chase called. "Pull the reins to the left."

Rebecca pulled on the reins, the muscles in her shoulders and arms straining.

"Damn it, pull hard!" Chase called.

"I *am* pulling hard!" Rebecca retorted, tears of pain stinging in her eyes as her muscles screamed. Then, seeing Chase was about to swing from his saddle and onto the seat beside her, she yelled, "No! I can do it!"

Chase sat back in his saddle and watched as Rebecca finally wrestled the oxen back into the line. Damn it, he had to hand it to her, he thought. When she set her mind to something, nothing— neither man nor beast—was going to change it.

For most of the morning Chase rode beside the wagon to observe Rebecca's driving. Then, around noon, satisfied that she could manage it, he said, "I'll see you tonight."

Rebecca watched as Chase galloped off, feeling a twinge of panic. She had felt relatively safe knowing he was beside her, but now that he was gone, she was on her own. She could only hope the oxen wouldn't take a notion to turn around and go back in the direction they had come. She could be back in Natchitoches before she could stop them.

It was a long, long day for Rebecca. She found if her attention strayed in the slightest, the oxen took the opportunity to leave the trail, and she'd have to wrestle them back in line. The third time it happened, she thought hotly, Chase was right when he said they were slow and stubborn. But they are *not* stupid. Oh, no, those devils knew what they were doing!

By evening, Rebecca was exhausted. Every muscle in her body ached, and her wrists were raw from where the leather had chafed them when she pulled on the reins. She sat on the hard wagon seat, her bottom numb, cursing the animals, calling them every ugly name she had ever heard.

Chase, thinking that Rebecca might have trouble getting the oxen to circle when they made camp, rode up to the wagon from behind and heard her. He was a little shocked that the well-bred Rebecca even knew such strong words, much less how to use them so well. Then he heard her say "You son of a bitch, if you give me any more hassle, I swear to God, I'll shoot you!"

Chase grinned, remembering how many times he had been tempted to do just that. He hadn't noticed that Rebecca had used the singular cuss word or realized that, at that moment, she was referring to him and not the oxen.

When Chase drew up beside her, Rebecca started, wondering how long he had been there or if he had heard her cursing and threatening him. The color rose in her face; she was horrified at being caught. But Chase didn't notice Rebecca's flush. He was shocked by how exhausted she appeared, and a twinge of guilt ran through him.

He swung from his horse and sat down beside her on the wagon seat. "Let me have the reins. I'll drive them into the circle."

"I can manage!" Rebecca said stubbornly, determined to complete her task.

"No, today you just watch. It's tricky business."

Rebecca slipped the reins from her wrists and handed them to Chase. Seeing the rawness of her wrists, Chase frowned, then turned his attention to the oxen.

As soon as they had stopped, Chase jumped down. Assuming that he was going to unhitch the wagon, as he had done the past two days, Rebecca turned and wearily started backing down from the wagon, wondering how she was ever going to find the strength to build a fire and prepare a meal. Then Chase's strong hands curled around her waist and swung her lightly to the ground, causing her to gasp in surprise. As soon as her feet hit the ground, she turned and saw him smiling down at her. Then she became aware of Chase's hands still on her waist, burning her through her clothing. And he was standing much too close. She could feel the heat radiating from him and smell his scent, a mixture of woodsmoke, pine needles, and a vague masculine muskiness that sent her pulses pounding. Suddenly his presence was overpowering.

She tore his hands away frantically and stepped back, almost staggering on her weak legs. "That wasn't necessary," Rebecca said, wondering why she felt so breathless.

"I was only helping you down," Chase replied.

"I can get down by myself. I don't need your help!"

Shaking his head in exasperation, Chase watched as Rebecca rushed away. Damn it, it seemed no matter what he did, it made her angry.

Hell, he couldn't even be polite without making her mad. He had thought to offer to cook supper tonight, since she was obviously so exhausted. Even though it was considered women's work by the other men in the camp, Chase was accustomed to cooking for himself and felt it would be a small price to pay for his freedom that day. But Rebecca was so damned independent, she'd probably refuse that too. Disgusted, he turned and started unhitching the oxen from the wagon.

Rebecca found driving easier and easier as the days passed and her muscles became accustomed to the hard work. And with the strips of lamb wool that Chase had given her, surprising her with his consideration, her wrists had quickly healed.

But even though the driving was easier, she found that she was bored to tears, for once Chase had assured himself that she was capable of the tricky job of circling the oxen, he was gone from dawn to dusk, and sometimes even later. When he did turn up, Rebecca was always happy to see him, a spontaneous reaction that irritated her. She kept telling herself that she didn't miss *his* company, but just the company of another human being, for everyone on the train, men, women, and children alike, was dour and unsociable, seemingly taking no pleasure from life.

She glanced over and saw Chase sidling his horse up to the wagon beside her. She was so pleased to see him that she didn't even try to hide her emotion. "You're back early," she commented with a wide smile.

Chase was stunned by that dazzling smile and

the sparkle in Rebecca's beautiful blue eyes. He was never sure what her mood would be. She might snap his head off, or give him the cold shoulder, totally ignoring him, or sometimes, on rare occasions, be almost civil. But today she actually looked glad to see him, and Chase felt a sudden surge of happiness, which he firmly told himself was only relief.

He smiled back. "Yes, there's nothing going on out there."

"You've seen no Indians at all?"

"No."

For a moment they rode in silence. Afraid that he would gallop off and leave her to her boredom again, Rebecca searched desperately for something to say. Then her eyes fell on his mount. "What did you say the name of your horse was?" she asked.

"Lightning."

"Lightning? Why did you name him that?"

"Because the first time I saw him racing across the plains, he looked like a flash of blue-white lightning."

Rebecca glanced at the animal's white coat. It did have a faint bluish tint to it. She examined the animal closer. He was smaller than most horses, but broad-chested and powerfully built. For the first time she noticed that his ears and muzzle were black and that his long mane and thick, sweeping tail were tipped with black.

"I never realized that he had so much black on him," she commented.

"Yes. Even his skin is black beneath his coat. That's what gives him that bluish cast."

Rebecca was amazed. She had never looked that close at a horse. She had just assumed that their skin was the same color as their coat.

"When I first saw Lightning, I thought he was the famous Winged Steed—or the Ghost Horse of the Prairie, as the Comanches call him—because of his color and his speed. And then I realized that he wasn't pacing but running."

"What did that have to do with it?"

"The Winged Steed never runs. He doesn't gallop or trot. The only gait he has, outside of a walk, is a pace. And he can pace faster than any other horse can run."

"Then you've actually seen this horse? He isn't just a legend?"

"Yes, I've seen him—just once, up near the Arkansas. He was the most beautiful horse I've ever seen, with splendid proportions. His tail and mane are so long, they touch the ground, and when he paced across the plains, with his long mane flying out on both sides, it did look like he had wings."

"Then you were disappointed when you realized that Lightning wasn't him?"

"No, not really. Oh sure, every mustanger dreams of capturing the Winged Steed. Some men have spent years chasing him. But I don't think anyone will ever capture him. So I was more than happy to settle for what I considered second best to him—Lightning," Chase said, patting his horse's neck proudly.

"Was he alone when you found him?" Rebecca asked.

"No, he had his mares with him. Sixty-two, if I

remember correctly. But Lightning was a young stallion. I'm sure, given time, he could have had a herd of mares, a *manada,* of at least twice that size."

"And you captured the entire *manada?*"

"You don't have to capture the *manada.* Just the stallion. The mares will follow him wherever he goes. They only scatter if the stallion is accidentally killed in the capture, and then you have a hell of a time trying to round them up. Then your best bet is to send in a tame stallion, but not just any stallion. It has to be one with a strong herding instinct."

Chase chuckled to himself. "I remember one poor tame stallion we sent into a herd of wild mares. Oh, he was eager enough, but he couldn't dominate them. They scattered, and he ran off with a group of them. Several days later he came limping back into camp. I've never seen such an exhausted horse in my entire life. Besides that, he was covered with bites and hoof scratches. I think he was glad to be home. He found out that having a harem wasn't all pleasure, but a lot of work too."

Despite Chase's tale being a little racy, for there was no doubt in her mind what had exhausted the stallion, Rebecca had to laugh. She could almost see the poor beaten-up animal limping in, looking, no doubt, sheepish too.

Chase was surprised at Rebecca's laugh. He had expected her to become outraged and icy. Encouraged, he slipped from Lightning's saddle and onto the wagon seat by her.

Rebecca was surprised when she heard the call

"Circle up!" being passed down the line of wagons. With Chase sitting beside her and telling her stories of his experiences as a mustanger, the time had flown by.

As soon as they had stopped, Chase jumped down, and Rebecca assumed that he was going to unhitch the oxen. But before she could climb down, he stepped back up to the wagon, holding two lifeless rabbits in his hand. Where had those been? Rebecca wondered, then realized that they must have been on the side of the saddle she couldn't see.

He handed them up to her. "I thought we'd have some fresh meat tonight."

That thought made Rebecca's mouth water. She was already tired of the smoked and salted meat they carried. But she had no idea how to skin a rabbit. She frowned.

"What's the matter?" Chase asked, seeing her expression. "Don't you like rabbit meat?"

"I love it, especially roasted. But I've never skinned a rabbit. My father or brother always did that."

Rebecca was afraid Chase was going to show disgust at her stupidity, but, to her surprise, he simply said, "Don't worry about it. I'll dress them for you as soon as I get back from taking the oxen to the corral."

That night, after they had eaten and Rebecca was washing their dishes, Chase walked to the wagon and took his rifle from it. On his way back to the fire he asked, "Are you going to be using any more of that boiling water over the fire?"

"No, I have enough."

Chase picked up a cup that Rebecca had just dried and walked to the fire. Sitting on a small camp stool, he removed the stock from his rifle, then dipped the cup into the pot of hot water and poured the water down the gun barrel. Over and over he repeated the procedure, flushing any remaining gunpowder residue from the barrel.

Having finished her chore, Rebecca dried her hands, removed her apron, and walked up to him, saying in a curious voice "What kind of a gun is that? I've never seen a rifle that short."

"It's a Hawkens—a plains rifle—and it's shorter than a Kentucky rifle because it's made for carrying on a horse. It also has a shorter range than a Kentucky, but it makes up for it in firepower, shooting a much bigger ball."

For a few moments Rebecca watched as Chase oiled the barrel and then pinned the stock back on the barrel. Then she noticed something missing on the gun. "Where's the priming pan?"

"This isn't a flintlock rifle. It's what they call a caplock. It uses percussion caps—pellets of fulminate—instead of flint, steel, and priming powder. With percussion caps you can load easier and faster."

"Why, I've never heard of such a thing! What if you lost those caps? Why, you wouldn't be able to fire your gun. At least if you lost your flint, you could always use a rock."

Chase chuckled. "Now you're sounding like some of those old mountain men I ran into when I went to St. Louis to pick up this gun. They were buying rifles from the Hawkens brothers too, but they insisted that their guns be fitted with flintlocks and not caplocks, for the same reason you gave. No, I won't lose my caps, any more than I'd lose the extra horn of priming powder I used to have to carry. Now I carry two pouches, instead of two powder horns, one for the balls and one for the percussion caps."

Rebecca glanced at Chase's chest where the two pouches hung, along with his powder horn. And then she noticed that there were four leather thongs hanging from his neck. The fourth held something concealed by his tunic. But what? Then she remembered seeing him naked in the lightning flash and that a pouch, smaller than the other two, had dangled from his neck. What was in that pouch? she wondered. What was so important to him that he slept with it, even wore it when he was completely naked?

Chase rose and carried his rifle back to the wagon. Rebecca bent and banked the fire, thinking that he had gone to bed and feeling disappointed. When she stood, she was surprised and pleased to see him striding toward her.

"You told McPherson that you had a rifle. I'd like to look at it, if I may."

"Why?" Rebecca asked irritably. She had thought he had come back to spend more time with her, and all he wanted to do was see her rifle.

"Because I want to see what condition it's in."

"It's in good condition," Rebecca replied tightly.

"Rebecca," Chase said, trying to be patient, "we'll be crossing the Sabine tomorrow—"

"Tomorrow?" Rebecca interjected, her eyes sparkling with excitement. "We'll be in Texas tomorrow?"

"Yes, we should reach the river about noon, and from then on we'll be in Indian country. Now, I want to be sure we have *two* good rifles. I need to check the vent on your gun to be sure it's clear. Unless you want it to explode on you and then go through life with your face permanently tattooed."

Rebecca had seen men with such powder burns, the side of their faces sprinkled with blue-black specks where the gunpowder had embedded itself in their skin. They hadn't bothered to clean their rifles after using them, leaving the sticky gunpowder residue to accumulate and clog the vent, or had loaded too fast and poured powder into the gun while there was still a piece of burning lint in it from the last shot. She was almost certain that the vent in her rifle was clear. She had cleaned it herself. But then, it wouldn't hurt to let Chase double check it. She certainly didn't want to be branded for life.

Rebecca walked to the wagon and climbed into it. Chase waited until she had lit the lamp before he joined her. Rebecca reached for a long, wrapped object resting against one of the crates, placed it on the floor, and unrolled the oilskin to reveal the rifle. Standing, she handed it to Chase.

Chase looked down at the Kentucky rifle in his hand. It was a good five feet long, but light, and it was one of the most beautiful rifles he'd seen. The stock was made of the prized tiger maple, or fiddle-back as it was commonly called, and the stripped wood had a rich patina that only time could give it. The butt, with its raised cheekplate, and the stock were decorated with silver and brass inlays. Even the long, brass patch box at the side of the butt had scrolled edges on it.

"It's a real beauty," Chase remarked in an almost awed voice, lightly running his fingers over the sleek gun.

Rebecca was very much aware of Chase stroking the gun, almost caressing it. She found herself wishing that he would touch her that way, so tenderly, so lovingly, and the thought shocked her.

"Where did you get it?" Chase asked.

Unable to recover from her shock, Rebecca stammered, "It—it was—was my father's. He was very proud of it. And very attached to it. It was the only thing the Mexicans allowed me to take with us that day."

Chase's head snapped up at Rebecca's words. "The Mexicans allowed you to carry a gun?" he asked in surprise.

"They knew it wasn't loaded. My father never got the chance. Besides, I wouldn't let them take it away from me. When they tried to, I went . . . berserk, I guess. When one of the Mexicans grabbed it from me, I attacked him, kicking and clawing. I finally wrestled it away from him and then started swinging it at the others who were trying to get it away from me. I guess they finally decided it wasn't worth getting a bashed-in head over. Besides, I think they thought I was demented and were a little afraid of me. So from then on, anytime they got anywhere near me, I'd start screaming and swinging. With my mother acting the way she was and me pretending to be insane, they left us alone."

Chase had wondered about that. With the East Texas garrisons manned with common criminals, he had wondered if Rebecca and her mother had been violated. He hated to think of any woman being raped, but the thought of that degradation happening to Rebecca had tortured him. Thank God Rebecca had had the presence of mind to pretend to be demented to keep the Mexicans at bay. All civilizations feared the insane; even the Indians were terrified of them. She was full of surprises, Chase thought with a grudging admiration. As small as she was, he'd never really thought she could handle the oxen, and now this. He had to hand it to her. Not only was she stronger than she appeared, but she was quick-witted too.

Chase examined the gun and found, as Rebecca had told him, it was in good condition. He handed it back to her. "It looks fine, but that gun won't do you any good if you keep it wrapped and tucked away in the wagon. From now on keep it beneath the wagon seat, along with your powder horns and balls. That way you can get to it in a hurry if you need it."

"I just didn't want it to get damaged," Rebecca replied, setting the rifle aside.

"I understand that, but you have to remember that guns are meant to be used, not heirlooms to be packed away. That gun might well save your life some day. Besides, as beautiful as they are, those Kentucky rifles aren't all that delicate. With reasonable care, you can't damage them much." Chase grinned, adding "Unless, of course, you start bashing in heads with them."

Rebecca smiled back.

"You do know how to load and shoot it?" Chase asked. "You weren't just telling McPherson that?"

"Yes, I know how."

Chase didn't question her answer. Over the past few weeks he had learned that Rebecca was very capable. Besides, he didn't think she'd lie to him about something as important as that.

Chase knew that it was time to leave, that he didn't have any reason to stay any longer, but he really didn't want to. He looked at Rebecca's hair, shining with red and gold highlights in the light of the lamp. So many times he had wanted to touch that beautiful hair, wondering if it could possibly be as soft as it looked.

As if it had a will of its own, his hand rose and touched a soft wave at Rebecca's temple, then dropped to a curl on her shoulder, fingering it.

Rebecca's heart beat crazily in her chest. She desperately wanted him to kiss her. Unconsciously she raised her head, her lips parting in silent invitation.

Chase gazed down at Rebecca's face, slowly taking in each feature, and then his eyes locked on her soft, full mouth. He had promised himself he wouldn't touch her. That was why he had stayed away from the wagon so much, trying to put distance between him and temptation. But now, with

Rebecca standing so close he could feel her heat, her mouth looking so inviting, her sweet scent filling his senses, resolve fled. He framed her face in both hands and lifted it, and Rebecca stood on tiptoe, meeting him halfway.

Rebecca had sensed that his kiss would be different from the other men who had kissed her in the past, but even her wildest imaginings couldn't have prepared her for Chase's sensuous kiss. His lips were incredibly tender and warm as they brushed back and forth across hers, then nibbled at the corner of her mouth. But it was when she felt his tongue glazing her bottom lip that her knees buckled and she caught his broad shoulders for support, weakly swaying toward him.

Chase slipped his hands around Rebecca's back, pulling her against his long length, his lips still coaxing, teasing, his tongue flicking like a fiery dart until Rebecca groaned, feeling as if she were being tormented. Then the kiss deepened as Chase slipped his tongue inside her mouth, sliding along the length of hers, tasting, searching every inch of her sweetness.

Rebecca had never been kissed so intimately or so passionately. Her heart raced, a heat suffused her, her legs trembled. She pressed herself closer to Chase, thrilling at the feel of his hard chest against her soft breasts and his muscles rippling beneath his buckskin tunic where her hands lay on his back.

Chase broke the kiss, raining hot, fiery kisses across Rebecca's forehead, her eyes, her temples.

She shivered when he nuzzled her neck, his warm lips at that ultrasensitive spot just below her ear.

And then, as his lips captured hers again, his tongue invading, demanding, Rebecca knew what it meant to be kissed until she was breathless. She felt as if her lungs would burst, and yet she didn't want Chase to stop. A low moan rose in her throat and her hands tangled in the dark hair at his nape, pulling him even closer.

Chase moved his hand down to cup one of Rebecca's soft, full breasts. His fingers brushed across the peak, feeling the nipple harden. His excitement rising to a heated pitch, Chase slipped both hands to Rebecca's back and cupped her buttocks, arching her hips into his and pressing her hard against him. Rebecca felt that rock-hard, throbbing testimony of his desire, its heat seemingly burning her right through his buckskins and her skirt. A brief twinge of fear flashed through her and then was gone, overridden by her passion. She pressed against him, squirming to get even closer.

Chase uttered a muffled groan and broke the kiss. Rebecca whimpered in objection and opened her eyes to see him looking down at her, his eyes dark with passion and his breath labored. He dropped his arms and stepped back. Without the support of his arms, Rebecca felt incredibly weak. She reached for him.

Chase touched her shoulder, stopping her. He searched her face, seeing her glazed eyes, her flushed skin, the racing pulse in her throat. "Do

91

you know what you're doing?" he asked in a husky voice. "Do you know where this is leading?"

Her senses still reeling, Rebecca stared at him dumbly.

Chase knew that Rebecca wasn't thinking clearly, that her mind was dulled by her passion, a passion that had surprised him. It was all he could do to try to keep a clear head himself. Even now his body was screaming for him to take her back in his arms, to quench the fire that she had lit in him, to throw all caution aside. But Chase knew Rebecca would regret it when it was over. Then she'd blame him, accuse him of taking advantage of her. They still had a long trip ahead of them, and one night of passion, no matter how promising, wasn't worth putting up with weeks of misery. No, she would hate him for it, and Chase didn't want that.

He was going to have to turn her down, but it was going to be hard to deny himself. She was so damn tempting, so utterly desirable. Every fiber in his body was begging for release, urging him to ignore his good sense. If only Rebecca fully realized what she was doing, then he wouldn't hesitate for a split second. Using all of his considerable will, Chase said in a soft, husky voice, "No, Rebecca. Not tonight. Maybe sometime . . . when you know what you're doing."

Chase turned and jumped down from the wagon. For a moment Rebecca stared after him, stunned. And then as her senses slowly returned, a flush of mortification rose on her face. She sank weakly to her rolled-up mattress. What in the world had come over her? she thought. She'd never let her senses rule her mind, and yet, when Chase had kissed her, she had become a mindless creature, melting like butter. And if Chase had continued, she would have surrendered to him. Then, in the morning, she would have hated herself for it, and him too, for taking advantage of her weakness. And what had he said? "Not tonight. Maybe sometime." Did he think she was so wanton that she'd beg him to make love to her? Well, she could hardly blame him, considering the shameful way she had behaved. How in the world could she ever face him again?

To Rebecca's immense relief, Chase had already left on his scouting duties when she emerged from the wagon the next morning. As usual, the triple yoke of oxen were already harnessed and hitched to the wagon. After a quick, solitary breakfast, she smothered the fire and loaded up. Then she climbed onto the wagon seat and waited for the wagons to pull out.

For a long while after the train had started moving, Rebecca was terrified that Chase would ride up to the wagon and she wouldn't know what to do or say. But as the morning progressed and she saw no sign of him, she relaxed.

Around noon, the train reached Gains Ferry Crossing on the Sabine, and Rebecca felt a surge of excitement as she gazed across the river at the Texas side. The wagons were loaded on the ferry, a huge log raft, planked on the top, with a weather-beaten, rickety railing around the sides. The ferry was moved from one side of the river to the other by a heavy rope attached to both ends and looped around a stout tree trunk on the bank, then harnessed to a team of horses. Two wagons were transported at a time, the draft animals unhitched from them in case they panicked and jumped into the river. That way at least they wouldn't take the wagons with them.

Moving the wagons across the river was a time-consuming chore, and because Rebecca's wagon was so large and would have to be ferried across by itself, she was the last to cross.

It was almost dark when Jamie McPherson rode up to Rebecca's wagon. "All right, Miz Winters, it's your turn. See if you can ease those oxen down on that ferry."

Rebecca looked down the sloping incline to the water and the bobbing raft. Suddenly the hill seemed very steep and the ferry very small. She wondered if she could get the big wagon on it. And God forbid! What if she couldn't stop the oxen once they were on the raft? Her hands turned clammy, and a lump formed in her throat.

"Come on, Rebecca. You can do it. Just take them down slow and easy-like."

Rebecca was startled by Chase's voice. She glanced over and saw him sitting on his horse beside the wagon. All day long she had been dreading their first meeting, and now she found that she was actually glad to see him. With him beside her, she wouldn't be nearly as frightened.

As the oxen started down the incline, the wagon picked up momentum and Rebecca was terrified the heavy wagon would run over the animals.

"Don't panic," Chase said calmly. "Ease the

brake back. Not hard. Just enough to slow the wagon."

Rebecca did as Chase told her and breathed a sigh of relief as the brakes caught and the wagon slowed.

"Now, when it levels out, let up on the brake and guide the oxen onto that planking," Chase said.

Again Rebecca did as Chase directed her, carefully guiding the oxen onto the planking that acted as a short bridge between the riverbank and the ferry. The wood creaked and groaned as the oxen stepped on it, and Rebecca held her breath, fearing it would break beneath the weight of the wagon, wishing the oxen would hurry before it did, and praying they wouldn't balk when they reached the bobbing raft.

But all of Rebecca's fears were unfounded. The oxen lumbered onto the ferry, their hooves clattering on the wooden planking, and stopped at the end of it, as if they knew exactly what was expected of them. Rebecca looked behind her in amazement, seeing the wagon parked neatly in the center of the ferry, still not believing she had actually done it.

Chase felt a twinge of pride at how well Rebecca had done, then dismounted and tied Lightning to the wagon wheel. While he disengaged the oxen from the wagon, the ferryman threw wooden blocks against the front and back of the wheels to keep it stable.

Chase rose, saying "I'm afraid I'll need your

help with the oxen, Rebecca. You stand by that lead ox on this side and I'll take the other."

Rebecca climbed down and walked to the lead ox. "Where shall I hold him?" she asked Chase, standing opposite her by the other lead ox.

"Grab hold of his throatlatch. If he starts cutting up, pull back and up on it—hard."

"But I'll choke him to death," Rebecca objected.

Chase chuckled. "You'll choke him, but only a little bit. Not enough to harm him. Just enough to make him think twice. I seriously doubt that anyone could choke an ox to death."

Rebecca looked at the massive muscles in the ox's neck and then at those in its shoulders and had doubts of her own. If the powerful beasts did panic and decided they wanted off the raft, she didn't think anyone or anything could stop them. She remembered how some of the horses had panicked on the previous runs, their owners fighting them all the way across the river to keep them from bolting. And then she remembered Chase's horse. "What about Lightning?"

"Don't worry about him. He's used to these ferry rides."

The ferryman waved, signaling the man across the river that they were ready to move. As the ferry lurched forward, the ox standing next to Rebecca began to snort and paw at the planking. Rebecca's heart raced in fear. "Sssh, big boy," she crooned, petting the animal with her free hand. "It's all right. There's nothing to be afraid of."

And then, as if panic was contagious, all of the oxen became restless, snorting and pawing. But

Rebecca kept crooning and soothing the one she stood by, and after what seemed an eternity they settled down. By the time they reached the middle of the river, they were as docile as kittens, and Rebecca felt a little twinge of pride. They were behaving better than any of the animals that had crossed earlier.

While the water had been smooth closer to the bank, it was choppy in midstream, the raft bobbing up and down and the water sloshing over the sides. Rebecca found herself holding on to the ox to keep her footing.

One of the ferrymen made his way across the raft and asked Chase, "What in the devil have you got in that wagon anyway, mister? I ain't never seen this ferry ride so low in the water."

Rebecca stiffened at his question, and Chase smiled. "Furniture."

"Furniture?" the man asked in disbelief. He turned and craned his neck, peering into the wagon. Then, seeing the huge crates, he said, "Hell, it must weigh a couple of tons."

Chase shrugged his shoulders, offering no other explanation. The man walked away, shaking his head in disgust.

When the ferry reached the opposite bank, Rebecca was vastly relieved. With the sun going down, the temperature was dropping fast, and the wind blowing over the water had chilled her to the bone. She shivered and pulled her wool shawl closer around her. She could hardly wait until she got into camp and had a warm fire going.

As soon as the wagon and oxen were unloaded

from the ferry, Chase mounted his horse. "McPherson wants me to do some scouting tonight," he said. "If everything looks clear, he's going to call a day of rest tomorrow. He said he'd have someone help you with the oxen when you get to camp. Think you can manage from here?"

Rebecca knew it was just a matter of driving up the riverbank and into the circle of wagons. And now that the dangerous crossing was behind them, she felt uncomfortable in Chase's company. "I'm sure I can."

Chase nodded, wheeled his horse, and galloped off. Despite herself, Rebecca felt a twinge of disappointment as she watched him ride away. She jiggled the reins and said to the oxen, "Okay, fellas, let's go. It looks like it's just you and me again."

After Rebecca had pulled the wagon into place and climbed down, she realized that she was actually standing on Texas soil. A thrill ran through her. She turned westward, looking at the setting sun, the sky streaked with vivid pinks, reds, and oranges, and a broad, victorious smile spread across her face.

"I'm back," she whispered. "Do you hear me, you damned Mexicans? You told me never to come back to Texas, but I have. And you'll never, *never* push me out again!"

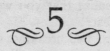

5

THE NEXT MORNING THE CAMP WAS BUSTLING with activity, but not with the usual preparations for departure. The men were busy greasing axles, taking wheels off the wagons, and gathering harnesses for repairs, while the women hurried to finish their breakfast chores so that they could get to their washing. A day of rest had been called, but the only ones that would rest would be the animals.

Rebecca was just finishing up her own breakfast chores when she looked up and saw Chase strolling up to her, leading Lightning by his reins. He's back, she thought in surprise. She hadn't heard him come into the wagon the night before.

Her eyes settled on his head where droplets of water glistened in the black tresses. Seeing her look, Chase ran his hand through his wet hair. "I just had a bath in the river."

"A bath in the river?" Rebecca echoed in disbelief. "But wasn't the water cold?"

"Nope. Felt just right to me."

Rebecca couldn't believe her ears. It was January. The water must have been freezing. Shaking her head, she turned to the fire. "I've already eaten. I didn't realize that you were back. I'll fix you some breakfast."

"Don't bother. I had breakfast with McPherson when I got back this morning."

"Then you *just* got back?"

"Yes, about an hour ago. They're getting together a hunting party and I'm going along. I just dropped by to pick up more powder."

Chase walked to the wagon, jumped on the wheel, and swung into the back of the wagon, as was his habit, instead of lowering the tailgate. A moment later he jumped back down and headed for his horse.

"Would you mind doing something for me before you leave?" Rebecca asked. "I want to wash today, but I can't reach the tub. It's too high for me." Rebecca pointed to the big wooden washtub hanging between the water barrels on the outside of the wagon.

Chase reached up and pulled the tub down, setting it on the ground, with an ease that both amazed and slightly irritated Rebecca.

"Do you have anything that needs washing?" Rebecca asked. "I wouldn't mind, since I'm doing it anyway."

"Nope. I wear buckskins."

"What about"—Rebecca flushed—"underthings?"

"You mean long johns? I don't wear them."

I should have known, Rebecca thought, remembering the night that he had stripped before her. She flushed even redder at the memory.

Chase knew what she was thinking and grinned. "Come to think of it, there is something you can wash for me. My blanket."

"You mean blankets."

"No, I just have one."

"You only sleep with one blanket? In this weather?"

"It's not that cold. I've never used two blankets in my entire life. I'll get it for you."

"That won't be necessary. I'll find it."

Chase shrugged and mounted Lightning. As he rode off, Rebecca shook her head in amazement. Bathing in the river in January and sleeping with only one blanket? And going both day and night? Didn't he ever get cold or tired? Wasn't he human? And running around with nothing beneath his buckskins. Why, it was disgraceful. Well, she thought ruefully, she supposed she should be glad he wasn't walking around in one of those skimpy rags that the Indian men wore, covering only the essentials.

Rebecca gathered her washing. Since she had not washed since leaving Natchez, it was a good-sized pile. She dumped it all in Chase's blanket, tossed a bar of lye soap on top of it, and tied it into a big bundle. Then she rose, wondering if she should carry the wash down to the river first, or the tub. Deciding on the tub, she bent and lifted it in her arms. She had never lifted it before, since it had been on the wagon when it was delivered, and she staggered under its weight. She might be able to carry it for a few feet, but not as far as the river.

She put it back down with disgust, thinking that she was going to have to tote water from the river. Then she looked up and saw one of the Kentucky women rolling her tub through the camp. Rebecca laughed. Now, why hadn't she thought of that?

Rebecca turned the tub on its side and rolled it through the camp. It almost got away from her when she reached the hill that sloped down to the bank. Then, leaving it sitting beside the river, she hurried back to camp for the bundle of wash.

When she returned to the river, a big fire was burning so the women could heat the water. Rebecca realized that she'd forgotten her pot. Once again she trudged up the hill and through the camp, thinking that Chase was smart, wearing animal skins that didn't need to be washed. Right then a squaw's buckskin dress looked very appealing to her.

Washing was a long, arduous chore. In the first place, Rebecca had to wait for her turn to heat the water. And then she had to scrub each piece by hand with the harsh lye soap. She looked enviously at the women with scrub boards, vowing that she'd pick one up in Nacogdoches. Once the clothes were washed, they had to be rinsed not once but twice. Rebecca decided to use the river water unheated rather than stand round shivering in the cold while she was waiting for her turn at the fire again.

She was shocked at how cold the water was and, once again, amazed that Chase had actually bathed in it. By the time she had finished rinsing the clothes, her hands were blue and numb. Now the real back-breaking chore began—wringing the water out—and Chase's blanket was almost more than she could handle by herself. Waterlogged, it seemed to weigh a ton. By the time she had finished, her dress was almost as wet as the laundry, and she was cursing herself for volunteering her services.

She stood and looked about her. Laundry was spread out everywhere to dry. It seemed as if every tree, shrub, and rock was already in use. Sighing in resignation, she picked up an armful of wet garments and walked farther upstream.

It took almost an hour for Rebecca to spread her laundry. And by the time she had finished, she was exhausted and chilled to the bone. After emptying the tub and turning it on its side, she hurriedly rolled it back up the hill to the camp. Then she climbed into the wagon and changed clothes, indulging in a cup of hot tea before she went back for her soap and pot.

That afternoon Rebecca returned to the river to gather up her dry laundry. She noticed that some of the poor women with large families were still washing and pitied them. If they had daughters, they helped, but if they were "blessed" with all sons, the woman was left to do the back-breaking chore by herself.

When she walked back through the camp with her laundry, Rebecca almost stumbled over a woman on her hands and knees. The woman was cleaning her husband's buckskins, which she had spread out on the ground. Rebecca sidestepped and watched as the woman continued brushing off the cornmeal she had sprinkled over them to absorb the grease. Rebecca was amazed. Before Chase, none of the men she had known had worn buckskins. She had no idea that was how they were cleaned.

As Rebecca walked into her campsite, she passed the washtub on her way to the wagon. Then she stopped and turned, staring at it. A glimmer came into her eyes. All day long she had thought about Chase bathing in the river. Had the weather not been so cold, she would have done the same thing. The only baths she'd had since she left Natchez had been from a bucket, often leaving more soap residue than the dirt she'd removed. She longed to soak in a tub. She slowly circled the washtub, eyeing it critically. It was deep, but not all that wide. It would be a tight squeeze, but she could make it.

Rebecca hurried to the wagon and tossed the bundle inside, then rushed back to pick up her pot. As she filled it from the water barrel, she thought that she might have to empty the entire container to fill the tub. But she didn't care. The barrels would have to be refilled tomorrow before they left the river anyway.

An hour later, Rebecca sat in the washtub inside the wagon, looking about her and feeling very smug. With the high tailgate up, no one passing by could see her, and the small opening on the canvas top let just enough light in that she didn't have to light a lamp. And the water felt absolutely heavenly. This was the first time she had felt warm since she had become chilled earlier that morning.

She scrubbed herself all over, then just sat luxuriating in the heat, absently soaping one of her knees. She wondered why she hadn't thought of this before and vowed that she'd have a real bath at every river they stopped by from then on.

She started as she felt the wagon dip and gasped as she saw a buckskin leg hook itself over the tailgate. A second later Chase's face and shoulders appeared.

Horrified, she crossed her arms over her breasts. "What are *you* doing here?" she demanded.

Chase could only stare. With her reddish-gold hair piled on top of her head, and her graceful neck, shapely shoulders, and the soft rise of her full breasts flushed to a rosy glow from the warm water, Rebecca was a breathtaking sight. Finally regaining his senses, Chase swung the other leg over and dropped to the wagon floor. "I'm back."

"That's obvious!" Rebecca said hotly. "But what are you doing here? In the wagon?"

"Since I didn't get any sleep last night, I thought I'd get a little shut-eye before supper. Besides, I should be the one asking what are you doing in here?"

"I'm taking a bath."

"That's obvious," Chase answered, throwing her own words back in her face. "But this is my end of the wagon. My private domain. My room, so to speak. Do you make a habit of making yourself at home in men's rooms—naked?"

Rebecca was very much aware of Chase's dark

105

eyes on her. His look made her feel as if he could see her breasts right through her arms. She glanced down and saw, with them pressed tightly against her chest, her breasts were pushed up, and there was a lot of cleavage showing.

"Well?" Chase asked in a taunting voice.

"I couldn't get the tub over the wagon seat at my end. I'm only borrowing your end for a little while."

Rebecca expected him to leave, but Chase sat down, leaning against the side of the wagon, one long leg casually drawn up, smiling at her blandly.

Rebecca stared at him in disbelief. "You're not just going to sit there, are you?"

"Yes, I am. Unlike some people around here, I'm not selfish. I don't mind sharing my end of the wagon with you. But I see no reason to leave. You're the trespasser, not me."

"Then turn your head so I can get out!"

"Nope."

Rebecca looked down at the goose bumps on her arms. "Chase, stop teasing me. The water is getting cold."

"I'm *not* teasing."

There was a husky timbre in Chase's voice that made Rebecca look up. His black eyes were smoldering with unconcealed desire. A sudden heat washed over her, warming her even more than the hot water had.

Suddenly she had to get out of there. She dropped her arms and tried to push herself up but, to her horror, realized that she was wedged in. She wiggled frantically, the water splashing over the sides of the tub and puddling on the floor.

Seeing her predicament, Chase threw his head back and laughed, and Rebecca caught a flash of sparkling white teeth against his bronzed skin.

His laughter infuriated her. With a sudden burst of strength, she gave a mighty shove and finally dislodged herself, sweeping up the first thing she saw—Chase's blanket—as she rose. Wrapping it hastily around her, she stepped from the tub, bent on making a beeline for her end of the wagon. Then, to her horror, she felt herself slipping as she stepped on the bar of soap on the floor. Her legs flew out from under her, and she would have tumbled back into the tub if Chase hadn't quickly jumped to his feet and caught her, laughing even harder.

"Get your hands off of me!" Rebecca shrieked, pushing his hands away. Then she turned and stalked angrily down the long dim corridor that ran between the huge crates in the middle of the wagon.

"Hey, that's my blanket you've got!" Chase called.

Rebecca was so angry that she didn't even care if Chase saw her naked. She whirled, whipped the blanket off, rolled it into a ball, and threw it down the corridor at him, screaming "Then take it!"

"It's wet," Chase complained, picking it up.

"That's just too bad!" Rebecca called back over her shoulder.

When she reached her "room" at the front of

the wagon, Rebecca quickly dried off and jerked on her chemise and pantaloons.

"Hey! What about the tub?" Chase called. "Aren't you going to empty it?"

"Empty it yourself, you half-breed bastard!"

Rebecca froze, horrified at what she'd said. She held her breath, expecting to see Chase come tearing through the corridor with murder in his eye.

There was a long silence. Then Rebecca heard a soft chuckle, the sound of the tailgate banging down, the scrape of the tub across the floor, and, finally, a splash of water. Weakly she sat down on her rolled-up mattress, sighing in relief.

That evening, the whole time Rebecca was cooking supper and they were eating, Chase kept watching her, amusement sparking in his dark eyes. Again, it infuriated Rebecca that he should take pleasure from seeing her humiliated. She had made a total fool out of herself, ridiculously getting stuck in the tub, then stupidly stepping on the soap and flying through the air as graceful as an ox. She wasn't concerned that Chase had seen her naked because she knew the corridor had been too dark. Thank God for that, she thought. It would have been the crowning humiliation.

As soon as her evening chores were done, she shot Chase a hot look, marched to the wagon, and angrily climbed into it. Then she lay on her mattress, seething long into the night.

Rebecca wasn't the only one that spent the better part of that night lying awake. Chase was burning too, but from a different emotion. With his Indian night vision, he *had* seen Rebecca standing naked in the dim corridor, and that vision tormented him. He wanted her. Now more than ever. And he could kick himself for not taking the opportunity when she had offered it to him that night he had kissed her. What in the hell had gotten into him, playing the role of a gentleman? So what if she hated him later? What should it matter? She was just another woman passing through his life.

As Chase finally drifted off to sleep, a last thought flashed through his mind. Or was she?

The next morning the wagon train left the Sabine River behind, heading due west. When they rolled through the East Texas canebrakes, Rebecca looked around her in surprise. On her last trip to Texas, in May, the shoots had been waist high; when she had passed back through in the late fall, when she was expelled from Texas, the cane had towered over them, blocking out the sun. Now, since the first freeze, the brown, mushy stalks lay in a big heap on the ground.

Beyond the canebrakes came the East Texas thicket, a curious blend of forests and swamps. With the peculiar greenish fog rising from the water, the swamps had an eerie look, and yet there was a haunting beauty about them.

They passed through St. Augustine, a small settlement consisting of nothing more than a few log cabins, without even stopping. As they approached Nacogdoches, the pine forests began, the trees so thick the sun never really penetrated them, the road covered with brown needles that crunched under the wheels of the wagons. To Rebecca, it looked as if they were traveling through a long, dark, winding tunnel.

During this time, Rebecca saw even less of Chase. Sometimes he would be gone for days, and she wondered whether he was really that busy scouting or just avoiding her and, if so, why? Was it her sharp tongue that had driven him off? Or, God forbid, was he afraid she would pounce on him, remembering with shame how wantonly she had behaved when he had kissed her?

He was the most disconcerting man she had ever met. She never knew when she would see him. He would be gone for days and then suddenly appear, acting as if he'd never left her side. At these times Rebecca would find herself either biting her tongue to keep from snapping 'Where have you been?' or ridiculously happy to see him. Now her time was measured not in days, with the rising and setting of the sun, but from one of the rugged Texian's appearances to the next.

His absence irritated her. He was the one who had been hired to take the cannons to the Alamo, and yet she was the one who was driving them there. To her, it was he who was just going along for the ride. For all practical purposes, she could have done the job alone. Except he had an uncanny way of always showing up when she needed him: the day they forded a dangerously flooded creek; the day one of the wagon wheels started wobbling; the day one of the oxen had gotten a rock stuck in its hoof and stood there bellowing, while she hadn't the slightest idea what was wrong with it. The stupid animal hadn't even had enough sense to raise its big foot and take the weight off it.

Ever since she had met Chase Winters, her emotions had been in a turmoil, swinging from one extreme to the other. When he was gone, she railed at him during the day and then, at night, listened anxiously for his footstep. If he didn't show up, she worried about him. She didn't know what was wrong with her. She should be glad he wasn't around interfering in her business. After all, she wanted to be independent, didn't she? And why she should worry about him was beyond her. He meant nothing to her. Once the cannons were delivered, they would go their separate ways. She frowned, wondering at the painful pang that thought had brought.

Suddenly Rebecca became aware of someone riding beside her. She knew that it was Chase. She could smell that distinctive scent of his, a scent that always excited her. Her heart pounded crazily in her chest and her spirits soared. She turned her head and smiled at him, hoping that she didn't look idiotic with her happiness to see him. Chase smiled back.

For a moment the silence hung between them, and then Chase said, "The train is making good time. We should reach Nacogdoches tomorrow."

Say something, Rebecca thought. Say something before he rides off and you don't see him for days again. "Has Nacogdoches grown much in the past few years?"

"I don't know. I have a few acquaintances that

live on the outskirts, but I haven't been to the town itself in over four years."

"But I thought you told me you drove your mustang herds through Nacogdoches."

"Not through the town itself. We always bypass it and use the *El Camino del Caballo*—the Road of the Horse. It's a hidden trail through a deep river-bottom woods, laid out long ago by St. Denis, one of the earliest mustangers. Up until the time the Mexicans pulled their garrisons out of East Texas, we had to use it to bypass the customs station. I guess it just became a habit."

"El Camino del Caballo," Rebecca repeated thoughtfully. "I've heard stories that there's buried treasure along that trail."

"Yes, so legend claims. But there's places all over the west where buried treasure is supposed to be. Ever since Coronado marched through in search of the Seven Cities of Gold, men have been lured by such tales. Even Jim Bowie tried his hand at treasure hunting when he and his brothers went searching for the lost San Saba Mine—and almost lost his life instead. They were surrounded by one hundred sixty-four Tawakonis, Wacos, and Caddos on the San Saba River. Only after a desperate Indian fight were they able to escape."

"Where did you hear that story?"

"From Jim himself."

"James Bowie? You know James Bowie?" Rebecca asked in surprise, feeling a thrill of excitement.

"Yes, we mustanged on one of my trips into

112

Texas. Besides, a lot of people know Jim. He's a man that gets around."

"Then you've seen his famous knife?"

Chase laughed, saying "Yes, I've seen it. It's big and wicked-looking, but not all that extraordinary. All of the Bowie brothers carry them, and they're all experts with them, but not because they've been in so many knife duels, as you hear rumored. Their expertise comes from using the knives to subdue the slaves they transport. Jim said it's easier than handling a gun, and once those Africans see him and his brothers tossing their mean-looking knives around, they don't give them any trouble."

"Bowie, a slaver?" Rebecca asked in a shocked voice. "But that's illegal."

"Yes, I know. When he and his brothers aren't running longhorns or mustangs across the Sabine, seeking lost mines, running their plantations in Louisiana, selling land with questionable titles, and God knows what else, they smuggle illegal Africans they bought from Lafitte on Galveston Island into Louisiana. Jim once asked me if I'd like to join him on that venture, but I turned him down. I told him I'd stick to herding animals, that herding humans was repugnant to me."

Rebecca gasped. "You said *that* to James Bowie? Didn't he take offense?"

"No, Jim admires honesty. He just told me if I change my mind to let him know."

Rebecca could only stare at Chase, wondering how many men would dare to risk offending James Bowie, a deadly knifeman, a famous Indian fighter, a man who wrestled alligators for fun, a man who was a legend in his day.

The train rolled into Nacogdoches early the next afternoon. As they passed the old customs house, where she and her mother had been imprisoned, Rebecca took immense satisfaction in seeing that it was deserted and falling into disrepair. And then, as they drove into the town itself, she looked about her in surprise. The town had grown very quickly. The street was lined with neatly planked houses and dogtrot log cabins—so named for the covered passageway between the two sections of the cabin. When they reached the center of the town where the stores were, the wagon train stopped, and everyone climbed down to hurry to do their shopping. To Rebecca, still sitting on her wagon seat, they looked like bees coming out of a honeycomb, flying in every direction. And the people of Nacogdoches didn't mind the train blocking their main thoroughfare. The merchants were eager for the trade, the townspeople for news from the East.

Much to Rebecca's delight, Chase didn't leave the wagon train to scout that day. She wasn't sure if he stayed to help with the purchasing of the provisions or, remembering his criticism of the oxen she had bought and the lack of coffee, to make sure she bought the correct items. But Rebecca didn't care what his motives were. All she cared about was that she'd have his company for a whole day.

As they walked to the general store, Chase asked, "Do you know what we need?"

Rebecca felt a little tingle at the word we. "Yes, I've made a list, if you care to see it," she answered, handing him a piece of paper. Then, remembering that she had put pantaloons on the list, she snatched it back. "I'll read it to you."

Chase grinned, guessing that there was something of an intimate nature on the list. "That's not necessary. I'll see everything when I carry it back to the wagon."

Not my pantaloons, you won't, Rebecca vowed.

The narrow aisles of the general store were crowded with people from the wagon train. The store sold everything from plows to watches, food staples to guns and ammunition, and the merchandise was packed wall to wall, floor to ceiling. The area where cloth was sold was particularly crowded, as the settlers were not only buying provisions for the rest of the trip but for their first year in Texas too, and the women knew that it would be a long time before they saw a bolt of calico again.

When Rebecca tried to make her way through to the ready-to-wear behind the table where the Kentucky women were rolling out the bolts of bright calico, she ran into a solid line of humanity. Then, seeing a brief break in the crowd, she quickly darted through it. She looked back over her shoulder to see that Chase was left standing on the other side of the material counter, blocked by the shoppers, and laughed in relief. She had feared that she wasn't going to be able to shake him, and she'd be damned if she'd buy pantaloons with him looking over her shoulder.

Rebecca found what she was looking for, which was an accomplishment, considering that everything was piled high on one table. There were calico and wool dresses, shoes, underwear, sunbonnets, cotton hose, wool mittens, and shawls. The pantaloons were made of a coarse, serviceable cotton and would undoubtedly be much rougher on her skin than her silk ones, but she picked out several pairs, snatched up a pair of wool mittens, and took them to the saleswoman on that side of the store. Then, with her purchases wrapped discreetly in brown paper, she made her way to where the washboards were, smiling smugly at how neatly she had outmaneuvered Chase.

As she made her way down the aisle to where Chase was waiting impatiently, she found her way was blocked by a tall, pleasant-looking, blond young man. He stepped back politely behind a cracker barrel so that she could pass. Rebecca smiled, muttered, "Thank you," and walked through, then felt a hand on her elbow.

"Rebecca?" the young man asked. "Rebecca Dryer?"

Rebecca turned and looked at the man. He was dressed in a broadcloth suit, and Rebecca knew that he wasn't from the train.

The man laughed softly. "Don't you remember me? I'm Tom Jeffries. I met you when you passed through Nacogdoches about four and a half years ago."

Rebecca frowned, searching her memory.

"The dance at the town square. Remember? I kept stepping on your feet."

Then Rebecca remembered. The town had thrown a dance for the wagon train her family had traveled with on her first trip to Texas, a sort of

welcome-to-Texas affair, and Tom Jeffries had bad-
gered her for dances. She had been only fifteen and
he a tall, gangly youth of nineteen. But now the
awkward boy was gone. There was an air of matu-
rity and self-confidence about him.

"I'm sorry. I didn't recognize you, Tom. Do you
still live here in Nacogdoches?"

"No. My parents still do, but I have a cotton
plantation on the Brazos now, south of here. I
came into town today to buy provisions." His blue
eyes swept admiringly over her. "I never dreamed
I'd run into you again. You're even more beautiful
than you were then."

Rebecca flushed at his compliment, aware of
Chase standing behind her and listening to everything.

"Is your father here?" Tom asked, assuming
that Rebecca had come with her father from the
plantation to buy supplies.

"No, I'm with the wagon train that's passing
through. We moved back to Natchez that same
year," Rebecca answered, hoping that Tom
wouldn't ask any questions that she didn't feel up
to answering.

"She's with me," Chase said, stepping forward.

Tom had been aware of the tall, darkly handsome man behind Rebecca and had assumed that
the man was scowling at them because they were
blocking the aisle. Tom had decided to ignore him.
But now he heard the warning tone in Chase's
voice and looked up to see a pair of fierce black
eyes glaring at him.

"Tom," Rebecca said, "this is Chase Winters, my—my husband."

Tom couldn't hide his disappointment. Then, remembering his manners, he said, "I'm pleased to meet you," and offered his hand.

Chase nodded his head curtly and gave Tom's hand a perfunctory shake. Then, taking Rebecca by the arm, he said, "Come, Rebecca. We've got supplies to buy."

Rebecca was embarrassed by Chase's rudeness. Ignoring the pressure on her arm that Chase was exerting, she smiled at Tom. "Good-bye, Tom. It's been good seeing you again."

As Chase and Rebecca walked away, Rebecca muttered, "That was rude of you. Don't you have any manners at all?"

"Not when I have business to attend to," Chase answered, tight-lipped, irritated at himself for being jealous, an emotion he had never felt before in his life.

They had to wait in line for their staples. The line curved around a potbelly stove, where two old men sat at a small table playing checkers, totally ignoring the activity around them.

When Chase and Rebecca came abreast of them, Chase asked, "What's the news from Bexar?"

One of the old men raised his head and glanced up at Chase with watery blue eyes, holding his checker in midair. Then he looked down at the board and made his move before answering. "If you're talkin' 'bout the Alamo, we still got it, as far as I know."

"Has Sam Houston sent reinforcements?" Chase asked.

"Don't know."

"Well, isn't the government doing anything?" Chase asked.

"Yeah, a lot of fightin' among themselves. Since the Alamo fell to the Texians, Governor Smith and the council have been at each other's throats. The governor givin' one set of orders, the council the opposite. Smith appointed Houston commander-in-chief, and he sided with the governor. Then, to get even with Houston, the council appointed Colonel James Fannin as supreme commander-in-chief, and now they're threatenin' to impeach Smith."

"Then who *is* in command of the army?" Chase asked in exasperation.

"Damned if I know. Some of the militia are takin' orders from Houston. Fannin's got a bunch of volunteers down at Copano takin' orders from him. And then there're some men that ain't takin' orders from nobody, just doin' what *they* think is right." The old man shook his gray head in disgust. "Damnest mess I've ever seen."

"What about Steven Austin?" Chase asked. "Can't he make peace between the governor and the council?"

"Hell, he ain't even in Texas. He's gone back East to try to raise money for the war."

Chase shook his head in disgust. Damned bunch of independent Texians, he thought. Everybody wanting to run the war their way and no one wanting to take orders. And while they're squabbling, the Mexican army is coming down on them.

"What about Santa Anna's army?" Chase asked. "Have they crossed the Rio Grande yet?"

The old man's head snapped up. "You crazy, mister? This is the middle of the winter. Ain't nobody gonna march an army that distance in this weather."

Chase had a gut feeling that the war was going to blow up in the Texians' faces and that their bid for independence would end up being a big fiasco. "Thank you," he muttered as he rejoined Rebecca in the line of waiting settlers.

6

THE WAGON TRAIN DEPARTED FROM NACOGDO-ches the next morning, still following *El Camino Real,* the old road to Bexar that dipped sharply southward. Rebecca could never understand why the road was named *El Camino Real*—the King's Highway—for there was certainly nothing royal or grand about it. Granted, it was the main road in Texas, stretching from the Sabine River on the east to Laredo on the Rio Grande on the west, but it was deeply rutted, full of bone-jarring holes, so narrow in some places that it almost disappeared. And when it rained, traveling over it could only be described in one word—miserable—for then it became just one long mud hole.

They crossed the Trinity River at Williams Ferry and, a week later, the Brazos River at Robbins Ferry. After crossing the Brazos, they took a more southwesterly course. There the land became flatter as the dense forests of East Texas were left behind.

During this time Rebecca hardly ever saw Chase, who was gone for days at a time because they were subject to attack by both the Comanches from the west and the Wacos and Wichitas from the east.

Rebecca had never spent a winter in Texas, so on one almost balmy afternoon, when she first saw the dark line on the northern horizon, she thought a thunderstorm was approaching. But as the strange bluish-black line moved toward them, filling more and more of the sky, she noticed there were no thunderheads or lightning.

Then Chase came riding out of nowhere, in one of his sudden appearances that always startled Rebecca and left her shaken. "I thought you were out scouting for Indians," she snapped.

"There won't be any Indians about for the next few days. Not with that blue norther coming down on us the way it is. No, they'll hole up in their warm tepees."

He slid from Lightning's saddle and onto the seat with Rebecca, a movement that always amazed her with its ease and fluidity. "Better let me have the reins," Chase said. "We're in for a blow."

And blow it did. Rebecca had never seen anything like it. The norther came howling down on them, an icy blast of wind that came straight out of the Arctic and buffeted the wagon, sending it rocking and the canvas crackling and popping. The temperature plummeted, dropping an unbelievable thirty degrees the first hour. The wind kicked up the sandy soil, stinging them where it hit exposed flesh, the gritty particles getting in the ears, the eyes, the mouth, the nostrils. Frightened, the cow in front of them started bawling and then the oxen snorted, only adding to the din of the shricking wind.

McPherson rode up to the wagon, his hair flapping wildly around his craggy face, calling to Chase. "Are we gonna have a blizzard?"

"No, this is a dry norther," Chase yelled back. "But even if it was a wet one, we won't have a blizzard. At least not like the ones you'll see farther north of here. Some sleet, a few snowflakes perhaps, but real snow is rare in this part of Texas."

"Well, God damn it, how long is it gonna keep blowing like this? A horse can't hardly walk against it."

"A day, maybe two. I advise you to find woods for protection and circle up. It's going to get even colder. Might be freezing by nightfall."

That night Rebecca lay on her feather mattress, huddled beneath every blanket she could find. She had put on two flannel nightgowns, heavy socks, her mittens, and she was still freezing. The wind still howled, sounding even louder and shriller in the dark. The wagon rocked as gusts of wind hit it, and Rebecca feared that the canvas would be ripped off it.

And then she saw Chase standing over her. "What . . . are . . . you doing . . . here?" she asked, shivering from the cold.

"I could hear your teeth chattering even from my end of the wagon," he answered.

"I'm sorry. I can't . . . help it. I'm . . . I'm cold."

"I know," Chase replied. He flipped Rebecca's covers off and lay down beside her, pulling them back over them.

"What do you . . . think . . . you're doing? Get out of . . . here! Go . . . back to your end."

"Stop it, Rebecca! You're freezing in here by yourself. Even animals have better sense than that. They huddle together and share their heat. Now come here," Chase said, pulling her firmly against him and wrapping his arms around her.

To Rebecca's relief, Chase was wearing his buckskins, but she was still frightened, more of her own emotions than of him.

"Relax, Rebecca," Chase said, his warm breath ruffling the hair on the top of her head. "Nothing is going to happen. We're just going to share our heat. It's too damned cold for anything else."

Rebecca could feel Chase's heat seeping into her chilled flesh. Slowly her shivering subsided and her teeth stilled.

"Feeling warmer?" Chase asked, smoothing her long hair back from her face.

"Yes," Rebecca admitted. "But my feet are still cold."

"Put them between my legs."

Rebecca hesitated. Somehow it seemed more intimate than just lying beside him with his arms around her. Chase muttered an oath, caught Rebecca's knees and bent them, then captured her feet with his calves.

"What about your hands?" Chase asked.

"They're still cold too. Despite the mittens."

"Mittens?" Chase asked in surprise. Then he

chuckled. Lying so close to him, Rebecca could feel the rumble in his chest long before it reached his lips. "Here. Tuck them under my arms," Chase said, raising his arms. "Now lean your face into my neck. I bet your nose is cold too."

It was. Her nose felt like an icicle on her face. Rebecca did as he directed, snuggling her face into the warm crook of his neck. A pleasant warmth and drowsiness crept over her. She closed her eyes and drifted off to sleep, luxuriating in the heat, the scent of Chase's skin, and the feel of his strong arms around her, thinking that it would be heaven to fall asleep every night like that.

As soon as the wind died down the next day, the train was on its way again. It was still bitterly cold, with a frost covering the ground.

Chase stayed with the wagon train that day, saying that it was too cold for any Indians to be out looking for trouble, and Rebecca took satisfaction in seeing that even he had bowed to the cold, wearing a leather jacket over his buckskins. That night Rebecca hoped he would come to warm her again, even though it wasn't nearly as cold since the wind had died down. But, to her disappointment, he didn't, and the next morning he was gone again.

He didn't return for three days, and Rebecca found herself even lonelier than before. On the third night, when she was brushing her hair before retiring, she could hear him moving about at his end of the wagon. She sank onto her mattress, pondering over her strange feelings. When he was gone, she was unbearably lonely, filled with an emptiness as if her life had left her. But when he returned, she was unbelievably happy, so full of joy she felt she would burst with it. Then she hung on every word he said, hungry for his every gesture, feasting on him when she didn't think he was looking.

The answer to her peculiar feelings came to her with a sudden insight that took her breath away. She loved him. It was as pure and simple as that. He irritated her and exasperated her as no one ever had, but still she loved him. She had never known a man like him, and doubted that there was another on this earth. Fierce and proud, he stood straighter and walked taller than any other, and there was within him a beautiful powerful spirit that defied all restraint—a force that excited her and brought all her senses vitally alive. In his presence the sun was brighter and warmer, the sky bluer, the air fresher, the world around her more beautiful. Yes, she loved him. That it was foolish was immaterial. Her heart had a will of its own.

It was a hopeless love, this one-sided love, for she knew that Chase didn't have any tender feelings for her. Oh, he wanted her. She had seen the look in his eyes the night he had kissed her and the day he had caught her bathing. But Rebecca was wise to the ways of men. She knew that just because a man wanted her didn't mean he loved her.

To be doomed to an unrequited love was bad enough, but Rebecca also wanted Chase, an admission that shocked her. She had never known that women could be driven by passion as men were. She had been taught that women were above such things. But, like her heart, her body refused to listen to the dictates of her mind. She ached for him, with a longing that was painful.

In less than a month they would reach Bexar. Then Chase would walk out of her life forever, and she would have nothing of him. Neither his love nor his passion. She remembered an old spinster in Natchez who had once confided that she had loved a man with all of her heart, but that he had gone away, leaving her behind. Rebecca had thought there had been a look of sadness in the woman's eyes. But Rebecca realized it was more regret than sadness. The old woman had admitted regret at having not taken what she could of him while she had the opportunity.

Well, she wasn't going to make that mistake, Rebecca vowed. She wouldn't go through the rest of her life wondering what it would have been like to know passion with the man she loved and regretting that she hadn't. That much of Chase she could have. A part of him, even for a short time, was better than nothing.

She tossed the hairbrush aside and rose to her feet. Walking to the passageway, she called softly, "Chase?"

Hearing her call, Chase peered around the corner of the crates and saw Rebecca. His breath caught in his throat at the sight of her. Her long hair hung around her shoulders in soft waves, a shimmering sheet of golden red under the light of the lamp. Her blue eyes were wide, dark and liquid, sensuous pools that a man could drown in. Her gown clung to her high, full breasts, rising and falling, seemingly beckoning to him.

His mouth went dry. He could feel his heat rising and that familiar ache becoming an unbearable pressure—an ache that he had lived with for weeks, since Rebecca had come into his life. Being near her and not being able to take her was an agony for him. That was why he spent so much of his time away from camp, still trying to put a distance between them. But he had found, to his own disgust, that he couldn't stay away from her for long. His days were plagued by visions of her, his nights tormented by the memory of her soft body in his arms. When it became too much for him, he returned, driven by an emotion that he refused to admit to.

"Chase?"

Chase heard the quiver in Rebecca's voice and frowned. He looked closer and saw her deathly white face. Alarmed, he crossed the narrow corridor in several swift strides, his broad shoulders brushing the crates that lined it. "What is it? Are you ill?" he asked, standing before her.

"No, I'm not ill. I just wanted to . . . to talk to you."

Beneath her gown, Rebecca's legs trembled. Stop it! she told herself firmly. This is no time to be afraid. Do you want to spend the rest of your life hating yourself because you were too cowardly to take what you wanted?

She took a deep breath and said, "I'm warm and willing, Chase. And I know what I'm doing."

Chase recognized his words. He had told her that he liked his women warm and willing, that maybe sometime, when she knew what she was doing . . . but he could hardly believe his ears. He looked into her eyes, seeking the confirmation there. She met his gaze unflinchingly.

A wild excitement rose in Chase, and he struggled to hold it in check. His body told him to take what was offered, to ask no questions, but he couldn't do it. Rebecca was hot-tempered, unpredictable, and sharp-tongued, but over the past weeks he had come to admire her determination and grit, to respect her. He didn't love her. He couldn't. He still loved Shining Water. But he did owe her his honesty. She deserved that much from him.

"Rebecca, I want you, but I don't love you. I can't. Once we've delivered these cannons to the Alamo, I'm leaving. It's finished."

"I know. You'll go your way, and I'll go mine. We'll never see each other again. I understand that, Chase. I told you, I know what I'm doing."

Chase cupped her face in his hands and gazed down at her. "You puzzle me, Rebecca. With you I never know what to expect. I've never known a woman like you."

"Don't try to understand me, Chase, just . . . just make love to me."

Chase's dark eyes moved over her features, hot and hungry, and Rebecca trembled under that searing gaze. One hand slid from her jawline, through her hair, to cup the back of her head, the other arm around her back to gather her close. As his incredibly warm lips covered hers, a moan of joy escaped Rebecca's lips. She had waited for this, hungered for it, and now she would savor it.

Chase's tongue explored her full lips before plunging into her mouth, gently ravishing. Tentatively Rebecca answered, then quivered with excitement as their tongues met and danced around each other. She leaned into him, pressing her body even closer to his long, hard length.

Chase left a line of fiery kisses across Rebecca's chin, her jawline, her throat. He nibbled at her delicate earlobe, before his tongue traced the tiny shell of her ear, then darted inside, sending a shiver of pleasure through Rebecca. Then his tongue traced the pulse beat down her throat to the soft crook of her neck while his hands moved over her back and hips.

God, she was so incredibly soft, Chase thought. So soft and sweet. But now he wanted to see her. He stepped back and began slowly to unbutton the front of Rebecca's gown, then slid it down over her shoulders, dropping it to pool at her feet. The impact of seeing her totally naked took his breath away.

He stood and drank in her beauty, the smooth, creamy skin of her shoulders, the high, full, rose-tipped breasts, the tiny waist, and gentle swell of her hips. His eyes drifted lower to linger at the golden-red triangle between her rounded thighs, then swept down her shapely legs. Rebecca shivered under Chase's bold look and, when he lifted his head to gaze into her eyes, saw the blatant, hot look of desire in his eyes, a look that left her weak-kneed.

"You're beautiful," Chase muttered hoarsely before pulling her back into his arms and capturing her mouth with his in a deep, searing kiss that seemed to suck the air from Rebecca's lungs. Her knees buckled, and Chase lowered her to the mattress, covering her halfway with his body, their lips still locked in that passionate kiss.

His hands swept over her curves as Chase dropped hot kisses over Rebecca's face and down her shoulders, leaving a trail of fire in his wake. Rebecca was floating on a warm, hazy cloud, and then her eyes flew open as Chase's mouth covered the rosy peak of one breast and his tongue swirled around the rigid nipple, sucking, nipping, sending a bolt of fire through her. She moaned, catching his head and pulling him even closer, never wanting the delicious sensations to end.

She muttered in protest when his mouth left the aching bud to drop love bites across the valley between her breasts and then sighed in bliss when he took the other nipple in his mouth, his teeth gently raking it before his tongue laved and rolled it. Rebecca's hands slipped lower to Chase's shoulders. Then she frowned, realizing that he was still fully clothed. She felt cheated. She wanted to see and touch him too.

"Chase," she whispered, "your buckskins."

Chase lifted his dark head and looked up at her. Rebecca stared at his dark eyes, black and blazing with desire. A tremble of renewed excitement ran through her. Then he smiled, a smile that tugged at her heartstrings.

He rose and started to blow out the lamp, thinking that Rebecca would be frightened by his nudity, particularly since he was so blatantly aroused. And if she should change her mind, say no, Chase wouldn't be able to stop at this point. He had to have her. Every fiber of his being demanded it.

"No!" Rebecca cried, seeing what he was about to do. "I want to see you too."

Chase was surprised at her urgent cry—and a little shocked too. Rebecca was well bred, the kind of woman he would have expected to want to hide everything in the darkness. He was still amazed that she had let him strip her naked, having halfway expected her to insist upon keeping on her gown.

Rebecca had to see him. She had to know if he was really as beautiful as she thought, or if the lightning had played a trick on her that night. Seeing him hesitate, she said, "It's only fair that I should see you too."

Rebecca watched as Chase slipped off his tunic and tossed it aside. Then he slipped the pouch from his neck and laid it beside the mattress, the muscles on his shoulders and back rippling sensuously. Rebecca's mouth turned dry as he unlaced his pants and then kicked them aside.

As he stood before her, Rebecca's breath caught. He *was* beautiful, a powerful primitive god, hewed in bronze. Her eyes drifted over him hungrily, taking in the exceptional breadth of his shoulders, the broad expanse of his chest, his lean flanks and long legs, noting that there wasn't a spare ounce of flesh on him. He was all muscle and tendons, hard and sinewy. No, the lightning hadn't played any trick on her. He was just as she remembered him, right down to the dark, blazing eyes—except for one thing. Tonight he was aroused, and Rebecca found that she couldn't take her eyes off him. A tingle of fear ran through her, to be quickly replaced with excitement. A sob tore from her throat, and she opened her arms to him.

Chase had been all too aware of Rebecca's scrutiny. It had excited him unbearably, as if it were her hands instead of her eyes that had touched him. When she had stared so long at his arousal, Chase had held his breath, still fearing she would change her mind. And then, when she had held her arms out to him, he felt a rush of relief.

He sank to his knees beside her, and Rebecca pulled him down over her. When their feverish bodies touched, skin to skin, both gasped, feeling as if a bolt of lightning had run through them. Chase rained fiery kisses over her while Rebecca ran her hands over his shoulders and broad back, loving the feel of those powerful muscles and filled with wonder at the smoothness of his skin.

Chase couldn't get enough of her, feeling drunk with her taste, her sweetness, marveling at her softness and the silkiness of her skin. His hands smoothed over her back and hips, then over the soft curves of her thighs. He eased from her slightly, and when Rebecca whimpered in objection, he silenced her with a long, drugging kiss.

Rebecca's senses were spinning dizzily. Her skin seemed on fire where Chase touched her, kissed her. When she felt his fingertips softly brushing her thighs, inching higher and higher, all of the blood in her body rushed through her, leaving her aching and throbbing for his touch. To her, it seemed an eternity before his hand finally found her. Then, as his fingers touched the core of her womanhood, she gasped, feeling as if she had been seared by a flame of fire.

Chase smiled at her reaction. Though he was throbbing for want of her, he wanted this first time to be good for her and was deliberately forcing himself to go slow. He was surprised at how much he was enjoying initiating her into the delights of lovemaking, finding pleasure in her pleasure. He watched her face as his fingers tantalized and stroked that throbbing bud, each shudder of her pleasure firing his passion even higher.

Rebecca was unaware of Chase's dark eyes on her face. She was too lost in sensation to notice. The sweet ripples became powerful undulations, and then she climaxed in a sweet rush of heat that burned all the way to the soles of her feet. Her eyes flew open at the wonder of it.

She watched with dazed eyes as Chase lowered his head and his mouth captured hers in yet another fierce, deep, penetrating kiss. She was still spinning from that intoxicating kiss when Chase rose over her, nudging her legs apart and kneeling between them. She was hardly aware when his hands slipped beneath her buttocks to raise her.

Chase slowly entered her, and Rebecca was filled with the wonder of it, amazed that he was actually inside of her. Even the brief, sharp pain of her maidenhead breaking brought only a gasp, and not the cry that Chase had steeled himself for. As Chase slid deeper, filling her completely, his slow, sensuous thrusts awakened nerve endings Rebecca had never known existed, and she sobbed with gladness. She caught him to her, arching her hips and wrapping her legs around him, moving against him instinctively, for she needed no instruction in this dance that was as old as time itself.

Her mouth caught his in a deep kiss that fired their passion into a blazing inferno. As Chase moved more rapidly, more urgently, his masterful strokes deeper, bolder, stronger, Rebecca felt herself spiraling higher and higher, her senses expanding, her heart pounding, her breath coming in short gasps. She seemed to be racing upward to some unknown lofty peak, an unbearable pressure building in her. She writhed beneath him, her fingernails digging into the flesh of his shoulders, as the strange tension grew to a frenzied pitch and then burst in her brain in a blinding flash of light, her body convulsing as wave after wave of ecstasy rushed over her. She was still shuddering with those powerful, rapturous waves when Chase followed her in his own shattering release, exploding inside of her and then collapsing on top of her.

For a long while they lay in each other's arms, still trembling with aftershocks, the sweat on their bodies glistening in the lamplight. Eventually Chase raised his head and looked down at Rebecca with awe. He had wanted it to be good for her but had never expected her to be so enthusiastic, meeting him with a passion that equaled his own. Once again she had surprised him.

Rebecca opened her eyes, still floating, and saw

Chase gazing down at her. She smiled and brushed back a damp lock of hair from his forehead.

Chase searched her face. "No regrets?" he asked.

"No regrets," Rebecca answered in all honesty. "How could I possibly regret something that beautiful?"

Chase rose from her and lay down by her side. His arm coiled around her, pulling her to his side, and Rebecca snuggled to him. Then, feeling warm and safe and wonderfully languid, she closed her eyes and drifted off to sleep.

But Chase didn't sleep. He lay staring at the canvas above him. It *had* been beautiful, he admitted. The most beautiful experience he had ever felt. Not only had he reached new heights of passion with Rebecca, but it had left him with a contentment he had never known. It had never been that way with any other woman he had made love to, not even Shining Water.

Why should Rebecca take him to such heights, satisfy him so completely, and leave him with a warm sense of peace that he had never known before, when he didn't even love her? She had given him the gift of her virginity gladly, putting aside her pain and then firing his passion with hers. Shining Water had meekly submitted, giving her gift as if it were a sacrifice, and at the time Chase had thought her behavior fitting for a young Indian maiden.

Was he doubting his love? Chase asked himself, disturbed at where his thoughts were leading him. No, he couldn't be. Love and passion shouldn't be confused. One was ruled by the body, the other by the spirit, and his spirit still belonged to Shining Water. But as Chase drifted off to sleep, a little seed of doubt lingered.

From that night on, Rebecca shared her bed with Chase, and to her delight, he spent his nights in camp more often. She treasured their lovemaking, locking every moment away in her heart to be relived when Chase had left her. Yes, long after Chase had walked out of her life, she would still have the memories of these stolen nights of passion to comfort her and she would never have any regret.

Chase was amazed by Rebecca in bed. She was more than warm, soft, and yielding. She was eager, surprising him again and again with her passion. Strangely, it was she rather than he who set the mood of their lovemaking, sometimes slow, leisurely, and incredibly sensuous; sometimes achingly sweet and tender; and sometimes fiery and tumultuous, leaving Chase shaken to the depths of his soul. He found that he could no more predict what their lovemaking would be each night than he could anything else about Rebecca.

That was another surprising revelation to Chase. He had thought, when they became lovers, that Rebecca would be more manageable, more docile, accepting his word as law, doing what he said without question. He was sadly mistaken. He found that Rebecca was just as stubborn and independent as ever, and if he pushed her, she could be just as hot-tempered and sharp-tongued. Rebecca was an enigma to him. She could irritate him to no end, then pleasure him beyond belief. He was fascinated with her.

One night, when they were both still floating in the warm afterglow of their lovemaking, a sudden, high-pitched, keening noise rent the air. Chase slammed to his feet and looked about him wildly. "What in the hell is that?"

Rebecca understood his reaction because the first time she had heard the noise, she had almost jumped out of her skin. "I believe it's a bagpipe," she answered calmly. "I've heard it once before, one night when you were out scouting."

"A bagpipe?" Chase asked in disbelief. "In Texas?"

"Yes. These people's ancestors were highland Scots. I suppose they brought their bagpipes with them when they came to this country."

Chase listened to the eerie, shrill sound, the hair on his nape standing on end and his heart wildly racing. Then he began to feel foolish. He sank back down on the mattress and lay for a few moments, then began to chuckle.

"What's so funny?" Rebecca asked.

"I was just thinking. Indians go to great lengths to develop their war cry. They strive for the most blood-curdling, spine-tingling sound they can possibly make to frighten their enemies. But that damned bagpipe beats them all."

7

AFTER THE WAGON TRAIN HAD CROSSED THE
yellow waters of the Colorado River, the terrain
changed abruptly, almost as if they had crossed an
invisible dividing line between east and west. The
vast grasslands of the Great Plains stretched before
them, a gently rolling land that was dotted with
clumps of cactus, squatty olive-green cedars,
dusty-gray cenizo, and twisted mesquites, bare of
their feathery leaves at that time of the year. As
they moved farther west, the ground became more
hilly and rocky, dipping sharply, then rising again.

Chase was driving the day they forded the Gua
dalupe River, where they would leave the wagon
train. They crossed the river where its bed was
almost solid rock, the crystal-clear water only a
foot deep. Just beyond them the rock shelf fell
away, and the water tumbled over a small water-
fall, then through fast-flowing rapids. As they
pulled up the bank, Chase continued driving on
the *El Camino Real,* while the other wagons
turned to their left to follow a trail beside the river.

McPherson rode up to them. "What in the hell

do you think you're doin', Winters?" he demanded. "Get back in line!"

Chase stopped the wagon and looked McPherson in the eye. "I'm afraid this is where we leave you, McPherson. We're not going up the Guadalupe with you. We're going on to Bexar."

"Bexar?" McPherson asked in surprise. Then his eyes narrowed dangerously. "Like hell you are! You signed a contract with me. You agreed to settle on the Guadalupe with the rest of us."

"I'm sorry about that," Chase said calmly, "but we never had any intentions of settling with you. We're going on to Bexar."

McPherson glared at Chase angrily. Chase stared back, totally unruffled by the Scot's hot look.

"You just used us then?" McPherson asked. "Traveled along with us for the protection?"

"Back off, McPherson," Chase said in a low, warning voice. "I scouted all the way for you, risked my neck looking for Indians. The way I figure it, we're even. You did me a service, and I did one for you."

McPherson couldn't argue with that. He had offered to pay Chase for scouting, but Chase had refused. And Chase had more than just scouted for him. On several occasions McPherson had gone to him for advice on other things. But if Winters left, others might take the notion to leave too. He looked at the determined set of Chase's chin. "What do you want to go to Bexar for?" he asked in exasperation. "There ain't nothing but a bunch of Mexicans there."

Rebecca knew Chase wasn't going to explain. Questioning him only made him more determined not to divulge any information. She said, "Mr. McPherson, we're not trying to be stubborn. We have a good reason for going to Bexar. An important reason. We're taking cannons to the Texians at the Alamo."

Chase's head snapped around, and he glared at Rebecca, a look that told her in no uncertain terms that he was far from pleased with her revelation. Chase didn't fully trust McPherson. It was his Indian blood coming out in him, a suspiciousness of all white men. But Chase was angry with Rebecca for another reason too. She had snatched the role as spokesman from him, stepping out of her woman's place, something no Indian woman would dare to do. It was none of McPherson's business what they did. Why hadn't she kept her mouth shut?

"What in the hell are you talkin' about?" McPherson asked. "What cannons?"

Rebecca knew what Chase was thinking, but her divulging the mission had not been the thoughtless act of a foolish woman. She had a gift for looking beyond the surface of others and reading their true character. Once satisfied with what she saw, she was completely open and totally honest with them. It was only with Chase she had trouble seeing into his heart and his mind. She knew they could trust McPherson with their secret, and if Chase was angry with her for speaking up, that was just too bad. She had a mouth as well as a mind, and she fully intended to use both as she saw fit.

Shooting Chase a defiant look, Rebecca said, "Mr. McPherson, there are three dismantled eight-pounders hidden in a false bottom in this wagon."

McPherson's gaze ran the length of the wagon, looking at it in disbelief. He turned his attention back to Chase. "Why in the hell are you takin' cannons to the Alamo? The war is over."

The damage was done, Chase thought in disgust. To deny the cannons' existence at this point would only make him look foolish. "No, the war isn't over, McPherson. Hell, it hasn't even begun! Santa Anna is going to come down on Texas with a vengeance. If you were smart, you'd turn that train around and head for the Sabine."

"Well, if it's so damned dangerous around here, how come you brought your little woman along?"

Rebecca was terrified that Chase would tell him that he'd been forced to bring her along and that she wasn't his wife. She answered before Chase had a chance to say anything. "Because I wouldn't let him leave me behind! I have reasons, personal reasons, for wanting to see the Texians win their independence."

If any other woman had said that she wouldn't let her husband leave her behind, McPherson would have scoffed at her. But he had seen Rebecca's determination when she tackled driving those oxen. He imagined that if she got a notion in her head that she was going to do something, no one, not even her husband, could stop her.

"I'm serious, McPherson," Chase said in an ominous voice. "Get your people out of here. Texas is a powder keg and it's going to blow up any minute.

As soon as I deliver these cannons, I'm going to high-tail it out of here myself."

McPherson frowned. He'd been assured before he left Kentucky that the war in Texas was over, but during the past two months he had come to respect Chase's judgment. Then he sighed. "We can't go back, Winters. There ain't nothin' to go back to. We sold everything before we left." He paused, looking thoughtful. "We've fought Injuns for years for our rocky, worthless pieces of land back in Kentucky. I reckon we can hold a few Mexicans at bay for a piece of Texas."

It wouldn't be a few Mexicans, Chase thought grimly. It would be an army. McPherson planned to settle on the headwaters of the Guadalupe, a sparsely populated area to the north of Bexar. If the Alamo held, the Scot would be safe, but even if it didn't, Santa Anna would probably march east, toward the heavily populated area around the Brazos.

Chase shrugged his shoulders. "Suit yourself."

McPherson turned his horse and rode away a few feet, then suddenly wheeled the animal around. "You're an obstinate cuss, Chase Winters —but I like you! Good luck to you and your little woman."

Chase grinned. "You're pretty stubborn yourself, Jamie, and good luck to you too."

The next afternoon Rebecca saw a rider coming toward the wagon, riding as if all the demons in hell were after him and leaving a thick cloud of dust in his wake. Her heart raced fearfully, expecting to see a horde of Indians following him, but the only thing she could see on the horizon was the outline of a few mesquite trees.

Chase saw the man too. "What the hell?" he muttered, pulling the wagon to a stop.

The rider galloped up to them and reined in hard, his horse rearing on his hind legs and pawing the air at the sudden stop. "Where're you heading?" the man asked when his horse had settled down.

"Bexar," Chase answered.

"Then turn around and go back," the rider said urgently. "Back to the Colorado at least. Santa Anna has the Alamo surrounded."

"Santa Anna?" Rebecca gasped. "He marched his army across Texas in the middle of the winter?" she asked in a shocked voice.

"He sure did! And now he's got the Alamo surrounded with almost a thousand Santanistas. A courier going from the Alamo to the Texas government stopped by my place and watered his horse. Said all the Anglos in Bexar have fled. Told me to ride around and spread the alarm."

"But what makes you so sure the Alamo will fall?" Rebecca asked.

"It's got to! There's only a hundred and fifty men in there, and there were even less until Davy Crockett arrived with his men from Tennessee."

Chase wasn't surprised at Santa Anna's sudden appearance. He had feared that all along. But he was shocked to learn that the Alamo was so poorly manned.

"Won't Houston send reinforcements?" Rebecca asked.

"Hell, Houston is on furlough."

"On furlough?" Chase asked in disbelief. "In the middle of the war, he went on furlough?"

"Yeah, he was disgusted with the whole mess. First he ordered the Alamo blown up and the men to fall back to Gonzales and they didn't obey. Then he had to go down to Goliad and talk Fannin and his volunteers out of attacking Matamoros. With Governor Smith and the council squabbling all the time, he finally got fed up and asked to be released of his command. Governor Smith talked him out of it and told him to take a furlough until the first of March. Houston is off with the Cherokees now, trying to get them to sign a peace treaty."

Chase shook his head in disgust. With everyone trying to run the war their way, he didn't blame Houston for wanting out. There could only be one commander-in-chief.

"Will the men at the Alamo surrender then?" Rebecca asked, sickened by the news.

"Nope. Colonel William Travis is in charge there now. When Santa Anna demanded his surrender, Travis answered him with a cannon shot. Then the Mexicans raised the red flag, signaling no quarter for the enemy. With Santa Anna refusing to take prisoners, Travis can't surrender."

"I'm curious," Chase said. "If the Alamo is surrounded, then how did that courier get out of there?"

"I wondered about that myself and asked him.

He said there's a deep drainage ditch that runs along the south wall of the Alamo and into the countryside a good ways. He just slipped out the south gate and escaped through that ditch."

"Then Travis and his men aren't trapped after all," Rebecca said in an excited voice. "If a courier can escape, then they can too."

"I reckon they could if they wanted to, ma'am, but Travis ain't abandoning the Alamo. In that letter that the courier was taking to the people of Texas, Travis wrote he wasn't going to retreat or surrender. And Travis signed it 'Victory or death.' No, he plans on fighting to the last man. Of course, I reckon he's hoping to get reinforcements. That's what that letter was, a plea for someone to come to his aid."

"Is there any of the Texas army nearby?" Rebecca asked, her hopes rising again.

"There's Fannin down at Goliad. He's got four hundred men. I reckon when he hears about Travis's plight, he'll go to his aid." The rider wheeled his horse. "I'd better get going. The Alamo might fall at any minute. The courier said it was already being bombarded when he left, and I got a lot of settlers hereabouts to spread the news to. Like I said, go back to the Colorado. It ought to be safe there."

Rebecca and Chase watched as the man rode off cross-country until he disappeared in the distance. Chase flicked the reins, pulled them to the left, and the oxen started turning.

"What are you doing?" Rebecca asked.

146

"Turning around and going back, like the man said."

"Go back?" Rebecca asked in disbelief. "But we can't do that! We still have these cannons to deliver."

Chase pulled back on the reins, stopping the oxen, and looked at Rebecca as if she had lost her mind. "Deliver the cannons," he repeated in an incredulous voice. "Are you deaf? Didn't you hear what that man said? The Alamo is surrounded!"

"But we can still get them to the Texians. Through the same ditch the courier used."

"Are you crazy? Drive this damned wagon right down that ditch? Hell, even in the dark the Santanistas could spot this big wagon from a mile off."

"I wasn't suggesting that! I'm not stupid!" Rebecca said angrily. "I was thinking that you could sneak into the Alamo and tell them we have cannons for them. Surely they could figure out some way to get them in."

Chase shot to his feet. "Me?" he bellowed. "You want me to sneak into the Alamo? Hell, that place is a death trap, fixing to blow up at any minute!" He shook his head. "Oh, no, not me! If a bunch of glory-seekers want to throw away their lives, that's their business. But I'm not committing suicide for anybody!"

Chase sat back down and picked up the reins. Rebecca jerked them out of his hands and glared at him.

"Give me the reins, Rebecca," Chase said in a hard voice. "We're turning back."

"No, not *we!* You can turn back, but I'm not! I'll deliver these cannons myself."

"You?" Chase asked in disbelief.

"Yes, me! I've driven this damned wagon practically all the way from Natchitoches by myself, and I can drive it fifty more miles to Bexar. I'll find some way to get word to the men in the Alamo. So go on back, you—you coward!"

No one called Chase a coward and lived to tell of it. He glared at Rebecca, and she shivered at the murderous look in those fierce, black eyes. Then she said, "Chase, I can't turn back. I'd never forgive myself if I didn't do everything in my power to help those men."

"But the Alamo may have already fallen," Chase argued.

"You don't know that. Maybe Fannin has already arrived. That would bring the fighting force up to five hundred fifty men. General Cos had a thousand men when the Texians captured the Alamo and they only had four hundred. If four hundred men could capture the Alamo, surely five hundred fifty men could hold it, particularly with cannons and sitting behind those thick walls."

Chase seriously doubted that Santa Anna only had a thousand men, as the rider had told them. He had seen Santa Anna's armies in Mexico. They had never numbered less than four or five thousand. But he knew if he told Rebecca that, she would only argue more.

"All right, Rebecca," Chase said, still trying to reason with her, "let's just suppose Fannin has already arrived at the Alamo, or is on the way. He'd bring artillery with him. Hell, he's supposed to be Texas's senior artillery officer."

"But he might not have wanted to be slowed down by dragging heavy cannons with him. After all, time is crucial."

Chase couldn't see an artillery officer abandoning his cannons. But then, if Travis had seriously considered that harebrained scheme to attack Matamoros, he just might have done so. Besides, he was leading a bunch of volunteers, many not even Texians but soldiers of fortune and glory-seekers who had come to fight from all over the South, and the Alamo would be just their piece of meat. They might be so fired up, Fannin would have to abandon his cannons to keep up with them.

Chase sighed deeply. "Rebecca, everything you're saying is just supposition. You're *assuming* that the Alamo hasn't already fallen, *assuming* that they don't have cannons, *assuming* that Fannin is going to their aid. Face the facts! Bexar is surrounded by Santanistas. They'll have patrols out watching every road leading into the city for reinforcements. If they catch you and discover those cannons, they won't just throw you out of Texas. They'll kill you! Even if you are a woman."

"I don't care, Chase. I'm not leaving Texas. *Ever!* Even if the Mexicans kill me, I'll at least be buried here." She looked him directly in the eye. "I'm delivering these cannons with or without you!" she said in a determined voice.

Chase seriously doubted that Rebecca would try to deliver the cannons without him. Hell, she would be a fool to try it by herself. A lone woman? And for all of her faults, Rebecca wasn't a fool. No, she was only threatening him, trying to force him to bend to her will. Once she saw that he meant what he'd said, she'd capitulate.

"Then I'm afraid it's going to be without me," Chase said calmly.

He jumped down from the wagon seat and walked to the back of the wagon, then saddled Lightning, expecting to see Rebecca coming around the corner of the wagon at any moment to tell him that she'd changed her mind. By the time he threw his saddlebags over the back of the horse, he was beginning to get a little uneasy. He mounted and rode up to the front of the wagon. Rebecca sat there stiffly, staring straight ahead of her.

Then Chase saw the tears glittering in her eyes. Despite her earlier show of bravery, she was scared, Chase thought. "Sure you won't change your mind and come back with me?"

"No, I'm going to Bexar," Rebecca repeated stubbornly, refusing even to look at him.

"For Christ's sake, Rebecca! Admit it! You're scared to go alone."

Rebecca's head snapped around. She glared at him, her blue eyes spitting sparks. "I'm *not* scared!"

"Then why in the hell are you crying?"

"I'm not crying!" Rebecca denied hotly. "I got sand in my eyes."

Stubborn, obstinate little fool! Chase thought. And mad as a wet hen. So mad she was even crying. Well, when she calmed down and realized that she was really on her own, she'd change her mind and turn around.

"Okay, have it your way," Chase said. He wheeled his horse around and galloped off, calling over his shoulder "Tell the boys at the Alamo hello for me!"

After Chase had ridden about a quarter of a mile, he looked back over his shoulder and saw the wagon moving off in the opposite direction. She'll change her mind, he assured himself, and kept riding. He glanced back about another quarter of a mile down the road. The wagon was steadily moving away from him. He turned his horse and watched as the wagon grew smaller and smaller.

Holy smokes! Chase thought. She wasn't threatening. She was serious! The crazy little fool was actually going to try to take those cannons to Bexar—right through the Santanistas' lines.

What in the hell was he going to do now? Chase asked himself. It wouldn't do any good to go after her and try to reason with her. She was obsessed with trying to get those damned cannons to the Texians. He had a choice. He'd either have to join her or leave her.

Well, he'd be damned if he'd risk his life to get some stupid cannons through the Santanistas' lines to a pack of glory-seekers who might already be dead by now. Just because she was crazy was no reason he had to be. And he didn't owe her anything either. Just because they'd been lovers was no reason why he should get himself killed. Hell, no woman was worth that. Besides, if he went back now, she'd get some crazy idea in her head that she could lead him around by the nose.

Chase watched, tight-lipped, as the wagon became a mere speck, tormented by visions of what the Mexicans would do to Rebecca if they caught her. And then, as the wagon rolled over the horizon and disappeared, he muttered in self-disgust, "You damned fool," nudged his horse, and galloped off after the wagon.

When Chase suddenly appeared riding beside the wagon, Rebecca felt a rush of immense relief and happiness. But then, as Chase rode beside her silently, acting as if nothing had ever happened, as if he had never left, her anger warred with her happiness. She wanted to hug him. She wanted to hit him. She did neither. She looked across at him and simply said, "You're back."

Chase was a little shaken at Rebecca's calm manner. Hell, he thought, she could have at least acted glad to see him. Why, she didn't even look surprised when he rode up. Did she think she had him wrapped around her little finger? That he'd follow her around like some damned stallion after a mare he'd caught the scent of?

He leaned over, jerked the reins from Rebecca's hands, and reined in the oxen. Then he dismounted, reached up and caught Rebecca by the waist, and swung her down so hard her teeth rattled.

Towering over her, his black eyes flashing dangerously, he said, "I'm just going as far as Bexar with you. No farther! Then I'm leaving! You can figure out how to get those damned cannons into the Alamo. Do you understand?"

"I understand."

"And another thing. I'm the boss! What I say goes. No questions and no back talk!"

"Yes, Chase. Whatever you say. I promise I won't interfere or ask anything else of you."

Chase looked down at Rebecca, looking so meek and docile. He didn't believe a word she said!

That night Rebecca huddled into herself, shivering with cold on her feather mattress. Another norther had come howling down on them and plunging the temperature to freezing, but Rebecca knew that there was no hope of Chase offering her the heat of his body this time. Oh, he still shared her bed, but he was lying as far away as he could get from her, with his back to her, ignoring her.

When she had told Chase that she wasn't crying, she *had* been lying, but not because she was scared. She had never even thought about being frightened. No, it was the realization that he was leaving her that had brought on the tears. All along she had steeled herself for the day Chase would walk out of her life—or so she had thought. The pain that had welled up inside her had shocked her with its intensity, and despite herself, the tears had come. That he was leaving with bad feelings between them had only made it seem worse. She had hoped that they could at least part on good terms.

And then, when she had seen him riding beside her, she had been filled with happiness, thinking that she had been given a reprieve, a few more days with him to add to her little treasure chest of memories that she kept secretly locked away in her heart. But she had been wrong to think that things would return to the way they had been. All day and evening he had been sharp with her, glaring at her hatefully. And now he wouldn't even offer her his body heat. Why, she could probably freeze to death, and he wouldn't care less! And he'd certainly never make love to her again. Not as angry as he was at her for forcing him into this position. It seemed the war had driven a wedge between them.

She couldn't understand Chase. Oh, she knew he thought that the Texians' bid for independence was foolish and doomed to failure, but how could he be so cold-blooded as to turn his back on those poor men at the Alamo? She couldn't. While there was life, there was hope. And she did have hope. Perhaps, even now, men were flocking to the Alamo. And tomorrow Houston's furlough would be up. Certainly, when he heard of Travis and his men's plight, he'd muster an army to come to their rescue.

Another frigid blast of wind rocked the wagon, and Rebecca shivered even harder. And then she heard a muttered "Damn!" and felt Chase's warm arms folding around her and pulling her to him.

Rebecca buried herself in his warmth and mumbled, "Thank you."

"Forget it!" Chase snapped. "I'm doing it as much for myself as for you. Hell, I'd never get any sleep tonight with your teeth chattering like that."

"I'm sorry, Chase," Rebecca said against his

chest. "I just couldn't turn back and leave them to their fate."

For a long while Chase was silent, wondering why he couldn't stay mad at her. Then he nuzzled the top of her head with his chin and said, "I know. I guess you can't help it if you're a little crazy."

He kissed the top of her head and whispered, "Now, go to sleep. We've got a long, hard day ahead of us tomorrow."

A silent tear ran down Rebecca's cheek. She had been given a reprieve after all.

8

THREE DAYS LATER CHASE SPIED SMOKE COM-
ing from a cabin in the woods and turned the
wagon down the small trail that led to it. "Let's
stop and ask those settlers if they've heard anything new about the Alamo. No sense in us going
there if it's already fallen."

When they drove into the clearing by the cabin,
the colonists were frantically packing a wagon, the
woman hastily arranging the boxes and small
pieces of furniture the children were passing up to
her. A young boy came around the corner of the
cabin, leading a lowing cow, and behind him, a
man followed leading four harnessed horses.

"Have you heard anything from the Alamo?"
Chase asked the man after the brief introductions
had been exchanged.

"Sure have. A Mexican and his family passed
through here this morning and stopped for water.
Said he'd come from Bexar three days ago. Said
there was at least four or five thousand Santanistas
in Bexar now. There's even a battalion of those
snappers."

Chase wasn't surprised to hear the number had swelled. Nor was he surprised to hear that Santa Anna had brought along his *Zapadores,* or snappers, as the Anglos called them. They were a tough, battle-hardened battalion of engineers, his best fighters.

"I was planning on sticking it out," the man continued, "until I heard that. Now I'm getting my family out of here as fast as I can."

"Then the Alamo hasn't fallen?" Rebecca asked. "They're still fighting?"

"No, Travis and his men are still in there. From what the Mexican said, there really wasn't much fighting going on. Santa Anna can't get his cannons up close enough to blast them out. Every time he tries it, Crockett and his sharpshooters pick off the Santanistas with their long rifles, and all the Mexicans have got is those short-range muskets."

"Has Travis received any reinforcements?" Chase asked.

"Don't know. The Mexican didn't say anything about that."

Chase glanced over at the corral. "What are you going to do with the rest of your horses?"

"Turn them loose, I guess."

"I'll buy them from you."

"Sure thing. Let me hitch these horses up to my wagon and I'll be right with you."

"What are you buying horses for?" Rebecca asked.

"Because I'm getting rid of these damned oxen, that's why!"

"But six horses can't pull as well as six oxen. They'll tire out too fast. We'll have to stop and rest them," Rebecca objected.

"Damn it! What happened to that promise of yours not to ask any questions or not to interfere? I know horses can't pull as far as oxen. And yes, we will have to stop and rest them. But if I see a Santanista patrol coming our way, I want to be able to move—and move fast! And those damned oxen have only one speed: slow!"

Chase jumped down from the wagon. Rebecca climbed down and watched as he removed the yokes and harnesses from the oxen. As soon as they were released, the animals ambled to a small creek by the side of the clearing and began to drink.

"What will happen to them?" Rebecca asked in a concerned voice.

"The oxen? Don't tell me you're worrying about a bunch of stupid oxen now?" Chase asked in disbelief.

Rebecca had become attached to the animals. For days and days on end, they had been her only companions when Chase was gone so much from the train. Many times along the lonely trail, she had talked to them. If she hadn't, she would have gone crazy.

"Yes, I am worried!" she snapped, then quickly added, "And they're not stupid! They may be big and awkward and dumb-looking, but they're not stupid. It doesn't seem right to let them bring us all this way and then just—just abandon them."

She's serious, Chase thought in amazement.

First she insists that she won't turn her back on the men at the Alamo, and now she doesn't want to abandon the oxen. Christ! What was she? The champion of all dumb animals?

"Rebecca, there are wild oxen all over out here, animals that have escaped from the supply trains going to Bexar. They'll survive."

The settler hurried back to Chase, and the two men walked over to the corral. The settler's wife approached Rebecca. "You're welcome to wait inside where there's a fire going. If you'll just put it out and close the door when you leave."

Rebecca looked at the settlers' open wagon. It would offer the family no protection from the cold or rain. Three young children huddled under a blanket in the back, their eyes wide with fright. The older boy sat on the wagon seat, trying very hard to be stoic. Rebecca's heart went out to the family. "Where will you go?" she asked.

"To Gonzales. I have a brother there. And then, if Santa Anna marches east, I don't know where we'll go."

The woman turned and looked back at her cabin. Rebecca knew that the woman was wondering if she'd ever see it again and, if so, in what condition. "It will still be here when you get back," Rebecca said, wanting to comfort the woman and yet not feeling nearly as confident that the Alamo would hold after hearing that Santa Anna's army had swelled to five thousand.

The woman smiled at Rebecca, but her doubts were visible in her eyes. Then she straightened her shoulders. "Well, if it isn't, we'll just have to rebuild," she said with determination in her voice.

Rebecca watched as the settler drove his wagon from the clearing. Just before they turned the corner of the road, his wife turned back and gave the cabin one last wistful look.

The next day Rebecca was surprised at the good time they were making, but she still didn't think the horses would be able to maintain that pace, not day after day. In her opinion, they would have been better off with the oxen in the long run.

She sensed rather than saw Chase stiffen. "What's wrong?" she asked.

"There's a patrol of dragoons coming over the horizon."

Rebecca strained her eyes, but she couldn't see anything. "Are you sure?"

"I'm sure. I caught the flash of one of those lances they carry, and now I can see them."

Rebecca was amazed at Chase's keen eyesight. She still couldn't see anything.

Chase glanced quickly around them, then turned the wagon sharply off the road and down a hill, urging the horses into a hard gallop. Rebecca hung on for dear life as the wagon bounced and lurched over the rocky ground, fearing that a wheel would sheer off at any minute. She held her breath as Chase drove down a steep side of a dry creek bed, terrified that the wagon would topple over. When they finally came to a stop under a group of live oak trees growing on both sides of the creek, Rebecca was amazed that every bone in her body hadn't been broken on the wild, rough ride down the hillside.

She looked around them, seeing the limbs hanging over them, and was thankful that live oaks weren't deciduous trees. Dead grapevines hung from them, looking like ropes, some as thick as a man's wrist, and screening them even more. But Rebecca fervently wished that the canvas wasn't on the wagon; the dragoons might spy the white through the leaves.

Shortly after they had stopped, the dragoons rode on the road above them. Rebecca heard them before she saw them, their sabers and canteens clattering, the hooves of their horses drumming. They passed at a hard gallop, their green-and-white uniforms a mere blur and the sunlight flashing off their metal helmets, breastplates, and beribboned lances, traveling so fast that she couldn't even count them. One of Chase and Rebecca's horses blew hard, winded from the frantic race down the hill. Rebecca held her breath, terrified that the cavalrymen would hear, then laughed at herself, realizing that they couldn't possibly hear over the din they were making.

At last the hoofbeats died away and the only sign that the lancers had passed was the heavy cloud of dust that still hung over the road. Rebecca sighed in relief. "You were right, Chase. Oxen could have never moved that fast. We would have been caught for sure."

"We were just lucky. If I hadn't spied that flash, we still might have been caught. From now on we're staying off the main roads. We'll take one of

161

the old Indian trails into Bexar. It may be slower, but it will be safer."

The ancient trail wound through old creek beds that were thick with tangled vegetation, sometimes so narrow the wagon could barely make it through. Then the trail crossed steep, rocky hills, studded with squatty cedar trees, the loose rocks hampering the horses' footing and crunching beneath the wagon wheels as they rolled over them. They spent a whole day looking for a place shallow enough to cross the San Antonio River, and early on the fifth night, when they finally crested a hill and looked down on the town of *San Antonio de Bexar,* Rebecca couldn't believe they had finally made it.

The town itself was dark and strangely silent, but all along where the river curved into a horseshoe bend and for what seemed like miles beyond, there were hundreds of campfires burning. They could see the interior walls of the Alamo in the distance, for in the middle of the fortress, a huge bonfire was burning, the firelight dancing eerily over the sand-colored walls. Rebecca strained her eyes and could barely see figures moving about the fire, looking like ants in the distance.

"Why in the world are they burning such a big fire?" Rebecca asked Chase.

"Damned if I know. Seems like a stupid thing to do to me. With that fire behind them, the men on those walls would be outlined like sitting ducks."

"There doesn't seem to be much going on," Rebecca observed.

"Maybe the Santanistas only bombard them

during the day," Chase suggested, an uneasy feeling creeping over him. "Let's find someplace to hide the wagon, and I'll go down and investigate. I've a friend who lives in Bexar. Maybe he can tell me what's going on."

"Oh, no!" Rebecca said in a fiercely determined voice. "You're not leaving me behind now. I've traveled halfway across Texas for this. I'm going with you."

An hour later they rode into Bexar, giving the area around the Alamo a wide berth. Rebecca rode behind Chase on Lightning as they moved cautiously down the deserted, twisted streets. There was an eerie silence in the town, the hush making Lightning's hoofbeats sound alarmingly loud to Rebecca's ears. Most of the houses were completely dark; only an occasional flickering lamp could be seen in the windows. The cold night air was heavy with the odor of smoke; oddly, it did not smell at all like woodsmoke, but had a peculiar, sweetish odor to it, a smell that left Rebecca's stomach feeling unsettled.

To Rebecca, the town seemed more like a graveyard than a place for the living. The deep darkness and strange silence made her feel jumpy, and the shadowy walls of the buildings around them seemed to be closing in on her, smothering her.

"How much farther is it to your friend's house?" she whispered nervously to Chase.

Chase was feeling uneasy himself, an uneasiness that had only grown ever since he had looked down on the Alamo. "Not far from here."

When they stopped before a two-story building,

Chase dismounted, then swung Rebecca to the ground. "It looks deserted," Rebecca remarked, looking at the darkened house.

Chase tapped the knocker on the heavy oak door, the noise sounding unusually loud in the silence.

They waited. Chase knocked again, this time even louder. Rebecca's eyes darted around her fearfully, expecting to see a horde of Santanistas jumping at them from the shadows at any minute.

"Maybe he's in back where he can't hear," Chase said. "Come on. There's a side gate that leads into the patio."

They found the heavily scrolled iron gate padlocked. From inside the courtyard, Rebecca could hear the tinkling sound of a water fountain.

"Señor Williams is not here," a male voice said from behind them.

Rebecca jumped at the sudden sound and whirled around, seeing the dim outline of a man standing in the shadows. Then she was temporarily blinded by the sudden light as the man quickly lit a lamp and held it up against her and Chase's faces.

"Ah, Señor Winters, it is you," the man said, and Rebecca could sense the tension leaving the stranger's body.

"Yes, Señor Seguin," Chase answered calmly, as if he had known who the man was all along. "You say Williams has left?"

"Sí, along with the other Anglos and many of the Mexicans in Bexar. He left the night that my son came with the news that Santa Anna's army was approaching the town, right in the middle of

164

the fandango we were having in the plaza to celebrate George Washington's birthday."

Rebecca couldn't believe her ears. The Mexicans had been celebrating Washington's birthday? An American President?

"But come into my house," Señor Seguin said. "It is dangerous for us to be out here in the streets. There are Santanistas patrolling everywhere in Bexar tonight." He glanced at Lightning. The stallion stood out like a white banner in the darkness. "And bring your horse into the patio, so he won't be seen."

Seguin blew out the lamp and led them to a gate next to the one that they had found padlocked, Chase leading his horse behind them. They walked through a cobbled patio and around a three-tiered fountain, the water cascading softly down it. When they stepped into the house, the Mexican shut the door firmly behind them and slammed in the bolt.

In the dimly lit hallway, Rebecca could see that Seguin was an older man, his dark hair sprinkled with silver. Slimly built, his features were aristocratic, and there was an air of self-confidence about him. Had he not been Mexican, Rebecca would have been impressed.

Placing the lamp on a small table in the hallway, Seguin turned to Chase. "Tell me, Señor Winters, why do you come to Bexar, when all of the other Anglos have fled?" he asked.

"We're delivering cannons to the Alamo," Chase answered.

Rebecca sucked in her breath sharply, shocked

that Chase would reveal their purpose to a Mexican.

"You have brought a woman with you on such a dangerous mission?" Seguin asked incredulously.

"It's a long story," Chase answered. "Too long to go into now. I came to Bexar tonight to find out what the situation is at the Alamo. From what we could see from a hilltop, there doesn't seem to be much going on."

There was a long silence before Seguin said in a quiet voice, "Come into the *sala, mis amigos.* We will talk there."

As Seguin stepped through the doorway and Chase started to follow, Rebecca caught his arm, pulling him back. "Are you insane? Telling that Mexican about the cannons?"

"Rebecca, Erasmo Seguin is a personal friend of Stephen Austin and has fought for separate statehood for Texas right along with the other Texians. If you're afraid he'll betray us to Santa Anna—forget it! He hates Santa Anna as much as we do."

Without another word, Chase took Rebecca's arm firmly and led her into the *sala.* When she stepped into the room, Rebecca looked around her wildly, half expecting to see Santanistas surrounding them, despite Chase's assurances that Seguin was a friend. To Rebecca, no Mexican was her friend.

The room was large, furnished with heavy, ornate furniture made of dark wood, the walls a stark white on which iron-grilled wall sconces hung, the candles in them flickering and sending shadows across the walls. A fire blazed in a small fireplace at one end of the room, and the windows were covered with heavy draperies that had been tightly drawn.

"Sit down, *mis amigos,*" Seguin said, motioning to two chairs by the fireplace. "I am sure you are chilled to the bone."

Chase slipped Rebecca's cloak from her shoulders and laid it across the back of a chair. Then he sat down on one of the chairs by the fire, looking completely at ease. Rebecca glared at him, then sank to the other chair, sitting stiffly. Seguin stood between them, his back to the fire.

"I am afraid I have some shocking news for you," Seguin began. He took a deep breath, as if steeling himself. "The Alamo has fallen."

Rebecca felt the quiet announcement as if she had been dealt a physical blow. The breath left her lungs, and the color drained from her face. Although Chase had expected that all along and had sensed that something terrible had happened ever since he had viewed the fortress from the hilltop, the news still came as a shock to him.

"When did it happen?" Chase asked, after he had recovered.

"This morning. They attacked before dawn, in a cold drizzle. They overran the Texians by sheer numbers."

"They're all dead?" Rebecca asked weakly.

"*Sí,* over a hundred and eighty men," Seguin said sadly.

Chase frowned, saying, "The last I heard there were one hundred and fifty men at the Alamo."

"Thirty-two volunteers slipped in from Gonzales under the cover of darkness a few days ago."

"I imagine it was all over within minutes," Chase commented, "if they were outnumbered that badly."

"No, *amigo,* they held them off for an hour and a half. Our Texians fought magnificently. Never has the world seen such bravery as was shown by the men at the Alamo. They repulsed two waves, the sharpshooters on the walls mowing the Santanistas down. Then, on the third wave, the Santanistas surged over their own dead while the band played the *Deguello*—the fire and death call that signaled total annihilation. This time they finally made it over the walls, but even then the Texians fought fiercely in a furious hand-to-hand combat, retreating until they made their last stand at the chapel. Bowie, who had been ill, was there in the chapel, on a cot. He fought like a tiger but the Santanistas bayoneted him. By six-thirty in the morning it was all over."

There was a long silence, all three staring out into space, lost in their own brooding thoughts. The only sound in the room was the crackling of the fire. Then Seguin whispered fervently, *"Por Dios,* my son was not there."

Chase lifted his head. "Juan?"

"Sí. Juan was with Colonel Travis from the very beginning. He would have been there today had not Travis sent him to Fannin at Goliad to plead for aid. He has not yet returned."

"Your son was with Travis?" Rebecca asked, shocked.

168

"Ah, I see that surprises you," Seguin said. He had been aware of Rebecca's suspicious glances earlier and knew that she did not trust him because he was a Mexican. "No, señorita, all Texians are not Anglos. Many of my people are fighting for independence too. There were others at the Alamo besides my son. Ten Mexicans fought and died there today, just as bravely as the rest of the Texians. One manned the cannon on the chapel roof. He died before his wife and four children."

"There were women and children at the Alamo?" Chase asked, shocked.

"*Sí.* The wife of Almeron Dickerson, who commanded the batteries, and their infant daughter were there. The rest were Mexicans, families of the men who fought there or friends of the Anglos."

"Were any of them killed?" Rebecca asked.

"No, Mrs. Dickerson was shot in the leg by an enraged Santanista, against orders that no harm was to befall the civilians."

"Thank God for that." Rebecca sighed in relief.

An angry look came over Seguin's face. "Oh, don't think Santa Anna was showing mercy, señorita. The man doesn't know the meaning of the word. No, he let them live for a purpose, to tell the horrors of what happened at the Alamo, to spread the word as a warning of what happens to those who rebel against him."

Seguin turned to stare at the fire in the fireplace for a few moments, then turned back. "But Santa Anna paid a heavy price for his victory, if that can be any consolation to us. I cannot give you an exact head count. Santa Anna was quick—too quick

—to bury his dead. What he could not bury in the cemeteries, he threw into the river. He did not want anyone to know that he lost roughly fifteen hundred men, a third of his army."

"And the Texians' bodies?" Chase asked.

"They were cremated on a huge funeral pyre in the middle of the Alamo courtyard. Santa Anna refused to give the Texians a Christian burial. He cremated them on purpose, for our religion teaches that those whose bodies are destroyed by fire cannot rejoin their souls on Judgment Day. It was the final outrage," Seguin ended bitterly.

That was the bonfire that she had seen in the Alamo, Rebecca realized. The Texians' funeral pyre. And that sickening-sweet odor in the smoke had been the smell of their bodies burning. Bile rose in her throat and her face paled.

Seeing her expression, Seguin said quickly, "I apologize for being so blunt, señorita. I keep forgetting my story is not one for such delicate ears. Let me get you some sherry."

Seguin walked to a small table. After picking up one of several decanters, he poured the liquid from it into a small crystal goblet and carried it to Rebecca.

Rebecca accepted the cup and sipped the sherry, but the warm wine did nothing to ease the icy feeling that had crept over her at Seguin's grim tale. She felt numb, stunned by the disastrous news.

Seguin poured a brandy for Chase, then one for himself. They sat, ignoring the goblets in their hands, once again lost in their own thoughts.

Finally Chase looked up, asking Señor Seguin,

"They never made any effort to escape? Or were they planning to, but got caught by surprise?"

"No, Señor Winters, they must have known the attack was coming. After twelve days and nights of constant bombardment, Santa Anna silenced his guns last night. That was when Travis gave his men the option to leave or stay. Only one left, Moses Rose, a soldier of fortune."

Chase sat for a long time, thinking. He had in the past called the men at the Alamo hotheads and glory-seekers, but now, after hearing about the battle, he had to admire the brave defenders of the Alamo. He thought of the men who had died there —Crockett, Travis, Bowie, and the others whose names would go down into the annals of history as the heroes of the Alamo.

"Señor Seguin," Rebecca said, breaking the silence. "You said something about cannons. Did the Texians have enough artillery? Could they have repelled the Santanistas' attack if they'd had more?"

"They had eighteen cannons. No, señorita, it was not for lack of artillery that the Alamo fell but lack of manpower."

So, Rebecca thought, their cannons weren't even needed. Even if they had gotten them to the Texians before the battle, the outcome would have been the same. She glanced at Chase, fearing his eyes would say I told you so, but his expression was unreadable.

For a few minutes the men talked, the Mexican asking questions about their mission. And then Señor Seguin glanced at the clock on the mantel and rose. "I do not wish to appear rude, but it will be daylight in a few hours. Under ordinary circumstances, I would offer you the hospitality of my home, knowing that you must be exhausted from your long trip. But just before you came, I heard rumors that Santa Anna was planning to arrest all of the Mexicans in Bexar who aided Travis and his men. It is well known that I was one of them. If the Santanistas should come here to arrest me and search the house and find you—"

"Then you must flee while you still can," Rebecca interjected, truly concerned for this man who had been such a revelation to her. She had thought that all Mexicans were her enemies, but Seguin had taught her differently.

"No, *mi amigo,* Bexar is my home. I will never leave it."

"But you could be killed!" Rebecca objected.

"The men at the Alamo didn't flee. Nor shall I."

"Come, Rebecca," Chase said, rising to his feet and picking up her cloak. "Señor Seguin is right. It's time we leave."

After Chase had slipped the cloak over Rebecca's shoulders, the three walked to the door. They paused in the hallway while Seguin unbolted the door and opened it. When they stepped out into the patio, Rebecca shivered and pulled her cloak closer. It was much colder than when they had arrived.

"Which way did you come into town?" Seguin asked Chase.

"From the north, down *Calle de la Soledad,*" Chase answered.

"The Santanistas are swarming all over town. It is a miracle that you weren't arrested," Seguin said. "Go south, until you cross *Calle Dolorosa,* a few streets down. Then cross the river. There is an old trail that follows it east."

"Yes, I know the one you mean," Chase answered.

Chase mounted Lightning and bent down, helping Rebecca up behind him. Seguin frowned at Rebecca's head, the golden-red curls tumbling down her back where it was tied with a ribbon. "Be sure and cover your hair, señorita. Even in the dark the Santanistas could see it."

"I'm afraid I don't have a hood on my cloak. Besides, it couldn't stand out any more than Chase's white horse."

"Ah, but in the distance a Santanista would only see two figures riding a white horse, but with that hair, they would know one is an Anglo. We Mexicans have red hair too, but not that light a color."

Chase had turned in his saddle and was looking at Rebecca's hair. "He's right. I never realized with you sitting behind me."

"Wait here," Seguin said. "I will bring you one of my wife's *mantillas.*"

A few moments later the Mexican was back, handing a lacy, black *mantilla* to Rebecca.

"Thank you," Rebecca said, as she tossed it over her head. "I shall see that it's returned."

"No, *mi amigo.* Consider it a gift from a Mexican Texian to an Anglo Texian."

Rebecca smiled sheepishly. "I still wish you would flee."

"No. I am not one to run from my enemies." Seguin cocked his head and looked at Rebecca thoughtfully before smiling. "And neither are you, I suspect."

Señor Seguin stepped back. *"Vaya con Dios, mis amigos,"* he said quietly.

9

CHASE AND REBECCA RODE DOWN THE DARK
streets of Bexar, the sickening odor of burning
flesh in their nostrils. Rebecca wondered if the
smoke was heavier and therefore the odor
stronger, or if it was just that knowing what the
smoke was made it seem more nauseating.

They entered a broad, cobblestoned plaza. At
one end sat the San Fernando Church, its belfry
towering into the dark, moonless sky. Farther
down, to their right, Rebecca could see the dim
outline of the Governor's Palace. Just as they
turned onto *Calle Dolorosa,* they heard the clatter
of hooves as a Santanista patrol approached. They
darted into a nearby alley and watched breath-
lessly as the soldiers passed, so close Rebecca
could smell the lather on their horses and feel the
heat from the animals' bodies.

From then on Chase stuck to the dark alleys,
weaving their way toward the *Rio San Antonio de
Padua.* The river was narrow but deep, and Lightning had to swim it to cross. Rebecca was surprised to find that the water was warmer than the

air, but soon after they had climbed the opposite bank and turned east, she was shivering from her wet skirts.

The old river trail they followed was narrow, and they had to thread their way through the tangled underbrush. A fog rolled off the river beside them, giving the low bottomland a ghostly appearance. When the river turned north, Chase left the trail, heading directly east through a thick woods. As they emerged from the trees and into a clearing, Rebecca could see the glow of the funeral pyre in the Alamo north of them.

"Alto!"

Rebecca jumped at the sharp command and looked about her wildly, then saw two Santanista sentries stepping from behind a cedar tree, their muskets aimed at them. And then, as Chase gave his horse a sharp kick and Lightning lurched forward, Rebecca's neck snapped at the sudden movement. They sped across the clearing, the sound of the sentries yelling and gunshots in their ears. Two balls whizzed by them, and Rebecca felt a stinging sensation on the outside of her thigh.

As they raced across the clearing, Chase suddenly veered sharply when two more sentries stepped out of the darkness in front of him, causing Rebecca to almost fall off the horse. As Lightning whirled, Chase swung his leg out and kicked one of the sentries in the chest, knocking him backward into the other sentry and sending his musket flying into the air as it discharged. The deafening roar left Rebecca's ears ringing.

"Damn!" Chase muttered, seeing four more sentries running from the nearby woods to the right of them. "We've run right into a picket line."

Musket balls peppered the dirt around them and flew through the air. *"Tejanos! Tejanos!"* the Santanistas yelled, sounding the alarm.

Chase gave Lightning his head, knowing that, with his animal's instinct for fleeing from danger, the mustang was a better judge of picking their escape route than he.

Rebecca clung to Chase's waist for dear life as Lightning raced into the countryside. The cold air rushing past her sent her skirts flapping and the mantilla whipping about her face as the ground flew past them, the clumps of cactus and cedars a mere blur from the corner of her eyes. Rebecca's heart raced, fearing that the animal would stumble on some obstacle in the dark and send both her and Chase flying through the air.

Lightning didn't bother to go up and down the sides of the deep ravines that crisscrossed the area. He jumped them. And each time Rebecca looked down at that deep, dark chasm below her, her heart sank. When they were far out into the countryside and miles from the sentry lines, the stallion slowed to a trot, and Rebecca was amazed that he wasn't even winded.

The sun was rising when they rode into the deep gully where they had left the wagon. The horses, confined in a roped corral where Chase had put them, whinnied their welcome to Lightning, and the stallion snorted in return.

As Chase helped her down from the mustang's back, Rebecca was still trembling from their wild

177

ride, and her thigh was throbbing. She hurried to the wagon, feeling exhausted and drained. Chase, who had turned his attention to unsaddling Lightning, didn't even notice the bloodstain on her skirt or her limp.

When Chase stepped into the wagon, Rebecca was in her nightgown and sitting on the mattress, the flannel bunched up on her lap. He looked down at the long red mark on her thigh as she dabbed at it with a flannel swatch saturated with antiseptic.

"How did that happen?" he asked.

"One of the balls grazed me," Rebecca answered calmly.

"You were shot?" Chase asked, horrified.

"No, I wasn't shot. I told you, the ball just grazed me."

Chase knelt before her and examined the wound closer. The long line was more skinned than lacerated, the blood oozing and not flowing freely, but an ugly, dark bruise was already forming.

"Why didn't you tell me a ball had grazed you?" Chase asked in an accusing voice, sitting back on his heels.

"What for? It's nothing serious. Besides, what would you have done about it? We certainly couldn't have stopped." Rebecca lay the swatch aside and flipped her gown back down.

"Aren't you even going to bandage it?" Chase asked.

"For heaven's sake, Chase! It's not serious enough for a bandage. Why, it's hardly bleeding anymore." She lifted the covers and slipped under them. "I don't know why you're making such a big thing of it. Now, please, I don't want to hear any more about it. I'm tired. All I want to do is go to sleep."

Chase watched as Rebecca rolled over with her back to him, wondering why he *was* so upset. The wound wasn't serious. Why, he'd certainly had worse, a bullet and a knife wound; he had even ridden for days with an arrowhead embedded in his shoulder. But Rebecca could have been killed, and that terrified him. Chase, who had known fear in his life but never terror, wondered at the intensity of his emotion.

When she awoke, Chase was watering the horses. Rebecca climbed down from the wagon and stood by the roped corral watching for several minutes, and then, realizing that the mustang stallion wasn't with the others, asked, "Where's Lightning?"

"Up there," Chase answered, pointing.

Rebecca glanced up and saw Lightning standing at the top of the gully. Against the azure-blue sky, with his head held high and proud, his powerful proportions, and his thick, flowing mane and tail, he looked magnificent.

"What's he doing up there?"

"Watching for danger. If he sees anyone or anything of consequence out there, or smells it, we'll know it."

"You've trained him to do that too?" Rebecca asked in amazement. "Act as a sentry, a lookout for you?"

"No, I didn't train him. It just comes naturally

to him, and he's not guarding us from danger. It's these horses that he's protecting."

"The horses? But why?"

Chase chuckled. "You're not very observant, Rebecca. Didn't you notice they're all mares, and Lightning has become very protective of them? You might not have been too happy with these horses, but Lightning has been delighted."

"Are you telling me that he considers them his . . . whatever you call it?"

"His *manada?* Yes, that's what it looks like to me."

"But these mares aren't mustangs," Rebecca objected. "They're tame horses."

"To a mustang stallion, all mares look alike. Given the opportunity, he'd steal tame mares."

"But what about the mares? Maybe they don't want to be in his *manada,*" Rebecca objected on behalf of the mares, resenting Lightning's attitude and thinking that he was just like his human male counterparts, domineering and arrogant.

"They'll accept him. There are tame horses that are herd stallions too, you know. In fact, these mares have already accepted Lightning as their leader. Didn't you notice how they welcomed him this morning?" Chase turned back to watering the mares. "I was only planning to take two back with us and turn the others loose. But now that they've accepted Lightning as their leader and protector, they'll probably tag along, whether we want them or not."

An uneasy feeling was creeping over Rebecca.

"What do you mean, only take two of them with us?"

"Well, we really only need two. One for you to ride and one as a packhorse. I can ride Lightning bareback and you can have my saddle."

"What about the wagon?"

"We don't want to drag that heavy wagon with us. I want to get the hell out of here as fast as I can," Chase answered in exasperation.

"You're going to abandon the cannons?" Rebecca asked, panic-stricken.

It was Chase's turn to feel uneasy. "What did you think I was going to do with them?"

"Take them to Fannin! That's what Paul told us to do. Take them to the nearest Texas army post if they weren't needed at the Alamo."

"Paul didn't know Santa Anna was going to invade Texas this soon," Chase argued. "He wouldn't expect us to try to deliver the cannons to Fannin now. Not with the territory swarming with Santanistas."

"But we've got to get those cannons to Fannin! It's even more important now that the Alamo has fallen. The Texians are going to need artillery desperately."

"Rebecca," Chase said, trying very hard to be patient, "I admire what the men at the Alamo did, but trying to beat Santa Anna's might is futile. What happened at the Alamo should prove that, if nothing else. When the people of Texas hear what happened at Bexar, they'll know independence was nothing but an impossible dream. Every Anglo in Texas will head for the Sabine as fast as he can."

"No, they won't!" Rebecca said hotly, her blue eyes flashing and dark with emotion. "What happened at the Alamo will only anger them, not frighten them. They'll seek revenge."

Chase looked at Rebecca closely. The determined gleam in her eyes that she usually had when she talked of independence for Texas had turned into a fanatical glitter. What happened at the Alamo had only fired her hatred more. He began to suspect that what Rebecca had said might be true.

"Don't you see, Chase? We've *got* to win this war now. If we don't, then every man who gave his life at the Alamo died in vain—for nothing!"

Yes, Chase thought grimly, the cause had its martyrs now. What happened at the Alamo would only leave the Texians with a deep hatred that would demand revenge. The Texians would continue to fight, despite the futility of it all. But winning a war takes careful planning and organization on the part of the leaders and a well-supplied, well-disciplined army, none of which the Texians had. Despite their desire to win, they would still fail.

"Chase, we've got to get those cannons to Fannin."

"It's too damned dangerous! Damn it, don't you realize that you could have been killed last night? Would have been, if that Santanista hadn't been such a lousy shot."

"I don't care what happens to me! All I care about is getting those cannons to the Texas army!"

Chase glared at Rebecca. "I told you I was only going as far as Bexar. No farther!"

182

"But, Chase, it won't have to be much farther. You heard what Señor Seguin said about his son going to Fannin for aid. Why, Fannin is probably marching to Bexar right now. We could meet them along the way."

Again Chase considered his options and once more found he didn't have any, not unless he was willing to abandon Rebecca to her fate.

Of course, he could force her to go along with him, he thought. Hog-tie her across his saddle if necessary. But then he'd have to gag her too, to keep her from raving at him, and blindfold her, to keep her from murdering him with her eyes. Then, once they reached their destination, she'd probably slip a knife between his ribs for frustrating her desire for revenge. If he could get his hands on Paul Blake right now, he'd strangle him with his bare hands for getting him involved with Rebecca. She wouldn't rest until she got those cannons to the Texians. He fervently wished the Santanistas had found the wagon last night and hauled the cannons away. He'd gladly give them to the Mexicans, just to get Rebecca off his back.

"Chase?" Rebecca implored, tears in her eyes.

"All right! We'll take the damned cannons to Fannin!"

"Oh, thank you," Rebecca cried, hugging him fiercely.

Chase could only shake his head in self-disgust, wondering what fool had said that women were the weaker sex.

* * *

As they rode westward, Rebecca could see the smoke still rising from the Alamo in the far distance.

"What does 'Alamo' mean?" she asked Chase.

"It's a Spanish word for cottonwood."

"Cottonwood?" Rebecca asked in a disappointed voice.

"Yes. The *presidio* was originally named *San Antonio de Bexar* and the mission *San Antonio de Valero.* To simplify matters, the Mexicans named the old presidio-mission *Los Alamos,* after a grove of cottonwood trees that grew nearby. So that's what it means, the cottonwoods."

Not any more it doesn't, Rebecca thought fiercely. From now on the Alamo will have an entirely different meaning. No one will think of trees when the Alamo is mentioned. No, everyone will remember the brave men that fought and died for freedom there. The Alamo would become synonymous with courage and dedication to the cause of liberty.

It took them four days to reach the old *La Bahia* road that led to Goliad. Again, to avoid the possibility of running into Santanista patrols, Chase followed an old Indian trail that twisted and turned in a seemingly aimless fashion. To Rebecca it seemed they were making more distance back and forth and sideways than forward. Then it rained, one of those sudden, violent thunderstorms that were so frequent in Texas during the springtime. The dry gullies became raging torrents as the water poured down out of the hills around them, blocking their path. When the floodwaters finally went down and they were able to cross, the wagon got stuck in the mud, and it took them the better part of another day to get it out.

When they reached the San Antonio River, they followed it south and passed, hidden in the river bottom, the abandoned mission, San Juan Capestrano. Rebecca looked at the crumbling mission with the three belfries in its front facade, thinking that at one time it must have been beautiful. Even then the mission had a quiet dignity about it.

They crossed the river below the mission and, when they rolled out of the woods, drove onto the old *La Bahia* road. After days of agonizingly slow travel and delays, Rebecca could have cried with relief and then with frustration, as their way was impeded by yet another obstacle, a human tide of refugees returning to Bexar after hearing that the fighting was over.

Some of the Mexicans rode on crude, two-wheeled carts, pulled by burros or a single ox, but most were on foot, carrying their meager possessions on their backs. There were men, women, and children of all ages, from the youngest babe in arms to the oldest bent, half-crippled grandparent. Despite being irritated at being slowed down to a snail's pace, Rebecca was filled with compassion, wondering where they had found shelter from the cold and how they had managed to eat during their long, self-imposed exile. It wasn't until the second day that the refugees finally thinned out enough for Chase and Rebecca to make any decent progress.

Chase drove the wagon, and Rebecca occupied her time by gazing at the scenery, amazed at how different it was from East Texas. Here, in this vast rolling grassland with its scattered trees and clumps of cactus, you could see for miles and miles. Here the stars seemed brighter, the moon closer, the sun warmer, the air fresher. Rebecca saw her first buffalo, which Chase said was a stray, a lone animal that had wandered off from its herd far to the north, in search of grass. Despite its disproportionate body, with its slim flanks and massive shoulders and huge, shaggy head, Rebecca thought there was a certain majesty about the animal. She wasn't impressed with the herd of longhorns she saw, another first for her. The animals were scrawny creatures, most of their bulk seeming to be in their long, wicked-looking horns, which sometimes stretched to seven feet from tip to tip.

One day Rebecca spied a strange-looking bird with a long tail and a crest of feathers on its head. "What kind of a bird is that?" she asked Chase.

"That's a chaparral cock. They can't fly worth a damn, but they can outrun anything. The Anglos call them roadrunners."

"What in the world is it pecking at so furiously? A worm?"

"No, probably a rattler. They seem to have a particular aversion for the snakes, and they can peck one to death before the rattler can even strike."

All along the road the San Antonio River played peek-a-boo with them, following the road, almost

186

as if it were hugging it, then wandering away to disappear for miles before suddenly reappearing again at their side. If the river was near them, they always pitched their camp on its banks, the horses drinking deeply of the clear waters and then munching the grass beside it.

When they made camp in the late afternoon on one balmy day, Rebecca decided to join Chase in his bath in the river. She stood on the bank and stripped, aware of Chase's dark eyes on her but not in the least embarrassed. She knew that Chase thought her beautiful and desirable. To pretend maidenly modesty when she gloried in his admiration would only be hypocritical, and for all of her faults, she wasn't going to sink to that.

She stepped into the river and gasped. The water was much colder than she had anticipated. Quickly she lathered and then waded in until she was hip deep, before she dipped down to her shoulders to rinse off the soap.

Shivering, she hurried out of the water and as she reached for her towel, Chase emerged from the river. She stared at him, thinking once again what a magnificent specimen of manhood he was, with his rugged looks, his wet bronzed skin glistening in the sunlight, and his sleek muscles rippling as he walked toward her. And then her breath caught in her throat as she saw he was fully aroused. Her eyes darted to his face, seeing the bold, hot look in those dark eyes.

Her mouth turned dry, and the towel dropped from her fingers. Then she was in his arms, his embrace crushing the breath from her as his mouth swooped down on hers in a fierce, possessive kiss, his tongue invading and ravishing the sweetness of her mouth. Rebecca's knees buckled, and she sank to the ground, Chase following her to the soft grass.

He straddled her legs and sat back on his heels, his eyes glued to the rapid rise and fall of her breasts. Then, spying a rivulet of water trailing down the side of her breast, he bent and licked it away, his tongue tracing lazy circles around the soft mound before his mouth closed over the hardened, throbbing peak. A low moan escaped Rebecca's throat as a bolt of fire shot through her.

His dark head lowered, his tongue seeking other rivulets of water, across her ribs and down her flat abdomen. He dallied at her navel before dipping his head to kiss the sensitive skin on the insides of her thighs.

Rebecca looked up and saw him sitting back on his heels, those smoldering black eyes boring into hers. He smiled as his slender fingers cupped her, then slipped inside her, sweetly probing, as his thumb circled the small bud. All of the heat of her body rushed to where Chase's fingers were, leaving her aching and throbbing for him.

She sobbed. "Please, now, Chase."

"If you want me, take me," Chase said in a husky voice.

She reached for him, and Chase groaned as her hand closed around him. A feeling of power surged through Rebecca, knowing that she had him at her mercy now. She stroked him, watching as Chase's breathing became ragged, his eyes darkening.

When Chase felt as if he would burst from need, he caught Rebecca's hips and plunged deeply into her warmth, Rebecca's breath catching at the electric sensation of his hard, masterful entry. And then, to her surprise, Chase rolled to his back, taking her with him.

"Ride me, Rebecca," Chase muttered.

Rebecca didn't need any urging. The feel of him deep inside her was driving her wild. Her movements were slow and sensuous at first, then, feeling those waves begin, urgent and demanding. Chase watched her above him, his eyes drinking in her beauty, his hands stroking her thighs, her hips, her breasts. He nipped at her shoulder, then her breasts, feeling that unbearable pressure building in him. And then, when a red haze drifted across his vision, a low groan escaped his throat as he flipped her to her back, his mouth taking fierce possession of hers, driving them over that peak in several powerful thrusts, until he exploded inside of her and the universe shattered into millions of glittering pieces.

When it was over, Rebecca held him tightly to her for a long while, loathe ever to let him go. Her need to tell him of her love grew until it was a physical ache in her throat. Instead she kissed the strong column of his throat, enjoying his salty taste and drinking in his exciting scent. Her tongue darted into his ear, and she felt him tremble with pleasure.

He lifted his dark head, his black eyes like fath-

189

omless pools as he gazed down at her. *"Bruja,"* he muttered before softly kissing her swollen mouth, then her eyelids. His mouth locked over hers and Rebecca felt him stir where he still lay inside her, then harden.

She cupped his head, kissing him back, wildly, feverishly, her heart racing in anticipation as he carried them once more to that peak of exquisite rapture.

Later, Rebecca trailed her hand over Chase's broad chest, still feeling deliciously languid. Her fingers brushed against the pouch that hung from his neck. She raised her head and looked at it in surprise, for Chase usually removed it before they made love. Curious, she reached for it.

Chase's hand shot out, catching hers as Rebecca's fingers closed over the eagle claws concealed in the leather pouch. Rebecca looked up at him, surprised at his fierce possessiveness, and saw a warning glint in his eyes.

"What's in it?" she asked, even more curious after the peculiar way he was behaving.

"It's my medicine pouch. I can't tell you, or anyone, what's in it. To do so would be to break my bond with my spirit guardian."

Rebecca might have laughed, had it not been for the conviction in Chase's voice and the serious expression on his face. "I see," she mumbled, withdrawing her hand.

She lay back down with her head on his shoulder, watching the forbidden medicine pouch as it rose and fell on his chest. What a strange man he was, she thought, her tender-savage lover, her bold, fierce half-breed.

The next afternoon Rebecca heard a sound like the rolling of distant thunder. She looked up at the cloudless sky above them and then searched the horizon for the signs of an approaching storm. Lightning, tied to the back of the wagon, began to snort, the loud, shrill sound startling.

Chase stopped the wagon abruptly. "Here, take the reins. That's broomtails coming."

"What?"

"Mustangs."

Chase jumped from the wagon, and Rebecca could hear him crooning to Lightning. "Easy, boy, easy." A moment later he stood on the ground beside Rebecca, holding the cheek strap of Lightning's bridle tightly, while the stallion continued to snort and move about restlessly.

Then Rebecca saw them, filling the whole horizon, for this herd was at least a hundred separate *manadas* running together, and the whole prairie seemed to be undulating as the mustangs ran toward them. The ground trembled, then shook, as they neared, the sound of their thundering hooves almost deafening.

The herd crossed the road before them in full gallop, their manes and tails flying, their necks stretched out and their ears flattened. One horse ran several yards before the rest of the herd, a beautiful bay that raced toward the river.

"Is that one of the stallions?" Rebecca asked in a raised voice to be heard over the din.

191

"No, that's a lead mare," Chase answered. "A good stallion doesn't lead his *manada* when he runs them. He drives them. But with this herd running so close, you probably won't be able to distinguish the stallions from the mares, not until the last *manada* has passed at the rear."

Rebecca looked back and saw that the herd stretched all the way back to the horizon. It seemed endless, and there was every possible color of horseflesh in it: sorrels, bays, red and blue roans, duns, grays, blacks, paints, and whites.

By then the herd had reached the river. Rebecca had expected them to stop, but the lead mare plunged into the water, and the others followed without hesitation. As they swam across the river, completely blotting out the greenish water, Rebecca realized that there were a few colts with the herd, the young horses resting their heads on their mothers' backs and lazily floating across the river. When the lead mare reached the other side, she lurched up the bank and continued her wild race across the prairie, the others following.

Forty-five minutes later the herd was still crossing the road in front of them and blocking their path. Rebecca couldn't believe that there were that many horses in the entire world. Then her eyes widened in disbelief as one animal raced past her. It wasn't a horse. It was a mule!

By this time the air was thick with a choking dust and the rank smell of horse sweat. Rebecca's eyes watered, and her head was pounding from the noise. And then she saw at the end of the herd the magnificent black stallion that was driving his *manada* there. He raced down the side of his mares, ramming the ribs of one mare and biting the ear of another, then doubled back to go to the opposite side, nipping at the mares' flanks.

Lightning saw the stallion too and reared on his hind legs, pawing at the air and squealing, eager to get away so that he could challenge the black stallion for his *manada*. Chase fought to maintain his hold on the bridle, then vaulted to Lightning's back, using his weight to help restrain the excited stallion, pulling hard on his reins to keep Lightning circling so that he couldn't follow. It wasn't until the herd had disappeared over the horizon that Lightning finally settled down, his muscles still quivering with excitement.

Chase dismounted and stroked his neck. "Sorry about that, boy, but you'll just have to be satisfied with your own *manada*."

Rebecca had watched as the herd disappeared over the horizon, amazed that they could run that far and long and wondering what had frightened them so badly.

She turned to Chase. "What happens to the stallions that don't have *manadas?* Obviously they all can't have their own herd of mares."

"Some of them are killed, challenging other stallions. Then many of the outcasts form their own herds of all stallions. Sometimes you'll even see a lone stallion in with a buffalo herd, just for the company of another animal."

Chase's words reminded Rebecca of the mules she had seen with the herd of mares. They hadn't seemed to belong to the herd, any more than a lone stallion to a buffalo herd.

"What were the mules doing with the herd?" Rebecca asked. "You'd think the stallion would chase them off or kill them."

"No. Somehow the stallion knows that those mules are no threat to him, and he allows them to stay. He uses them as lookouts. I've even seen mules take over a herd if the stallion is killed."

"And the mares follow the mule?" Rebecca asked in surprise.

"If that mule's herding instinct is strong enough and the mares think it can protect them, yes."

The next day Rebecca saw a dust cloud in the distance and knew a rider was approaching them. She hoped that it was a scout from Fannin's army, for so far they had seen no sign of it. In fact, the road to Goliad had been virtually deserted since they had left the refugees behind.

Chase handed the reins to Rebecca and picked up his Hawkens, then relaxed when he saw that the rider did not wear a Mexican uniform. As the man neared Chase called, "Hold up!"

The man reined in and trotted his horse over to the wagon. When both the wagon and the horse had come to a halt, Chase asked, "Have you seen anything of Fannin's army on the road?"

"What'd you want to know for?" the man asked suspiciously.

"I'm delivering some . . . some supplies to him."

"Yeah, I've seen him. But not on the road. He's still back in Goliad."

"Goliad?" Rebecca asked in surprise. "But we thought he was coming to relieve the Alamo."

"Yeah, so did I. Twice!" the man answered in disgust. "We started out once in February, after we heard about it being surrounded by Santa Anna. We only got two miles from the fort when word arrived that General Urrea was marching down on us, and we turned back. Fannin said his last orders from the council was to defend Fort Defiance. Then, when Houston heard about the Alamo being surrounded, he ordered Fannin to go to Travis's aid—"

"Then Houston is back from his furlough?" Rebecca interrupted.

"Yeah, he's back. He was down at Washington-on-the-Brazos, drafting the Texas Declaration of Independence, when he heard the news. He sent word to Fannin to go and reinforce Travis."

"Then why didn't Fannin do as he was ordered?" Rebecca asked angrily.

"We were going to, but part of our force had been sent to evacuate some civilians down at Refugio and ran into some of Urrea's calvary, and Fannin sent another hundred men down to rescue them. Hell, we were still waiting around for them to get back when Houston heard about the Alamo falling and ordered Fannin to retreat to Guadalupe Victoria."

Chase groaned in disgust. Things were still in a muddle. "Then Fannin has retreated?"

"Hell, no! He's still down there at Goliad. He's waiting for wagons to be brought from Victoria so he can haul off his artillery. I just finally got so disgusted I left."

Rebecca's head shot up at these words. "Then you aren't a scout for Fannin?"

"Hell, no, I ain't no scout. I just got fed up and left. I came to Texas to fight, and I ain't seen a Mexican soldier yet. And now Houston is ordering Fannin to blow up Fort Defiance and retreat. Hell, I'm going back to Georgia. I ain't never gonna see any fighting here!"

"You're deserting?" Rebecca asked angrily.

The man's eyes narrowed. "Look here, lady, I ain't regular army. I'm a volunteer. I don't owe nobody nothing, particularly a bunch of jackasses that don't know what they're doing."

With that the man kneed his horse and galloped away.

"What are we going to do now?" Rebecca moaned.

"Well, there's no use of us dragging these cannons to Goliad if Fannin's not there."

"But the man said he was waiting for wagons to move his artillery. He might still be there."

"Rebecca, we can't take the chance of running into Urrea's army with this heavy wagon we're pulling. Let me ride down there and check it out. I can make it in a day if I ride hard. If Fannin's there, I'll ask him if he wants these cannons or not. If so, he can send a detachment to haul them back."

Rebecca could see the wisdom in Chase's plan. There was certainly no point in taking the cannons to Goliad if there would be no one there to accept them.

Chase looked around them thoughtfully. "If I'm not mistaken, there's an old abandoned shack not too far from here that the Mexican mustangers used to use. It's back far enough that it can't be seen from the road, in case Urrea's army comes marching up it while I'm gone. You should be safe there until I get back."

They found the old shack, hidden in a wooded area beside a small creek. The mesquites around it were just starting to bud, but there were several wild plum trees already in full bloom, their delicate white blossoms fluttering in the breeze. To Rebecca they were a welcome sight. She was sick and tired of winter.

Chase looked about him. "This is perfect. There's water for the horses and even that old corral over there we can pen them in."

Rebecca climbed down from the wagon while Chase unharnessed the horses. She walked to the shack to investigate its interior. Seeing her, Chase called, "You better let me check in there first."

Rebecca turned, her face ashen. "You think it might be some wild animal's lair? Like a panther or a bear?"

"There aren't any bears in this part of Texas, and panthers prefer caves. No, if any animal is making it its lair, it's most likely a family of skunks. But what I was really thinking of was rattlers."

Rebecca looked wildly at the ground around her

and then, seeing none of the reptiles, beat a hasty retreat to the wagon.

After Chase had put the horses in the corral, he searched the cabin. Rebecca stood outside, peering fearfully into the dim interior, expecting to hear the buzzing sound of a rattler at any minute. After a few moments Chase came to the door and said, "All clear."

"You didn't find anything?"

"Just a spider or two, but I killed them."

Rebecca stepped into the shack. It wasn't much. The floor was packed dirt, and the walls and roof were made partly of logs and partly of dried mud mixed with grass. A natural stone fireplace sat in one wall, its ends crumbling with age. In the middle of the shack were two rickety chairs, their straw seats half rotten, and a table that looked as if it would collapse if you placed anything on it. The only other furniture was a built-in bunk in one corner, totally bare except for its crude rope springs.

"Well, it's not much, but it will keep the rain off," Chase remarked.

Rebecca looked up at the gaps in the roof, where the dried mud had fallen from between the logs, and seriously doubted that.

"As soon as I get some firewood chopped for you, I'll be going," Chase said.

"I thought I saw some firewood stacked beside the shack."

"Mesquite wood. It's just about the best wood there is for burning, particularly the roots, but it has one distinct disadvantage. It smokes. This shack might not be visible from the road, but smoke would be. I'll see if I can find some cotton-wood. It doesn't burn as well, but it won't give your position away."

Rebecca was amazed. She had no idea there was such a thing as a smokeless wood.

Chase found a cottonwood farther down the creek and chopped it down. When he had a good-sized pile stacked beside the shack, he went to saddle Lightning. Rebecca stood behind him, feeling a growing fear filling her and trying desperately to convince herself that she was just being silly, that Chase was a man more than capable of looking after himself.

Chase turned and saw her pale face. "Are you afraid to stay here by yourself?"

Rebecca knew she couldn't admit that she was terrified—for him. She longed to throw herself in his arms and beg him not to go, to tell him that she had bad feelings about this, that she loved him and the cannons weren't important anymore. But Chase had made it clear from the very beginning that he wanted no emotional entanglements, and Rebecca knew that such an outburst of feelings would send him from her faster than anything else.

She took a deep breath. "No, I'm not afraid."

"You're sure?"

"Of course, I'm sure. After all, if Jane Long could manage by herself for a whole winter in a deserted fort in Galveston Bay, then I can certainly manage by myself for a few days."

Every settler in Texas knew Jane Long's remark-able story, and she was often called "The Mother of Texas" because she had borne the first Anglo child in Texas. She was the wife of a filibuster, a breed of men who plagued the Spanish during the early part of the century by invading Texas with their own personal armies in hopes of wresting the territory away from them. Jane's husband had built a small fort on Galveston Island, then left his wife and two small children behind while he marched with the rest of his army to attack La Bahia. His expedition was a failure, and Long was captured by the Spanish and taken to Mexico. When word of him had arrived at the fort, the men who had remained there sailed away, leaving Jane, a young Negro girl, and the two children behind. They had survived the long winter through sheer courage and fortitude, once even firing the cannons in the fort at attacking Indians to frighten them away. Chase smiled, thinking that Jane and Rebecca had a lot in common. Both were courageous and fiercely determined women.

Chase turned and tossed his saddlebags over his horse. "If I'm not back in a couple of days, don't panic. I may have to take some detours to avoid the Mexican army."

Chase's comment irritated Rebecca. What did he think she was, a child? Why, she had never panicked in her life. "I won't," she answered tightly.

"I'm serious, Rebecca. You stay put until I get back. I don't want you wandering around out there with Santanistas swarming all over the area." He gave her a long, steady look.

"I won't budge," Rebecca promised him.

Chase's eyes searched Rebecca's face. Again, he was puzzled by her. How could she be so passionate one minute and then so cool and self-composed the next? He wished that she would act as if she were going to miss him, show some regret at his leaving, instead of looking so maddeningly calm.

Chase had no idea of how much that calm demeanor was costing Rebecca, how hard she was struggling to control her inner turmoil. She blinked back tears and smiled bravely up at him.

Chase hooked a roughened finger under her chin and bent to kiss her tenderly, lingeringly, before he mumbled "Good-bye" against her lips.

Rebecca was stunned by his kiss. Chase had never kissed her like that, so—so caring—without the slightest hint of passion. By the time she had recovered from that surprising kiss, he had swung into his saddle.

Lightning was reluctant to leave his *manada,* and Chase had to give the animal a sharp kick in the flanks to convince the stallion that he meant business. Then Lightning galloped off, and Chase called over his shoulder, "Remember, Rebecca. Stay put!"

Rebecca watched Chase as he rode from the clearing and then disappeared in the trees, that strange feeling of impending doom growing steadily stronger and silent tears streaming down her cheeks. She fervently wished that she had thrown caution to the wind and told him that she loved him before he had left.

10

It was midafternoon the next day when Chase reached Goliad. Thinking to save time, he skirted the small town. When he spied the dark smoke rising in the sky to the south, he knew that it came from Fort Defiance. Chase questioned a bent, old Mexican who was taking firewood to Goliad and learned that Fannin and his army had pulled out a few hours before, after dismantling the fort and setting it on fire.

As the Mexican and his cart lumbered away, Chase wondered what to do. Both he and his horse were hot, tired, and hungry. The last thing he wanted to do was go chasing after Fannin and spend another half day in the saddle. But if he didn't find out from Fannin whether he wanted the damned cannons, once and for all, he'd never get Rebecca off his back. Sighing with a mixture of resignation and disgust, he kneed Lightning and galloped off.

Fording the San Antonio River below Goliad, Chase found Fannin's trail and followed it. Then, hearing the sound of gunfire in the distance, he reined in sharply. Moving cautiously, he rode over a small rise to see the battle taking place in the middle of the Coleto Prairie below him. He had found Fannin's army.

Fannin had formed a fragile fortress by pulling his wagons into a square, his artillery placed at the four corners. The whole prairie around the Texians was swarming with General Urrea's calvary and infantry, and dead Santanistas and horses littered the ground. Through the thick, rolling smoke, Chase could see that Fannin's men were outnumbered at least six to one.

Chase watched, grim-lipped, as the Mexican cavalry raced toward the Texas line with trumpets blaring and bright pennons flying. They were mowed down by a murderous fire from the Texians' rifles, joined by Fannin's artillery.

While the Mexican cavalry was retreating in confusion, Chase made a split-second decision. He urged Lightning forward and sped across the prairie, leaning out of his saddle and hanging to the stallion's side, Comanche fashion. He raced right through the milling Mexican lines as balls whizzed through the air all around him. Just before he reached Fannin's fortress, Chase righted himself, so that the Texians would know that he was friend, not foe, and Lightning flew over the barricade between two wagons with a powerful lunge.

Chase was out of the saddle and running for the barricade, his Hawkens in his hand, even before his horse came to a halt. He threw himself to the ground between two lanky, sandy-haired men who quickly made a space for him at the barricade of boxes and saddles. The Texian who was wearing a solid red uniform clapped him on the shoulder. "I don't know who in the hell you are, mister, but if you can shoot half as good as you can ride, I'm mighty glad to see you."

Chase ignored the man's compliment. "How many charges have the Mexicans made?" he asked.

"Three," the other man answered. "Reckon they know by now that they can't break our lines. Look! They're dismounting and coming on foot."

Then all three men were busy with firing, loading, refiring, over and over. The heat from the guns combined with the sun overhead, and soon the men's clothing was drenched with perspiration, their faces blackened by the powder.

In a brief lull in the battle, the men introduced themselves to Chase. "I'm Louis Johnson of the Red Rovers," the man in glaring red uniform said, "and this is Ben Ritter of the Mustang Company."

Chase shook hands with the two men. "Chase Winters here." He looked about the pitiful fortress and wiped the sweat from his brow with his forearm. "How long have you been out here?"

"Since we stopped to eat at noon," Ben answered.

Chase frowned, asking "Then why didn't Fannin stop over there by the creek, where there's trees for protection and water, in case you were attacked?"

The two men exchanged disgusted looks, then Ben answered. "Hell, somebody forgot to feed the oxen we used to pull the cannons. When they got out here and saw all this grass, they kept straying off to graze. Fannin decided to stop, since we weren't getting nowhere anyway, and just let them eat their fill. The next thing we knew we were surrounded by Mexicans."

"Yeah," Louis said. "And if that wasn't bad enough, some damn fool got carried away this morning when we were burning and dismantling everything and burned *all* the food. So here we are stuck out in the middle of the prairie with no food and water." An angry look came over his craggy face. "But we got plenty of cannons. Damn it, if we'd retreated right away when Houston ordered us to instead of waiting for that fool Will Ward and his men to get back from wherever they ran off to, and sunk these blasted cannons in the river like Houston told Fannin to, we wouldn't be in this fix right now. Hell, those damned cannons just slowed us down, and what good are they gonna do us now? You can't eat them," Louis finished bitterly.

Chase felt sick. It was the same old story. Independent men taking off on their own and officers disobeying orders. Disorder and chaos. Now Fannin's men were trapped, and he was trapped with them.

"Here they come again," Louis said in a grim voice, peering over the barricade and seeing another wave of Mexicans rushing down on them. "God, what I wouldn't give for a drink of water."

For the next hour even water was forgotten in the furious fighting. Just before sundown, Ben caught a ball in his shoulder.

As Chase bent over him to examine the wound, Ben said, "It ain't all that bad. Just lodged in the fleshy part. But damn it, that's my right shoulder, and I can't shoot no more. I'd just ram that ball right into my shoulder bone." He grinned gamely. "But I can still load. Do me a favor and tie something around my shoulder, will you? Then I'll load and you can shoot both our rifles. Hell, you're a better shot than me anyway."

From then on Ben loaded and Chase alternately shot his Hawkens and Ben's Kentucky rifle, firing with a deadly accuracy that amazed both men beside him. By the time the sun set and the battle ended for that day, Chase's shoulder was throbbing and his arm felt numb clear down to his fingertips.

Shortly after nightfall, with Chase holding the lamp and shielding it with his body so that the Mexicans couldn't see it, the harried doctor finally got around to removing the ball from Ben's shoulder. By the time he had finished, Ben's face was covered with cold perspiration, for the small supply of pain medication had been used up long ago.

After the doctor had bandaged Ben's arm and left, Chase walked over to Lightning, still standing beside the wagon and waiting patiently. Taking his canteen from the saddle, he carried it back to Ben.

Gently lifting him by the shoulders, Chase placed the open canteen at Ben's lips. After drinking the water, Ben lay back. "Thanks. Hope I can return the favor sometime."

Louis rejoined them, sank down beside them, and, after inquiring about Ben's condition, said, "Colonel Fannin has been talking to the men. He said it's possible that we could escape under cover

206

of darkness, but Fannin said he's gonna stay. He don't want to leave the wounded behind. The men all talked it over and agreed to stay with him. Almost everybody's got a friend or relative that's wounded."

Louis stopped and gazed at Chase's horse. "What about you, Chase? You planning on jumping that horse of yours back over that barricade? You could make it, you know. The way you ride, you'd be through those Mexicans' lines in no time. And no one here would blame you for leaving. You ain't part of this army."

Chase glanced down at Ben. He could take him out with him. But Chase knew that Ben wouldn't leave his friend Louis. "Nope, I'll be staying."

It proved to be a long, miserable night for everyone. In anticipation of the morning's battle, trenches were dug and everything they could find was piled on the mounds of dirt. As the men worked, hot, exhausted, and thirsty, they could hear the moans of the wounded and their delirious pleas for water, which only added to their misery.

Even before the sun had fully risen the next morning, they could see the Mexicans preparing for an attack. When the Santanistas moved out of the timber, it was apparent that they had been heavily reinforced during the night, and one company was an artillery company, something that Urrea hadn't had the day before. Any hope of winning the battle was dashed once the Texians laid eyes on Urrea's huge twelve-pound cannons that outranged Fannin's nine brass ones.

After a furious Mexican bombardment that sent

dirt, wood, and debris flying everywhere, the big guns were silenced. Shortly thereafter, a Mexican with a white flag appeared, signaling that they desired a parlay.

The battle-weary, thirsty Texians waited anxiously while the terms of surrender were decided, each wondering what their fate was to be. Finally Colonel Fannin called his men together and read the document to them. The Texians would be held as honorable prisoners of war until exchanged or liberated on their word of honor not to engage in war against Mexico again—at the option of the Mexican commander-in-chief. An audible sigh of relief was heard throughout the small, battered enclosure.

Chase and the others were rounded up and forced into lines headed for Goliad. Chase allowed himself to be pushed in line, waiting for the right opportunity to make his break for Lightning. He had no intention of being taken a prisoner of war. Rebecca was waiting for him, and he fully intended to fulfill his promise to be back in a few days.

When a shoving match began in the line in front of him between the Mexican guards and several unruly Texians and the guards at Chase's end of the column ran to their *compadres'* aid, Chase glanced over his shoulder, his body tense in anticipation.

At that precise moment, a Mexican officer walked over to Lightning and tried to take his reins. The mustang snorted a warning and backed away. The officer swore, lunged for the reins, and caught them, jerking on them hard. Lightning squealed in outrage, reared on his hind legs, and struck out with his sharp hooves, knocking the officer down and then pounding on the fallen man. A group of nearby Santanistas ran to subdue the white horse, brandishing their sabers. As they circled him, Lightning broke away and sped for the barricade, jumping it and racing across the open prairie.

Chase watched bleakly as Lightning sped across the prairie, knowing that he'd lost his one and only means of escape. Seeing the stallion heading west, Chase knew that Lightning was going back to the mustangs, back to his wild, free life. And Chase would go to some dank, filthy, stinking prison in Mexico.

The Texians were marched to the old La Bahia mission that afternoon, passing through Goliad in order to further humiliate them before the predominately Mexican population.

As they passed Fort Defiance, the old *presidio* that Fannin's men had shored up then destroyed, Chase spied the remnants of a flag flying over the still-smoldering timbers. Seeing his gaze, Ben said, "The Georgia Greys brought that flag with them. It was sewn by a Georgia woman that lives here in Texas. We raised it the day Texas declared its independence, but it got caught in the ropes and the wind tore it up like that. We just left it up there. It's a shame it happened, though. It was a real pretty flag. White silk with a lone azure-blue star on it."

209

Unlike the thirteen American colonies that had fought together for their independence from the British, Texas fought Santa Anna's tyranny alone, the other Mexican states cowering in fear. Yes, Chase decided, the single, lone star was appropriate.

That night, inside the crumbling walls of the old mission, Chase found himself worrying about Rebecca and cursing himself for a fool. Never once had he considered the predicament he was placing her in when he rushed to help the Texians. He wondered at his sudden, rash decision. It wasn't like him to act before thinking things through. But seeing the Texians surrounded and outnumbered had triggered some deep sense of outrage in him, an outrage that had precluded all rational thought. Now he had left Rebecca totally unprotected and alone in the wilderness. He wondered how long it would take her to realize that he wasn't coming back. Once she did, he could only hope that she would take one of the horses and head east and that she wouldn't get lost in that rugged, desolate hill country.

Alone in the mustangers' cabin, Rebecca had set her fear of impending doom aside, firmly telling herself that she was just behaving like some silly female, that if any man could take care of himself it was Chase. To keep her mind from what might be happening to him, she threw herself into a frenzy of physical activity, first tackling the old cabin and trying to make it more habitable, then currying the mares until their coats shone, then chopping more firewood, then washing everything that she could lay her hands on, and finally rearranging the wagon.

But as the days passed without any sign of Chase, her fear returned, stronger than ever, clawing at her stomach and making her nerves crawl. She alternated between railing at him for being so slow to return and praying fervently for his safety, interspersed with sudden crying jags over which she had no control.

On the seventh night she sat gazing off into space, the tears on her cheeks glistening in the firelight. "Oh, God, please bring him safely back to me," she prayed.

Time passed at an agonizingly slow pace for Chase, who spent most of the time listening to Louis and Ben talk and offering only an occasional story of his own frontier experiences. But their fighting together at the Battle of Colcto had created a strong bond, and the three men had become fast friends.

On March 25, eighty men from William Ward's Georgia Battalion were herded into the mission, the very same men whose disappearance had delayed the others' retreat. Upon hearing the story of their defeat and capture at Dimitt's Landing, Chase sat back, a grim look on his face. Now the five hundred men in Fannin's army, practically the entire Texas army, was either dead or held prisoner, to say nothing of the supplies and artillery that had been lost. While it was just as he had predicted—the Texians were going to lose their bid for independence—Chase took no satisfaction in knowing that he had been right.

The next day the prisoners were moved from the mission plaza and into the chapel itself, a small, musty building, its walls completely crumbled in some places.

"Hell, why did they move us in here?" Ben asked in a disgusted voice. "It's so crowded a man can hardly breathe, much less lie down."

"Maybe they were afraid we would try to overpower the guards and escape," Chase suggested.

"Now, why would we want to do that, when we're going to be exchanged?" Louis asked. "All we gotta do is be patient."

"You're crazy if you think we're going to be exchanged!" Chase spat. "Hell, we're headed for a prison in Mexico, and compared to them, this place is a castle."

"Do you really think the Mexicans might do that, Chase?" Ben asked nervously, for both he and Louis were new to Texas and realized that Chase knew the enemy better than they. "Go back on their word?"

"If you're expecting Santa Anna to behave like an honorable man—forget it!" Chase answered in a hard voice. "That bastard doesn't know the meaning of the word. Anyone who says 'Man is nothing, power is everything' is capable of anything."

"But what about General Urrea? He's the one we surrendered to," Ben argued. "I've heard he's an honorable man, a gentleman."

"He's also a soldier—a good soldier, and he

takes his orders from Santa Anna," Chase reminded him bluntly.

Early the next morning the prisoners were awakened and told that they were to be freed on parole, that they would be marched to Copano on the coast, where vessels awaited to transport the Texians to New Orleans. Ben and Louis were elated, since both had spent a sleepless night worrying over Chase's warning.

Chase had listened to the Mexican officer as he explained the plans for the prisoners, the hair on his nape standing on end. His Comanche blood warned him not to trust the Mexicans, reminded him of all the times the Mexicans had lured the Comanches into a death trap with promises of a peace parley or gifts. Quietly he packed his belongings, strongly suspecting treachery.

As the prisoners filed out of the mission and lined up into three separate columns, Ben said, "Hey, would you look at those Mexicans, all gussied up? Those must be their Sunday-go-to-meeting uniforms."

"That's right," Louis said. "Today is Sunday. Palm Sunday. You suppose we'll be in New Orleans by Easter?"

Chase looked at the Mexicans' parade uniforms, then glanced around. There were no baggage wagons being prepared. His uneasiness grew.

When the Mexicans marched the columns out of Goliad on three different roads, Chase knew. They were being taken into the countryside to be executed. The bastards! The Santanistas didn't even have the decency to tell the prisoners their fate.

No, they had lied to them, so that the prisoners could be blindly and willingly marched to their deaths, like so many dumb cattle to the slaughter.

"Ben, Louis," Chase whispered to his two friends walking side by side in front of him, "don't show any sign you hear me. We don't want to alert the guard behind us. These bastards aren't marching us to Copano. They're taking us out into the countryside to shoot us."

Chase knew by the stiffening of both men's bodies that they had heard him. The man walking next to Chase was staring at him, dumbfounded, having also heard.

After a moment had passed Ben whispered back apprehensively, "What are we gonna do, Chase?"

"Try to escape. But not now. Wait until they stop the column and the guards on one side move to the other side, to form the firing squad. At least then half of them will have their backs to us. When I say so, duck and run like hell for the river. Whatever you do don't take off across the open prairie."

"*Silencio!*" the guard behind Chase commanded, having finally heard Chase whispering.

When they were about a mile out of town, the column was halted. Before them, they could see the prisoners being forced to kneel. When the guards walking on the right side of them walked to the left side, Chase yelled at the top of his lungs, "Run! They're going to shoot us!" Then Chase shoved the guard, who had just passed him, into the guard by his side, who was already raising his musket to shoot.

Chase lurched from the column, running in a

half crouch, as the muskets of almost two hundred guards exploded behind him. As he cleared the rolling smoke, he straightened and raced for the river, zigzagging as balls whizzed around him. In his peripheral vision he saw two other men running slightly behind him.

When he reached the river, he whirled, then, for the first time, realized that the two men who had been running beside him weren't Ben and Louis. As the two prisoners tore past him and dove into the river, Chase scanned the area behind him. What he saw sickened him. Those prisoners who weren't killed by the first volley were being bayoneted by the Mexicans. He saw Louis lying in the middle of the road, apparently killed by the first volley. And then, seeing Ben, Chase sucked in his breath.

Ben had been hit by a ball in his leg and was limping badly as he tried to run across the clearing to the river, a look of desperation on his face. But before Chase could reach Ben, a Mexican drove his long bayonet into Ben's back. The soldier was joined by another, and the onslaught continued on Ben's lifeless body until Chase reached them. Enraged, Chase snarled, wrested the musket from one of the Mexican's hands, and slammed the butt into the man's face. Then Chase whirled and sunk the bayonet deep into the second Mexican's stomach, jerking it upward in an old Comanche knife trick.

Chase glanced up and saw a horde of soldiers running toward him, reloading as they ran. He whirled and again raced toward the river, then, taking a flying leap, dove deep into the water, hearing the muskets roar as he hit the surface.

Thankfully, the river was deep, and Chase dove to the sandy bottom. He could hear the balls spattering the water above him and actually saw a few as they passed him, the water having slowed their momentum. Chase swam upstream, underwater, fighting the swift current, until he thought his lungs would burst and he heard a ringing in his ears.

When Chase surfaced, he breathed deeply and looked quickly around him. Several other former prisoners were swimming upstream. Then, hearing the Mexicans yelling, he glanced up the bank and saw them running along the side of the river, their muskets aimed at the men in the water. Again Chase dove to the bottom, and again he heard the spattering of balls all around him.

The next time Chase surfaced, sucking in a deep breath of air, he spied a small cavelike opening in the riverbank. The cave was on the side where the Mexicans were, screened by a few bushes. Chase knew that because of the steep bank the Mexicans wouldn't be able to see the cave behind the bushes from above.

Chase hurriedly climbed the bank, using the bushes to pull himself up the steep side, his feet slipping on the mud. He crawled into the small opening. He barely had room to sit hunched over in the cave. Just minutes later Chase heard the drumming of the Mexicans' feet above him as they ran beside the river. He held his breath as dirt, dislodged from the roof of the cave, splattered all around him.

As the sound of the running feet faded into the distance and the dirt stopped falling away, Chase relaxed. Catching his breath, he decided to stay in the cave until nightfall, hoping that he could escape under the cover of darkness.

About thirty minutes later Chase heard a loud volley of shots coming from the direction of the fort. He knew what those gunshots meant. Fannin and the wounded men that the Mexicans had claimed would later be transported by wagon had also been executed.

Chase waited until several hours after the sun had set before leaving the safety of his small cave. Then he climbed up the riverbank, his legs numb and tingling from sitting in a cramped position for so long. As he made his way from the woods around the river and into the open prairie, he spied the glow in the night sky. Chase knew that glow only too well because he'd seen it over the Alamo. Again Santa Anna had denied the Texians a Christian burial, had inflicted upon them the last insult by cremating them.

Chase thought of the 342 Texians who had been brutally massacred on that Palm Sunday. But if Santa Anna thought he had taught the Texians a lesson, Chase mused, he was sadly mistaken. Instead he had given them their second set of martyrs who had died for the cause. Chase knew that the Texians would be even more enraged once they learned of the massacre at Goliad and the Mexicans' treachery, for at least the men at the Alamo had died fighting and not been brutally slaughtered in cold blood.

Chase stood and stared at the glow in the dark sky, his anger growing until it became a hard core of seething hatred deep inside him, a hatred that cried out for revenge. He had witnessed the treachery of the Mexicans, had seen his friends brutally massacred before his very eyes. No longer could he remain impassive to the Texians' cause. Now he was one of them.

11

CHASE DIDN'T COVER MUCH DISTANCE THAT night. He was forced to move slowly and cautiously, having almost stumbled into a Mexican patrol that was still out searching for the prisoners who had escaped. Had the infantrymen not been wearing their white uniforms, Chase might not have spied them first in the darkness.

An hour before daylight he found a gully, screened by mesquite brush, where he spent the day, alternately dozing and watching the prairie for Mexican patrols. When he had seen nothing of the Santanistas by that evening, Chase assumed that the soldiers were concentrating their search on the east side of the San Antonio River, thinking that the escaped prisoners would head east toward the Brazos, not north.

That night Chase made excellent time. He was still running the next morning, in that easy lope he had learned from the Comanches, when he spied a rider coming toward him on the road. Chase dove for cover and peered out from behind the clump of cactus. Then, seeing the white horse and the unmistakable golden-red hair of the rider, Chase rose, muttering "I'll be damned!"

Chase stepped from behind the cactus and waved to catch Rebecca's attention. As she galloped toward him he thought, I should have known Rebecca wouldn't stay put, like I told her to. And the crazy little fool. Where in the hell did she think she was going, riding straight into Urrea's lines like that?

Chase felt a mixture of emotions wash over him: relief to know that Rebecca was safe, pure joy at seeing her, and anger at her for being foolish enough to ride off looking for him and placing herself in danger. The emotions waged inside him, and his anger won out. As soon as Rebecca pulled up beside him, he yelled, "I thought I told you to stay put! Can't you *ever* do anything you're told?"

Rebecca had been terrified when Lightning had returned to the mustangers' shack without Chase. At first she had hoped that the stallion had just thrown Chase, frightened by a rattler or some wild animal, since she could find no signs of blood on the saddle or the animal. And then, when Chase hadn't shown up by the next evening, Rebecca's fear had become more than she could bear. Early that morning she had saddled Lightning and given the stallion his head, hoping that the horse would lead her to Chase. But when Chase stood there, glaring up at her, Rebecca's fear died a quick death, to be replaced with anger. Here she had worried herself sick over him, gone out to look for him, and all he could do was yell at her.

She swung from the saddle and stood, glaring

back at him. "Where in the hell have you been?" she spat, her hands on her hips.

"I told you it might take awhile."

"Awhile? It's been ten days since you left! And then when Lightning showed up two days ago—"

"Two days ago?" Chase interjected in surprise. "Is that when he got back? Where'd he go? He ran away from me in Goliad nine days ago."

"It took you nine days to walk from Goliad?" Rebecca asked in disbelief. "Why, it couldn't be more than twenty-five miles away."

"I didn't start walking until the day before yesterday, and then only at night. I've been a prisoner of war, along with Fannin's men. I didn't escape until then."

Rebecca turned pale at Chase's words, her anger disappearing like a puff of smoke. "Oh, Chase, I was afraid something terrible was going to happen, even before you left." Tears glistened in her eyes, and Rebecca didn't even care if Chase saw them. She couldn't hide her true feelings for him any longer. She threw herself in his arms, hugging him tightly, muttering against his chest "I've been so worried about you."

She does care about me, Chase thought, feeling a thrill run through him. He hugged her back, crushing her to him fiercely and stunning Rebecca with the intensity of his embrace.

Finally Rebecca pushed herself away. "Tell me what happened."

A brief flicker of pain crossed Chase's dark eyes before he answered tersely, "Not now." Then, taking her hand, he said, "Come on. Let's get out of here."

Chase leapt to the saddle on Lightning's back and held his hand down to help Rebecca mount. Then he kneed Lightning, and the stallion galloped off.

As they rode, Chase asked, "You say Lightning didn't show up until two days ago?"

"Yes. And when he returned, he brought three new mares with him. But they weren't wild horses. They were shod."

Chase grinned, thinking that he'd figured out what had happened. Lightning had headed back to his *manada* at the shack but couldn't resist taking a detour to steal some mares from one of the *rancheros*. And apparently he'd had to hang around for a while, waiting for the right opportunity. Now Chase was glad that the stallion had delayed his return. If he hadn't, Rebecca might have rode right into Goliad and been captured herself. And just thinking about what might have happened to her then made Chase's blood run cold. Instinctively Chase tightened his grip around Rebecca and pulled her closer.

Rebecca didn't wonder at Chase's protectiveness. She was too busy relishing the feel of his heart pounding against her back and his warm breath fanning her neck. They were proof that he was alive and whole, and that was all that mattered to her. She didn't even care if she had betrayed herself in showing her feelings toward him or that he might leave her all the sooner for knowing them. His life was more important than her stolen time with him, more important than anything.

On the trip back to the shack, Rebecca longed to ask Chase what had happened, but she sensed that he was deeply disturbed and not ready to talk about it yet. Wisely she held her tongue.

When they reached the cabin late that afternoon, Chase was surprised to see that the mesquites surrounding it had completely leafed out during his absence, the new feathery leaves a golden green. The mares had also fattened up on the tender grass while he was gone. He gave the three new mares a quick scrutiny, admitting that Lightning had good taste when it came to horseflesh.

As soon as they had dismounted, Rebecca said, "I'll fix you something to eat. I know you must be starved."

"Don't hurry," Chase answered, unsaddling Lightning. "I want to take a bath in that creek before I do anything. Since Lightning ran off with my saddlebags, I haven't even been able to change into fresh buckskins."

"I put your saddlebags in the shack," Rebecca answered. "I'll get them for you."

By the time Rebecca returned, Chase had unsaddled Lightning and put him in the corral with the mares. Rebecca handed Chase his bags. "I'll start supper while you're bathing."

Chase ambled off to the creek. After he had bathed, he dried off and pulled his buckskins from his saddlebags, then frowned, realizing that Rebecca must have cleaned them. Ordinarily, knowing that someone had handled his personal belongings would irritate Chase, but strangely, that wasn't what was bothering him. What he couldn't figure out was where she had learned to clean buckskins. Damn it, she was just full of surprises, Chase thought as he slipped on the soft leather garments.

He walked back to the shack and stepped inside, ducking to keep from hitting his head on the low doorway. Then he gazed about him in wonder. Rebecca had made the old shack almost livable. The table and chairs had been repaired, the table covered with a tablecloth made from what Chase recognized as one of Rebecca's old calico dresses. The same material hung over the two small windows. In the middle of the room, close to the fire, Rebecca had laid her feather mattress and covered it with a patchwork quilt. Every cobweb had been swept from the walls, and even the dirt-packed floor looked as if it had been swept. An inviting fire crackled in the fireplace and the odor of fresh coffee filled the air.

"Sit down," Rebecca said, placing a cup of coffee on the table before Chase.

Chase sat down and, sipping his coffee, watched Rebecca as she cooked supper. A strange sense of contentment crept over him. He could almost feel the tension of the past ten days slipping away. For the first time in his life, he felt like he'd come home. Hell, you must be going crazy, he thought. How can this hovel possibly be compared to a home? And yet Chase felt it—that peacefulness, that contentment, that feeling that he belonged.

He puzzled over his strange feelings, then said, "Thanks for cleaning my buckskins."

Rebecca turned from the fire. "I hope you don't mind. I was going crazy around here, trying to find something to do with my time."

The truth was Rebecca was going crazy worrying about Chase. She had fixed up the cabin not out of boredom but in hopes of distracting herself from her worries. As far as cleaning Chase's buckskins, just touching something that belonged to him had made her feel better, soothing her ragged nerves in some strange way.

Rebecca placed the eating utensils on the table and then a pan of piping hot cornbread and a pot of beans with salt pork. Chase lit into the simple fare as if it were a gourmet's feast, shocking Rebecca with his ravenous appetite. Noticing the leanness of his face for the first time, she realized that he had been literally starving. She was dying of curiosity to know what had happened—how he had been captured, how he had fared during his imprisonment, how he had managed to escape. But she knew if she pushed Chase that he'd clam up on her and she might never hear the story. Oh, she thought in frustration, he could be the most exasperating man!

When they had finished eating, Rebecca cleared the table and poured hot water in a bucket to wash her dishes. Chase sat back and watched her, thinking how beautiful she looked with the firelight playing over her golden-red hair and her face flushed to a rosy glow from the heat. A new hunger rose in Chase, a hunger that stunned him with its intensity.

He rose and walked to Rebecca. Slipping his arms around her, he pulled her back to him and nuzzled her neck. "Forget the dishes tonight," he said in a husky voice.

Chase softly kissed the column of Rebecca's throat, then nibbled at her earlobe, his hands rising to cup her full breasts, and Rebecca felt a tingle of pleasure run up her spine. When he buried his head in the soft crook of her shoulder and his fingers brushed over the peaks of her breasts, Rebecca felt that familiar heat rising in her. She turned in the circle of his arms, wrapping her arms around his shoulders, as Chase tightened his embrace and his mouth closed over hers.

It was a long, sensuous, breathtaking, spine-tingling kiss, and still, it didn't last long enough for Rebecca. As his mouth left hers to nibble at her chin, then trailed across her cheeks, she turned her head to capture those warm lips again. But Chase was brushing her eyelashes with kisses before he kissed each eyelid in turn, then dropped soft, butterfly kisses over her hairline.

Chase's fingers trembled with excitement as he undressed Rebecca, stopping to caress each inch of her skin. When she stood before him totally naked, he reached for the laces in his tunic, his eyes hotly devouring her.

Rebecca stopped him. "No, let me do that."

Chase stood, waiting impatiently while she stripped off his tunic and tossed it aside. But then as Rebecca began unlacing his buckskin pants and he felt her warm fingers brushing against him, he trembled, his excitement rising even higher. As she slipped the soft leather down his legs, he stepped from them, then saw her sitting on her heels and looking up at him. The sight of her breasts rising and falling was enough to make his blood course hotly through his veins, but the look in her eyes made his bones melt. When she reached up and stroked him, standing boldly and proudly before her, Chase had to clench his teeth to retain control.

As her fingers slowly explored him, Chase couldn't stand it any more. With a low moan, he lowered himself, caught her shoulders, and rolled them both to the mattress, capturing her mouth in a fierce, penetrating kiss as his hands roamed hungrily over her curves.

Rebecca was spinning in a maelstrom of heady sensations as Chase kissed and nibbled, his hands stroking, caressing, tantalizing. She felt as if her skin were on fire as he kissed her from her shoulders to her breasts, across her flat abdomen to her navel, where he lingered, his tongue circling, then darting, sending shivers of delight through her.

Then, aware of him kneeling between her legs, she arched her hips, eager to have him buried deep inside her. And then she gasped in disbelief as she felt him stroking her with his tongue.

She raised her head and saw his dark head buried between her thighs, the sight shocking her. She started to reach for him, to pull him away, muttering "No, Chase!" But it was too late. If she had thought Chase's fingers magical, they were nothing compared to what his lips and tongue and teeth were doing to her. The sweet ripples began, then turned to powerful waves of rapture.

Her sweet-salty taste and womanly scent were powerful aphrodisiacs to Chase, driving him even wilder. When her body convulsed with pleasure, he couldn't stand the excitement any longer. In a frenzy of passion, he plunged into her. Then, feeling her hot spasms surrounding him and clutching him, he fought for control, fearing he would burst any second.

Rebecca had felt Chase's powerful thrust like a bolt of lightning that sent shock waves dancing up her spine. Her eyes flew open and she gazed up at him in a daze, feeling him hot and throbbing inside her.

Once Chase had regained control, he bent and kissed Rebecca's breasts, then captured her mouth with a deep, searing kiss that seemed, to her, to burn clear down to her toes. He moved in slow, sensuous strokes that rapidly brought her body to that feverish pitch once again. She sobbed when he retreated, moaned with rapture as he thrust deeply, boldly. Over and over he brought her to that shuddering brink, and Rebecca thought she would go out of her mind if he didn't end his exquisite torture. And then, when his tempo increased, she felt herself spiraling weightlessly up those lofty heights and finally exploding in a starburst of blinding colors, her cry and his groan of ecstasy mingling in her ears.

For a long while they lay with their sweat-slick bodies still entwined, their breath coming in quick gasps, both too weak to move, each feeling utterly contented. Finally Chase rolled from her and lay on his back, bringing her to his side possessively.

Rebecca nestled to him, her head resting on his shoulder. She looked down at their naked bodies, one so dark, one so light, one so hard muscled, the other so softly curved, thinking that they were a sharp contrast. Her hand played across his broad damp chest, her fingers tracing those powerful muscles there, muscles that glistened in the firelight with the fine sheen of perspiration that covered his skin. Once she had seen a statue of a Greek god. At the time, Rebecca had thought it beautiful, each muscle and tendon superbly sculptured. But the white marble god had been cold and lifeless, only suggesting power and strength. In Chase the power and strength was real—alive— the muscles still quivering beneath his warm, bronzed skin.

She raised her head, her eyes drinking in his features—the high forehead and cheekbones, the thick, dark lashes on his closed eyelids, the long, slender nose, sensuous lips, and strong jawline— committing each to memory for the day when he would leave her. Tenderly she brushed a lock of dark hair from his forehead, and Chase opened his eyes.

Rebecca startled. She had thought him asleep. She gazed down into those black, fathomless eyes, eyes that could smolder with passion, blaze with anger, and even, sometimes, twinkle with amusement. No, no sculptor could ever capture the rugged male beauty of Chase, his strength, his power, his remarkable eyes, any more than any woman could capture his heart.

She sighed, feeling a tug of pain, and laid her head back down in the crook of Chase's neck, tasting his saltiness there. Loving Chase was heaven, but giving him up was going to be hell. Now she wondered if she had been wrong to steal this time with him, to allow herself to know his passion. True, they were memories she would carry for a lifetime, but would they be worth the pain of the loss? There was an old adage that said you could never miss what you had never had. And she would miss Chase, unbearably so, not just the unbelievable heights of ecstasy he had brought to her, but the security and warm contentment she felt just being in his presence. He had become her life, and it was he, not she, who was the thief. She had stolen this time from his life, but he had stolen her heart and soul and when he left, he would take them with him, leaving her with nothing but an empty shell.

Tears welled in Rebecca's eyes. Stop it! she told herself firmly. The next thing you know you'll be crying and blubbering out your feelings, and that would only disgust Chase. At least maintain your dignity. And find something to distract yourself from these sad thoughts. Then she remembered that Chase had yet to tell her what had happened to him while he had been gone.

Tentatively she asked, "Will you tell me what happened now?"

Chase hadn't been ready to relate the story earlier. Its disastrous ending had left a deep wound on his soul, and Chase wasn't the kind of man to bare his soul to anyone. But lying beside Rebecca now, feeling totally satiated, he found he wanted to tell her, sensing that sharing his pain with her would somehow lessen it. Already the rawness of it was seeping away, as if by her very presence alone Rebecca had been a balm, easing it.

Rebecca lay and listened silently as Chase related the story from its very beginning to its horrible ending. Many times she was tempted to stop him and ask questions, but she repressed the urge, knowing that Chase had to tell it at his own pace, in his own way, or it would never be told at all. When he spoke of Louis and Ben's deaths, Rebecca could tell by the subtle change in his voice, a huskiness, that Chase was reliving painful memories. She bit her lip and fought back tears, feeling his pain as if it were her own and wishing that she could take all of it for him.

And when it was over, she wisely refrained from making any comment, sensing that Chase was feeling vulnerable. Instead she drew his head down to rest between her breasts, gently stroking his dark hair, in that age-old manner women have comforted those they love since the beginning of time.

Finally, after long minutes had passed, she asked, "What will we do now?"

Chase raised his head and looked her directly in the eye. "Deliver those cannons to the Texas army."

Rebecca couldn't believe her ears. "But you believe the fight for independence is hopeless, that the Texians can't possibly win against Santa Anna's might. After the fall of the Alamo, you said that was proof of the futility of it all. Isn't this new disaster just further proof?"

Chase sat up and gazed off into space for a minute before answering. "Reason tells me it's still futile." Then he turned his head and looked at her again. "But a part of me refuses to listen to reason, demands this of me. I owe something to those men who died at Goliad, not just my friends, Ben and Louis, but all of them. I know it sounds unbelievable, even melodramatic, but that night, when I stood out on the prairie and gazed at the glow from their funeral pyre, I could almost hear them crying out to me, begging me not just to avenge them but to take up their cause and see it through. Now I'm going to do everything in my power to get those cannons to Houston—even if it kills me!"

Rebecca sat up, her eyes sparkling. "And I'm going with you," she said with determination.

Chase didn't want to take Rebecca with him. From then on the mission would be even more dangerous than before. He wasn't sure just what his feelings for her were, except that he felt strongly protective of her. The thought of anything happening to her filled him with fear. He started to refuse, to tell her no, that he would find a safe place to leave her and deliver the cannons himself. But then he looked at her and saw the determined set of her chin. It wasn't her determination that changed his mind, but rather the fervent look in her eyes. For the first time he understood the true depths of her need to avenge her family's deaths.

How could he deny her soul its peace and yet seek to find rest for his own?

He nodded grimly and pulled her back into his arms. Lying back down on the feather mattress, he said, "I guess we're in this together."

Rebecca sighed in relief. "Thank God! I was afraid you would refuse, and then I don't know what I would have done."

Chase chuckled. "I do. First you would have ranted and raved, and then, when that didn't work, you would have probably held a gun at my back."

Rebecca looked thoughtful for a moment. "Yes, I probably would have," she finally admitted.

Chase could only shake his head in amazement at Rebecca's candid admission. Then, becoming very much aware of her heat and softness against him, he began to stroke her back and softly kiss her forehead.

Feeling him stir against her thigh, Rebecca objected. "No, Chase. You're exhausted. You need your rest."

Chase hooked a finger under her chin and raised her head. Rebecca gazed into his smoldering eyes. "No," he whispered huskily. "What I need is you."

"But—"

"Hush, woman! You talk too much," Chase muttered against her lips, before his mouth silenced her with a deep, burning kiss that melted any resistance and obliterated all rational thought.

CHASE AND REBECCA LOADED THE WAGON THE next morning, preparing to leave the relative safety of the shack. Rebecca would have liked to delay their departure, feeling that Chase could have used a day of rest after his ordeal, but Chase was anxious to be on their way, arguing that time was of the utmost importance.

"What are you going to do with the three new mares? Turn them loose?" she asked as she watched him harness the six mares to the wagon.

Chase chuckled. "And have Lightning go chasing after them? No, I don't think he'd take kindly to that, not after all of the time and effort he spent stealing them. Besides, I've decided we can use them. This way we can rotate the horses, giving all of them a chance to rest. We'll make better time."

When the horses were harnessed and Lightning tied to the back, Chase took Rebecca's arm to help her up into the wagon. "What about the new mares?" she asked. "Aren't you going to tie them to the wagon too?"

"No need to. They'll follow Lightning."

234

As they drove off, Rebecca discovered Chase had been correct. Lightning gave a short snort and the three mares followed dutifully, never questioning his authority over them. In a way, the mares' docility irritated Rebecca. She wished that they had shown more independence, more spirit. Stupid animals, she thought, chasing after Lightning as if he were the only stallion in the world. Well, when Chase left her, she'd be damned if she'd go chasing after him. At least she had her pride and her independence. She might love him with all her heart, but she'd never bow and scrape to him. And if their paths ever crossed again after this mission had been completed, he would have to seek her out.

When Chase drove onto the main road and turned north, Rebecca didn't question him, assuming that he would turn east when they got closer to Bexar and take the same bypass around the town that they had used on their trip south. But two days later, when Rebecca spied the half-hidden ruins of San Juan Capestrano and Chase didn't turn off, she asked apprehensively, "We're not going to drive straight through Bexar?"

"No, we're making a little side trip."

"Side trip? Where to?"

"To my Comanche relatives," he said casually.

Rebecca's first reaction was one of total horror. He intended to take her into an Indian camp? Not just any Indian camp, Rebecca reminded herself, but a Comanche camp, no less, the most fierce and dangerous Indians in Texas. Her mouth turned dry with fear. Then she remembered their mission, and her irritation overrode her fear.

"Are you crazy?" she asked. "This is no time to be dropping in for a visit with your relatives, even if they are close by! We've got to get these cannons to General Houston."

"I'm not just dropping by for a visit, Rebecca. I thought you knew about the other part of my agreement with Paul, but obviously you don't. Paul didn't hire me to just haul those cannons to the Alamo. Any man with any frontier skills at all could have done that. He chose me because I'm half Comanche and the Texas government needed someone who knows the Comanches personally to approach them about signing a peace treaty. I guess you could say I'm an emissary, since they couldn't find anyone else to send."

Rebecca was stunned. Paul had told her nothing of this. But then, she supposed he saw no reason to, since it didn't involve her. Once they had reached Bexar and delivered the cannons to the Alamo, she had planned on staying with a friend of his until the end of the war. What Chase did after he left her was none of her concern. Paul couldn't have anticipated what had happened, nor that Rebecca would fall in love with Chase.

"At the time Paul approached me," Chase continued, "I had serious doubts that the Comanches would sign. I still doubt it. But I think, in view of how badly the war is going for Texas, I should at least try. An all-out Indian attack would put the finishing touch on any hopes for winning this war."

Rebecca could see Chase's point. The Texas army would be hard pressed fighting one superior, powerful enemy, but two? Why, even Indian skirmishes would be disastrous to them, depleting their already meager ranks and small supply of ammunition. But Houston needed those cannons too.

As if reading her mind, Chase said, "I'm not going to take any more time than I absolutely need to. I'm only going to talk to my grandfather, who is chief of some of the *Penateka,* in hopes he will intercede for us with the other chiefs of that tribe, since its the one that would be the most likely to get involved in this war."

Rebecca was surprised to hear that Chase's grandfather was a chief, and then she wondered why. She should have known that Chase didn't have ordinary Indian blood running in his veins, but that of a proud, fierce leader. No, there was nothing ordinary about Chase. He was a cut above other men, whether white or Indian.

But Rebecca knew very little about Indians, and certainly nothing about Comanches. "I thought the Comanches were a tribe, under one chief."

"No, Rebecca, the Comanches are a nation unto themselves, just as the Sioux and Apaches are. There are twelve tribes in the Comanche nation, but only six are of importance, and only three of those tribes roam in Texas. The *Nolonis*—or Wanderers—on the upper Brazos and Red River; the Antelope band, to the southwest, along the Llano Estacado; and my tribe, the *Penateka*—or Honey Eaters. And all of those tribes have subtribes, with

237

their own chiefs. There is no single chief of the Comanche nation."

"My God! How many Comanches are there in Texas?"

"Around thirty thousand or so."

Rebecca turned pale. Why, the Anglo population in Texas was estimated at only twenty thousand. Add the other Indian tribes to that of the Comanche, and the red men outnumbered the white by . . . By what? Three to one? Six to one? Ten to one? Compared to the force the Indians could amass if they combined their might, Santa Anna's army looked small and insignificant. No wonder the provisional government was worried about what the Indians would do in this time of unrest.

"So you see," Chase continued, "my grandfather can't speak for all of the *Nim-ma,* only for his own tribe. That's why it would be impossible to get the Comanches to sign a peace treaty in such a short time. There are simply too many subtribes, and what one chief signs does not commit the others."

"Nim-ma? Is that what the Comanches call themselves?" Rebecca asked.

"Yes, it means the People."

Rebecca stared at him, astonished. "Is that all it means? Just the people?"

"Yes. The Comanches believe in keeping things simple. You're either one of them, or you aren't."

"How long will it take us to get to the Comanches?"

"Actually we're in *Comancheria*—Comanche

territory—right now. Comanches consider the land from the Nueces River to the Arkansas as their hunting grounds, and they don't necessarily pitch their camps in the same place, unless it happens to be their winter camp. I'm hoping my grandfather still makes his winter camp in the same place. It's been years since I've been back to the tribe. And then, they may have already moved out, since its spring. To be honest, I'm taking a gamble that he'll still be there. But we'll know, one way or the other, by this afternoon."

"But how do you know your grandfather hasn't died, if you haven't been back in years?"

"He hasn't. I keep up with him through other tribes. Besides, my grandfather will live to be a hundred."

"Why do you think that?"

A warm look came into Chase's eyes. "Because he's tough and resilient. He defies time. His body might age, but not his spirit. Just wait until you meet him. Then you'll know what I mean."

Rebecca saw the warm look in Chase's eyes, the look of love. It surprised her. She had thought that Chase was incapable of deep emotional attachments, since he was so independent, so restless. But then last night she had known he felt a deep remorse over the loss of his friends. Apparently this man she loved had depths to his emotions that she had never dreamed of. She realized how little she really knew of him.

Chase drove the wagon from the main road and headed cross-country, in a northwesterly direction. She looked about her, thinking that the land on this side of Bexar was even more desolate than that south of the town. They went up one steep hill covered with cactus and mesquite brush, then down, then up again. Then the land leveled out on a flat plateau, and Rebecca could see for miles around her.

Her eyes caught the sight of something shiny to the east of her. She strained her eyes, seeing the dome and the twin bell towers in the distance. "Look!" she cried. "Another mission!"

"Yes, that's Mission Conception. It's been abandoned by the church too. There was a battle there between General Cos's men and the Texians before the Texians captured the Alamo. Thirty-three Texians repelled four hundred Mexicans. Bowie and Fannin were there."

"You mean Travis?" Rebecca asked, remembering that Bowie and Travis had died together at the Alamo.

"No, Fannin. It was in October, before he went east to gather together his companies of volunteers."

It was always the same, Rebecca thought bitterly. The Texians drastically outnumbered. But Bowie and Fannin had fared better in that battle than in their last confrontation with the enemy: Bowie killed at the Alamo and Fannin executed at Goliad.

Hoping to distract herself from her gloomy thoughts, Rebecca looked for more deserted missions. For a long while, she saw nothing that looked like it might be the walls or bell towers of a crumbling mission. Then the corner of her eye caught the glitter of metal. She turned in her seat and looked behind the wagon. Her breath caught at the sight of the riders in the distance, their lances and helmets glittering in the sun.

"Chase, look!"

Chase leaned out and glanced around the wagon. "Dragoons! Where in the hell did they come from?"

"They're chasing us!"

"We'll see about that," Chase said in a sharp voice, whipping the horses into a hard gallop.

The wagon lurched ahead, the mares pulling with all of their strength and speed. They raced across the open prairie, the wind whipping around their faces, the dust kicked up stinging their eyes. Rebecca held on for dear life as the wagon bounced over the rough terrain. She ventured a quick glance backward, and her heart fell. Despite their speed, the lancers were gaining on them.

"It's no use, Chase!" she cried with a half sob over the deafening hoofbeats. "We can't outrun them. Not with this heavy wagon."

"I'm not trying to outrun them. I'm just playing for time."

Rebecca glanced over at him, wondering what he could mean. And then, as he stood and squinted, peering intently at the horizon, then smiled, she thought he had lost his mind. She craned her neck, straining her eyes, and saw the solid line of Indians rolling over the horizon and racing toward them. Rebecca's blood turned to ice water. One terrifying look at that horde of howling savages bearing down on them, and she quickly decided she would rather take her chances with the Mexicans.

"Turn back!" she shrieked. "They're Indians!"

"No, they're Comanches!" Chase yelled. Then he laughed, a laugh that sounded absolutely diabolical. "Here," Chase said, "take the reins. And keep those mares running straight ahead."

"But where are . . ."

Rebecca's voice trailed off as Chase disappeared inside the wagon. She was much too busy trying to control the wildly racing horses in front of her to wonder at Chase's sudden desertion. A minute later Lightning tore past her, with Chase riding on his back.

Chase had stripped off his tunic and rode bareback, and at that minute, with his dark hair whipping about his face and his bronzed upper torso bare, he looked just as fierce and frightening as the Indians racing toward them.

He's crazy! Rebecca thought wildly. He doesn't know what tribe of Comanches those are. He couldn't. Not at this distance. And all the Indians knew was that there was a white man's wagon coming toward them, followed by a patrol of Mexican dragoons. My God, they'd all be massacred!

Frantically Rebecca tried to turn the horses. They totally ignored her jerking on the reins. Lightning was in front of them now, and the mares were racing after him.

"Turn around!" Rebecca yelled to them, pulling hard on the reins. The mares ignored her. She stood, fighting to maintain her balance on the wildly bouncing wagon bed, and shrieked at the top of her lungs, "Turn, damn you! You stupid mares, turn!"

But it was futile. Rebecca might just as well not had reins, or lungs, for all the good they were doing her. And then Chase let out a blood-curdling yell, a yell that made the hair on her nape stand on end and goose bumps rise on her skin.

She watched in total horror, helpless to do anything, as the Comanches sped closer, expecting to see arrows flying all around her at any second.

Had she not been so terrified, she might have admitted that the Indians were a magnificent sight. Dressed only in breechclouts and moccasins, their sinewy muscles rippling beneath their dark skins and their long braids flying out behind them, they rode with such mastery and skill that man and horse blended into one superb animal. The sun glittered off their brass earrings, and the feathers tied in their horses' manes fluttered about their red-painted faces. Some carried shields of buffalo hides decorated with a circle of feathers and held long red lances, while others carried bows and arrows. Most were bareheaded, a single yellow or black feather in their scalp locks, while a few wore headdresses of buffalo horns.

A new fear filled Rebecca as the Comanches swept down on them. The savages looked as if they were going to ride them down, collide with the horses and wagon. However, when they reached Chase and Lightning the Indians divided, half going to one side of the wagon, half going to the other. Rebecca watched in astonishment as they flew past her, paying no more attention to her than they would have a boulder they had veered to avoid, their glittering black eyes glued on the dragoons behind her.

Chase whirled Lightning around and rode back to the wagon, grinning from ear to ear. "You can stop now!" he called.

Rebecca glared at him. How dare he sit there looking so sure of himself! Why, he could have gotten them both killed!

She pulled hard on the reins and the mares slowed, then stopped, blowing hard after their frantic race, their coats lathered with sweat. Rebecca was so angry with them for ignoring her commands to turn, she couldn't even feel any pity for them.

Chase slipped from Lightning's back and onto the seat beside her, still grinning. "That was some driving you did there."

"I wasn't driving!" Rebecca countered in anger. "Those fool mares were following Lightning. The stupid idiots are so enamored with that damned stallion, they'd follow him to the ends of the earth!"

"But I thought I heard you urging them on."

"I wasn't urging them on!" Rebecca said hotly, her anger at the mares once again rising. "I was yelling for the stupid things to turn around."

"Turn around?" Chase asked in surprise. "But why? I told you those were Comanches."

"You didn't know what tribe of Comanches they were! And even if you did, they certainly couldn't recognize you from that distance. It's a miracle they didn't shoot first and ask questions later. No, you were still gambling—but this time with our lives!"

"I wasn't gambling, Rebecca. When I saw those Indians, I knew they were my tribe, because my grandfather makes his winter camp just over that rise. I knew when they saw the Mexican patrol heading toward their camp, they'd come out in force. That's what I was waiting for."

"But they might have thought we were with the Mexicans!" Rebecca objected hotly.

"No, Rebecca. Their lookouts have probably been watching us for some time. One lone wagon ambling along didn't particularly bother them. It was the sight of that patrol racing toward their camp that alarmed them. I was almost certain they knew the Mexicans were chasing us, but just to play it safe, I rode out front and gave the Comanche war cry. I knew once they heard that cry and saw the color of my skin they'd know I was a friend and not an enemy. From then on we were in no danger."

"Why didn't you tell *me* that?" Rebecca demanded angrily.

"I was in a bit of a hurry at the time," Chase answered ruefully. "Things were moving too fast for me to take the time to explain. Besides, I don't know why you're so angry. Nothing happened."

Rebecca had just gone through the most terrifying experience in her life and all Chase could say was nothing happened. His calm, unconcerned manner angered her even more. She wanted to throttle him, and the stupid mares, and Lightning. Instead, she shot daggers at him with her eyes.

Chase picked up the reins and urged the horses into a walk, aware of the murderous looks Rebecca was sending his way. She was the most exasperating woman he'd ever met, he thought for the hundredth time. Any other woman would have been relieved that it had ended so well. But not her. He could understand her being afraid, but he couldn't, for the life of him, understand why she was so mad, particularly after he'd explained everything. Well, he'd be damned if she'd get a rise out of him.

"Well, at least we got rid of those dragoons," Chase commented.

In her fright and subsequent anger, Rebecca had completely forgotten about the Mexican patrol. She leaned out of the seat and looked behind them. Far off in the distance, she could see the dragoons fleeing for their lives, but the Comanches were gaining on them, and Rebecca knew the Mexicans weren't going to escape. And then . . .

She sat back, her face pale. "Will they kill them all?" she asked, her voice low.

"Yes."

"And scalp them?"

"Yes."

Rebecca shivered.

"Don't feel sorry for them, Rebecca," Chase said in a hard voice. "Any Mexican who ventures into *Comancheria* knows he's taking that risk. Besides, remember Goliad. If it hadn't been for leaving you stranded out here and not knowing what was going on, I would have gone with them."

"But you wouldn't scalp them."

"Oh, yes, I would," Chase said in a steely voice.

Rebecca gasped. Chase turned to her, his black eyes glittering angrily. "Did the Mexicans treat the Texians any better? The men at the Alamo and Goliad were mutilated. And do you know why the Indian scalps his victim? To prevent him from gaining immortality! Isn't that the same thing the Mexicans tried to do to the Texians when they burned their bodies?"

Rebecca sat back, stunned by Chase's vehemence. Then she remembered the Mexican dragoons repeatedly shooting her dead father and brother. Had they had bayonets on their muskets, they would have probably cut them to pieces too. No, she couldn't fault Chase.

When they rode over the crest of the small hill and looked down at the Comanche camp, Rebecca stared in awe. She had assumed, because Chase had said his grandfather was a chief of a subtribe, that he had meant it was a small tribe, but the camp stretched for miles along a clear-running stream. That alone was a surprise to Rebecca, but the herd of horses grazing to the side and rear of the camp was even more stunning. She had thought the herd of mustangs that had passed them on the road was large, but this herd was even larger, stretching to the horizon.

"I've never seen so many horses," Rebecca muttered in wonder.

"The only thing a Comanche truly values is horseflesh," Chase explained. "Besides his weapons, it's the only thing he can personally own. The tepee is considered the wife's property, and everything else belongs to the tribe. An average Comanche warrior has around two hundred fifty horses, a war chief as many as fifteen hundred to two thousand. Even Comanche women are allowed to own their own string of horses, something that you won't see in most of the Indian tribes. The white man has his gold and land, the Comanche his horses."

Rebecca spied four Comanches riding up the hill toward them and tensed.

"There's nothing to be alarmed about," Chase assured her. "They're just our escort into camp."

The horses pulled up to the wagon and stopped. Chase exchanged what Rebecca assumed must be a greeting with them and then they resumed their drive down the hill and into the camp, the four Comanches riding two abreast beside them.

As they rode, the warriors blatantly stared at Rebecca, making her very nervous and self-conscious. "Must they stare so rudely?" Rebecca finally complained to Chase.

"They don't mean to be offensive, Rebecca. It's just that they've never seen a woman with skin as white as yours or hair the color of yours. For that matter," Chase said, his eyes sweeping over her hair admiringly, "neither had I."

Knowing that it was her hair that the Comanches were so enthralled with didn't make Rebecca feel any easier. She had once heard that Indians prized blond scalps over others and couldn't help but wonder if that was why they were eyeing her hair, thinking how handsome it would look beside their other scalps. She sat stiffly, staring straight ahead, afraid to look them in the eye for fear she would see greed there.

When they rolled into the camp, a curious crowd had already gathered, babbling in excitement. But when they saw Rebecca, they stopped talking and stared at her, just as openly as the warriors had done.

Chase chuckled. "You're creating quite a sensation, Rebecca. The whole tribe is fascinated with you."

Rebecca didn't feel at all complimented by all the attention. She was beginning to feel more like an oddity, a freak of some kind. The only inhabitants of the camp that seemed oblivious to her were the camp dogs that barked and snapped at the mares' hooves as they drove down the road between the tepees.

They stopped before a tepee that was much larger than the others. Two standards stood before the entrance, the eagle feathers on them fluttering in the breeze.

"This is my grandfather's tepee," Chase said.

Chase helped Rebecca down, and they stood before the tepee. Rebecca waited for Chase to lead the way, but he made no effort to move.

"What are we waiting for?" Rebecca asked.

"No one enters the chief's tepee without an explicit invitation, not even the chief's grandson."

They stood before the tepee, the only sounds the restless pawing of the mares and the whispering of the wind across the prairie. Even the camp dogs were silent. The hushed quiet gnawed at Rebecca's nerves. Finally the flap on the tepee was pushed aside and a man, his hair white as the snow and hanging in two long braids, startling against the dark, weathered skin of his face, emerged. Rebecca saw that he wasn't as tall as Chase, and yet, with his proud, erect carriage, he gave that impression. The muscles on his bare chest were hardy and sinewy and his abdomen taut. Now Rebecca knew what Chase had meant when he said his grandfather defied time.

As Chase and his grandfather clasped each other's upper arms in what Rebecca assumed was the Comanche version of a hug, Rebecca took the opportunity to study the chief further. On his head he wore a beaded headband, and silver loops dangled from his pierced ears. Around his neck a simple silver necklace hung, along with his medicine pouch. His breechclout, leather leggings, and moccasins were completely unadorned. Despite his surprisingly simple clothing, Rebecca thought he looked magnificent. He was a man who needed no adornment, no feather bonnet, no elaborately beaded buckskins to proclaim his station. Anyone who saw him would know he was a chief. He radiated power and dignity. For the first time Rebecca knew what people meant when they spoke of the majesty of kings.

The two men stepped apart, then Chase pulled Rebecca forward and said something to his grandfather. All Rebecca recognized was her name. Then Chase turned to her. "Rebecca, this is my grandfather, Eagle at Sunrise."

Eagle at Sunrise turned his head and gazed at Rebecca with his black eyes, eyes that were identical to Chase's, his look so penetrating that Rebecca felt he was peering into her soul. She trembled, fearing that he might find her lacking. Then the chief glanced briefly at her hair, smiled slightly, and turned his attention back to Chase.

Chase and his grandfather talked for several minutes before Eagle at Sunrise turned and ducked beneath the skin flap at the door and disappeared inside his tepee.

"My grandfather said he's had a tepee prepared for us close by," Chase said.

"But aren't you going to visit with him?" Rebecca asked in surprise. "You said you haven't seen him for years."

"Not today. The war party will be returning soon, and there will be a victory celebration, which my grandfather will preside over. I told him I wanted to have a long talk with him about something important, and he told me we would talk tomorrow morning."

"Did he ask who I was?"

"Yes. I told him you were a friend but that I intended to tell everyone else in camp that you were my wife. I don't want any of these warriors getting the mistaken idea that you're up for grabs."

Rebecca wasn't sure what Chase meant by "up for grabs." Did he mean they might take her by force, or try to woo her? Either way, she didn't want the Indians getting the wrong idea either.

Chase led her to a tepee a short way from his grandfather's. "You can wait inside or out here."

"Where are you going?" she asked apprehensively.

"To move the wagon to the side of the tepee, where it will be out of the way, then take care of the horses."

Rebecca looked back at the tepee behind her. To her, it didn't look very inviting. "I'll wait here."

Chase climbed on the wagon and circled the tepee, stopping on the opposite side, between theirs and the tepee next to it. As he started unharnessing the horses, three warriors rushed up to help him. When one of the Indians started to lead the mares away to put them with the other horses, Chase stopped him. Another brief conversation in Comanche followed and the Indians burst into laughter at the end of it.

One of the Indians eyed Lightning, where the stallion stood tethered to a stake beside the tepee, nodded his head in approval, then said, *"Mucho huevos,"* bringing on another wave of laughter.

After the Comanches had left, Rebecca walked to where Chase was roping the mares into a small corral he was making between the wagon and their tepee. "What was that all about?" she asked.

"They were going to put the mares in with their herd, but I told them I didn't think it would be a good idea. I explained how Lightning seemed to think they were his *manada* and warned them he just might take the notion to go and get them out and take a few of their mares in the process."

Rebecca smiled, thinking, Yes, Lightning probably would do just that, greedy horse that he was.

252

"What does *mucho huevos* mean? It sounded Spanish."

"It is. The Comanches have picked up a lot of Spanish from the Mexicans. It's sprinkled all through the Comanche language, which otherwise is exactly like the Shoshone's, far to the north, from which they branched."

"But what does it mean? *Mucho huevos?*" Rebecca persisted.

Chase wondered if he should tell her the explicit translation. The Indian had been admiring the stallion's testicles, something that Spanish and Comanche men were very proud of in their horses— as well as in themselves—and the reason why they never gelded them. He decided against it, thinking that it was probably just as well Rebecca didn't understand Comanche or Spanish. Indians were very frank about sexual matters, men and women alike, and undoubtedly Rebecca would be shocked by their openness. "It means very manly," Chase answered, watering down the Comanche's remark to suit Rebecca's ears.

Chase led Rebecca into the tepee, lifting the flap for her to pass. The interior was dim, and Rebecca had to wait until Chase had lit the fire before she could see much of it. Then she gazed around her in surprise, for it was much larger than it looked from the outside. It stood about fourteen feet high, its framework consisting of eighteen poles over which the buffalo hides had been thrown. The smoke escaped through an ingenious flap at the top, and the door faced away from the prevailing wind. There was no furniture, only buffalo skins for sitting and sleeping on.

"It must be cold in the winter," Rebecca remarked.

"No, to the contrary. These tepees are warmer than any log cabin. Those hides overlap so snugly no drafts get in, like they can between the chinks in logs, and the skins hold in the heat better than wood does."

Rebecca heard a scraping noise at the flap and turned to look at it, expecting to see one of the camp dogs sneaking under it. Chase walked to the flap, lifted it, and spoke briefly to someone. He returned with two wooden bowls heaped high with roasted meat.

When he handed one of the bowls to Rebecca, she asked, "They eat their evening meal this early?"

"No, it's customary for the Comanches to feed their guests as soon as they arrive."

Rebecca was surprised at their hospitality. Chase sank to the buffalo hides and sat cross-legged, with his bowl in his lap. Since it was either stand and eat or do the same, Rebecca sat down beside him. She picked up a piece of meat, wondering what it was.

Seeing her expression, Chase said, "It's buffalo meat. It has a taste a little stronger than venison."

Rebecca took a tentative bite and discovered what Chase had said was true. The buffalo meat did have a strong, gamey taste. She also discovered that the meat was almost raw inside. Rebecca had never cared for rare meat, much less raw, but she was wise enough to force herself to eat it, not wanting to offend the Indians.

They had just finished eating when the camp seemed to explode with noises. The ground shook as the sounds of horses running through the camp and loud whoops filled the air, followed by excited cries. No one had to tell Rebecca what was happening. The victorious warriors were returning, undoubtedly brandishing fresh scalps over their heads. The thought along with the raw meat already sitting uneasily in her stomach nauseated Rebecca.

The flap suddenly opened, and Rebecca jumped as she saw a warrior entering the tepee, his face painted red. Fearing that the Indian had decided to add her scalp to the others he had taken that day, she cringed.

Chase rose, smiling broadly, and the two men greeted each other in the same manner Chase and his grandfather had. Then Chase pulled Rebecca to her feet. "Rebecca, this is my brother, Two Feathers."

Rebecca looked at Two Feathers. He was much shorter than Chase, and his features were much more Indian. His hair also looked coarser, and, she realized with surprise, his eyebrows were completely plucked. But the eyes were the same, black and fierce.

Two Feathers asked Chase a question. As Chase answered, the Comanche stared at Rebecca. There was something about his scrutiny that made her even more uncomfortable than when the other Indians had looked at her so rudely. Finally she realized that he wasn't just staring at her hair, but her breasts too. Instinctively she stepped back, a sudden revulsion running through her. Two Feathers grinned at her, a grin that seemed even more threatening to Rebecca, then turned to Chase and said something.

Chase nodded, and Two Feathers stepped back outside. "Two Feathers has asked me to attend the victory dance with him," Chase told Rebecca. "In view of the fact that they saved us from the dragoons, I feel I should go. I assume you don't want to go, since they'll be exhibiting their scalps."

Rebecca repressed a shiver. "No, I'll stay here."

"You won't be afraid to stay alone?"

Rebecca *was* a little nervous about staying by herself in the middle of an Indian camp, but she couldn't admit that to Chase. Then he would either insist she go along and witness something that she had no desire to see, or tell his brother that he had to stay with her because she was afraid, causing the Indians to scorn them both. "No, I'm not afraid," she lied adroitly.

Chase turned to leave, and Rebecca remembered something. "Chase, would you mind bringing my trunk in from the wagon for me before you leave?"

Chase nodded, then left the tepee. A few minutes later he returned, dumping the trunk on the ground in the tepee. Rebecca thought he looked irritated about something and asked, "Is something wrong?"

In truth, Chase *was* irritated. His brother had chided him about doing women's work when he saw Chase carrying the trunk. The remark rankled, and yet he knew the trunk was too heavy for Rebecca to lift. She might shove it all over the wagon, but it was much too heavy for her to carry. "No," he snapped, then said over his shoulder, "Don't wait up for me. I'll be late."

After Chase had left, Rebecca stared at the tepee flap where he had disappeared, wondering what had gotten his dander up. Then, shrugging her shoulders, she knelt and opened the trunk, removing her sewing basket and the calico dress with the torn hem. She sat down, hoping the sewing would distract her from remembering where she was.

She was only halfway through when she was very much reminded of where she was. She startled when the loud drums began, followed by whoops and hollering. From then on, the din got steadily worse. When it turned dark, she could see the glow of the big bonfire through the buffalo skins and an occasional shadow as someone walked between the light and her tepee. She told herself it was only the Indians making their way through the tepees to the dance, fighting her imagination's persistence that there was someone lurking around outside her tepee, about to pounce on her. After pricking her finger several times because her hands were shaking so badly, she finally set her sewing aside.

Two hours later the drums were still beating and the hollering and yelling still going on, and Rebecca had a throbbing headache from all of the noise. She decided to go to bed, finally having convinced herself that the Indians—and Chase—had forgotten that she was even there. She undressed and slipped on her flannel gown, then sat down on one of the buffalo pallets. She bent and sniffed it suspiciously, only to find that it had no bad odor. In fact, it smelled much like sage. She lay down and pulled the buffalo robe over her, wishing that she had remembered to ask Chase to bring in her blanket too.

A few moments later the flap of the tepee was raised and a dark head appeared. Rebecca sat up in fright, then sighed in relief when she saw it was Chase. Spying Two Feathers entering the tepee behind him, she jerked the buffalo skin up to her chin.

When Chase realized that Two Feathers had followed him, he turned and frowned at his brother. Then, seeing his brother looking at Rebecca with lust-filled eyes, his blood came to a slow boil.

Two Feathers turned to Chase, saying in Comanche "Your wife is very desirable. I will take her to my pallet tonight."

"No!" Chase said in English, then repeated it in Comanche.

Two Feathers was shocked by Chase's refusal. The warrior scowled. "Have you forgotten the Comanche ways so soon? I am your brother. Your only brother. Brothers share everything."

"We don't share this woman," Chase answered in a hard voice.

"I will bring my woman to warm your pallet tonight," Two Feathers offered.

"I don't want your woman. And you can't have mine. Not tonight. Not ever!"

Two sets of fierce black eyes glared at each other

angrily. Then Two Feathers sneered, saying in a voice dripping with contempt "You are no Comanche. You have been weakened by the white man's way." He spat a Comanche insult, whirled, and jerked the flap open.

After Two Feathers had left Rebecca asked, "What were you two arguing about?"

"You."

"Me?" Rebecca asked, shocked.

"Yes. He wanted to sleep with you tonight."

Rebecca knew Chase didn't mean just sleep. She was struck speechless.

"I told everyone in camp you were my wife, completely forgetting that it was Comanche custom for brothers to share everything—including their wives. That's why he was so shocked and angry when I refused him. He expected me to agree."

"*You* to agree? What about the woman? Doesn't she have anything to say about it?"

"No. Comanche women are totally subservient to their husbands. They do anything they are told to do."

"Anything?" Rebecca asked in horror. "Including prostituting themselves?"

"It's not the same as prostitution. The loaning of wives is just between brothers. Comanche women know the custom and accept it. They marry with the understanding that they will be shared with their husband's brother."

"It's indecent!" Rebecca cried in outrage. "Loaning their wives out, like they were a horse or blanket, for their own brothers to satisfy their lust. I've never heard of anything so disgusting!"

"It works two ways, Rebecca. If a warrior is killed, his brother is expected to marry his widow to provide for her, regardless of how he might feel about the woman personally."

"That doesn't mean he *has* to sleep with her. He still has a choice. The woman doesn't!" Rebecca argued back.

"Well, what are *you* so upset about? I told him no."

Rebecca wondered, if they had been married, whether Chase would have loaned her to his brother. The thought hurt deeply and fired her anger. She started to say something, but Chase stopped her. "Don't say another word! I don't intend to stand here and argue about Comanche customs with you. Just forget it even happened."

With that, Chase went to the pallet on the opposite side of the tepee and lay down, turning his back to her. Rebecca glared at him, then flounced to her side with her back to him.

The minutes passed. Then Rebecca turned back. It was a hard question to ask, but she had to know. "Why did you say no?"

The question hit Chase like a physical blow. Sexual jealousy between Comanche brothers was unheard of, and yet, when Two Feathers had looked at Rebecca with lust in his eyes, Chase had wanted to kill him. The intensity of his jealousy had surprised and shocked Chase. Rebecca's question delved into emotions he himself didn't understand.

260

"You're not my wife," Chase answered evasively.

Tears glittered in Rebecca's eyes. He hadn't refused because he felt anything for her, she thought bitterly, just because he didn't have any authority over her as a husband. She knew that Chase didn't love her, but she had hoped that he desired her enough to be a little possessive. Even Lightning felt more for those dumb mares than Chase did for her. At least he wouldn't share them with another stallion. No, Lightning would kill another stallion if he got anywhere near them.

Rebecca and Chase lay in their separate, lonely pallets, Rebecca miserable with hurt, Chase struggling with emotions he didn't understand. It was a long time before either of them slept that night.

13

CHASE WAS GONE FROM THE TEPEE THE NEXT morning when Rebecca awakened. She was glad because she needed time to compose herself. Whatever Chase did, she'd never let him know how deeply he had hurt her. Nor would she ever let him touch her again. She wanted nothing to do with a man who could be so cold-blooded, so unfeeling.

She had hardly finished dressing when the flap opened and Chase stepped into the tepee. "We've been summoned to the chief's tepee."

"We?" Rebecca asked, completely forgetting her anger.

"Yes, both of us."

"But I thought you were going to talk to your grandfather about the peace treaty this morning. That doesn't have anything to do with me."

"I thought so too, and frankly, I'm just as puzzled as you. Women other than his wives are never allowed in the chief's tepee, and even *they* are asked to leave if there is official business being discussed."

"Then what does your grandfather want me for?"

"I didn't ask. You don't question a chief's summons. You just obey, even if you're a relative. And you don't dally. So come on."

Chase took Rebecca's arm and led her away. Rebecca was so worried, she didn't even notice his dictatorial attitude. Had she unknowingly done something to offend the Comanches? she wondered. Something taboo? Was Chase's grandfather going to demand punishment?

As soon as they stepped into the chief's tepee, Chase stiffened, seeing Two Feathers sitting in one corner and smiling maliciously. He shot his brother an angry look and turned to face his grandfather.

Eagle at Sunrise sat cross-legged on a buffalo pallet and, despite his simple dress and surroundings, looked as regal and commanding as a king. "Your brother has come to me with a disturbing complaint," he said to Chase in Comanche. "He charges you with brotherly selfishness, a disgraceful attitude for a *Nim-ma* warrior. He says you have forgotten *Nim-ma* ways."

"I assume my brother is talking about our disagreement last night, when I refused to loan him my woman," Chase replied, tight-lipped.

"Did you refuse because the white woman is not your wife? If so, you should have told your brother this."

Two Feathers's head shot up at this revelation. He jumped to his feet. "If she is your captive, I will buy her from you," he said to Chase. "I offer fifty horses."

"She's not for sale!" Chase snapped.

"Then we will gamble for her," Two Feathers said, drawing a pair of dice from within the waistband of his breechclout.

"No, we will *not* gamble for her," Chase said angrily. "She's not a captive. She came with me willingly. She's a . . . a friend."

"He lies!" Two Feathers told Eagle at Sunrise. He pointed to Rebecca. "If the woman came willingly, she is his wife. Men do not have women as friends," he scoffed. "It is as I told you. He refused me, his brother, the use of his woman, while I offered mine freely. He is selfish!"

When Rebecca saw Two Feathers, she suspected that the summons had something to do with the brothers' argument over her the night before, but when Two Feathers pointed at her, she knew. She stepped forward. "He's still angry about last night, isn't he?"

"Stay out of this, Rebecca," Chase said in a warning voice.

"To hell I will!" Rebecca spat. "I know you're discussing me. Do you think I'm a complete idiot? That just because I don't understand Comanche, I'm too stupid to know what's going on?"

"I told you, don't interfere," Chase said in a firm voice.

"Don't you tell me not to interfere," Rebecca answered angrily, her blue eyes glittering dangerously. "I'm not some Comanche squaw to be pushed around by a bunch of egotistical, domineering men!"

"I'm not pushing you around. I'm just telling you to shut up. I'll handle this."

"No! It concerns me, and *I'll* handle it! I don't need some man to speak up for me—or protect me. And I'll be damned if I'll stand by and have you two squabbling over me, like two mangy dogs fighting over a bone. You can tell that brother of yours that nobody owns me—ever! I'm not a possession. I'm a person. My body belongs to me. Me! I decide who I give it to, not my husband, not anybody!"

Two Feathers stared at Rebecca in disbelief. Even though he didn't understand English, he knew she was defying Chase, something that a Comanche woman would never do to any man.

"Rebecca, calm down," Chase pleaded.

"Calm down?" Rebecca shrieked. "Haven't you heard anything I've said. *I'm* saying, no! You tell that brother of yours that even if I were married to you, and a Comanche, I'd still refuse. And if you tried to force me to, I'd kill you. Then I'd kill him!"

She turned and glared at Eagle at Sunrise. "I came to this village willingly. Not as your grandson's woman, but as my own woman. Is this how you treat people who come to you as friends?" she asked angrily.

Chase caught Rebecca's arm and whirled her around. "You crazy little fool! Don't you know who you're talking to? The chief! No one talks to a Comanche chief in anger."

"You mean *you* don't talk to a chief that way. I do! No one tells me what to do with my body, or anything else. Not even a chief!" Tears of frustration glittered in her eyes. "Besides, he doesn't even know what I'm saying, because you're too—too cowardly to interpret for me."

"But he does understand English, Rebecca," Chase said in a grim voice. "I taught him the language when I was here years ago."

Rebecca's eyes widened at this revelation. But she was still too enraged at being treated like a piece of property to be afraid of what the chief might do to her for daring to talk to him in such a manner. "Then why are you speaking Comanche? Just to leave me in the dark?"

"Because Two Feathers does not speak your tongue," Eagle at Sunrise said in a quiet voice.

Rebecca turned. Chief Eagle at Sunrise sat, his face impassive, every inch of him radiating dignity. Suddenly she felt ashamed of herself for losing her temper. Under his quiet, dignified perusal, she felt childish. "I apologize for losing my temper and speaking in anger to you," Rebecca said to the chief. "But I meant every word I said. I won't be pushed around by anyone."

"This is your people's way?" Eagle at Sunrise asked. "Women do not obey their men?"

"Some white women obey their men blindly. Others can be led, but not dominated."

"And you are of the latter?"

Rebecca smiled and replied in all honesty, "No, I am not a follower either. I'm a woman who chooses her own path. If I walk that path with a man, I walk beside him, not behind him. I will not live my life in any man's shadow."

Eagle at Sunrise was intrigued with Rebecca's words. The idea of equality of the sexes was a totally new concept to him. He knew that it was a concept that weak men would reject, fearing that they would be the dominated one. No, it would take a strong man to meet a woman on equal grounds, one so sure of his own strengths that he did not fear giving up his age-old right to dictate to his woman. Was it a concept that conflicted with nature? Eagle at Sunrise asked himself, giving it the test he always used to judge if something was right or wrong, using the Great Spirit's example as his rule of thumb. In animal life, there was always a dominant sex, either male or female. He frowned, not particularly pleased with his answer. Then he remembered seeing two rivers of equal size and strength, far to the north, when he was a young man hunting buffalo on the prairie. One had come from the west, its waters filled with mud, the other from the north, clear and sparkling. When the two rivers joined and their waters mingled, they became one mighty river, the longest and most powerful he had ever seen. He smiled, knowing that he had found his answer.

Eagle at Sunrise turned to Two Feathers and said in Comanche, "This woman belongs to no man. She has come to our village as a visitor, just as a warrior from another tribe would. She is to be treated with honor and given the same consideration."

Two Feathers was shocked that Eagle at Sunrise

would give a lowly woman the same status as a warrior, but he knew from his grandfather's firm tone of voice not to argue with his decision. He shot Chase an angry look and stalked from the tepee.

Eagle at Sunrise turned his attention to Chase. "And now we will talk of this important business that brings you here."

Rebecca turned and started to walk from the tepee.

"Why do you leave?" Eagle at Sunrise asked her.

Rebecca turned back to the chief. "Chase said women are not allowed to remain in the chief's tepee when men are discussing important business."

"Then you leave because my grandson told you to?" Eagle at Sunrise asked her, feeling disappointed in Rebecca.

"No, he didn't tell me that I must leave, simply that it is your custom. You have shown respect for my ways, and now I show respect for yours. I leave willingly, without being asked or told."

Eagle at Sunrise smiled, pleased with her answer. "You may stay, if you wish."

Rebecca's eyes widened. Then she said, "Thank you, Eagle at Sunrise, for your invitation. I would like to hear what you have to say."

Chase had been stunned when Rebecca had talked so boldly to his grandfather and the chief hadn't shown anger or even disapproval at her words. His grandfather's invitation to her further surprised him. His grandfather was giving Rebecca a great honor, one he had never afforded to any other woman.

Chase related the entire story to his grandfather, starting from the night Paul had called him into his drawing room in Natchez and ending with the massacre at Goliad and his escape. The only thing he deleted was his and Rebecca's intimate relationship, in respect for Rebecca's feelings.

When Chase had finished his story, Eagle at Sunrise scowled. "The Mexicans' treachery does not surprise me. Many times they have lured the *Nim-ma* with false promises and then ambushed us or fed us poisoned food. Now the Mexican government pays bounty hunters for our scalps, like we are so many wild animals to be disposed of."

Chase nodded. He knew of the bounty hunters. But he also knew they killed more Mexican peons than Comanches or Apaches, for whom the bounty was also paid. It was much easier and safer for the hired killers to attack an unarmed Mexican village than an Indian camp. And the officials couldn't tell the difference, since the Mexicans' hair was black too. Again it was the innocent Mexican people who had to pay the price for their government's incompetence in dealing with its *Indio* problem.

"And now you come to me with this peace treaty from the Texians?"

"Yes."

"For what purpose? Do the Texians think because the Mexicans are our common enemy that we will join them in their fight?"

"They would like that, but I don't think they

really expect it. Even the tribes they are friendly with probably won't go that far."

"Then what do they want from us?"

"First, the *Nim-ma*'s word that they won't help the Mexicans either, that they will at least remain neutral in this fight. But I told Paul the Texians didn't have to worry about that, that the Comanches would never side with the Mexicans, not the way the *Nim-ma* hate them."

Eagle at Sunrise frowned. "I would not be so sure of that, my grandson."

"Why? Have there been alliances signed between the Comanches and Mexicans?" Chase asked apprehensively.

"I am not sure that an alliance was signed, but there was one Comanche chief who visited Santa Anna's tent at Bexar while the Alamo was under siege. He was so impressed with the Mexican general when he left that he now calls himself Santa Anna. The fool!"

"Have you heard of any others?"

"No, and as I said, no one knows if he agreed to help Santa Anna or if the general even asked him for his aid."

Chase looked thoughtful, then said, "You have a point there. One that I never considered. As egotistical as Santa Anna is, I wonder if he would ask for anyone's help. He seems determined to crush the Texians himself, just to prove how powerful he is."

"Then the only thing your Texians are asking is that we remain neutral?"

"No, they're asking for peace between themselves and the *Nim-ma* too."

"But we are not at war with the Texians," Eagle at Sunrise objected. "The *Nim-ma* have never waged war against these Anglos, as you call them."

"I know. They're only asking that things remain that way, that you don't decide to attack them, while they are fighting the Mexicans."

"I am only one chief. I can give my word, providing my tribal council agrees, but I cannot speak for the others. You need to call a council of the *Nim-ma* chiefs."

"I haven't got time to do that. It would take months, and I have to deliver those cannons to the Texas army. I was hoping that you could talk to some of the *Penateka* chiefs informally. They respect your judgment. Just telling them that you have given your word would pull a lot of weight, hopefully enough that they won't jump on the Texians' backs too."

"To use my influence with the other chiefs, I would have to know more of these Texians. Who is their leader?"

"They have many leaders."

"Then who is their war chief?"

"Houston. Sam Houston."

"The man the Cherokees call Big Drunk?" Eagle at Sunrise asked in surprise.

"Where did you hear that?"

"I was at the council that your Great White Chief called between the Cherokees and the *Nimma* near here four years ago. I have seen this

Houston you speak of. He was one of the men who negotiated the peace treaty. He is a big man, even taller than you, and powerfully built."

"Yes, so I've heard. I've never seen him personally, but I do know he lived with the Cherokees for six years and they adopted him into their tribe. I understand he did quite a bit of drinking during that time. He was despondent over his broken marriage. That's probably why the Cherokees named him Big Drunk."

"He was not drunk that day, and the Cherokee chiefs I talked with spoke of him with great respect. The name was not said with scorn, but affection. They said he is a brave man, a strong leader."

Chase fervently hoped that the Cherokees were correct in their estimation of Houston's leadership capabilities. Texas had more than its share of brave men, but it was going to take a very strong leader to shape a disciplined army out of that bunch of independent frontiersmen and bring order out of chaos. He wondered if Houston—or any man, for that matter—were up to it.

"I will talk to the other *Penateka* chiefs. I will tell them of the Mexican's treachery and that the Texians are led by a powerful war chief who once lived with the red man."

"Thank you," Chase said gratefully.

"I cannot promise you anything, my grandson."

"I understand that, but if they won't listen to you, they certainly won't listen to me."

Chase looked up as Rebecca walked up to them. She had been so quiet, he'd forgotten that she was even there.

"Thank you for allowing me to stay, Eagle at Sunrise," she said. "And I too thank you for helping the Texians. Now I will leave you and Chase to your more personal conversation. I know that it has been a long time since you have seen each other."

After she had left, Eagle at Sunrise said, "Flame Woman is a most unusual woman."

Chase couldn't argue with that. He'd never known a woman like her. "Why do you call her Flame Woman?" he asked.

"Have you not noticed that her hair is like the flame of a fire? Red one second, gold the next, then red again, constantly changing."

"Yes, I've noticed," Chase admitted, "but I thought you were referring to her temperament. That too is fiery and always changing."

"She will go with you to deliver those cannons?"

"Yes."

"Are you not concerned about the danger to her?"

"Yes, I'm concerned, but Rebecca knows the danger and insists upon going along. And when Rebecca gets something in her head, no one can stop her. She's the most determined, strong-willed woman I've ever known. And outspoken," Chase added in exasperation. "You saw that today for yourself."

Eagle at Sunrise smiled in remembrance of Rebecca's earlier outburst. She was a strong, brave woman, and he admired her spirit. Apparently his grandson was having trouble coping with that spirit. They were two of a kind. He remembered

Rebecca's words, that she would walk in no man's shadow. Nor would Soaring Eagle walk in anyone's shadow, man or woman. But could the two learn to compromise, unite their strength, as the two rivers had?

"So you see," Chase continued, unaware of his grandfather's close scrutiny, "I couldn't stop her if I wanted to. But she has personal reasons for insisting on coming with me. She saw her father and brother killed by the Mexicans. Her mother later died from shock. She hates the Mexicans with a passion, and this is her way of getting revenge, just as I seek to avenge the massacre of my friends at Goliad."

Eagle at Sunrise nodded. "As a *Nim-ma,* I can understand revenge against the Mexicans, but as an old man, I wonder at the wisdom of your plan. It seems a big risk to take for such useless weapons."

"Useless?" Chase asked.

"Yes. I have seen those cannons you speak of. They are useless. They are too big to be carried on a horse."

Chase smiled. To a Comanche warrior, anything that couldn't be carried on his horse was totally useless. "The Texians do not consider them useless. The Mexicans have cannons, so the Texians must have them too, to fight them with equal weapons."

"The *Nim-ma* have fought the Mexicans, and the Spanish before them, for hundreds of years without the use of cannons."

"Yes, but the Texians can't ride a horse like the

Nim-ma can," Chase replied, hoping to distract his grandfather from what he knew would be a pointless argument on the choice of weapons.

Eagle at Sunrise grinned. "That is true. No one can ride a horse like a *Nim-ma* can. We can ride circles around the Mexicans' cannons. I must show you my herd of horses before you leave."

"I'd like that."

"Will you leave today?"

"No, tomorrow, I think. I noticed one of the wheels squeaking when I parked the wagon yesterday. I need to repair it. And then I'd like to get rid of some of those crates to lighten the wagon as much as I can. Your people can use them as firewood."

"Where will you go when you leave here?"

"To Gonzales. That's where Houston was, the last I heard."

"I will give you an escort around Bexar."

"Thank you."

Eagle at Sunrise rose. "Come to me when you have finished making your preparations. I will show you my herd of horses. Perhaps we will even race."

Chase stood. "Yes, but let me warn you, Grandfather. You won't want to wager with me. I have a stallion that no horse can beat."

The old man's black eyes twinkled. "We shall see."

Rebecca was eating her breakfast of meat and ash cakes when Chase returned to the tepee. He sank down on the pallet opposite her and started eating.

"Where did the Comanches get the corn for their ash cakes?" Rebecca asked. "Do they raise corn like the Indians in East Texas?"

"No, they don't grow any crops. They scorn those who are farmers, calling them women. The *Nim-ma* are hunters and totally nomadic. They trade their horses for the provisions they eat, but their diet is mostly meat."

Chase's remark about the Comanches scorning other Indians brought on a new wave of anger in Rebecca. "And they gamble their women too, don't they?"

"How did you know that?"

"I told you I'm not stupid. I saw those dice Two Feathers pulled out. I know what he wanted to do. Gamble for me."

"Yes, I'm afraid the Comanches do have a weakness for that vice. Even before they picked up the dice from the Mexicans in Santa Fe, they were that way. Like all Indians, they're compulsive gamblers. They'll gamble anything, not just their women."

"But not their precious horses, I'll bet."

Chase frowned at the bitter tone in Rebecca's voice, then answered, "There are only two things an Indian will never gamble away, his medicine pouch and his war horse. But he will wager the rest of his herd. I've seen as many as three thousand horses change hands on one roll of the dice."

Chase's answer didn't make Rebecca feel any better. She was still smarting under the scornful way the Indians treated their women and thinking that Chase would have treated her in the same degrading way if she'd been his wife and she'd allowed him to. The Comanches were awful, she thought. Valuing their stupid medicine pouches and precious war horses over their wives. She had been correct in assuming Chase wasn't capable of any tender emotions. No Comanche man was.

Now when she thought of how they had made love, she had felt Chase and she were sharing their passion, that neither was using the other. But now she knew that the Comanches shared nothing with their women. They didn't even consider them human. They just used the women to slave for them and to satisfy their lust.

Chase glanced up and saw the angry look on Rebecca's face. Damn it, she's getting all riled up again, he thought. He couldn't understand why she got so upset over Indian customs. What the Indians did was their business. It didn't concern him and Rebecca. Well, he'd be damned if he was going to let her drag him into another pointless argument.

He tossed his bowl aside and rose. "I'm going to check that squeaky wheel on the wagon. Then I'm going to throw those crates away."

Deliberately, Rebecca stayed in the tepee, nursing her hurt and anger, until she heard Chase leave. Then she cautiously stuck her head out of the tepee and saw him and his grandfather walking toward the huge herd of horses, Chase leading Lightning behind him.

She stepped out of the tepee and looked around her, determined that she would ignore the Indians if they started staring at her again. But apparently the novelty of her coloring was no longer an attraction.

She surveyed the camp, noting that a few tepees down from her there was a larger tepee, and before it sat a circle of older, gray-haired Indians, soaking up the sun and talking and gesturing wildly. Rebecca knew what they were doing—reliving their old battles. Apparently the Indian and white man were not so different in that respect. Almost every Anglo town in Texas had a general store where the old men gathered and sat around a potbelly stove, reliving their adventures.

Rebecca turned her attention to the women, thinking bitterly that they seemed to be the only ones working. They chatted gaily and laughed as they tanned the buffalo skins staked on the ground or tended their fires, their children running and playing around them.

She studied them closer. They wore two-piece buckskin dresses, ornamented with beads and fringes, their moccasins painted every color of the rainbow. Their hair hung loose and was parted in the middle, surprisingly short, considering how long the men's braids were. But what astonished Rebecca was their painted faces, their eyes accented with red or yellow lines, and both cheeks daubed with a solid red circle. Even the insides of their ears were painted red.

Rebecca was also amazed to see that none of the women looked haggard or worn down, nor did they appear unhappy with their lot. In fact, they seemed to be taking more joy out of their lives than the women she had traveled with on the wagon train.

Rebecca was forced to stop and take stock. She had to admit that many white men didn't treat their women too well either, some abusing them badly with beatings, some drinking or gambling their families into starvation. Rebecca had seen no signs of such abuse of the Indian women.

She walked back into her tent, a pensive look on her face.

Several hours later Chase walked through the camp, still grinning. Lightning had beaten his grandfather's swiftest horse and then had won four other races. The Comanches had been impressed, and Chase was feeling very proud of his stallion.

Chase felt a hand on his arm and turned, then sucked in his breath, seeing Shining Water standing before him, smiling shyly. When he hadn't seen her at the victory dance the night before, Chase had assumed that she had married and moved to another tribe. Now, as she stood before him, his eyes warmed as they swept over her, thinking that she was just as beautiful and sweet-looking as he had always remembered her.

"May I speak with you, Soaring Eagle?" Shining Water asked in a meek voice, her voice so soft he had to strain to hear her.

"Yes, of course," Chase answered, stepping out of the main path and leading Lightning over to the side.

When they stood beneath a small tree, Chase turned to her. "I didn't see you at the ceremonies last night. I assumed that you had married into another tribe."

"No, I have not married," she answered in a small voice. She lowered her head. "I could never find another warrior I could give my heart to."

Chase would have expected her words to send a surge of joy through him, but strangely, he felt nothing. He frowned as she shifted her feet and twisted her hands nervously, wishing that she would look him in the eye.

Still staring at the ground, Shining Water said timidly, "I was wrong not to go with you when you asked me to, Soaring Eagle. I have regretted it all this time. If you still want me, I will go with you now."

Again Chase wondered why her words brought him no joy. If anything, he felt uncomfortable. "I'm afraid that's impossible now."

"Because you have another wife? I do not mind. I will be your second wife. And I shall be a good second wife. I will obey her, just as I will obey and please you."

Shining Water's meek and docile manner strangely irritated Chase and grated on his nerves. When she said she would be happy to accept the position of second wife, Chase felt disgust, thinking that Rebecca would certainly never accept such a degrading position. Had the woman no pride? No dignity?

Finally she lifted her head, her soft brown eyes adoring and filled with love, a look that would have melted Chase years ago. Now all he could feel was embarrassment for her, hating her groveling, pleading manner.

"Do you not want me any more?" she asked, her eyes glittering with tears.

The truth came to Chase in a burst of sudden insight. No, he didn't want her because he no longer loved her. He wondered how it was possible to stop loving her after he had carried her in his heart all those years. But he had remembered her as being so perfect, and now the very things that had drawn him to her repulsed him.

"Soaring Eagle?" Shining Water asked, her hand trembling as she tentatively touched the sleeve of his buckskins to gain his attention.

Chase no longer loved her, but he didn't want to hurt her either. Shining Water couldn't help the way she was, and Chase owed her at least that much. But he knew that rejection would totally destroy her. She simply wasn't strong enough to accept the truth. "You're still a very beautiful woman, Shining Water," Chase said gently. "You'll make some Comanche warrior a very fine wife. But I cannot take you for a second wife. I live by the white man's customs now. They do not allow more than one wife."

She dropped her head, a tear running down her cheek. "Then it is too late?"

No, not too late, Chase thought. It was wrong from the very beginning. Marriage to Shining Water would have been a serious mistake. With her meek, docile manner, Chase would have soon tired of her. Then she would have become like a rock around his neck, dragging him down with her utter dependency, smothering him with her blind adoration. In the end, he would have hated her for binding him to her.

"Yes, I'm afraid it is too late," Chase answered. "But perhaps it is for the best. You would have never been happy in the white man's world, and I cannot come back to the Indians'." He smiled. "Good-bye, Shining Water," he said gently.

Then he turned and walked away, fighting down the urge to run like hell.

Rebecca had been standing in front of their tepee and saw Chase and Shining Water when the Indian woman approached him. The warm look in Chase's eyes when he first saw Shining Water had stunned Rebecca. The only time she had seen that expression in Chase's eyes was when he had talked of his grandfather. She had watched, dumbfounded, as he and the Indian woman walked to the side of the road and talked. Chase's back had been to Rebecca, but she had seen the adoring, loving look in Shining Water's face when she lifted her head and gazed up at Chase. She knew then that Chase was capable of loving a woman after all, and the woman he loved was this beautiful Comanche woman.

A pain unlike any she had ever known tore through her. Tears welled in her eyes. Quickly, she retreated into the tepee, before either of them saw her, fearing she would make a fool of herself in front of them.

Rebecca wasn't the only one who had witnessed Chase and Shining Water's meeting. Eagle at Sunrise had seen too and frowned when he saw the two old lovers talking. Then he had noticed Rebecca standing in front of her tepee and seen the pained look in her eyes before she fled.

He scowled deeper and turned, retreating into his own tepee.

14

It was dark when Chase went to his grandfather's tepee. After his unexpected meeting with Shining Water, he had spent the rest of the afternoon wandering about the camp, deep in troubled thought. Unable to find the solution to his emotional turmoil, he had gone to Eagle at Sunrise, seeking the old man's counsel, as he had done when he was much younger.

As Chase sank down on the pallet beside his grandfather, Eagle at Sunrise said in a quiet voice, "My grandson is disturbed."

Chase had never hidden anything from his grandfather. He had always been able to reveal his deepest emotions and thoughts to the old man, without the slightest embarrassment. Eagle at Sunrise had never laughed at him, or scorned him, or scolded him. The chief had simply listened quietly and then imparted his words of wisdom, always leaving the decision, if there was one to be made, up to Chase. So Chase wasn't surprised when his grandfather guessed why he had come to him.

"Yes, I am troubled," Chase admitted. "You

would think, at my age, that I could find the answers myself, but instead of untangling them, they seem to get more raveled."

"A man is never too old or too wise to seek the counsel of another. It is the *Nim-ma* way to do so."

"But certainly at your age, and with your wisdom, you don't," Chase commented.

"You are wrong, Soaring Eagle. I too seek the counsel of my elders. And they will tell you that a man never attains full wisdom. He only becomes wiser. Wisdom has no limits, nor does everyone have the capacity for it. There are some who will never show good judgment, who never learn from their mistakes or experiences, while others seem to be born with an inherent understanding."

"Perhaps I'm one of those who doesn't even have the capacity for it," Chase said in disgust. "I thought I knew myself, at least well enough to know what I wanted. For years I thought that I loved a woman, that she was as perfect as any woman could be. I carried her memory in my heart and cherished it. Now I find that I don't love her, that the very things that had attracted me to her now repulse me. How could my feelings change so drastically?"

"What a man truly wants and what he thinks he wants are often two entirely different things, and the young have difficulty distinguishing one from the other. Often they are influenced by those around them, accepting their wants and needs as their own. It isn't until they have matured that they realize their mistakes."

Eagle at Sunrise looked Chase deeply in the eyes. "Shining Water is not the woman for you."

"How did you know I was speaking of her?"

"I know of your love affair with her many years ago."

Chase's eyebrows rose. "You knew we were lovers and yet you said nothing to me?"

"Our people do not encourage this. Nor do they condemn it. They only ask that you be discreet, which you were. I knew that you planned to take Shining Water as your wife, and *this* I did disapprove of. But it was not for me to say, unless you sought my counsel, as you have tonight."

"I thought she was everything I wanted in a woman," Chase said, shaking his head in confusion.

"No, your natures are not suited. You are air. You must be free to move about as you wish, totally unencumbered. She is still water. The two do not mix. Have you not seen air that has been trapped beneath water? The bubbles rush to the top, anxious to be rid of the burden of the water, until they burst free. But I think you already know this truth. It is the truth of your feelings for Flame Woman that you seek."

Chase smiled. "You've always been able to read me like a book."

"Yes, I can sense your feelings and your thoughts. Perhaps it is our sharing the same guardian spirit that gives me this special insight where you are concerned. I do not have it with any of my other grandsons."

Chase frowned. "How do you know my guardian spirit is the same as yours? I've told no one, not even you."

"I might ask you the same question. How do you know my guardian spirit?"

"I—I sensed it."

"You see. Those under the guardianship of the eagle spirit know their own."

Chase was shocked at his grandfather's words.

"No, do not be alarmed," Eagle at Sunrise said. "We of the same spirit do not need our guardian's permission to speak of it. If that were true, as it is of all others, we would not be able to recognize one another."

"Is that why you named me Soaring Eagle?"

"No, at the time I only *hoped* we could share the same guardianship. It was up to the eagle spirit itself to accept you."

Chase nodded, a thoughtful expression on his face. Eagle at Sunrise waited patiently. Finally Chase spoke. "What you said is true. It's my feelings for Rebecca that I'm having trouble sorting out. She's so different from what I thought I wanted in a woman."

"The same rule applies to her as Shining Water. Look to nature for your answer. Flame Woman is fire, and fire and air do mix. Fire needs air. The more it has, the brighter it blazes. And air is drawn to fire. If air goes away, fire dies down, smoldering until it returns, to blaze anew."

"I can't deny I'm drawn to Rebecca. I can't seem to stay away from her, but yet she infuriates me with her obstinance and her fierce independence."

Eagle at Sunrise smiled. "I said that your natures were compatible, not that your wills might not sometimes clash. Have you not seen a prairie fire blazing out of control? The air around it becomes a roaring wind, feeding the fire even more."

Chase chuckled. "Are you suggesting that if I stop doing so much roaring, she won't flare out at me as much?"

"Perhaps," Eagle at Sunrise answered with a twinkle in his eyes. Then he said in a serious tone of voice, "I am thinking, my grandson, that you know the answer in your heart. Your mind fights it, because you have lived so long with the preconception that a woman should be weak and subservient. Flame Woman is a strong woman, not just strong-willed, but strong in all ways. I would advise a lesser man to stay away from her. She would dominate him, trample him, consume him. You must learn not to fear her strength but to glory in it, for once you are truly united, her strengths will become yours, and yours hers."

Chase smiled and rose to his feet. "Thank you for your counsel," he said, feeling as if a burden had been lifted from him.

"You leave tomorrow?" Eagle at Sunrise asked sadly. Of all his grandsons, Soaring Eagle had held the greatest promise. Eagle at Sunrise had hoped he would follow in his footsteps and become the next chief. Chase's decision to go back to the white man had been a big disappointment to the old man. But wisely, Eagle at Sunrise had not tried to hold Chase back. Still, that didn't stop him from missing his favored grandson.

"Yes, but I will not wait so long this time to visit you again," Chase promised, feeling sad himself.

Chase turned and walked to the door.

"Soaring Eagle," the old chief called gently.

Chase turned, a questioning expression on his face.

"Remember one thing," Eagle at Sunrise cautioned. "If air leaves fire for too long, fire will die completely."

"I've already told you the answer to that, Grandfather. I can't stay away from Rebecca for too long."

When Rebecca had fled into the tepee after her heartbreaking discovery, she had been terrified that Chase would come in and find her crying. But as the afternoon wore on and Chase didn't return, she was left to assume that he and the Indian woman had slipped off someplace for a lovers' tryst. She had believed that she couldn't possibly hurt any more, but the thought of Chase making love to someone else was unbearable. She felt as if her soul was being wrenched from her body.

She told herself that she had no right to feel so hurt, so bitter. She had no claim on Chase's heart. He had offered her nothing but physical passion. And yet Rebecca felt terribly betrayed.

She admitted that she couldn't blame Chase for being attracted to Shining Water. She was beautiful, with her black hair and doelike eyes; the picture of sweetness, softness, and femininity, the kind of woman it seemed all men desired. And she certainly couldn't fault the Comanche woman for loving Chase and yet, raw jealousy ate at her.

She had been a complete fool, she realized. She had told herself that she would be satisfied to have Chase's passion for a short while, to steal a part of him, assuming that was all Chase would ever give any woman. The memories that she had carefully committed to her mind and heart would offer her no comfort in the future, in the long, lonely years ahead of her. Now they would only serve to torment her, to make the rest of her life an agony.

It was dark when Rebecca slipped from the tent to the wagon, feeling she had to put a distance between her and Chase. She couldn't stand the thought of being anywhere near him, knowing his feelings for Shining Water. She wondered how she would ever survive the rest of the mission, and yet she knew she had to go through with it. After her insistence on going along, Chase would question why she had changed her mind, and she could never tell him the real reason. Nor could she ever let him touch her again. Not now when she knew that he loved another. She would simply tell him their affair was over. She owed him no explanations. She had made no promises to him either. At least she could salvage a part of her pride.

When Chase left his grandfather's tepee he hurried to Rebecca, his pulse racing in anticipation of seeing her, just being near her. He knew, and now accepted, that his feelings had nothing to do with passion, but a much deeper emotion. He lifted the flap and stepped inside, aware that he was grinning like a fool. But he couldn't help it. After months of trying to suppress his feelings, he could no longer contain his happiness.

He glanced quickly around the firelit tepee, then frowned when he realized that Rebecca was not there. Where could she be? he wondered. He knew that she didn't feel comfortable enough in the Indian camp to wander on her own. A sudden, terrifying thought came to him. Had Two Feathers come and forced her to go with him? No, Chase thought, Two Feathers might be hotheaded, but he was no fool. He'd never defy his grandfather, knowing that Eagle at Sunrise would severely punish him.

And then Chase remembered that Rebecca had been angry with him over the way Comanche men treated their women the last time he had seen her. Obviously she was still angry, determined to make him pay for not giving her the satisfaction of arguing with him. He knew where she was—in the wagon sulking. Well, he'd be damned if he'd let her ruin his happiness with her stubbornness.

Chase stalked from the tepee and across the clearing between it and the wagon. He vaulted to the wagon bed and stepped inside. Rebecca, who had almost drifted off to an emotionally exhausted sleep, bolted up when she saw the dark shadow of a man standing over her.

"Come back to the tepee," Chase demanded.

"No—no, I want to stay here. I—I don't feel comfortable in there."

It was Rebecca's tone of voice, rather than her words, that gave Chase pause. She didn't sound angry. There had been an unmistakable quiver in her voice.

"Are you upset about this morning?" Chase asked.

"No. I—I just want to stay here."

Chase frowned. She sounded hurt. "What's wrong, Rebecca?" Chase asked quietly.

"Nothing is wrong."

"Rebecca, I know better than that. I can tell there's something wrong by the tone of your voice."

"Please, I don't feel like arguing. Nothing is wrong. I'm just tired. I just want to get some sleep."

Chase knew now there was something drastically wrong if Rebecca didn't feel like arguing. He crouched beside her and reached for her. "Rebecca . . ."

"No! Go away!" Rebecca cried, scurrying away from him into a corner in the wagon.

To Chase, seeing her huddling in the corner, she looked like a little wounded animal. Damn it, he wished he could see her face. He caught her wrist and pulled her to her feet as he rose.

"What are you doing?" Rebecca asked, frantically jerking on her wrist as Chase pulled her to the back of the wagon.

"We're going inside the tepee where I can see your face when I talk to you," Chase answered. He shoved the tailgate down and jumped from the wagon, taking Rebecca with him.

"Put me down!" Rebecca cried.

"Sssh! Do you want to wake up the entire camp and have them out here ogling us?"

That was the last thing Rebecca wanted. Chase had already made a fool of her with one Comanche. She'd be damned if she'd let him humiliate her in front of the whole tribe.

Chase carried Rebecca into the tepee. As soon as he had set her down, she backed away from him. "Stay away from me," she said with a wild look in her eyes.

"Damn it, what's wrong with you?" he asked, stepping closer.

"No, don't touch me!" Rebecca cried. "Don't you ever touch me again!"

Chase was at the end of his patience. He caught her shoulders and jerked her to him. "To hell I won't touch you! Do you think after two months of struggling with myself and finally admitting I love you, I'm going to keep my hands off you?"

Rebecca didn't believe her ears and stared at him dumbly.

"Did you hear what I said? I said I love you," Chase said, throwing the words out as if they were a challenge.

"What—what about her?"

"Who?"

"Her! The Indian woman! I saw you with her this afternoon. I saw how you looked when you first saw her, *and* how she looked at you."

"So that's what this is all about," Chase said, finally understanding why Rebecca was so upset. He smiled and shook his head. "I don't love her, Rebecca. I thought I did—for years! It wasn't until

293

today that I realized the dream woman I'd been carrying around in my heart all those years wasn't at all what I wanted. I was a boy then. I'm a man now. I want more woman than Shining Water could ever be. I want you."

"Have you forgotten that I'm sharp-tongued and bad-tempered?"

Chase's dark eyes twinkled. "And obstinate, opinionated, and argumentative? No, I haven't forgotten. But I love you anyway."

"Well, you're not so perfect yourself, you know!"

"And?" Chase prompted. He held his breath, feeling very vulnerable. He had blurted out his love and really didn't know what Rebecca's feelings were for him.

Rebecca saw the expectant expression on his face and the fear in his eyes, which tugged at her heart. "And I love you too," she said in a low voice, for the first time allowing all of the love in her heart to show on her face.

Chase felt a surge of pure joy. He brought her to him, embracing her fiercely. Rebecca clung to him, tears of happiness glistening in her eyes, basking in the warm euphoria of knowing that he loved her.

For a long while they stood that way, content just to hold one another. Then Chase leaned back. "Were you jealous?" he asked.

Rebecca started to deny it, then remembered that she no longer had to hide anything from him. "Yes. I wanted to scratch her eyes out."

"You couldn't have been as jealous as I was of Two Feathers last night. Just the thought of another man touching you made me see red. I wanted to kill him!"

"Then why didn't you tell me that?"

"Rebecca, jealousy between brothers is taboo in the Comanche culture, particularly sexual jealousy. I was having a hard time admitting it to myself, much less to you."

Chase reached behind her neck and untied the ribbon that held her hair there. He smoothed the long, reddish-gold tresses over her shoulders, then lifted one strand, bent his head, and brought it to his lips.

The tender act shook Rebecca to the depths of her soul. Chase raised his head, and Rebecca saw the look in his eyes. It wasn't the blazing hot look of passion but the warm look of love, filling her so full of joy and happiness that she felt she would burst. Tears shone in her eyes.

Chase frowned and wiped his finger gently across her eye. "Why are you crying?"

"I never dreamed you could fall in love with me," Rebecca admitted.

Chase smiled. "I think I fell in love with you the first time I saw you, but I was too stubborn to admit it." His eyes drifted over her face. Then he said, "I want to love you. Not make love to you, but truly love you."

Rebecca nodded, wanting that too.

They undressed each other slowly, taking their time, touching, caressing, kissing, saying with their lips and hands the deep feelings that seemed so inadequate when put into words. When they were both naked, his dark eyes drifted over her, warmly, lovingly, and Rebecca reveled in that look, knowing that it was motivated by love and not just passion.

They sank to the pallet by the fire, their kisses achingly tender and sweet, their hands touching, caressing, exploring each inch of the other's body as if this were their first time. Both strove to keep their passion at bay, wanting to prolong this special loving, to savor their wondrous feelings.

In expressing their mutual love, their lovemaking took on a new, higher form of ecstasy, as souls and bodies together blended in the ultimate, perfect union.

Each tried to give the other the most pleasure possible and, in giving, received much more in return. Chase kissed every inch of her satiny skin, and Rebecca adored him in return. He brought her to the shuddering peak with his mouth, and Rebecca eagerly reciprocated, her tongue an instrument of exquisite torture, both surprising and pleasing Chase. Their kisses were deep and sensuous as their tongues danced and intertwined and their breaths mingled. Soon their senses were spinning, their pulses pounding, their blood racing like liquid fire.

When Chase had reached an almost unbearable peak of excitement, he rose over Rebecca, his body trembling with need. He entered her slowly—ever so slowly—savoring the feel of her surrounding his pulsating flesh, feeling as if he were drowning in that sweet, tight warmth. Then, when he was buried deep inside her, he sighed. If there had been any doubts in his mind as to what his feelings were for Rebecca, they had been firmly put to rest. He felt as if he had come home, a deep contentment stealing over him.

For a long time they lay, just savoring their joining, their closeness, his hard muscular flesh pressing against her soft comforting flesh, chest to chest, hip to hip, thigh to thigh, her soft warmth surrounding him where he lay deep inside her.

Chase lifted his dark head from where he had buried it in the crook of her neck. "Open your eyes, Rebecca," he whispered. "I want to see your eyes when I love you."

He bent and kissed her, tenderly, lovingly, as he began his thrusts—slowly, exquisitely, sensuously. Each deep, powerful stroke was pure rapture, each fiery passionate kiss ecstasy. Breaths quickened, hearts raced against each other, lips met with feverish abandon, sweat-slick bodies strained with urgency as they climbed steadily toward that glorious pinnacle. They held at that quivering zenith, breathless, trembling, until they felt they would burst. Then they soared over in a shattering explosion that tore their souls from their bodies and hurled them through time and space.

They slowly drifted back to reality, still trembling and still locked in that tight, sweet embrace. When their ragged breathing had finally returned to normal, Chase lifted his head and looked deeply into Rebecca's eyes. "I love you," he said in a voice thick with emotion.

"I love you too," Rebecca whispered.

He kissed her forehead, her nose, her lips, then started to rid her of his weight. Rebecca pulled him back down to her fiercely. "No, stay with me."

She placed his head between her breasts. Chase nuzzled and kissed the soft mounds, slipping his hands around her back, lying half over her. Soon Rebecca knew by his deep breathing that he was asleep.

Her hands drifted over his broad shoulders and muscular back, then cupped his head and held him to her. She fervently wished she could absorb him, take him totally inside of her and carry him beneath her heart forever, for although Chase had told her he loved her, she knew he would still leave her when their mission was over. He had made no commitment other than his love, nor would he. And while she would have the knowledge that he loved her as the greatest jewel in her treasure chest, she knew that Chase was not a man to be tied down by something as fragile as his heart. He was a man who could be bound to no woman, not by love, not by obligations, not by anything. No, she would still lose him in the end.

A silent tear slid down her cheek.

15

THE NEXT MORNING WHEN THEY WERE PREPARing to leave the Comanche camp, Eagle at Sunrise came to say farewell. He and Chase talked quietly for a few minutes, and then the chief walked over to where Rebecca stood at the side of the wagon.

Rebecca smiled at him. "Thank you for your hospitality, Eagle at Sunrise, and for being so patient with me yesterday during my outburst," she said.

"There is no need to thank me, Flame Woman."

"Flame Woman?" Rebecca asked in wonder.

"Yes, it is *Nim-ma* custom to name another after some distinguishing feature or attribute, particularly when those people have names that have no meaning to us."

"But Rebecca does have a meaning," Rebecca objected. "It's an old Hebrew name, meaning 'ensnarer.'"

Eagle at Sunrise smiled, thinking that the name was appropriate, after all. This Rebecca had snared his grandson's heart and, to be honest, a little of his too.

"And who are these Hebrews you speak of?"

"A very old race of people."

"As old as the *Nim-ma?*"

Rebecca suspected the Hebrews were older, but answered, "Yes, probably."

"Are they a wise people?"

"Yes, I suppose so. There was one man who was particularly noted for his wisdom. His name was Solomon. He was one of the Hebrews' kings."

Eagle at Sunrise gazed at Rebecca thoughtfully. His perusal made her feel uncomfortable. Again she felt as if he were gazing into her soul.

She smiled nervously. "Good-bye, Eagle at Sunrise."

"No, not good-bye, Rebecca. That sounds too final. We will meet again."

Rebecca knew differently. Once Chase had left her, she'd have no occasion to see his grandfather again. Her eyes drifted to Chase, who was occupied giving the harnesses a last minute check. At that minute all of the love and pain in her was mirrored in her eyes.

Eagle at Sunrise saw and said in a quiet voice, "It is not easy to love an eagle. It takes a very strong and wise woman to do so."

Rebecca glanced over at him. "I'm afraid that I don't understand what you mean," she said, confused.

So, she doesn't know his grandson's guardian spirit, the old chief realized. He had assumed Chase had told her, since they were so very close. The chief smiled, pleased that his grandson was holding to his Indian heritage so faithfully, for a

Comanche *never* revealed his guardian spirit to anyone, not even the woman he loved. But the chief was surprised that Rebecca hadn't guessed the nature of his grandson's spirit. She was unusually perceptive. He decided that it would only be a matter of time before she did.

The chief smiled at Rebecca. "Do not worry about it now. The time is not right. But someday you will understand my words and make a decision." He cocked his head and studied her thoughtfully. Then he said, "I think it will be a wise one."

Rebecca watched as Eagle at Sunrise turned and walked back to his tepee, wondering if the Comanches always talked in riddles.

Just as he had promised, Eagle at Sunrise gave them an escort to see them safely around Bexar. For a while the ten Comanches rode sedately beside the wagon, but once they had reached the open prairie, they grew restless and started racing their horses back and forth, exhibiting their remarkable riding skills.

One of the Indians raced his horse past their wagon and then disappeared over the animal's side, grinning at them from beneath the horse's neck. Another stood on his horse's back juggling three arrows as his mount sped across the prairie. Rebecca's eyes widened as another wiry Indian did flips back and forth on his horse's back, and yet another, holding his mount by its long mane, did flips while running beside the animal. Rebecca had never seen anything like it, these acrobats on horseback.

Chase chuckled. "They're just showing off."

"I've heard that Comanches were superior horsemen, but I never dreamed such things were possible. It's a wonder they don't break their necks."

Chase shrugged. "It's not all that dangerous. It's just a matter of skill and perfect coordination between man and horse."

Rebecca looked at him in wonder. "Can you do those things?"

"Most of them."

Rebecca looked at him incredulously.

"You don't believe me?" Chase asked. "Here, take the reins. I'll show you."

Suddenly Rebecca was afraid for him. "No, Chase," she objected, but Chase had disappeared into the wagon.

A moment later Lightning sped past her, with Chase on his bare back. Chase had stripped off his tunic to keep it from getting in his way, and as man and horse sped across the open prairie, Rebecca thought they were a beautiful sight. And then, as Chase joined in the performance, Rebecca was amazed. He *could* do all of the tricks the others were doing, plus a few others, including standing on his head.

As if not to be outdone, the other Indians began to perform even more amazing and dangerous feats. But it wasn't until she saw two braves standing on their horses' backs with their arms locked together galloping up to Chase that she became alarmed. She held her breath as Chase nimbly jumped from Lightning's back to the back of one of the horses racing beside him. Then, seeing what he was about to do, she called in a terrified voice, "No, Chase!"

But Chase either didn't hear, or ignored her. She watched, fear clutching at her heart, as he climbed to the shoulders of one brave, then stood, a foot straddling the shoulder of each Indian. Seeing they were going to jump a clump of cactus, she closed her eyes, then opened them, the agony of not knowing what had happened even worse. Miraculously, Chase was still standing on his lofty perch. It wasn't until he flipped backward to the ground and landed on his feet that Rebecca sucked in a deep breath.

A few minutes later Chase rode up to her and slipped to the wagon seat, grinning from ear to ear. Rebecca felt like throttling him. "Don't you ever do anything like that again!" she yelled. "You scared me to death."

Chase reached for the reins and said in a calm voice, "There was no reason for you to be frightened. I told you it was just a matter of coordination."

"You could have been killed!"

Chase said nothing, staring straight ahead. Rebecca realized that he was disappointed in her reaction. He had gone out to perform for her, wanting her to be proud of his skill, and here she was railing at him. Suddenly she hated herself for her unthinking words. She chewed her lip, then said tenderly, "But, Chase, you were magnificent."

The smile that came to his face more than made up for all of the terror she had experienced. She hugged his arm, thinking how very special he was and how proud she really was of his remarkable horsemanship.

During the two days and one night Rebecca was in the company of the Comanches, she discovered something that amazed her. The warriors who could be such fierce and deadly fighters could also be playful. Not only did they take pleasure in showing off their riding skills, but that night they wrestled and took delight in playing practical jokes on one another. But that didn't mean they weren't vigilant. Rebecca was very much aware of the two sentries patrolling farther out on the darkened prairie.

When they reached the road to Gonzales, the Comanches left them with much hooting, hollering, and waving, and Rebecca was sorry to see them leave. She realized that she would miss them.

Just as Rebecca had never been in Texas in the winter and witnessed a blue norther, she had never been in Texas in the springtime and seen the bluebonnets blooming. At first there were just a few patches of the flowers here and there, and then, almost as if overnight, the whole landscape was filled with them. A solid mass of deep blue stretched across the horizon, so blue that the white tips on every individual flower was obliterated. It was a breathtaking sight, rolling hill after rolling hill of blue, broken only by an occasional oak tree or clump of cactus. Rebecca hated to see the wagon rolling over the wildflowers and the horses trampling the delicate plants, but Chase assured her that they would be back next year, just as they had for thousands of years.

The ride to Gonzales was tense, for they had no idea where Santa Anna's army was, whether in front or behind them. When they rolled into the town, which lay beside the Guadalupe River, they were shocked. The entire town had been burned, its houses nothing but blackened shells.

Rebecca looked at one burned-out home. The only thing left standing was its fireplace. "Do you think Santa Anna did this?" she asked Chase.

"It's possible, considering his fondness for burning things," Chase answered bitterly.

The silence was eerie. A lone mockingbird sang in the woods on the other side of the river, the sound somehow making the stillness all the more ominous.

"What do you suppose happened to the people?"

Chase had been wondering that himself. Had they fled, or had Santa Anna taken them all prisoner?

"You don't think Santa Anna killed them?" Rebecca asked, horrified.

"It's possible," Chase replied in a grim voice.

"But they're civilians! Surely he wouldn't kill civilians."

"Have you forgotten what he did to the honorable prisoners of war at Goliad? That bastard is capable of anything!"

Rebecca looked about her, feeling sick to her stomach. Chase stopped the wagon and climbed down, walking to one of the ruins. He bent and felt a blackened timber, then rose and walked back to the wagon, brushing the charcoal off his hands.

As he climbed back into the wagon, he said, "Whatever happened, it wasn't recent. That timber is stone cold."

Slowly they drove through the deserted streets of Gonzales, shocked by the utter destruction they saw. Everything had been burned—all of the buildings, wagons, stables, even the fences. Rebecca saw a rag doll laying in the middle of the road. Somehow it had managed to escape the holocaust. The sight tore at Rebecca's heart as she wondered what had happened to the little girl it had belonged to.

Then suddenly an old, gray-haired man stepped out from behind a fireplace and limped into the road in front of them.

Chase stopped the wagon and, motioning to the burned-out town, asked, "Did Santa Anna do this?"

"Nope," the old-timer replied, spitting a mouthful of tobacco juice on the ground. "Houston did."

"Houston?" Rebecca gasped. "But why?"

"When Deaf Smith, Houston's scout, found Mrs. Dickerson and that bunch of Mexican women out wandering on the prairie, he brought them back here to the general. That was the first we heard about the Alamo falling. Houston didn't know where Santa Anna was. For all he knew, he could've been marching down on us right then. So he ordered an immediate retreat. Took all the civilians with him and left a rear guard with orders to burn everything and sink the cannons in the river."

"He sank his cannons in the river?" she asked, shocked.

"Sure did. He couldn't take those cannons with him. Not in the condition the roads were in. And he sure wouldn't leave them behind for Santa Anna to capture."

"What was wrong with the roads?" Chase asked.

The old man peered out from beneath bushy, gray eyebrows, then asked, "Where in the hell you been, mister?"

"West of Bexar."

"Well, I don't know what the weather was like over there, but it's been doing a heap of raining around here. Was raining hard that day, and cold too. The roads were muddy clear up to your ankles. He couldn't drag no heavy cannons in that muck. Slow him down too much. Took his supply wagons, but he wouldn't let most of the townspeople take theirs, 'cause he was afraid they'd get bogged down. Most of them went on foot."

"When was that?" Chase asked.

The old man scratched his tobacco-stained beard thoughtfully. "The night of March thirteenth."

"That long ago, huh? Well, where was Houston heading?" Chase asked.

"All I know is he was heading for the Colorado. Heard him telling the rear guards to meet him at Burnham's Crossing."

Chase nodded. "Have any idea where Santa Anna might be?"

"Well, I can tell you one thing for sure. He ain't

307

in Bexar no more. I know 'cause I watched him march through here. Biggest damned army I ever seen. Infantry, cavalry, artillery. Had more than a dozen cannons and a couple of them short, funny-looking ones. What do you call them?"

"Howitzers?"

"Yep. And I ain't never seen so many baggage wagons, two-wheel carts, and pack mules in all my life. Took those Mexicans hours to pass through here."

"When was this?" Chase asked.

"Couple of days ago."

Why had Santa Anna waited so long to march? Chase wondered. It had been over a month since the Alamo fell.

"You're sure it was Santa Anna and not General Urrea's army, coming from Goliad?" Chase asked.

"Nope, it was Santa Anna, all right. I saw all of them fancy, gilded coaches he takes with him when he goes on campaign. I reckon you've heard of them. The coaches he uses to tote his silk tent and his special sheets, furniture, gold-plate dishes, and do-dads in?"

"Yes, I've heard of them," Chase answered in disgust.

Rebecca had been observing the old man while he talked. He was thin and stoop-shouldered, his buckskins in tatters. "Was one of these your home?" she asked in concern.

"Nope. I got me a shack back in them woods," he answered, motioning to the thick woods that ran along the clear-flowing Guadalupe. "I tole them rear-guard fellas iffen they tried to burn my shack, I'd put a ball through their heads." He grinned, showing a lot of gaps in his teeth. "Reckon they believed me. Didn't see hide nor hair of them 'round my place."

"Why didn't you leave with the others?" Chase asked.

"Hellfire! I ain't running. I ain't 'fraid of a few Mexicans."

A *few* Mexicans? Rebecca thought in disbelief.

Chase asked the old man the best place to ford the Guadalupe, and while they talked, Rebecca turned her attention back to the burned town, her thoughts again on the refugees who had fled, taking only those possessions they could carry. And when they returned, they would come back to this, she thought sadly. But then, if the Texians lost this war, the refugees would never come back. The land would revert to a wilderness.

As they drove away Rebecca felt heavy-hearted. She looked back over her shoulder and saw the old man standing in the blackened ruins. "Maybe we should make him come with us," she said in a worried voice.

"*Make* him?" Chase laughed. "If Houston couldn't make him leave, then we sure can't."

"But he's just an old, half-crippled man, all alone out here by himself."

"Stop worrying about him, Rebecca. He's a tough old cougar. One of those rugged mountain men. Those kind can survive anything."

They crossed the Guadalupe River and followed the road that led to Burnham's Crossing. At first they moved slowly and cautiously, half expecting to run into a rear guard of Santanistas or stumble into a skirmish between the two armies. But the road was completely deserted, and despite their caution, they made good time. When they reached the Colorado, they could see no signs of either Houston's or Santa Anna's army, or anything that might hint of a battle taking place there.

Chase and Rebecca stood on the banks of the wide, muddy river, looking perplexed.

"Maybe Houston didn't even come this way," Rebecca suggested.

"No, he crossed here and the river was flooding when he did. Look at those wagons."

Rebecca looked downstream to where Chase was pointing. The wreckage of several wagons were strewn on the banks. "Will we be able to make it across?" she asked fearfully.

"Yes. The water's down. It might be a little deep in the main channel though." Chase looked at the horizon and frowned. "But I know one thing. We'd better get across before *that* hits, or it will be too late."

Rebecca's eyes swiveled to the horizon. A line of dark, angry thunderheads was rapidly approaching. She glanced back down at the river, seeing the waves that the wind preceding the storm was kicking up.

Chase handed her the reins. "You drive. I'll get Lightning and guide the horses across."

A few minutes later Chase was mounted and rode up beside the lead mare on the downstream side. "Move them out!" he called back to Rebecca.

Rebecca glanced at the river. At that minute it

looked just as angry as the sky above them, the water reflecting the dark sky as the thunderheads obliterated the sun and gusts of wind buffeted it. She swallowed hard and flicked the reins. The mares moved ahead, splashing into the water, the heavy wagon lumbering behind them. The water rose to the horses' bellies, then their sides. Rebecca's heart sank when she saw the horses suddenly dip in the water and realized that they were swimming.

"The channel's deeper than I thought!" Chase called back. "If that wagon starts sinking, get the hell out of it while I cut the horses loose!"

"Get out?" Rebecca shrieked in terror, for she couldn't swim. "Jump in the river?"

"No! Jump onto the horse's back in front of you!"

Rebecca felt the wagon wheels leave the riverbed as the wagon dipped, and the back of the wagon swayed in the current. She held her breath, terrified that the wagon, with its heavy load of cannons, would sink to the bottom. Realizing her feet were wet, she glanced down and saw the wagon bed was flooded. She stood, ready to jump to the horse's back, then realized that the wagon was floating, that the water was coming from the waves being washed over it. Weakly she sank back to the wagon seat.

A crash of thunder followed by a blinding flash of lightning made Rebecca jump and frightened the horses, who were already nervous as they labored to swim across the thrashing river. They whinnied in terror, wall-eyed, veering sharply and trying to swim downstream with the current. Chase yelled at them and slapped the lead mare's flank, while Lightning, sensing the danger, nipped at her neck and snorted a shrill warning.

The wagon rocked as the gusts of wind hit it, followed by another deafening crash of thunder. Then the rain came, sudden and torrential, drenching Rebecca in seconds. She looked at the solid sheet of water before her, straining her eyes to see the bank, thinking that they would never make it across that damned river. And then, just as suddenly as they had dropped into the depths of the main channel, they emerged from it. Rebecca felt the wagon wheels catch on the solid sandy bottom, saw the horses' flanks, then their legs. She sobbed as the horses rushed up the bank, her tears of relief mingling with the rain that was lashing her face.

Chase rode back and slipped from Lightning to the wagon seat, taking the reins. And not a minute too soon. Another crack of lightning sent a jagged blue-white streak across the darkened sky, and the mares reared, trying to bolt. Rebecca would have never been able to control the frightened animals. Finally they settled down, stamping their feet, their harnesses jingling.

Within minutes the worst of the storm had passed, and Chase climbed down and unsaddled Lightning, then took him to the back of the wagon to tie him. There the three loose mares stood, still trembling after their frantic swim to follow Lightning across the river.

When Chase climbed back on the wagon seat,

Rebecca was shivering from her wet clothes. He frowned. "You'd better get something dry on before you catch cold."

Rebecca nodded and climbed into the back of the wagon. She looked down at the water in the wagon bed, and then, seeing that her feather mattress was soaked, she felt fresh tears in her eyes. She stooped and opened her trunk, only to discover that the water had seeped in there too, and everything was wet. Then, as the wagon lurched when Chase called to the horses, she snatched up her cloak, which had been hanging on a hook, wrapped it around her, then climbed back on the wagon seat.

Chase glanced over at her questioningly. "Everything is wet back there, including the mattress," Rebecca explained in disgust.

"It'll dry out."

"Yes, but not by nightfall," she answered, wondering what they were going to sleep on.

Chase guessed her thoughts. "I still have my bedroll. It's wrapped in oilskins, so it should be dry."

But it's only one blanket, Rebecca thought, not in the least encouraged by his words.

Not far from the river, two smaller roads forked from the main road. Chase stopped the wagon. "Damn it, I don't know which road to take. I don't know if Houston went north to Bastrop, or south to Columbia, or east to San Felipe."

Rebecca scanned the area. The rain was a miserable drizzle now, and everything looked gray and gloomy. She was still cold beneath her cloak, and all she wanted to do was snuggle up to a warm fire. Then her eyes caught the sight of smoke drifting up into the sky to the right of them.

"Look, Chase!" she cried in an excited voice. "Maybe Houston is camped near here after all."

Chase looked to where Rebecca was pointing. "No, I don't think so. If that were true, there'd be more fires. That's probably a settlers' cabin. But we might be able to get some information from them."

Chase turned the wagon and followed the road leading south, turning onto a small trail that wound through a thick woods and led to the isolated cabin.

When they drove into the clearing, Rebecca was pleasantly surprised. The cabin was much larger than the usual two-room, dog-trot cabin frequently seen in Texas. She gazed longingly at the chimney towering over it, knowing that inside there was a warm fire burning.

They had no sooner stopped the wagon than a middle-aged, short, chubby woman stepped out of the cabin and onto the small porch. Rebecca gasped, seeing that the rifle the woman held was pointed at them. Then, noticing Rebecca, the woman frowned and lowered the rifle.

"Land's sake!" the woman said. "Where'd you two come from?"

"West of Bexar," Chase answered. "I'm Chase Winters and this is Rebecca."

"Well, you look like two half-drowned cats. Climb down off that wagon and come in where it's warm."

Rebecca supposed they did look awful, with their soaking wet clothes and their hair plastered to their heads. And she certainly didn't need any further encouragement to go inside where it was warm. She scrambled from the wagon seat before Chase could even help her down.

After Rebecca hurried to stand before the warm fire, she looked about her. Two toddlers and a boy of about five were playing by the fireplace. From the corner of her eye, she caught a glimpse of a girl about eight peeking around from what Rebecca assumed must be a bedroom.

Shutting the door behind Chase as he walked in, the woman said, "I'm Martha Johnson. Have a seat at that table over by the fire."

Chase and Rebecca walked to the split-log table and benches. Before they sat, Chase slipped off Rebecca's cloak and tossed it down on one of the benches.

"Gracious, child!" Martha said to Rebecca. "You're soaking wet clear to the skin."

"Yes, I know," Rebecca replied. "I got wet crossing the river in the storm. I was going to change, but everything inside our wagon got wet too."

"You crossed the river in that storm?" Martha asked, shocked.

"We were afraid if we didn't cross then, the water would rise and we wouldn't be able to," Chase explained.

"You're probably right," Martha said. "Seems like all that river's been doing lately is flooding. Never saw such a wet spring." She turned to Rebecca. "You're welcome to wear one of my dresses till yours dries out."

Rebecca knew the dress would swallow her. Martha could make two of her. "No, thank you. It will dry out quickly, now that I'm near a fire."

Martha placed a cup of hot coffee before each of them. "I thought you were kinda late for runners when I saw your wagon drive up, but I reckon if you're coming all the way from Bexar that explains it."

"What do you mean, runners?" Rebecca asked.

"I'm talking about the Runaway Scrape."

Seeing the bewildered looks on their faces, Martha said, "Ain't you heard 'bout that? When Houston pulled his army back from the Colorado, after he heard that terrible news about Fannin's defeat at Coleto, 'most everyone in East Texas started running for the Sabine, including the new Governor and the government," Martha added in anger.

"Do you know where Houston went when he left here?" Chase asked.

Martha poured herself a cup of coffee and sat down opposite them. "I sure do. My husband and oldest son went with him. Jacob, my husband, came home for a few days to see how we were doing and told me everything. First Houston marched them to San Felipe and then—" Martha stopped in midsentence and slapped the hand of her small son as he reached for a pan sitting on the table. "Git your hand out of there, Tommy! That cornbread is for supper." She turned to Chase and Rebecca. " 'Cuse me. These pesky young'uns git into everything, if you don't watch them. Now, where was I?"

"You were going to say where Houston marched his army after they left San Felipe," Chase prompted.

"They marched north, following the Brazos River. Jacob said that was a terrible trip, rainy and cold, wagons gitting stuck in the mud or overturning in the flooding creeks. To make things even worse, the roads were full of runners, and everyone was sick with colds, flu, and pneumonia. By the time they finally reached Groce's plantation, a fourth of the men were too sick to march. That's where they're at now. Groce's plantation on the Brazos. Houston has been fattening them up and drilling them there."

"Aren't you afraid to stay here by yourself?" Rebecca asked.

"Nope. We're far enough off the trail not to be noticed. I'll admit I was a little nervous the day the Mexicans crossed the Colorado though. Had my son keeping an eye out for them. We doused our fire and hid in the woods, but they didn't come down this way. They took the main road to San Felipe."

Martha rose and walked to the fireplace. Grinning, she took the cake that was sitting on the high mantel down and carried it back to the table. "I have to keep it up there, or the young'uns git into it," she explained.

After she had served Rebecca and Chase a slice of cake and refilled their cups of coffee, Martha cut a small slice for the children, who had crowded around her like bees to honey.

Martha looked a little sheepish. "I know I shouldn't let them have this cake. It'll spoil their supper. But I guess I have a tendency to spoil them, particularly with Jacob gone and all."

Rebecca took a bite of the pound cake and savored its sweet taste. It had been so long since she'd had dessert of any kind, not since she had left Natchez. She gazed about the cozy kitchen, then, noticing the shingles missing on the roof at one corner, asked, "Did the wind blow your shingles off?"

"Nope," Martha said, an irritated look coming over her face. "I told Jacob 'fore he left that I was running low on firewood and he needed to chop some more for me 'fore he went back to the army. He said he was in a hurry and knew how capable I was, that I could manage to git it done somehow. So I've just been using the shingles on the roof for firewood."

Chase, who was just swallowing a piece of cake, choked on it and looked at the woman, astounded. Was she crazy? he thought. Making those shingles was hard, tedious work, shaving them from the log at just the right depth.

Martha smiled smugly. "I reckon when he comes home and sees the roof, the next time I ask him to chop some wood for me, he won't be in such a danged hurry to git away."

Rebecca thought Martha's method of teaching her husband a lesson both apt and funny. She laughed outright. But Chase couldn't see the humor in it. He was horrified.

The front door slammed open, and a blond boy of about nine rushed in, crying in an excited voice "Ma, there's a wagon sitting out—" The boy came to an abrupt halt, staring open-mouthed at Chase and Rebecca.

"I know all about it, Will," Martha answered. "It belongs to Mr. and Mrs. Winters here. Now you run back out and unharness those horses for Mr. Winters and put them in the corral."

Neither Chase nor Rebecca bothered to correct Martha when she said Mr. and Mrs. Winters, knowing that a long explanation would be called for, something which neither wished to take the time or trouble to do.

"You will stay the night, won't you?" Martha asked them. "Ain't no need in you trying to make any more distance today. It'll be dark in an hour or so. You can sleep in my bedroom."

"But we can't take your bedroom," Rebecca objected.

"Sure you can. I'll sleep in the other bedroom with the girls. That way you can get a fresh start in the morning."

The thought of sleeping in a real bed with a roof over her head sounded heavenly to Rebecca. But it was really up to Chase. She looked at him with pleading eyes.

"Thank you, Mrs. Johnson. We'll stay. It's very kind of you to ask us." He looked at the boy and said, "Leave the white stallion that's tied to the back, Will. He's skittish. I'll take care of him later."

"Yes, sir," Will answered. He eyed the cake sitting on the table, saying "Ma, can I have—"

"Later, after you've put the horses up," Martha interjected. "And while you're out there tell Betsy to stop dawdling with her milking. She needs to git busy on the butter, if we're gonna have any for supper tonight."

"Yes'm," the boy answered, hurrying out the door.

Rebecca offered to help with the evening meal, but Martha refused her. "No, thanks. I got my girls to help me. You jest make yourselves comfortable. Or maybe you'd like to bring in your trunk and lay your clothes out, so they can dry. You said everything got wet when you was crossing the river."

"Yes, I would, if you don't mind," Rebecca replied.

"Shucks, no. Been so wet this spring, I've been having to do most of my clothes drying in the cabin. We're used to it."

Chase went out to get the trunk. While he was outside, he put Lightning in the corral with the other horses and fed them. Will followed him around, asking questions about the white stallion. Chase related the story of how he had captured Lightning.

When they walked back into the cabin, Will said in an excited voice, "Ma, you should see the fine horse Mr. Winters has. He says he's one of them wild horses he captured and he can run faster than any horse he'd ever seen and—"

"Calm down, Will," Martha said in a firm voice. "You can tell us all 'bout it after supper. Now run out to the smokehouse and git me some of them sausages."

Will frowned. It was obvious he didn't want to leave Chase. "Go on, now. Stop your dawdling!" Martha said.

The boy left the cabin reluctantly, and Martha said to Chase, "I hope he ain't been pestering you. Land's sake, that boy can ask more questions."

"No, Mrs. Johnson. I've enjoyed his company. He has a sharp mind," Chase answered.

Martha smiled with maternal pride. "Yep, he's smart as a whip. Don't know what I'd do without him with his pa and older brother gone off to war."

"How old is your oldest son?" Rebecca asked.

"Sixteen." A worried look came over Martha's face. "I didn't want him to go. Told him he was too young. But ever since he heard there was a fifteen-year-old boy at the Alamo, he'd been itching to join the army."

"There was a fifteen-year-old boy at the Alamo?" Rebecca repeated in a shocked voice.

"Yep. We found out about it when some of the Gonzales refugees passed through here, after Houston saw them safely across the Colorado. The boy was with the men from Gonzales that slipped into the Alamo after it was surrounded. He was their cannon boy."

Martha was quiet for a while, and Rebecca knew that she was thinking of the boy who had died at the Alamo and that his mother had probably not wanted her son to go to war either. And then, with that special fortitude and bravery that marked the Texas frontier woman, she smiled and said cheerfully, "Let me hang up that line, so you can git your clothes dried out."

While Martha cooked supper, and Betsy, a pretty, shy eleven-year-old, churned the butter, Rebecca hung up her wet clothes. She looked over and saw that Chase was cornered by Will, the boy asking questions about mustanging. Soon the younger children crowded around, and Chase bent and pulled one toddler up on his lap. Rebecca felt a pang, seeing the little girl snuggle up to Chase. At that minute she wished desperately that she could bear Chase's children, that they could share a home like this one some day, but she knew that it was impossible, and a deep sadness invaded her.

But Rebecca couldn't remain melancholy for long—not around Martha. The woman chattered gaily, obviously pleased to have some adult company. When they sat down to eat, the food looked like a feast for the gods: sausages with pan gravy, mashed potatoes, home-canned green beans and spiced crabapples, cornbread dripping with fresh-churned butter. Rebecca thought that the food was the best she had ever tasted and said so.

Martha laughed at her compliment. "It ain't all that special. It's jest that you've been eating camp food for so long. I know when Jacob and I traveled out here, the trip took so long, I didn't think I'd ever see a decent home-cooked meal again." She paused, then asked, "Jest where is your home? You said you come from west of Bexar. Ain't too many white folks out there."

Rebecca and Chase exchanged looks, then Chase said, "We're not actually from Bexar. We were taking some cannons to the Alamo, but we arrived too late. Since then we've been chasing all over Texas, trying to deliver them to Houston."

"I didn't see any cannons," Martha objected.

"They're dismantled and hidden in a false bottom in the wagon," Chase explained.

"Land's sake!" Martha said in amazement. If she thought it strange that Rebecca would accompany her husband on such a dangerous mission, she was too polite to say so. "Well, I reckon the army really needs them. Jacob said they jest have those two the citizens of Cincinnati, Ohio, gave them."

"Oh? When was that?" Chase asked.

"Jest since they arrived at Groce's plantation. Jacob said the men named them the Twin Sisters."

Later that evening Martha shooed her brood off to bed. The boys climbed the ladder to the loft above the main cabin, each taking a toddler with him, and the two girls disappeared into a small bedroom off the side of the big room.

The adults talked for another hour or so, and then Martha showed Rebecca and Chase where they would sleep. Rebecca grabbed one of her nightgowns off the line of clothes that were drying and followed her, Chase ambling behind them.

The bedroom was small and far from luxurious, but Rebecca thought the bed looked absolutely heavenly. As soon as Martha left the room, closing

323

the door softly behind her, Rebecca undressed and slipped on her gown, then made a beeline for the bed. The sheets were made of a coarse but fresh-smelling cotton, and Rebecca knew that Martha must have sent one of the girls in to change them while the adults were talking. She snuggled in, thinking that nothing felt as good as a soft feather mattress—on springs.

Chase blew out the candle, stripped, and slipped under the covers beside her. He pulled her to him and frowned when he felt Rebecca's gown between them.

He fingered the loose sleeve. "I don't know why you persist in wearing these damned things."

"Because they keep me warm," Rebecca answered sleepily.

"I'll keep you warm," Chase whispered huskily, running his mouth down the slim column of her throat and pulling her even closer. Rebecca shivered at the feel of his lips nibbling at her earlobe and then his tongue at that ultrasensitive spot just below her ear, thinking that this was what heaven was made of, lying in the arms of the man you loved on a real bed.

Chase swept soft kisses across her cheek and captured her mouth in a deep, fiery kiss that left her breathless. She gasped softly as his warm hand cupped one of her full breasts, his slender fingers massaging, then brushing across the sensitive peak through the material of her gown, the bud hardening and rising under his hand. As Chase lowered his head, kissing and nuzzling her neck, Rebecca heard one of the girls in the next room asking her mother a question—and froze.

"Chase!" she whispered.

Chase muttered incoherently, nuzzling her breasts where he had bared them after unbuttoning her gown.

Rebecca caught her breath as Chase's mouth closed over one throbbing peak. She caught his head and tried to pull him away, whispering urgently "No, Chase! I don't think we—"

Her eyes widened as Chase's hand slipped between her thighs. And when his hand cupped her there, it was all Rebecca could do to struggle for reason.

"Chase, no!" she muttered.

"No, what?" Chase muttered back, shifting his weight.

Rebecca could feel him, hot and throbbing, against her thigh. But it was the squeak of the bedsprings when Chase had moved that caught her attention. To her ears, the slight sound had sounded as loud as a cannon shot.

"The noise. They'll hear. These walls are paperthin."

Chase raised his head, his eyes darkened with passion. "What noise?" he asked, his voice thick with desire.

"The bed springs. They squeak."

Chase moved tentatively. The bed squeaked. Another slight movement brought the same results, only louder. He lay for a moment, listening, hearing every movement of the woman and two girls in the bedroom next to them.

325

"God damn it!" he muttered, flipping Rebecca's gown down and rolling to his back.

For a few minutes they lay side by side, both tense, still aching for fulfillment. Finally Chase threw the covers back and climbed from the bed, jerking on his buckskins.

"Where are you going?" Rebecca whispered.

"Out! For a walk," Chase whispered back.

"But it's still raining out there," Rebecca objected.

"I know. And I hope to God it's cold too. Maybe it will cool me off."

After Chase had slipped from the room, closing the door quietly behind him, Rebecca wondered if Martha had heard him leave and guessed what had happened. Rebecca flushed hotly, hoping the woman would think that he'd gone out to check on the horses. Rebecca lay on the big bed, feeling very lonely, her body still burning from Chase's touch. She fervently wished that they had turned down Martha's invitation to spend the night. Even if her mattress was damp, with no springs, she would have been in Chase's arms—and therein lay real heaven.

16

THE NEXT MORNING REBECCA FOLDED HER clothes and put them in her trunk while Martha cooked breakfast.

"Your husband is sure a fine-looking man, Rebecca," Martha commented.

He isn't my husband, nor will he ever be, Rebecca thought sadly, then smiled. "Thank you. I think so too."

"Where'd you meet him?"

"In Louisiana."

"I figured he had some French blood in him, with his dark skin. 'Course you're a right purdy woman yourself. Land's sake, you two sure do make a striking couple."

Rebecca wished Martha would stop talking about her and Chase. It wasn't making her feel any better. The closer they came to Houston's army, the more Rebecca was dreading delivering the cannons. Then her time with Chase would come to an end.

Chase walked in, thankfully distracting Martha.

"I chopped you some firewood, Mrs. Johnson," he said.

"Why, you didn't have to do that, Mr. Winters."

"It's the least I could do after your hospitality," Chase answered. In truth, Chase had chopped the firewood because he couldn't stand the thought of her burning any more shingles.

"Well, that's right nice of you," Martha answered. "Don't know how long this war might last." She turned and winked at Rebecca. "Now I'll have something to burn when I've used up all those shingles."

Chase choked back a gasp and stared at her. Rebecca suppressed a giggle.

After a huge breakfast of bacon, eggs, and flapjacks, dripping with butter and molasses, Rebecca and Chase prepared to leave. Martha stood talking to Rebecca while Chase saddled the horses, looking sad at their leaving. Rebecca felt sorry for the woman, knowing that she must be lonely, being isolated out there in the wilderness. Texas wasn't heavily populated anywhere, but there were more settlers east of the Brazos.

"If you ever get in these parts again, you come visit," Martha said as Rebecca climbed into the wagon.

Rebecca sat and smiled down at her. "We will."

Will ran up to his mother, followed by the other children, saying excitedly "Look what Mr. Winters gave us, Ma. A Comanche arrow. He said it's for the whole family."

Rebecca's eyebrows rose in surprise when she

saw the arrow in Will's hand. She had seen it in Chase's saddlebags and assumed it was a keepsake.

Chase saw Martha frown and peer at the arrow, as if she expected to see bloodstains on it. "That's not an ordinary warrior's arrow, Mrs. Johnson. It's a ceremonial arrow."

"Land's sake! A ceremonial arrow?" Martha said, her eyes wide with wonder. "Why, I didn't know there was such a thing. Where did you get it?"

"From a Comanche chief who's . . . a friend of mine."

"Well, I'll be," Martha said, obviously impressed. "We thank you kindly, Mr. Winters. I'll put it over the mantel, along with the old flintlock that belonged to my husband's grandpappy."

When they pulled away from the Johnson homestead, Chase turned east, toward San Felipe. In the days that followed, as they moved farther east, Chase and Rebecca saw more and more deserted cabins left by settlers who had panicked and fled. Throughout the countryside around these homes, pigs, chickens, and an occasional cow roamed, turned loose to fend for themselves.

At one cabin, the door was left wide open, and Chase stopped the wagon to close it, fearing that some wild animal might enter it in search of food and destroy any valuable furniture inside, or the rain might blow in. As he crossed the clearing he noticed the clothes still hanging on the line and the full corncrib. When he reached in to pull the door shut, he saw the unmade beds and the half-eaten meal on the table, all testimony of the haste with which the settlers had abandoned their home.

And then he saw a flintlock hanging above the mantel. He looked at it thoughtfully, then walked to the fireplace and snatched it down from its wooden mounting. Spying two powder horns and a pouch of balls lying on the mantel, he picked them up too. Then he turned and walked from the cabin, closing the door firmly behind him.

When Rebecca saw the flintlock, her eyes widened. "You're not going to steal their gun?" she asked.

"No, I'm going to borrow it. This gun isn't doing them any good, wherever they are. And since I lost my Hawkens at Goliad, we can use it. At the end of the war, if the Texians win, I'll bring it back. If they lose, these people won't be coming back for it."

Chase looked about him. "I hope to God the Indians stay quiet and don't take advantage of this hysterical exodus. Can you imagine the looting and burning they could do to these homes, to say nothing of the mayhem they would cause if they attacked those settlers on the open road? And I wonder how many settlers are totally unarmed."

Rebecca shivered, saying a silent prayer.

When they reached San Felipe, they found the same thing they had found at Gonzales—blackened rubble. The small settlement on the Brazos River had been burned to the ground, and this time there was no stalwart old-timer around to tell them if the destruction had been ordered by Santa Ana or Houston.

They stood on the banks of the Brazos where the ferry landing had been before it had been burned, gazing across the wide river, whose water had a reddish tint from the iron-rich sandy soil around it. The area around the river was heavily wooded, the trees covered with thick wild grape-vines.

Rebecca squinted and pointed downstream. "There's some kind of a canoe down there, under that pecan tree."

Chase looked in the direction Rebecca had indicated. Seeing the crude dugout, bark still on the log, his eyes quickly scanned the river bottom. "Come on! Let's get out of here!" He took Rebecca's arm and rushed her to the wagon.

"Why? What did you see?" Rebecca asked, running to keep up with his rapid strides.

"That's a Kronk canoe," Chase answered in a grim voice.

Rebecca came to a dead halt, her face ashen. "Do you mean those Karankawa Indians who live on the islands off the coast? Those cannibals?" Rebecca's voice squeaked on her last words.

"Yes. Now come on," Chase said, pushing her forward.

"You saw them?" Rebecca asked over her shoulder as Chase shoved her into the wagon so fast that she stumbled.

"I didn't have to see them to know they're around!" Chase snapped, thinking that she could pick the damndest times to ask questions.

Chase snapped the reins loudly, startling the mares and sending them lurching forward. Strug-

331

gling to hold on, Rebecca glanced to the side and froze as she saw the Indians running at them from the woods.

There were only six of them, but to Rebecca, there might as well have been six hundred, for the Karankawas were the most terrifying sight she had ever seen. A good foot taller than other Indians she had seen, their bodies were powerful and muscular, and they were totally naked, their skin completely covered with wild, bluish tattoos, their bows almost as long as the Indians were tall. The Kronks' noses, lower lips, and breasts were pierced with bone or cane cuttings, and they didn't howl like other Indians, but shrieked, a nerve-shattering sound that sent Rebecca's skin crawling and her heart racing in fear.

Chase raced the wagon up the incline of the riverbed through a narrow trail, the trees beside them a mere blur, the wagon bouncing on the rutted road. "Here," Chase said, handing Rebecca the reins, "take these and keep them running fast."

"Where are you going?" Rebecca asked.

"To the back of the wagon to untie Lightning before they kill him." He snatched up the rifle from under the seat. "I'll pick them off from there."

Rebecca's heart was pounding as loud as the horses' hooves as she tried to guide the speeding mares down the narrow, twisting trail. A moment later Lightning and the three mares rushed ahead of her and the six mares pulling the wagon. Seeing Lightning in front of them, the mares harnessed to the wagon ran even faster, and it was all Rebecca could do to hold on to the reins.

Ahead of them, Rebecca could see the narrow road turning sharply. She tried frantically to slow the racing horses, pulling hard on the reins, terrified the wagon would roll over if the mares tried to make that turn at the speed they were going. But her efforts were useless. The mares took the turn at full gallop, and for a long moment that seemed a lifetime to Rebecca, the wagon leaned precariously, rolling on two wheels. Then, when it slammed back down, the back wheels skidded on loose rocks and the back of the wagon whipped around, slamming violently into a big tree. Rebecca felt the impact and heard the sound of wood splintering, then a loud thump as Chase was flung from one side of the wagon to the other.

Over the pounding hooves, Rebecca could hear him cursing. "Are you all right?" she called over her shoulder, afraid to look back for fear of taking her eyes off the speeding mares.

"Yes, it just threw me," Chase called back. "But I can't get a clear bead on any of those bastards until we get out of these woods."

A moment later they raced into a broad meadow, and several arrows whizzed by them. Lightning circled back to the side of the mares pulling the wagon, nipping at their ears and biting their flanks, driving them to an even faster speed. Rebecca heard the rifle explode as Chase fired, then fired again. The wind rushed past her, flapping her hair wildly around her face as Rebecca counted the shots. Chase was firing and loading as fast as was possible with a flintlock, getting off two shots a minute, but to Rebecca it seemed a lifetime between shots.

Then she glanced to her side and blinked, not believing her eyes. A Karankawa warrior ran beside her, loping effortlessly, not even appearing in the least winded. Rebecca had heard that Kronks could run as fast as the swiftest horse but had always thought the tale a gross exaggeration. Now the proof of their running skill raced right beside her.

She stared at the warrior, terrified. His face was splotched with multicolored tattoos, his nose and lower lip pierced with bones. He had an unusually large head and flat forehead. His dark hair had a reddish hue about it, and the long, greasy strands flew out behind him, while a necklace of shells dangled from his neck and bounced on his chest, looking incongruous against his nudity. He reeked of some overpowering odor, the stench almost suffocating.

He turned his head and looked at Rebecca. With his lower lip dangling from the weight of the bone, he seemed to be grinning at her fiendishly, as if he were taking perverse pleasure in her horror. Rebecca watched, mesmerized, as he raised his tomahawk, his black eyes glittering with gruesome anticipation of his kill. She stared at the brutal stone club, knowing that she was looking death in the eye, yet too frightened to move or even scream.

Suddenly she was pushed forward to her knees. The tomahawk whizzed by her head, and Chase's rifle roared in her ears. The Karankawa's chest seemed to explode as he was flung backward from the impact of the ball.

Chase took the reins from Rebecca's trembling hands. He helped her back to the seat with one hand as he pulled the reins back with the other. "Whoa!" he called to the frantic horses. "Whoa, girls!"

But the horses had smelled the Karankawa's stench too, a smell that had terrorized them even more. Chase had to hold the reins with both hands and pull with all of his strength before the animals finally slowed and came to a stop.

Rebecca had been in a daze since her near brush with death. The first thing she heard when she drifted out of it was the horses' labored breathing and nervous stamping at the ground. Then she realized that Chase was talking to her. "What?" she muttered.

Chase had been as scared for Rebecca's life as she had been and was feeling a little weak himself. "I said he must have slipped to the side of the wagon while I was loading. All I knew was I'd killed five and couldn't figure out where the sixth had disappeared to. I'm sorry you took such a fright."

Rebecca remembered the Karankawa's hideous leer and shivered. "Are they all dead?"

"Yes." Chase looked at her closer. She was deathly pale. "Did I hurt you when I pushed you off the seat?" he asked in a deeply concerned voice.

"No, I'm not hurt. I just keep remembering that horrible Indian. Please, let's just get away from here."

By the time they made camp later that afternoon, Rebecca was feeling more composed. Chase helped her down from the wagon and strode to the back to examine the damage there. Seeing his frown when he stood looking at it, Rebecca walked back and joined him. One whole corner of the back of the wagon was badly crushed, and there was a huge gaping hole in the false bottom. Rebecca bent and peered into the dark hole, and saw the muzzle of one of the cannons. "I didn't realize it had done so much damage when we hit that tree. Do you think the cannons are damaged?"

"I doubt it. Cannons aren't exactly delicate weapons, you know."

Chase crawled beneath the wagon to assess the damage. When he emerged he said, "There's a good-sized hole in the bottom too, but thank God, both rear wheels and the axle look all right."

Rebecca frowned as Chase rubbed his left shoulder. She had seen him doing that several times since the Indian attack. "What's wrong with your shoulder?"

"I hit it when I lost my footing, when we slammed into that tree."

"Is it hurt badly?" Rebecca asked, alarmed.

"No, just bruised," Chase answered in an unconcerned voice. He turned, saying over his shoulder "I'll find some firewood after I've unharnessed the horses."

After Chase released the horses, they trotted to the meadow where the other three mares were already grazing. Lightning stood off, on higher ground, first looking about him alertly, then grazing, then looking again. When one of the mares approached a small stream that ran beside the woods near their wagon, the stallion snorted a shrill warning, trotted up to the mare, and nudged her aside. Cautiously he pawed at the water, sniffed it, then took a small drink. Satisfied that it was safe, he stepped back, allowing the mare to drink.

After they had eaten supper that night, Chase and Rebecca sat around their small campfire, Rebecca staring out into space. Then she looked at Chase. "Are the Karankawas really cannibals?"

"Yes, they are," Chase answered. "But I think it's mostly ceremonial cannibalism, a part of their victory feast. They believe it transfers the courage and fighting skill of their victim to themselves, and also prevents the victim from having a second or third life. They don't eat human flesh to satisfy their hunger. Their diet consists of oysters and other seafood."

Rebecca shivered, thinking that it didn't matter what their dietary preferences were. If she and Chase had been captured, they would have been a most unwilling part of the victory ceremony.

"But what were they doing up here?" Rebecca asked. "I thought they stayed on the islands."

"No, the Kronks make raids up the rivers, sometimes as far north as a hundred miles. And they don't all live on the islands. Some live on the lagoons around the mouths of the rivers, from the Brazos to the Nueces."

"They're the most hideous-looking things I've ever seen," Rebecca said with a shiver. "And filthy! I've never smelled anything so rank. Why, the stench was overpowering."

Chase chuckled. "That was the alligator grease and shark oil they smear on their bodies to keep off the mosquitoes that you smelled. Actually, the Karankawas have a fetish for bathing."

Rebecca gazed off thoughtfully for a moment, then asked, "How do you suppose they learned to run so fast and with such endurance?"

"I don't know. They claim they aren't Indians, that they didn't come from the north, that their origins go back to an ancient people who always lived on the Texas coast. If that's true, perhaps their exceptional running skill is an inherent trait of their race. But I do know one thing for sure. There aren't many Karankawas left. When those few are gone, their tribe will have died out."

Noticing Chase rubbing his shoulder again, Rebecca said, "You'd better let me have a look at that."

"It's just a bruise, but I think I will let you rub some liniment on it."

Rebecca took the liniment from the medicine chest and carried it to the fire. Chase slipped his tunic off. When Rebecca saw his shoulder, she gasped. His entire shoulder was blackened. "Are you sure it's not broken?" she asked, alarmed.

"No, it's not broken. If it were, I'd never have been able to stop those horses. Now, stop frowning and rub some liniment on it for me."

It was a miserable night for them. Chase was restless because of his aching shoulder, and every time Rebecca closed her eyes, she saw the hideous face of the Karankawa who had almost killed her.

The road they took to Groce's plantation followed the Brazos River and was deeply rutted from Houston dragging his supply wagons through the mud a month earlier. A few days after their encounter with the Karankawas, Chase spied a heavy dust cloud hovering over the road in the distance. He stopped the horses and reached for his gun under the seat. Sighting it on the road, he waited, tight-lipped. If the rider was a Santanista courier he'd never know what hit him when he rounded the bend in the road, nor would his message ever be delivered. Chase almost hoped it was a Santanista. His need to avenge his friends' deaths had only grown with the passage of time.

When the rider came into view and Chase saw that he was an Anglo, he lowered his rifle and called, "Hold up, there!"

The man trotted his horse up to the wagon, obviously displeased at the delay. "What do you want?" he asked in a surly voice.

"I'd like to know if you've heard anything about Houston," Chase asked. "Is he still at Groce's plantation?"

"Hell, no, he ain't there! He pulled out the day before yesterday. Crossed the Brazos and is retreating—again! He's nothing but a damned coward! Afraid to stand and fight. He's gonna run all the way to the Sabine!"

Rebecca and Chase were stunned by the news. Here they had almost caught up with Houston and he was on the move again.

"Which way was he headed?" Chase asked.

"Hell, I don't know. We camped on the east bank of the Brazos the night we pulled out. The men were mad as hell about retreating again. A lot of them, like me, were just flat fed up. Houston knew there were going to be a lot of desertions, so he had some graves dug and told us anyone who tried to leave would be shot. But he didn't scare me. I packed up and snuck out that night."

"Then he could still be there, for all you know," Chase said, giving the man a disgusted look.

"Maybe. But the way old Donoho was complaining, I don't think he'll stick around there for long."

"Who's Donoho?"

"The man who owned the pasture we were camped on. He was complaining to Houston about us chopping down his trees for firewood. Houston reprimanded us, asking us why we were taking Donoho's timber, when it would be easier to burn his split-rail fence. Houston's always making smart remarks like that to people. If he was half as good at fighting as he is at making gibes, we'd have won this war a long time ago."

"So you just left?" Rebecca asked angrily.

"Damn right, I did! If Houston's gonna run and never fight, I've got to get my family out of Texas. That's where I'm heading for now. To my family in Columbia."

"What about Santa Anna? Do you know where he is?" Chase asked.

"Yeah. He's marching to Harrisburg, trying to catch the government down there. He tried to cross at San Felipe, but Mosely Baker burned the town and took all the boats to the other side of the river. Mosley's men held Santa Anna's men there for four days, firing across the river at them. I should of stayed with them. At least they got to do some fighting. Santa Anna finally gave up and went south. Crossed the Brazos at the Fort Bend crossing, near Richmond. But I don't know where the rest of Santa Anna's army is."

"What rest of Santa Anna's army?" Chase asked.

"Santa Anna split his army into five columns when he left Bexar. I guess they're all supposed to meet up somewhere. Anyway, Santa Anna ain't waiting for them, wherever they are. I guess he figures he can beat a coward like Houston without their help—providing he can catch the yellow-belly before he runs across the border!" the man added in a voice full of contempt.

With that, the man wheeled his horse and galloped away, leaving a thick cloud of dust in his wake. Rebecca sat on the wagon seat, feeling sick with despair at Houston's last retreat. Finally she asked, "Do you think it's true, Chase? That Houston is a coward? That he *is* running for the border?"

Chase looked thoughtful for a long moment, mulling over everything the man had said, then answered, "No, I don't, Rebecca. It looks to me like Houston has been deliberately leading Santa Anna on. He'll fight. But he'll pick the time and the place. It's an old military tactic, pull back, keep retreating until the enemy splits its forces in hopes of trapping you, stretch your enemy's supply lines, then turn and fight when he least expects it. Even the Indians use it. What I can't understand is why Santa Anna can't see what Houston is doing. He's supposed to be such a military genius. The only thing I can figure is that Santa Anna is convinced Houston is a coward too and, in his contempt and his own egotism, has lost sight of the first rule in warfare—never underestimate your enemy."

Chase grew quiet then said, "No, I've got a gut feeling that Houston has just about got Santa Anna where he wants him—out in the open and isolated from the rest of his army. The day of reckoning is coming—and soon."

"Then we've *got* to get these cannons to him in a hurry."

"I know, but first we've got to figure out a way to get across the Brazos. We can't ford it, not with that hole in the bottom of the wagon. If that false bottom fills with water, it will sink like a rock."

"Where's the closest ferry crossing?"

"Groce's Ferry. But that's two days away. Then we'd have to backtrack. We'll be losing valuable time."

"I don't see where we have any choice," Rebecca replied.

"You're right. We don't," Chase answered grimly, flicking the reins.

That afternoon, as they were following a stretch of road that ran right beside the river, Rebecca gazed upriver. Then she leaned forward, peering closer, hardly believing her eyes.

"Chase, am I hallucinating, or is that a steamboat I see?"

"It's a steamboat," Chase confirmed, his voice taking on an excited edge.

"But I didn't know there were any steamboats in Texas."

"Only one, the *Yellowstone,* and it steams up and down the Brazos." Chase laughed, saying in an exhilarated voice "And by God, that's a steamboat and this is the Brazos!" He handed Rebecca the reins. "Wait here. I'll flag him down."

Chase jumped from the wagon and ran down the riverbank to the water's edge. There he stood, waving his arms and calling.

The steamboat veered to the bank where Chase stood and slowed down, but didn't stop.

"I need a lift across the river!" Chase called.

"Yeah, you and every other God damned runner!" the crusty, gray-haired captain yelled back, leaning from the pilothouse. "I tote people and cargo up and down the Brazos between towns, not across it. I ain't running no God damned ferry!"

"I'm not a runner!" Chase called back. "I'm trying to deliver some cannons to Houston's army!"

The captain leaned farther out, craning his neck and peering at the wagon. "I don't see no cannons! All I see is a wagon!"

By this time the steamboat had passed Chase. He ran along the bank to keep up with it, yelling "They're dismantled and hidden in a false bottom in the wagon!"

The captain thought Chase's words over for a minute, then pushed his cap back from his head and yelled, "Okay! But you better not be trying to pull any tricks on me, young fella!"

The *Yellowstone* turned around in the river and steamed back to where Rebecca and the wagon were. By the time the engines had stopped and the boat had floated up to the bank, Rebecca had eased the wagon down to the river. No sooner had the cargo gangplank been lowered than the captain was walking down it, a fiercely determined look on his face.

When Chase walked up to him, the captain glared at him. "All right, now, young fella. Before you get on my boat, I want to see those cannons. I don't rightly take to people trying to pull the wool over my eyes."

Chase grinned. "Come right back here and you can see for yourself."

Chase led the captain to the back of the wagon and pointed to the huge hole in it. "Look right in there."

The captain bent and peered into the hole. Then his eyes widened. "Well, I'll be damned. You're telling the truth. How many you got in there?" he asked as he straightened.

"Three eight-pounders. We've been chasing Houston all over Texas trying to deliver them to him."

The captain removed his cap and wiped the sweat from his brow with his forearm. "Yeah, he has been moving around a bit. And now I see why you couldn't ford the river. How'd you get that hole in there, anyway?"

"Hit a tree while we were trying to outrun some Karankawas."

"Did you outrun them?"

"No. I finally had to kill them."

"I ain't surprised. Those God damned Kronks followed me upriver for damned near thirty miles one time, with me going full steam ahead and them shooting those long arrows at us the whole time. I thought I was going to bust my boilers before they finally tired and fell back."

The captain put his cap back on, turned, and said over his shoulder, "Okay, young fella, see if you can ease that wagon up that gangplank."

It turned out not to be an easy thing to do. The heavy wagon sank in the wet sand just before it reached the gangplank, and Chase and three Negro stevedores had to push from behind while Rebecca urged the horses forward, before the tenacious sand finally gave up its captive. Everyone breathed a sigh of relief as the wagon clattered up the gangplank.

After the wagon was lashed down, the captain gave the order to pull away. The wheels turned slowly, and the steamboat backed away, then turned and headed for the opposite bank. Soon the wheels were spinning rapidly, throwing reddish-yellow water behind them, and the small boat shuddered with the vibrations from the engines. The horses didn't like the shaking sensation, or the loud boiler noises, or the hot cinders that floated down around them from the smokestack. This boat didn't just float across the river, as did the ferries they were accustomed to. The mares neighed, pawed at the deck, and moved about nervously. Lightning's eyes took on the same wild look that they'd had when he'd seen the herd of mustangs, and he snorted his displeasure. The entire trip across the river, Chase and Rebecca were kept busy trying to calm the frightened animals. As soon as the gangplank was lowered, the horses lunged for the riverbank, anxious to be away.

Chase reached into the coin pocket on the waistband of his buckskins. "How much do I owe you?"

"Forget it, young fella," the captain answered. He scratched his thick muttonchops and said with a grin, "I reckon if I can ferry Houston and his entire army across the Brazos for nothing, then I can do the same for you too, since you're taking cannons to him. I figure it's an investment in the future, 'cause if Houston doesn't win this war, I sure ain't got any steamboating future here in Texas."

"You ferried Houston across the Brazos?" Chase asked, surprised.

"Yep, up at Groce's."

"Do you know where he was going?"

"Nope. But I'd guess he's heading for Harrisburg to defend the Texas government. Don't know if I'd do it if I was him, though. Not after the Governor Burnett called him a coward. Of course, I don't think the new governor was ever too fond of Houston."

"Thanks for the lift," Chase said, offering his hand.

The captain accepted it and gave it a hardy

346

shake, saying in a solemn voice, "Good luck, young fella."

A day later Chase found Houston's trail. It wasn't hard to do. His army had left a wide swath of trampled grass across the coastal flatland.

Shortly after they had picked up the trail, Rebecca saw a wagon up ahead in the distance. "Do you think that could be one of Houston's supply wagons lagging behind?" she asked Chase.

Chase squinted his eyes and then sat back, laughing. "I'll be damned if that's not Rose."

"Rose who?"

"I don't know her last name. I don't think anyone does. Everyone just calls her the Yellow Rose of Texas, because she always wears a yellow dress made from flower sacks printed with roses. She bakes cakes in an oven in the back of that chuck wagon of hers and takes them all over East Texas, selling them to travelers."

Chase watched as the wagon in the distance turned off the trail and then smiled. "I knew Rose wasn't a runner. Look! She's turned west, not east toward the Sabine."

As Houston moved farther south, both Chase and Rebecca felt a growing urgency, sensing that the long-awaited confrontation between Houston's and Santa Anna's armies was drawing nearer and fearing that they wouldn't be able to get the cannons to the Texas army in time. They took to traveling at night too, Chase dozing during the daytime, while Rebecca drove the wagon.

Periodically, Chase stopped and checked the

burned-out campfires of the Texas army. After doing so early one afternoon, he smiled. "Those embers are still warm. I'd guess we're only a half a day behind them."

Rebecca was elated. But later that afternoon, when Houston's trail ran right into Buffalo Bayou, Rebecca could have cried with frustration. There was no way they could ford the narrow but deep creek with the gaping hole in the bottom of the wagon.

"Now what are we going to do?" she asked, blinking back tears.

Chase looked about him. "Houston might have been able to float his wagons across, but he needed a raft to get those cannons over that bayou. It must be around here somewhere."

It was almost dark before Chase found one of the crude rafts the Texas army had built to use as a ferry. He poled it back upstream to where Rebecca was waiting.

As he stepped from it he said, "We'll have to wait until morning to cross. It's going to be tricky enough getting that wagon on this small raft, without trying to do it in the dark."

They were up with the sun the next morning. A silent, ghostly fog rolled off the bayou. The chore wasn't only tricky, but slow and tedious too. Since the raft wasn't big enough for the horses to pull the wagon onto it, the wagon had to be backed onto it.

Finally they secured the wagon and poled it across the stream. Then Chase called to Lightning, and the stallion plunged into the murky water and swam across to them, the mares following, six of them still in their harnesses.

By the time they had the horses harnessed to the wagon and were ready to be on their way, it was noon. They had lost at least half a day crossing a muddy bayou that wasn't over forty feet across. Rebecca glared at the bayou and silently cursed it.

As they drove farther south, following Houston's trail, Chase shook his head in exasperation. "Damn it! How much farther is Houston going to go? Galveston Bay can't be much over ten miles from here. Where's he going to fight Santa Anna, anyway? In the middle of the Gulf of Mexico?"

When they reached Vince's Bayou, Rebecca's heart sank. "Don't tell me we're going to have to take the wagon across on a raft again," she said, feeling suddenly very discouraged.

"No, there's a bridge a little farther down. We'll cross there."

The bayou twisted and turned. The road following it was surrounded by willows and live oaks. When the wagon rounded another bend and the bridge came into view, Chase stiffened, seeing a man setting a torch to it at their end.

"He's burning the bridge!" Rebecca cried.

Chase snapped the reins and raced the horses and wagon to the edge of the bank, leapt from the wagon, and ran toward the man, yelling "What in the hell do you think you're doing?"

The man was startled, apparently not having heard them drive up. "You'll have to talk louder, mister. I'm kinda deaf."

"I said what are you doing?" Chase yelled louder.

"What Houston told me to," the man called over the crackling fire, backing a few more feet and lowering his torch to the bridge again. "He said to destroy this bridge. Burn it, chop it down if I had to, but get rid of it. So I'm burning it, since that's easier," he added dryly.

"Houston ordered this?" Chase asked, stunned.

"Yep. We're *finally* gonna fight!" the man yelled excitedly.

"Where is Houston?"

"About eight miles from here, back by the San Jacinto River. Santa Anna and his army are there too. We were waiting for him when he arrived yesterday afternoon. The men thought Houston was going to let us fight then, but after a couple of cannon shots, Houston called it off. The men have been as mad as hornets since then."

Rebecca rushed up, screaming "Stop! You can't burn this bridge yet. We've got three cannons for Houston in that wagon. We have to get across."

The man's head shot up. "Cannons?" He looked at the wagon and then back at the burning bridge. "I'm sorry, ma'am. If I'd known that, I'd put off firing this bridge for a few minutes, but as you can see, it's too late now."

Rebecca's eyes dropped to the end of the bridge near her. The dry timbers had caught and the bridge was blazing, the flames leaping into the air. Desperate, she rushed to the bridge and began stamping at the flames with her feet.

Chase jerked her back. "Have you gone stark

raving mad? Do you want to catch yourself on fire?" He pulled her away from the burning bridge and down the bank of the bayou.

"But we've got to put it out," Rebecca objected.

At that second, the end of the bridge near them collapsed, the blazing planking falling into the water and making a sizzling sound, while the pilings still burned.

"It's too late, Rebecca."

"Is there another bridge farther downstream?" Rebecca asked.

"No, this is the only one over Vince's Bayou," Chase answered, then turned back to the man, still busy firing the opposite end of the bridge, and yelled, "How can you be so sure Houston is going to fight? You said you thought he was yesterday, but he called it off. How do you know he won't retreat again?"

The man tossed his torch into the middle of the burning bridge and shouted, "He can't retreat! Some of our men captured Lynch's Ferry on the east side of the San Jacinto yesterday from the Santanistas and took all of the boats back to that side of the river."

Chase stared at the man in disbelief, then yelled, "Houston's crazy to burn this bridge! If those boats are on the other side of the river, this is the only way out of there. He's trapped!"

The Texian swung on his horse and yelled back, "He knows that! But Santa Anna is trapped too. There ain't gonna be any retreating in this battle, mister. On either side. It's gonna be a fight to the death. And only one side can win!"

With that, the man whirled his horse and galloped away. Chase stared at him, knowing that the confrontation between the two armies had finally arrived. And he wanted to be a part of it—desperately! Damn it, it might be his only chance to avenge his friends' death. But he couldn't take Rebecca into a battle.

He turned and saw Rebecca staring at the burning bridge. Suddenly, remembering her terror the day they had crossed the Colorado, he asked, "Can you swim?"

"What?" Rebecca asked, still in a daze.

"Can you swim?"

"No, I can't. But why do you ask?"

Thank God, Chase thought, then answered, "Never mind."

He rushed to the horses and unharnessed them. Once freed, they hurried over to where the other mares were grazing in a meadow a short distance away. Then Chase walked to the back of the wagon, a purposeful look on his face.

Rebecca followed him and rounded the back of the wagon just in time to see him throwing his saddle on Lightning's back. "Where are you going?"

Chase ignored her, tightening the cinch, then tossing his saddlebags over the horse's back. He reached into the wagon and pulled out the long coil of rope, looping it over his saddle horn.

"Are you going to try to find another way across the bayou?"

His lips firmly compressed and a determined gleam in his eyes, Chase walked right past her to

352

the front of the wagon, leading Lightning behind him.

Again, Rebecca followed him. "I asked you where you're going."

Silently Chase mounted, leaned down, and reached under the seat, pulling out the rifle.

Rebecca rushed up to him. "Chase, answer me!"

Chase bent, framed her face in his hands, and gave her a quick, fierce kiss. Then he looked her directly in the eye. "I'm going to join Houston's army in that fight."

Before Rebecca could even open her mouth, Chase nudged Lightning, and the stallion leapt forward and galloped down the bank of the bayou. As the horse splashed into the water, Rebecca tore after them, screaming "Wait for me! I'm going too!"

Chase ignored her, the stallion already swimming for the opposite bank.

"Chase, did you hear me?" Rebecca called, coming to a dead stop at the water's edge. "Don't you dare go off and leave me! I've traveled all over Texas for this! I have as much right to be there as you!"

When Lightning emerged from the sluggish bayou and stepped onto the bank, Chase whirled him around. "Sorry, Rebecca, but this is one time you can't come along. War is men's business."

"The devil it is! I have deaths to avenge too!"

Chase looked at the tiny woman standing on the opposite bank and felt a pang of doubt at leaving her in this isolated place. But it would certainly be safer than a battlefield, and he knew that Indians

353

were no danger, not with the two big armies so close by. No, there wouldn't be an Indian within twenty miles of this place, and if Rebecca would just follow a few simple instructions, she'd be perfectly safe.

While Chase was mulling over these thoughts, Rebecca's hopes had risen, thinking his hesitancy meant he was coming back for her. Her hopes were dashed to the ground when he said, "It's too dangerous for you to go along. Keep your rifle loaded and by your side at all times. And stick close to the wagon. Whatever you do, don't go wandering off. You might get lost."

The look on Rebecca's face was murderous, and Chase was glad that she didn't have her rifle with her at that moment. As angry as she was, he wouldn't put it past her to take a shot at him. Oh, she wouldn't shoot to kill. No, she'd aim that ball just close enough to scare the hell out of him. Chase grinned. No, he didn't have to worry about Rebecca. She was one little lady who could take care of herself. She had more than proved that to him when she had to fend for herself in the wilderness while he was a prisoner at Goliad.

Chase grinned across the bayou at the woman glaring at him and called, "Now, you be a good girl, and I'll see you later."

As Chase whirled Lightning around and galloped off, Rebecca screamed, "Damn you, Chase! You come back here!" Seeing him disappear around the bend, she shrieked, "Chase!"

Rebecca's eyes darted to the murky water of the bayou as she considered throwing herself in and thrashing her way across. She quickly decided against it, her fear of drowning bringing her to her senses. Then, remembering the mares, she turned and gasped, seeing them racing toward her. She knew where they were headed. They had seen Lightning speed away and were frantically trying to follow him.

"No! Stop!" Rebecca yelled, running toward them and waving her arms wildly to frighten them back, but the mares rushed past her so fast Rebecca couldn't even catch one of their manes or tails. They plunged into the water, swam the bayou, and climbed the opposite bank, racing down the road where Lightning and Chase had disappeared, with Rebecca yelling at them all the while "Come back here! Come back here, you stupid mares!"

She watched as the horses disappeared down the road, realizing that Chase had known that they would follow, had planned it to further assure her being unable to get across the bayou. Her anger at him rose even to greater heights.

"Damn you, Chase Winters!" she shrieked in the direction Chase had ridden. "I hate you! Do you hear me, you bastard? I hate you!" Her eyes glittered with rage. "And if I ever lay eyes on you again, I'll blow your brains out!"

Rebecca sank to the ground, sobbing in anger and frustration, her only companions the blazing bridge and the huge wagon, its false bottom filled with cannons that would never be used by the Texas army.

17

CHASE DIDN'T RIDE TOO FAR FROM REBECCA AF-
ter he had left her on the muddy bank of the
bayou, just far enough that he was certain he was
out of her sight. Then he reined in and waited for
the mares to appear.

When the horses ran around the bend in the
road, Chase rode to a thick copse of trees and dismounted. Catching the mares with Lightning
standing there was no problem, for they had all
crowded around their leader. As he tied each mare
firmly to a tree, Chase turned and saw Lightning
watching him. The stallion did not look at all
pleased with what Chase had done to his mares.

Mounting the stallion, Chase said in a firm
voice, "Don't get your hackles up, boy. If Rebecca
can't come along with us, neither can your fe-
males."

Chase turned Lightning back onto the road and
gave him his head, the plaintive neighs of the
mares in his ears as he galloped away. With his
amazing speed, it didn't take Lightning long to
catch up with the man who had burned the bridge.

The man looked at Chase in surprise as Chase sidled up to him. "Thought I'd join you in this fight, if you don't mind," Chase called across the space between them and over the hoofbeats of the horses.

"Sure, glad to have you. Every man helps," the man called back, then added, "I'm Erastus Smith, but most people just call me Deaf."

Chase remembered the old-timer at Gonzales telling them Deaf Smith was one of Houston's scouts, the man who had found Mrs. Dickerson and the Mexican women wandering on the prairie. "Chase Winters here," he answered, then asked, "Do you know what happened to the government officials at Harrisburg? Did Santa Anna capture them?"

"Nope. They were gone when the Mexican army got there, and Santa Anna was so mad he burned the town to the ground. But he almost caught the governor down at Galveston. The governor barely had time to get on one of our naval ships and sail away."

"*Our* naval ships?" Chase asked. "Texas has a navy now?"

"Sure do. Where you been, anyway?"

For the last four months halfway across Texas and back, Chase thought in disgust, chasing an army to deliver cannons to them and, after all of that, arriving only minutes too late. Chase wondered just how badly Houston needed those cannons. Was the Texas army as badly outnumbered as they had been at the Alamo and Goliad? "How many men does Houston have?" he asked.

"Between eight and nine hundred, I'd say," Smith answered.

"And Santa Anna?"

"After General Cos arrived this morning with his army, I'd guess over twelve hundred."

"General Cos? I thought he promised never to come back to Texas when they let him go, after he surrendered at the Alamo."

"He did. But he ran smack-dab into Santa Anna when he reached the Rio Grande and Santa Anna made him turn right back around." Smith laughed. "I don't guess that Mexican's life is any bed of roses, having Santa Anna for a brother-in-law."

The men fell silent as they rode. Well, Chase thought, the Texians might still be outnumbered, but the odds were much better than they had been at the Alamo and Goliad.

Chase looked around as the two men rode into the woods where the Texas army was camped. The trees were a tangle of live oaks, dripping with Spanish moss and skirting the Buffalo Bayou behind them. To his left he saw the San Jacinto River and Lynch's Ferry. Across from him, in another grove of trees, was the Mexican army. A wide meadow of grass, as tall as a man's knees, stretched between the two armies. Chase squinted and could see the white-and-green silk tent of Santa Anna. Above it fluttered the white-and-green flag of Mexico with its eagle standing on a cactus, a serpent dangling from its beak.

"There doesn't seem to be much going on over there," Chase remarked to Smith, his eyes still on the Mexican camp.

"Nope. They worked all night building their fortifications and then, a couple of hours ago, they stacked their arms and have been taking a siesta ever since."

"A siesta?" Chase asked in an incredulous voice. "Is Santa Anna crazy? He's letting his army nap with Houston's army within seeing distance?"

Smith shrugged. "I guess when Houston called off the battle yesterday, Santa Anna figured he ain't so anxious to fight, so he'd just take it easy too. Hell, I don't know what Santa Anna is thinking about," Smith continued with a shake of his head. "I ain't never been able to figure out those Mexicans. I'm married to one myself, and I still can't figure them out."

Chase and Deaf Smith rode up to a massive oak tree. Beneath it stood a tall, heavily muscled man, dark haired, with thick sideburns. No one had to tell Chase who the man was: Sam Houston. His calm yet commanding appearance identified him. Houston radiated strength and self-assurance, every inch of him the competent leader.

"Well?" Houston asked Smith.

"It's down. Burned it clear to the water line," Smith answered.

Houston nodded, then glanced up at Chase on his horse.

"This here is Chase Winters," Smith told the general. "He was trying to deliver some cannons to us, but I had the bridge half burned before I found out. Now he's joining us."

"I appreciate your efforts, Mr. Winters," Houston said, looking Chase directly in the eye.

359

At that moment Chase sensed a strange kinship with this man who commanded the Texas army. From the puzzled look on the general's face, he knew that Houston had sensed something too. Then a man rushed up to Houston, and the general broke eye contact, turning away.

Chase and Smith dismounted and walked a short distance, then stood, watching Houston anxiously. But the general seemed to be in no hurry to order the battle to commence. He walked about, talking to his men, acting as if Santa Anna and the battle was the last thing on his mind.

"What's he waiting for?" Chase asked impatiently.

"Hell, I don't know. He never tells anyone what he's thinking. I guess he's still trying to decide if the time is right."

Chase felt his nerves stretched taut as he waited for Houston to make his decision. Now he knew how the men who had been marching with him must feel. For weeks they had been kept at bay, waiting, waiting for the order to fight, then retreating, always showing the enemy their backs. No wonder they were mad as hornets, as Smith had said.

Chase watched as Houston left the men and walked out onto the meadow that separated the two armies. The general stood and looked thoughtfully at the Mexicans' camp for a few minutes, and then he glanced up at the sky. Chase looked up too and saw the lone eagle circling high overhead. Suddenly Chase realized what the kinship he had felt with Houston was. Houston had been adopted by the Cherokees. His guardian spirit and Chase's were the same. Just as Eagle at Sunrise had said, those under the eagle guardianship recognized their own.

Chase knew what Houston's decision was, even before the general turned and walked back to the Texians' camp, a smile on his face. Houston had been waiting for an omen and had received it. His guardian spirit was with him. The time for the long-awaited confrontation was at hand.

The word spread like wildfire through the Texas camp. Quick, last-minute preparations were made as the men checked their rifles, powder, and balls. The long flintlocks were primed and loaded, freshly sharpened knives slipped into waist scabbards. Houston mounted his big white stallion, Saccren, and led his troops, dressed in tattered rags, silently out onto the meadow.

Chase sat on Lightning with the Texas cavalry in a woods on one side of the meadow. For a long time the only sound in the open field was the whispering gulf breeze as it blew the tall grass in undulating waves of green. And then a new sound caught Chase's attention, the gentle flapping of the standard they would fight under.

Chase looked up at the flag being carried by the flag bearer at the front of the Texas infantry. It depicted the goddess of liberty on a blue circle, one breast bared, her saber outthrust, a banner on which was written "liberty or death" dangling from it.

Then Chase's attention turned back to the men in the meadow and the Mexican camp in the distance. He held his breath, waiting for the shot that would signal that the Mexicans had seen their approach, but, unbelievably, the Santanistas continued to nod in the late-afternoon sun, apparently unaware of the impending attack.

Houston, riding at the front of the infantry column, unsheathed his saber and gave the command to attack. It was as if the floodgates had suddenly been opened. Kept at bay by Houston for weeks, driven half mad with frustration, the Texians charged wildly at the Mexican camp, running through the tall grass and yelling at the top of their lungs "Remember the Alamo! Remember Goliad!"

In the background Chase heard the fifer playing "Will You Come to the Bower?" He listened for a second to the totally inappropriate music, hardly believing his ears as the lyrics ran through his mind.

Will you come to the bow'r I have shaded for
   you?
Our bed will be of roses all spangled with dew
There under the bow'r in roses you'll lie
A flush on your cheek but a smile in your eye!

Chase shook his head. The Santanistas attacked to the stirring, rousing *Deguello,* the ancient Moorish fire and death call, and the Texians to a silly romantic ditty.

"Fire away!" Houston ordered, the call ringing through the air. But the Texians continued running blindly toward the enemy, the ground shaking beneath their trampling feet, yelling "Remember Goliad! Remember the Alamo!"

"God damn you, fire!" Houston yelled, then stared in horror as the Texians raced toward the enemy barricade. Then Houston shouted incredulously, "Aren't you going to fire at all?"

"What in the hell is wrong with them?" Chase asked Smith, mounted and ready next to him. "The Mexicans will mow them down!"

"Damned if I know. They must be in some kind of a trance from being kept back for so long, and now all they can do is run and yell."

Smith kicked his horse's flank and raced across the charging Texas line, yelling at the top of his lungs "Vince's Bridge is down! Fight for your lives! Vince's Bridge is down!"

The news apparently roused the Texians from the strange daze they were in. Rifles were raised, a thunderous roar filling the air as hundreds of guns were fired almost simultaneously. Fast on its heel, a new roar followed: the Twin Sisters were fired, the cannons belching fire and smoke as their missiles flew through the air and crashed into the Mexican barricade.

A split second later the cavalry shot from the woods, joining in the battle. Chase raced Lightning through the Texas lines, firing his rifle. As the Mexicans swarmed over the barricade to meet them, he heard the whizzing of balls all around him as he reloaded. Then he fired again, never missing his enemy.

Soon the whole field was a swarming mass of Texians and Mexicans. A cavalry officer, brandishing his saber, rushed at Chase, whose rifle was unloaded. Chase swung the gun around and used the butt to knock the saber from the man's hand, then clubbed the officer over the head with it. No sooner had the officer fallen to the ground when Chase felt a hand trying to pull him from Lightning. He kicked out at the Santanista, then again used his rifle as a club.

The whole field was filled with rolling smoke, burning his eyes. With the cannons roaring, the rifles cracking, the men yelling, the wounded screaming in pain, the noise was horrendous. From the corner of his eye Chase saw Saccren go down and Houston jump free to keep from being crushed under the huge animal's weight. A moment later a Texian caught a Mexican horse whose rider had been unseated, and Houston flew into saddle, waving his saber and urging his men on.

Chase fought his way to the barricade through a crush of men on foot, alternately firing his flintlock and using it as a club. And then Lightning sailed over the fortification made of saddles and packing cases, just seconds behind Houston, riding yet another horse. The resistance here was much less than Chase had expected. Most of the Mexicans, caught completely off-guard and not even able to reach their stacked muskets, had fled across the open field, bent on escape. A senior Mexican officer, standing on a crate, waved a white flag, and Houston ordered a cease-fire. From the time the Texians had marched out of their camp to the Mexicans' surrender had been only eighteen minutes.

But the killing didn't end. While the Texian officers yelled "Cease fire! Cease fire! They have surrendered!" to their men, to their dismay and horror, the slaughter continued. Enraged Texians chased the fleeing Mexicans across the field. Even Santanistas who knelt and begged for mercy were not spared. Despite their officers' pleas to stop, the carnage continued, as if the floodgates of hell had been opened. When the Texians' lust for revenge had finally been satisfied, 630 Mexicans lay dead on the bloody battlefield.

Chase rode Lightning to a tree and dismounted, sitting and leaning against the tree trunk, his breathing still labored after the frenzied fighting. He too had sought revenge, but he had been stunned by the senseless killing of the unarmed Mexicans. And yet he couldn't blame the Texians either. Not after the massacres at Goliad and the Alamo.

Smith walked up to Chase and sat down beside him. "Houston took a copper ball in his right leg when that second horse was shot out from beneath him. Shattered both bones in his lower leg, and when he pulled off his boot, it was full of blood. The doc is bandaging it up right now," he finished, pointing to the huge oak tree that Houston was lying under, propped up against the huge trunk.

"Is it serious?" Chase asked, seeing the worried look on Smith's face.

"Well, it ain't good, but he ain't in any danger of dying. What is worrying me, and Houston, is that Santa Anna escaped. He and most of his staff fled, leaving the common foot soldiers to do the fighting. Houston's worried that Santa Anna will make his way back to the rest of his army at Fort Bend. Hell, there must be close to five thousand of them there."

"And if he does manage it, all that happened today will be for nothing," Chase added grimly.

"Yep. Houston was hoping the fight today would be the end of it. The men are forming search parties right now. We've got to catch that little bastard. You want to go with us?"

Chase thought of Rebecca. She was alone back at Vince's Bayou, and he had planned to go back to her as soon as he had rested up from the battle. But if Santa Anna wasn't caught . . . Then he remembered that Rebecca was a woman who was very capable of looking out for herself. Chase rose, saying "Yeah, I'll go along."

As he and Smith rode across the still-smoky battlefield strewn with Mexican dead, Chase asked, "Do you know what our casualties were?"

"Yep. Heard one of the officers telling Houston when I was over there. We had two dead and twenty-three wounded, including Houston. The Santanistas lost over six hundred, and so far we've taken over six hundred prisoners."

Chase could only shake his head in utter amazement. Caught napping, the Mexicans had suffered overwhelming, almost unbelievable losses, while the Texians had lost only two men.

As Chase and Smith rode off into the sunset, that great orb in the sky blood red, Chase thought Santa Anna had paid a great price for his contempt of Houston and, as usual, at the expense of his common foot soldiers.

18

AFTER CHASE HAD LEFT HER STRANDED BY THE
bayou, Rebecca had cried in anger and frustration.
Finally she rose, muttering angrily "I'll show you,
Chase Winters. I'm not about to be stopped by
something as silly as not being able to swim. You'll
see—you bastard!"

With renewed determination not to be cheated
of her revenge, she spent the next fifteen minutes
searching for something large enough to support
her weight, hoping she could float across the
bayou. She stumbled over exposed tree roots and
tore her skirts on thorny berry bushes as she
looked through the thick underbrush skirting the
bayou for a fallen log. Then, spying one on the
bank near the murky water, she cried out in delight and ran toward it. When the log moved, she
froze in horror as she realized that it wasn't a log.
It was an alligator!

She watched, afraid even to breathe for fear the
motion would attract the reptile's attention to her,
as the alligator rose and lazily lumbered to the
bayou's edge and slipped into the muddy water.

She glanced around, terrified that there might be more about. Seeing none, she beat a hasty retreat to the wagon.

Taking her gun from beneath the seat for added protection, she sat in the wagon, looking about her in total disgust. She might have been able to risk floating across the bayou, but nothing, not even her need for revenge, could make her go into that murky water now, knowing that there were alligators lurking about. No, the thought of being eaten alive was much more frightening than the possibility of drowning.

A few minutes later she heard the muffled sound of cannon shots in the distance and knew, with a sinking feeling, that the battle had commenced and she had lost her chance. She strained her ears, fervently wishing she were at San Jacinto. But then, when the cannon shots ceased in less than fifteen minutes, she was left to assume that the armies had only exchanged shots, as they had the day before. She knew that battles between two major armies were long and drawn out, lasting hours, if not days.

She considered her position. She could climb down from the wagon and start a fire and keep it burning brightly all night. That would keep the alligators and any other wild animals away. Then she remembered how close she was to Galveston Bay, one of the Karankawas' favorite campsites. Undoubtedly they traveled up and down these bayous on their raiding forays into the mainland. No, she wouldn't light a fire, she decided. That would be too risky. The last thing she wanted to do was catch the attention of those horrible savages.

She watched as the sun set, wondering at its blood-red color. She had never seen a sunset like it. She fervently hoped that it wasn't a bad omen for the Texians in their impending battle with the Mexicans.

With that thought came a new terror. For the first time she realized that Chase could be killed; her earlier anger at him had overridden all rational thought before. As darkness fell, she climbed into the back of the wagon and huddled on her mattress, sick with worry over him.

It was a long, miserable night for Rebecca. Fear for Chase's life and safety was added to the apprehension of the night itself. A gray fog rolled off of the bayou, giving the area around it a ghostly appearance. Crickets chirruped, bull frogs croaked, and, every now and then alligators roared, a sound that left the air vibrating and sent shivers up Rebecca's spine. She thanked God that the ugly, scaly creatures couldn't climb.

And then a sudden hush fell over the bayou, an eerie silence that sent Rebecca's nerves crawling, for she knew that the night creatures had heard or seen something and were waiting to see if it was friend or foe. She held her breath, hearing a splash, followed by yet another one a few minutes later, terrified that the Karankawas were creeping up on her. She clutched her rifle to her, her eyes darting wildly from one end of the wagon to the other, wondering from which direction they would attack, desperately trying to convince herself that it wasn't Indians she had heard but a racoon, or a possum, or one of those strange armor-plated armadillos swimming across the bayou.

It wasn't a Karankawa that Rebecca heard. Nor was it some wild nocturnal animal. The noises were made by a Mexican officer fleeing from the battle. In his haste to be gone, the officer had caught the first horse he had laid eyes on, a black stallion that had been seized by the Mexicans after being abandoned by his owners. With the officer on his back, the stallion had headed for home and plunged into the river. That was the first splash Rebecca heard.

Utterly disgusted, the officer looked down at the hapless animal stuck in the mud beneath him, the slime almost reaching the stallion's chest. The Mexican carefully reversed his position, shimmied to the back of the horse, and jumped for the bank, catching a bush that grew there as he flew through the air and splashed in the water, then pulling himself from the muck.

Standing on the bank, his pointed red shoes and long johns covered with slime, his fine silk shirt splattered with mud, the Mexican glared at the bayou, cursing the obstruction to his flight under his breath, for this particular Mexican could not swim and was terrified of deep water.

Still muttering curses, Santa Anna turned and walked down the bayou, heading for the shallow narrow spot he had spied earlier on his ride from the battle.

Rebecca was immensely relieved when the sun finally rose the next morning. She had spent a sleepless, terrifying night and had decided that, if the Karankawas were out there, she would rather see them coming than be tortured wondering from which direction they would jump her. She peeked out of the wagon, but all she could see was the drifting fog and the vague outline of the nearby trees. Not until the fog had burned off and she could see that the clearing around her was free of wild animals and Indians did she venture to climb down from the wagon.

Still afraid the smoke might draw unwelcome visitors, she decided not to risk a fire for breakfast. Instead she cautiously circled a clump of dewberry bushes that were just beginning to bear fruit. She checked them first for snakes by poking them with a long stick. Then, after gathering a huge handful, she sat on the bank of the bayou and ate the juicy berries, her gun beside her, her eyes constantly on the alert for alligators.

There she sat for the entire morning, anxiously awaiting the sound of cannon shots that would announce the battle's beginning, but all she heard was the soft whispering of the gentle breeze through the tall grass and the cheeping and warbling of the birds in the trees behind her. She wondered if the wind was coming from a different direction that morning; that might be why she didn't hear anything. She raised her head to look for smoke in the sky, but all she saw was fleecy white clouds racing across the blue dome. Everything around her was peaceful and serene, and Rebecca could detect no sign of a blood battle taking place in the distance.

She frowned in puzzlement. Was Houston still trying to decide whether or not to fight, or, God forbid, had he retreated once again? Then she remembered that the man who had burned the bridge had said that Houston *had* to fight, that there was no escape route. As the hours slowly crept by, Rebecca became even more puzzled, then finally she began to feel irritated at being kept in suspense for so long.

Absently she snatched a wildflower from the grass and twirled it between her fingers. Then she looked down at it, really seeing the wine-cup for the first time. She gazed around her at the banks of the bayou. They were covered with wildflowers: pink primroses, yellow dandelions, salmon-color Indian paintbrush, delicate Queen Anne's lace.

The sun rose to its zenith, bathing her with its warmth, and bees droned lazily in the wildflowers and clover all around her. Rebecca grew lethargic and was barely able to keep her eyes open after her long, sleepless night. Then she heard it, not the sound of cannon shots but hoofbeats on the road across the bayou from her.

She jumped to her feet, holding her gun and straining her eyes to see through the thick maze of trees. She was just on the verge of running to hide, fearing that it might be Santanistas, when she saw the flash of a white horse. Seconds later Chase rode Lightning into the clearing, the mares following eagerly behind them.

At the sight of him, Rebecca's heart soared. He had returned safe and sound. Then she remembered how he had left her the day before, deliberately trapping her on the other side of the bayou, and her anger flared anew. She glared as Lightning splashed into the muddy water, the other horses fast on his heels. Chase grinned back at her, which only infuriated her more.

Chase was very much aware of Rebecca's angry look as Lightning swam the bayou, but he was much too euphoric to let her displeasure ruin his happiness. "It's all over!" he yelled. "We won!"

In her anger, Rebecca had completely forgotten about the battle. She stood, momentarily stunned by Chase's announcement, and watched wordlessly as Lightning climbed the bank and Chase dismounted. She didn't come out of her daze until Chase was hugging her fiercely, then twirling her about, his husky laughter in her ears.

When he sat her back on her feet, his dark eyes sparkling with excitement, Rebecca caught her breath, then asked, "When? I didn't hear anything today."

"Not today. Yesterday afternoon," Chase answered. "And, Rebecca, it was all over in eighteen minutes. Can you imagine? Why, the Battle of San Jacinto must have been one of the shortest decisive battles ever fought."

"Yesterday?" Rebecca asked in surprise. Then she remembered her long, miserable night. While she was worrying herself sick over him and terrified of an Indian attack, Chase had probably been celebrating the victory, undoubtedly getting stinking drunk in the process. "Then why didn't you come back then?" she asked, her eyes flashing dangerously.

"I was going to, until I found out that Santa Anna had escaped. I stayed to join one of the search parties."

"He fled the battle? Deserted his men?"

"Yes. It seems that Santa Anna doesn't like to fight when the odds aren't overwhelmingly in his favor," Chase replied contemptuously. "Santa Anna showed his true colors yesterday. After months of accusing Houston of cowardice, *he* turned out to be the coward. He was trying to get back to the bulk of his army at Fort Bend. He crossed the bayou and spent the night over at Vince's Ranch. Then, this morning, our search party caught him napping in the grass about a half a mile past that bend," Chase said, pointing. "He had found some slave garments at the ranch, an old cotton jacket and a pair of tattered pants, but we knew we had an officer because he still had on his elegant silk shirt. It wasn't until we marched him into the prison compound and the Mexicans started yelling *'El Presidente!'* that we realized who we'd captured."

Rebecca was amazed at the story. "I bet he was furious at his men for giving him away."

"No, he was too damned scared to be mad. All the time we were marching him back to General Houston, the men kept crowding around us and threatening him. There was a time there when I feared they'd overpower us and tear Santa Anna apart with their bare hands or take him away to lynch him. When we finally reached the oak tree where Houston was, Santa Anna was trembling so badly that he asked for his medicine box. He needed his opium to give him courage."

"Opium?" Rebecca asked in amazement.

"Yes. Didn't you know Santa Anna was an opium eater?"

"No, I didn't," Rebecca answered.

"After he'd taken his opium," Chase continued, "he was feeling a little braver. He told Houston that he should be generous to the vanquished. Houston reminded him of the Alamo. Santa Anna replied that the Texians had refused to surrender. Then Houston reminded Santa Anna of the massacre of Fannin's men at Goliad, men who *had* surrendered under honorable terms. Santa Anna began to shake. His face broke out in sweat. He was terrified that Houston planned the same fate for him. And I don't blame him for being scared to death. The look in Houston's eyes when he said it was enough to send shivers up any man's spine."

"Is Houston going to execute the prisoners?"

"No, Houston just wanted Santa Anna to sweat blood for a little while. He finally told Santa Anna that, if he wanted to live, he must order all of his remaining forces out of Texas, and that he would be kept prisoner to assure the Mexicans' retreat. When I left the Texians' camp, Deaf Smith, the man who burned this bridge, and a man named Burlenson were preparing to leave to take Santa Anna's order to withdraw to the Santanista troops at Fort Bend. It's over, Rebecca. Not just the battle but the entire war! It seems impossible, doesn't it?"

Yes, it does seem impossible, Rebecca thought. From beginning to end, the Texas War for Independence had lasted only seven months, from the refusal of the Texians to give up their old cannon at Gonzales to the Battle of San Jacinto. While Steven F. Austin was still pleading for funds to aid the Texas army in the United States, Andrew Jackson was still trying to decide what he was going to do, and the Texas settlers were still fleeing eastward across the Sabine, the war had come to a sudden, unexpected end. It seemed unbelievable that after all of the Texians' stunning defeats under Santa Anna's might, after all of the utter disorganization and chaos, the Texians had won their independence in one fierce battle that had only lasted eighteen minutes.

Then Rebecca remembered that Chase had cheated her out of her revenge. The war was over, and she hadn't done anything to get back at the Mexicans for killing her family. She pushed away from him angrily and stalked away. When she was standing beside the wagon, her back still to him, she spat, "Damn you, Chase Winters! Why didn't you let me go along? It was bad enough that we couldn't deliver these damned cannons, but to cheat me of everything was too much. Now I'll never be able to avenge my family's—" Rebecca came to a dead halt, remembering what Chase had said about Santa Anna crossing the bayou and where they had found him. Suddenly, with that strange insight she had, she *knew* that it was he who had made those splashes last night. Why, the bastard had been within shooting distance of her! She'd had her chance to get her licks in on the Mexicans, could have shot Santa Anna himself, but instead she had been cowering in fear in the wagon like some silly female. Even more furious at herself for missing her golden opportunity than she was at Chase, she kicked the front wheel of the wagon—hard!

Chase had followed Rebecca to the wagon and had assumed her silence was because she was impotent with rage. He took her shoulders and whirled her around to face him. "It was too dangerous to take you with me, Rebecca. I couldn't let you take that risk."

Neither noticed the wagon moving, just as neither had ever realized how precariously close to the edge of the riverbank the wagon had been parked the previous afternoon. Rebecca's kick had been just enough to move the wheel forward. For a second the wagon hovered on the crest, and then, caught by the force of gravity, the front wheels rolled over the brink and down the incline.

By the time Chase noticed it, it was too late. The wagon had gained momentum and was racing toward the bayou. He stared at it in disbelief. Wondering what had caught his attention, Rebecca turned just as the wagon plunged into the bayou's murky waters. For a moment or two it floated, and then, as the water rushed into the massive holes and filled the false bottom, the wagon slowly sank out of sight, until the only thing that could be seen was the very tip of its canvas top.

Chase was the first to recover. He threw back his head and laughed. Rebecca looked at him as if he'd lost his mind. Finally, becoming aware of her expression, he struggled to control himself. "For months we've been chasing all over Texas trying to deliver those damned cannons to the army—and the army didn't even need them! I'm glad to be finally rid of the stupid things. I only wish we'd sunk them months ago."

Rebecca didn't wish they had sunk the cannons months ago. If they had, she wouldn't have had her time with Chase. Suddenly she realized that the war wasn't the only thing that was over. What she had been dreading all along was finally at hand. Chase would leave her now. There would be no more precious memories to file away in the treasure chest of her heart. Oh, she knew that he would take her to someplace safe before he left her, but her brief, wonderful love affair was over. She could feel the life ebbing from her, to be replaced with an unbearable, almost painful emptiness.

Chase saw the look of sadness on Rebecca's face and assumed that she was still disappointed at being cheated out of her revenge. "Rebecca, the Santanistas are leaving Texas. That's what you wanted. Don't feel so bad because you didn't take a more active part in it. The war has ended, but not the struggle. That's just beginning for Texas. Do you realize that we're a republic now? A nation in our own right? Hell, we're not Texians any more. We're Texans! And it's going to take strong and determined men and women to build this infant republic of ours into a nation that we can all be proud of, a nation that the rest of the world will respect. And, Rebecca, *you* can be a part of that, an important part."

Rebecca continued to stare out at the bayou.

"Where did you say your father's land in Texas was?" Chase asked.

When Rebecca didn't respond, Chase frowned, wondering what was wrong with her. She didn't act as if she had heard anything he'd been saying. He took her shoulder and turned her to face him. "Rebecca, I'm talking to you."

"What?" Rebecca asked in a dazed voice.

"I asked you where's the land your father settled."

So that was where he would take her before he left her, Rebecca thought. Back to her land. "On the Brazos, north of *El Camino Real.*"

Chase caught her hand and walked rapidly to Lightning. "Well, come on, then! We don't want any of those settlers that will be swarming into Texas now that the war has ended beating us to it. After all, we worked for that land, dragging those stupid cannons all over Texas. We've earned our right to it."

Rebecca, who had been half running to keep up with Chase's quick, long strides, came to an abrupt halt. Chase turned and saw Rebecca watching him. "What's wrong?"

"What do you mean, *we?*"

Chase grinned and shrugged. "I've discovered that I like being married to you. I think we make a pretty good team."

"We *aren't* married," Rebecca reminded him bluntly.

"No, we aren't," Chase replied calmly. A twinkle came into his eyes. "I guess we'll have to remedy that as soon as we can find a preacher."

Rebecca stared at him, unable to believe her ears.

Chase laughed at her expression and said, "Rebecca, don't look so shocked. It's customary for men to ask the women they love to marry them, you know."

But that wasn't the only thing that had stunned Rebecca. She couldn't believe that Chase was serious about settling down. *"You're* going to be a *planter?"*

"If men like Houston, Bowie, and Travis can be planters, I don't know why I can't. I'm ready to put down some roots. I've had enough chasing around these past few months to last me a lifetime."

Rebecca watched as Chase turned and walked to Lightning. At that moment, she knew him better than he knew himself. Oh, he might be satisfied with the life of a planter for a while, but eventually he would become bored with the repetitive planting, waiting, harvesting, planting, waiting, harvesting, and get restless. Then he would leave, and she wouldn't be able to hold him, married or not. No, Chase wasn't the kind of man to put down roots. It just wasn't in his nature.

She glanced up and saw an eagle circling high in the sky. Yes, Chase is like that eagle up there, she thought. He has to be free. To bind him to her, to hold him back would destroy his spirit, that beautiful spirit that made him the remarkable man he was. No, she loved him too much to do that to him.

She wondered if it wouldn't be better to refuse his marriage proposal and give him his freedom now. Somewhere in the future she might find a man with whom she could share her interest in the land, a man who would be willing to give his entire life to her and their plantation. Oh, she knew she could never love another man, but perhaps she could learn to accept another as a companion. And she did want children. Otherwise the long, hard work of building a successful plantation would all be for nothing. But the thought of spending her lifetime with another man did nothing to ease the depression that was slowly creeping over her.

And then she remembered that an eagle mates for life, that no matter how far they fly or how high they soar, they always come back to their nest and their mate. If she married Chase, their life would be much as it had been during those first weeks on the wagon train. He would leave her for long periods of time, perhaps weeks or months, and she would be left to manage the plantation and raise their family, feeling all the while an emptiness, as if her life had left her. And then, when he returned, she would be filled with an incredible happiness and joy. She wondered if she could live a lifetime of such emotional extremes. Suddenly Eagle at Sunrise's words came to her: *It is not easy to love an eagle.* Now she knew that he had been referring to Chase. Yes, to love him was both heaven and hell. There would never be any in betweens.

"Rebecca? Are you coming?"

Rebecca looked up and saw Chase mounted on Lightning and watching her intently. She knew that he was waiting for more than an answer to his question, that he was waiting for her decision—and that he wouldn't ask again. Rebecca had a choice. She could have this remarkable eagle of a man on a part-time basis or have all of a lesser man. In essence, Rebecca had made that decision long ago. She would rather share the life of an eagle than spend the rest of her life alone.

"I'm coming!" she cried, running to the man she loved.

When she stopped in front of him, her eyes shining with happiness, Chase looked down at her warmly, lovingly. He held down his hand to help her mount. Rebecca took it, and Chase swung her in front of him on the saddle, then nudged Lightning with his knees.

The big stallion leapt forward, and Chase and Rebecca rode westward, to the Brazos and their future together. The mares, seeing their master leaving, stopped their grazing and raced after him.

Behind them the wagon, with its heavy load of cannons, sank another foot in the deep, slimy mud of Vince's Bayou.

WIN A FREE BOOK
AND SEND ONE TO A FRIEND!

You can win a brand new, top quality, passion-filled historical romance from Dell for yourself and a friend just by being among the first 500 respondents* who mail in the coupon below. You will receive the exciting and unforgettable novel **DESIRE'S MASQUERADE** by bestselling author Kathryn Kramer as well as the opportunity to have the book sent to a friend ABSOLUTELY FREE! Send the attached coupon with your name and address and the name and address of a friend and YOU MAY BE A WINNER!

In addition, please help us to bring you the best in historical romance by answering the four questions on the reverse side of this page.* *

Look for these future titles from Dell:
AVENGING ANGEL by Lori Copeland
CLOUDCASTLE by Nancy Henderson Ryan
NO CHOICE BUT SURRENDER by Meagan McKinney

Mail your responses postmarked no later than August 15, 1987 to:
Dell Publishing Co., HISTORICAL ROMANCE OFFER, 6 Regent St., Livingston, NJ 07039

Please enter my name to win **DESIRE'S MASQUERADE** by bestselling author Kathryn Kramer.

Name_____

Address_____

City_____ State_____ Zip_____

And send a copy to my friend:

Name_____

Address_____

City_____ State_____ Zip_____

*In the event of tying entries, winners will be chosen at random.
* *Completion of survey not necessary to win.

1. Try to remember back to when you were picking out this book at the store. What ONE thing attracted you most to this book? (Please read the full list before you make your ONE selection.)

☐ the artwork on the cover
☐ the title
☐ the author
☐ the price
☐ the recommendation of someone working in the store.
☐ the recommendation of a friend
☐ an advertisement in a newspaper
☐ comments in a newspaper or newsletter
☐ the historical time period and setting
☐ the description of heroine
☐ the description of hero
☐ the description of the plot on cover
☐ the excerpt from the book on first page
☐ other:_____

2. Would you buy another book by this author?

☐ definitely yes ☐ possibly yes ☐ probably not

3. Would you like to see more humor in historical romances?

☐ yes, a lot more ☐ yes, a little more ☐ no

4. In your opinion, what makes a historical romance a really good one?

_____
_____
_____
_____